THE WRONG PLAYER WORLD SO FAR

The Wrong Player Series

The Wrong Quarterback

The Wrong Play

The Pucking Wrong Series

The Pucking Wrong Number

The Pucking Wrong Guy

A Pucking Wrong Christmas

The Pucking Wrong Date

The Pucking Wrong Man

The Pucking Wrong Rookie

THE WRONG QUARTERBACK

C.R. JANE

Podium

All rights reserved. No part of this publication may be reproduced, stored in a retrieval system, or transmitted in any form or by any means electronic, mechanical, photocopying, recording, or otherwise without prior written permission from Podium Publishing.

This is a work of fiction. Names, characters, places, and incidents are either products of the author's imagination or used fictitiously. Any resemblance to actual events, locales, or persons, living, dead, or undead, is entirely coincidental.

Copyright © 2024 by C. R. Jane
Cover design by Emily Wittig
Photography by Wander Aguiar
Editing by Stephanie H./Hannotek, Ink

ISBN: 979-8-3470-0428-7

Published in 2025 by Podium Publishing
www.podiumentertainment.com

To my own thanK you aIMee.
The stars are stunning up here. Thanks for beating my spirit black
and blue all those years ago.
P.S. I know you read my books.

Dear Red Flag Renegades,

While I'm known for my red flag men . . . one of the other defining markers of my writing is the emotion I like to infuse into my characters. No matter how different we are, humans share emotional characteristics that none of us can escape from. No matter where we come from, there are certain human experiences we all will feel. In The Wrong Quarterback, the shared emotion I chose to write about . . . was grief. At some point in our lives, we all encounter it. It wears many faces—the loss of a loved one, the end of a relationship, or the quiet fading of a hope-filled dream. Many of you have shared with me how deeply you resonated with my attempt to capture that aching solitude, that unbearable stillness when your world stands still, yet the rest of the world moves forward without pause.

The world would be a far better place if Parker Davis was there to pick up our pieces in the midst of that experience.

Parker Davis and his friends were so fun to write. And I needed fun. While I was writing this book, I suffered some failed infertility treatments, and I experienced my own form of grief. Parker and Casey's story was the balm my soul needed to get past the darkness I was feeling.

I hope you enjoy Parker and the rest of his "No Drama Llamas" #IYKYK. And hopefully they can bring the smile and warmth to your life that they did to mine.

I'll reread the words that I wrote . . . but the story is yours now.

XOXO,

TEAM ROSTER

OFFENSE

QUARTERBACK:
Parker Davis | #12
Trent Maxwell | #07
Malik Harper | #16
Owen Matthis | #14

RUNNING BACK:
Garrett Harper | #22
Griffin Tillman | #30
Trevon Brooks | #29
Elijah Rivera | #33
Jordan Wright | #20
Marcus "Speedy" Hayes | #28

WIDE RECEIVER:
Jace Thatcher | #77
Hunter Manning | #63
Chris Jordan | #19
Caleb "Ace" Thompson | #11
Ethan Vance | #36
Isaiah Turner | #18
Brandon Holt | #17
Trey Anderson | #84
Quentin Scott | #89

TIGHT END:
Matthew "Matty" Adler | #23
Eric Simmons | #86
Logan Mendez | #80
Cam Richards | #82

OFFENSIVE LINE:
Hunter "Tank" Thompson | #67
Sam Carrington | #65
Connor Wright | #55
Chapman "Chappie" Cordell | #68
Derrick Morgan | #73
Connor Steele | #71
Blake McAllister | #75
Jared Foster | #54
Grayson Lee | #72
Noah Chambers | #74

TEAM ROSTER (CONT.)

DEFENSE

DEFENSIVE LINE:
Darwin Harrison | #90
Matt Santiago | #92
Elijah Reed | #99
Anthony Williams | #94
Jacob Tanner | #96
Jalen Fields | #69
Wyatt Cook | #98
Damien Ward | #91
Sean Little | #97

LINEBACKERS:
Brandon Scott | Outside Linebacker | #44
Marcus Steadman | Middle Linebacker | #52
Andre Carter | Outside Linebacker | #41
Malcolm Spencer | #51
Aiden Cruz | #57
Cole Anderson | #53

SAFETIES:
Xavier Hawthorne | Free Safety | #21
Malik Greene | Strong Safety | #93

CORNERBACKS:
Tyrell Brooks | #24
Dante Jefferson | #66

SPECIAL TEAMS

KICKER:
Ethan Collins | #3
Will Torres | #6

PUNTER:
Ryan Matthews | #2

RETURN SPECIALIST:
Chris Reddick | #46

LONG SNAPPER:
Colton Ramsey |

COACHING STAFF

HEAD COACH	Clint Everett
OFFENSIVE COORDINATOR	Dale Malone
DEFENSIVE COORDINATOR	Bryce Thompson
SPECIAL TEAMS COACH	Reggie Caldwell
STRENGTH AND CONDITIONING COACH	Travis Richards
QUARTERBACKS COACH	Evan Houston
WIDE RECEIVERS COACH	Trey Winston
RUNNING BACKS COACH	Nathan Grant
OFFENSIVE LINE COACH	Doug "Grizzly" Callahan
DEFENSIVE LINE COACH	Marcus Hayes
LINEBACKERS COACH	Jerome Brooks
DEFENSIVE BACKS COACH	DeAndre Moore

THE WRONG QUARTERBACK
PLAYLIST

OVER YOU	MIRANDA LAMBERT
IRIS	THE GOO GOO DOLLS
PRETTY WHEN YOU CRY	LANA DEL REY
NUMB/ENCORE	JAY-Z AND LINKIN PARK
RISK	GRACIE ABRAMS
LOOK AFTER YOU	THE FRAY
THE SMALLEST MAN WHO EVER LIVED	TAYLOR SWIFT
CALL ME WHEN YOU'RE SOBER	EVANESCENCE
STRAWBERRY WINE	DEANA CARTER
SO HIGH SCHOOL	TAYLOR SWIFT
YELLOW	COLDPLAY
HEAR YOU ME	JIMMY EAT WORLD
LOSE CONTROL	TEDDY SWIMS
SOMETHING TO REMEMBER	MATT HANSEN
FADE INTO YOU	MAZZY STAR
UNLOVABLE	DELACEY
THE ALCHEMY	TAYLOR SWIFT

LISTEN TO THE FULL PLAYLIST HERE

TRIGGER WARNING

Dear readers,

Please be aware this is a dark romance and as such can and will contain possible triggering content. Elements of this story are purely fantasy and should not be taken as acceptable behavior in real life.

Our love interest is possessive, obsessive, and the perfect shade of red for all you red flag renegades out there. There is absolutely no shade of pink involved when it comes to what Parker Davis will do to get his girl.

Themes include football, stalking, manipulation, dark obsessive themes, grief after the death of a family member, mention of a car accident, mention of gambling addiction, drugging (not of the heroine), captor/captivity, and sexual scenes.

There are no harems, cheating, or sharing involved. Parker Davis only has eyes for her.

Prepare to enter the world of the Tennessee Tigers . . . you've been warned.

THE
WRONG
QUARTERBACK

"FOOTBALL IS EASY IF YOU'RE CRAZY AS HELL."

—Bo Jackson

PROLOGUE

CASEY

Ben: *Gray and I will be there in ten.*
    Maria was telling me something about a girl at school, but I was having trouble focusing on what she was saying because of the text my brother, Ben, had just sent me.

Gray Andrews. The object of every daydream I'd had since the moment he'd come through our front door four years ago. Ben's best friend. Assistant captain of the school's basketball team last year. Two years older than me.

Completely out of my league.

I self-consciously ran my fingers through my hair, wishing I was wearing something cuter than cutoff jean shorts and an old T-shirt.

"Did you hear what I just said?" Maria huffed as we stepped out of the theater, the warm evening air a welcome contrast to the chilliness inside. I really needed to remember to bring a sweatshirt—or better yet, a blanket—next time. The sidewalk outside the movies was crowded with people milling around, talking and laughing. I recognized a few people from class. Maria immediately started waving at them, but I ducked my head and stood there awkwardly, hugging my phone to my chest, waiting for Ben and Gray to show up.

While my brother had been the most popular guy in his grade . . . I was the exact opposite. A quiet nerd who preferred to stay in the shadows and who played the piano for fun.

Just another reason that Gray was always going to be nothing but a daydream to me.

"OMG, Caleb's over there," Maria hissed, hitting me in the arm to get my attention. "Hi, Caleb!" she yelled in a weird, high-pitched voice.

6 C.R. JANE

Grumbling as I rubbed the sore spot, I kept my eyes on the road next to the theater, not particularly caring if *Caleb* was here or not. He may have been one of the cool kids in our grade, but he was nothing compared to Gray.

I was saved from Maria pushing me into an awkward conversation by the familiar headlights of Ben's Jeep pulling up to the curb. He was sitting in the passenger seat, which means he'd been drinking at the party they'd been at. And he looked pissed.

Ben was my favorite person in the whole world, but he was so annoying to deal with when he was mad.

I scowled, my stomach twisting; it wasn't like I wanted to call him, but Mama was stuck at work late, and there was no other option.

This was going to be fun. Gray was probably pissed too—and that only made it worse.

I swung open the back door of the Jeep, and Ben didn't even wait for me to get in before he started.

"Seriously, Casey?" His voice came out sharp, cutting through the air. "You couldn't get a ride from anyone else? You had to call me?"

I waved goodbye to Maria, who immediately joined another group of girls, and slid into the backseat with a sigh. "You know Mama's working late . . . and I don't know anyone else here well enough to ask them for a ride. You were *literally* my only option."

Ben groaned as I slammed the door and buckled my seatbelt. "What are you going to do next year when I'm gone?"

I frowned, not wanting to think about that. Ben and Gray would both be going to the University of Tennessee in the fall, and I didn't like the idea of being in a silent house with nobody but Mama for company. Ben might be annoyed with me right now, but he was my best friend—somehow not minding all the things that made me weird and drove Mama crazy.

Gray glanced at me in the rearview mirror, his lips twitching into a small grin. "Hey, Case," he said, his voice casual, as if Ben wasn't pitching a fit in the seat next to him. His blond hair caught the last of the evening light, turning the strands almost golden, like the sun had dipped down just to brush against him. It always seemed effortless with him—his hair, his smile, the way he moved through life without a care.

I managed a small wave, trying to ignore the way my heart fluttered at the sound of his voice. "Hey."

Ben wasn't done yet, though. "I had to leave the best party of the summer because you didn't plan ahead. Again. Whitney was all over me."

THE WRONG QUARTERBACK 7

I grimaced at that. Whitney was gross, and it was in Ben's best interest to stay far, far away from her. He wasn't wrong, though, about the other part. Ben *was* constantly needing to save me. I was so socially awkward that I felt weird asking people for rides. "I'm sorry," I muttered.

"Yeah, sure," he grumbled, crossing his arms and leaning back in his seat. But his voice had lost its edge. He never could stay mad at me for long.

"She probably saved you from being a baby daddy at eighteen, though, bro," Gray commented, shooting me another quick look in the rearview mirror and giving me a wink, mouthing "Grump" before he pulled the Jeep away from the curb when Ben scoffed at what he'd said.

And just like that, the butterflies were back.

Winking should be illegal. Or maybe just for him. I was quite sure that a wink from any other guy wouldn't have quite the same effect on me. I could feel my face heat up as I shifted uncomfortably in the backseat, hoping neither of them noticed that my face resembled a tomato at the moment.

Gray turned up the music, tapping his fingers against the wheel, and I let myself relax into the familiar comfort I always felt when it was just the three of us. When I was with people at school, I was always on my toes, trying not to do anything that would push me further down the social pyramid, but with Ben and Gray, I didn't need to pretend so much. They already knew I was a dork and still tolerated my presence.

For a while, the drive was smooth, and the night was quiet outside the car. I could almost forget how annoyed Ben was. Almost.

"Maybe we can just go back," Ben muttered from the front seat, turning to look at me. "You wouldn't completely hate that, right?"

Before I could answer, headlights flooded the road in front of us, blinding, too close. "Fuck!" Gray cursed, jerking the steering wheel hard to the left. The tires screamed, and the Jeep veered off the road. I felt the drop in my stomach as we flew down the embankment, the trees rushing toward us in a blur.

"Hold on!" Gray shouted, his voice panicked.

The impact hit like a punch to the gut. The front of the car crumpled against a tree; the sound of metal crunching so loud it drowned out everything else. My head snapped forward, and pain exploded behind my eyes. The airbags slammed into Ben and Gray, but in the back, all I felt was the glass shattering against my skin.

Everything slowed. The world became a blur of noise, of pain. My head throbbed, and my right hand . . . I looked down at it, how blood was dripping onto my legs from a deep cut . . . was that my bone I could see? The metallic smell of the gash filled my nose, and I blinked, trying to get my bearings.

8 C.R. JANE

"Casey!" Gray's voice cut through the haze. I blinked again, focusing on him as he twisted in his seat, panic etched into every line of his face. "Are you okay?"

I tried to nod, but my head swam. "I . . . I think so," I whispered, the words slurred, like my mouth wasn't working right.

Gray's eyes flicked from me to Ben, and suddenly everything shifted. His expression changed, terror flashing in his eyes. He leaned over, shaking Ben's shoulder. "Ben! Ben, man, wake up!"

Ben didn't move.

Gray's voice broke, his hands trembling as he shook him harder. "Come on, Ben! Wake up!"

I couldn't breathe. My body felt heavy, and I tried to call out to them, but the world was spinning too fast. I watched Gray, his face desperate, his voice fading as everything around me blurred into darkness.

When I was five years old, I'd fallen into the lake behind our house. I remember sinking below the murky depths and a sense of calmness washing over my skin. The water was warm, and it felt like it was almost calling for me. For a second, I hadn't even tried to get back to the surface. I'd just stared out at the darkness.

It was only when my oxygen had totally disappeared that I'd begun to struggle, kicking my legs violently as I tried to get to the surface.

Ben had been the one to save me and pull me out of the lake before I could drown.

Waking up felt like trying to swim through that thick, dark water again. Everything was heavy, pulling me down, my body refusing to cooperate. I blinked, but my eyes wouldn't focus. The light was too bright, stabbing through my head like a knife. The steady beeping of machines filled the air, but it all felt distant, like I was hearing it from underwater.

I tried to move, but even the smallest shift sent pain shooting through me. My hand . . . my head . . . everything hurt. I forced my eyes open, slowly, the world coming into focus in pieces. A white ceiling. Harsh fluorescent lights.

Where was I?

Something bumped my leg, and my gaze darted down to a figure slumped over me on the bed. Mama. Her eyes were closed, but her lips were moving, like she was talking in her sleep.

Only, I couldn't hear her clearly because sound was still coming in all garbled and messed up. I blinked a few more times, and more details came into focus in the room. The hospital. That's where I was. There was an IV pump next to me, and my right hand was bandaged.

I stared at Mama again. She looked pale, like she hadn't slept in days, her hair tangled, dark circles smudged under her eyes. Her hands were clutched to her chest, so tight her knuckles were white.

And I could finally understand what she was saying. "Ben." Over and over again she was saying my brother's name.

I glanced around the room again, looking for him. Was he in the hospital, too?

I tried to speak, to call out to her, but my throat felt raw, like sandpaper had scraped it clean. The word wouldn't come, caught somewhere between the pain and the fog in my head. I swallowed, forcing it out, a weak croak.

"M—Mama."

It took a minute, but the sound of my voice eventually cut through her sleep. She opened her bloodshot eyes, and the second she saw I was awake, her face crumpled. A sob broke from her lips, and she leaned forward, grabbing my hand. Tears streamed down her face as she clung to me, her whole body shaking with the force of it.

"Casey," she gasped, her voice barely holding together. "Oh, Casey . . ."

I blinked, still groggy, my mind fuzzy, trying to piece together why she was so upset. Was my hand really that messed up? How long had I been here?

And then it hit me. The car and the headlights and the crash . . . Gray shouting . . . and Ben . . .

Ben.

My heart twisted, and I lurched up, my arm yanking at the IV and sending sharp pain shooting down my arm as the IV stand clattered against the floor and blood ran down my arm, staining the white sheets I was lying on.

A beeping sound that was more of a wail filled the air as the machines all seemed to go off at once.

"Mama . . . where's Ben?" I asked, my voice shaky, slurred with confusion. "Is he . . . is he okay?"

Her sobs got louder, her whole body trembling. She looked at me, her lip quivering, and the silence that stretched between us felt like a million lifetimes. My throat tightened as dread curled in my stomach.

She couldn't say it.

But she didn't have to.

The words came out broken, barely a whisper. "He's gone, Casey. Ben's gone."

The world shattered.

And I knew I'd never be the same again.

———————

The back door screeched as it swung shut behind me, the metal grinding in that familiar, sharp way that made me wince when it went too long without some oil. It didn't usually sound like that. Ben had been the one to oil the hinges after Daddy died, making sure the house didn't fall apart on us girls. But now . . . it had been a week since we'd put Ben in the ground, and it was already screeching.

I stepped out onto the porch, the warm southern night wrapping around me like a heavy blanket, thick with humidity. The air smelled of magnolia and honeysuckle, the same way it always did this time of year, but it felt different now. Everything did.

Crickets chirped, a soft hum rising and falling in the stillness. A light breeze stirred the trees, rustling the leaves, but even that felt wrong. The night was too alive, too full of sound. How could life continue on when Ben wasn't here? The world hadn't stopped like mine had. It just kept moving, indifferent to the gaping hole his absence had left.

I sat down on the porch steps, my fingers trailing across the weathered wood. I could still see him, clear as day, sitting here with me. Laughing. Telling me I worried too much, making me feel better after some kid made fun of me at school, protecting me when Mama became a little too hard to handle . . .

The warm air felt stifling, the sound of the crickets suddenly unbearable. It felt like a betrayal—for the world to just keep moving on. The stars still hung in the sky, the wind still whispered through the trees, the door still screeched on its rusty hinges. It was all the same, but so, so different. And Ben wasn't here to fix it. He wasn't here to make it all okay.

Grief is like that, I guess. You think the world should stop, should fall apart with you, but it doesn't. It keeps going. And you're left standing in the middle of it, feeling hollow, watching everything move on like the person you loved wasn't the very center of it all.

The ache of missing him was sharp, and I was sure it was a wound that would never heal. It hit me then what the sound of the screech was—it was the sound of grief. Of losing someone who was supposed to always be there, like a part of the air you breathe, a part of the ground you stand on.

A hitched sob burst from my lips, and I covered my mouth, not wanting Mama to come out and demand I come back inside to talk to the guests she had over for the reception in Ben's honor.

THE WRONG QUARTERBACK   11

I jumped from the steps and started across the lawn, running toward the dock that stretched out on the placid, dark lake. The faint sounds of voices drifted from the house behind me, my mother inside, shaking hands, accepting condolences. But I couldn't be in there anymore. Not with all those people telling me how sorry they were.

Sorry didn't get me anywhere—it certainly didn't get Ben back.

Slowing when I got to the weathered wood of the dock, I took my time walking down it until I reached the edge. I sat down with a clunk, my legs dangling over the water, the cool wood rough against my skin. A pebble caught my eye, and I picked it up, turning it over in my hand, the smooth surface somehow grounding me. I tried to throw it, to watch it skip across the water like Ben had shown me a million times, but my hand started to shake, like it had since I'd woken up in that hospital bed. The pebble slipped from my fingers, falling uselessly into the water with a soft plop.

My chest tightened as I stared out at the dark water, a tear slipping down my face. It felt wrong to think about what else I'd lost that night.

The ability to play the piano.

The doctors weren't sure that the nerves in my hand would ever get better. It felt stupid to cry about that, though. Even if it was something Ben was so proud of me over. He'd always been convinced that I was going to be a big star someday, and he'd see me perform on the stage in front of a huge crowd. Staring down at my hand and the scar that still marred my skin, I tried to clench it, my nails digging into my palm for just a second before I lost control of my fingers and my hand opened up again.

Ben's absence already felt like a sharp knife in my mind. Maybe it was fitting that I had a physical reminder to remind me of that night as well.

Footsteps sounded behind me, soft and careful. I didn't have to turn around to know it was Gray. He sat down beside me without saying a word, the dock creaking under his weight. I side-eyed him, noting how he'd undone his tie and how it was hanging loosely down his shirt. He still had a black eye from the airbag going off in his face, a cut that sliced through his right eyebrow, and his shoulders were slumped, the same despair hovering in the air around him that I was sure was a permanent fixture around me now.

We didn't talk, not at first. The silence stretched out between us, broken only by the gentle lapping of the lake against the shore and those infernal crickets that never stopped.

Finally, after what felt like forever, Gray sighed, his voice low and quiet. "It's going to be weird going to school without him."

I swallowed hard, my throat burning with unshed tears.

He shook his head, staring out at the water. "I don't even know how to do it. We had it all planned, you know? The dorms, the games . . . everything."

It was hard to breathe. I could hear the grief in his voice, the way it pulled him down, the same way it was pulling me. Ben wasn't just my brother—he was Gray's best friend. And now, he was gone, leaving this gaping hole in both our lives.

A sudden wave of panic washed over me, sharp and unforgiving. My heart started to race, my chest tightening so fast I couldn't catch my breath. I felt like I was drowning again, like everything was too much, pressing down on me until I couldn't think straight.

"Casey? You okay?" Gray's voice broke through the haze, concerned now, as he shifted closer to me.

I shook my head, trying to suck in air, but my throat was too tight, my lungs too constricted. "I . . . I can't . . ." The words wouldn't come, stuck in my throat as the panic clawed at my chest.

Gray's hand was on my shoulder, steady and warm, grounding me in the storm. "Hey, hey, it's okay. I'm here, Casey. Right here."

"I can't . . . breathe," I gasped, my hands shaking uncontrollably.

Gray's hand slid down my arm, his touch gentle but firm, like he was trying to pull me back from the edge. "Casey," he said frantically.

And then he kissed me.

I froze, my mind going blank. His lips were warm, soft against mine, and for a moment, everything around me stopped—the panic, the fear, the overwhelming sense of loss. It was like being jolted out of a nightmare, waking up suddenly to find everything still.

He'd never looked at me like that before, like I was something more than Ben's little sister. And yet, here he was, kissing me. It shocked me so completely; it snapped me out of the spiral I was in, yanking me back into the present.

Before I could second-guess myself, I kissed him back. My heart pounded, not from the panic anymore but from something else, something raw and unexpected. For the briefest moment, everything felt . . . right. His hand cupped the side of my face, gentle but sure, and I leaned into the kiss, letting myself get lost in it, in him.

When he finally pulled back, his blue eyes searched mine. I blinked, still shaken, still trying to catch my breath as he pushed up from the dock and stared down at me.

THE WRONG QUARTERBACK   13

"I'll wait for you to get older. But in the meantime, you don't have to worry about being alone, okay? I'm here, and I'm not going anywhere."

His words hung in the air between us, heavy and strange, and I wasn't sure what to say. I didn't even know what I was feeling anymore. I watched him as he walked away, giving me one last, long look once he'd gotten to the shore.

"I'll see you, Casey," he called out, giving me a sad wave before he turned and walked back across the lawn.

As soon as he was out of sight, I turned back to the water, staring at it as I listened to the crickets and I felt the warm breeze, and I heard the sound of the screen door screeching as he went back into the house.

Standing, I slipped off my black dress, and I dove into the dark, murky depths.

Sinking down, down, down into the silence. I let myself sit there for a moment before I finally kicked back up to the surface.

Knowing there wasn't anyone around who was going to save me anymore.

CHAPTER 1

CASEY

Two Years Later

Freedom. That's what it felt like as I drove toward my dorm in my beat-up Honda.

It felt like I could breathe again.

The weight that had pressed on my chest for the past two years seemed to be lifting as I took in the sprawling expanse of the university. The orange brick buildings lined with trees, the wide open spaces, the students walking in groups or rushing around. It was alive here, vibrant. So unlike the house I'd left behind, that felt like it had died the night that Ben did.

I'd been afraid that I'd get here and immediately burst into tears thinking about my brother. But so far so good.

That felt like a good sign.

I'd held out hope for about six months after the accident that my hand would heal, and I'd still be able to try for piano performance at Juilliard or the New England Conservatory of Music. It had soon become apparent, though, that my hand wasn't going to be improving anytime soon.

And so I applied here. The University of Tennessee.

Where Ben was going to go before the accident and where Gray was now.

I told myself that the death of my dream had nothing on what Ben had lost, but even now, I felt guilty, like I was walking in his would-be footsteps. Mama had wanted me to go to the local community college, something small and safe and close to home. But I couldn't do that. I couldn't take one

THE WRONG QUARTERBACK 15

more day of her grief. I'd insisted on coming to Tennessee right away, and she hadn't even bothered to say goodbye when I left.

Rolling to a stop, I watched a group of girls cross the street in front of me. I didn't even need to see Greek letters to know they were sorority girls. I'd read that rush week was during move-in, and judging by their matching high ponytails, shirts, and red lipstick—it was in full swing. I wondered if I would have had enough courage to do something like that if that night hadn't happened.

But then again, I never would have been here in the first place, right?

My phone buzzed, and I glanced at it, a smile crossing my lips when I saw it was from him. Gray.

> Gray: Almost here?

Butterflies sparked to life inside me, and my hands started to sweat. This was it. I was about to see him again.

I hadn't seen him since he left for school, despite everything he'd said that night by the lake. I'd replayed that night over and over in my head, especially the kiss. But it had been two years since he'd been home, and although he'd invited me several times to come visit him, Mama had barely let me leave the house to go to school, much less to go visit a university hours away. He'd told me it was too painful to come home, but he'd texted me here and there.

I'd lived for those texts.

Gray was like a lifeline when things got too lonely. I'd changed after everything that had happened, and it felt like he was the only one who could understand.

Taking a deep breath, I reminded myself this was a fresh start. I didn't need to think about the past. It was time for once to focus on the future.

The campus was bigger than I remembered from the tour we'd gone on with Ben. Neyland Stadium rose up in the distance, hovering over all the buildings like it wanted to remind them who was really in charge. The trees along the main quad were just starting to change color, a hint of gold creeping into the green leaves. Sidewalks wound through the grassy areas where students sat or played Frisbee, some sprawled out in the shade of massive oaks.

Pulling up to the curb, I turned off the car and sat there for a moment, soaking it all in, trying to make sure I was calm enough to actually see Gray without doing something like flinging myself into his arms . . . or fainting.

16   C.R. JANE

I typed out *I'm here* and then hesitated, my finger hovering over the send button as I glanced into the rearview mirror, making sure I looked okay.

This was as good as I was going to get, I guess.

I'd lost weight in my grief. When food tasted like ash on your tongue, it wasn't hard to do. The gauntness in my cheeks made me look older, and my weird gray eyes hadn't stopped looking haunted. But maybe Gray would think I looked old enough now. Maybe he would be ready to stop waiting for me to grow up and just be *ready*.

A girl could dream.

I finally pressed send, my nerves twisting in my stomach.

A few minutes passed, and nothing. My nerves twisted tighter, not releasing until a familiar ping of a message made my heart skip.

> Gray: Almost there.

A minute later, I spotted him. He was walking toward my car with a group of guys, laughing at something, his head thrown back, carefree. He looked . . . different. Not drastically, but there was something in the way he carried himself. Like he'd become more confident. His blond hair was longer than I remembered, brushing just above his collar. His tan was darker, and the way his muscles filled out his shirt made it clear he'd spent a lot of time in the gym. He was wearing a polo shirt and boat shoes—a look Ben would have mocked him endlessly for. He looked every bit the preppy college guy. But not really like my Gray.

He's not "your Gray," creeper, I reminded myself.

My heart was trying to beat out of my chest as I watched him get closer. He hadn't seen me yet, he was too busy laughing with his friends. I was jealous of him for a moment, that he'd been able to escape the miserable memories that now came with our hometown, while I'd been caged within.

I was hoping that college could have that effect on me, too, because I could hardly remember what laughing felt like anymore.

I got out of the car, too nervous to stay there and watch him. Gray finally glanced around and spotted me.

And his eyes moved right past.

"Gray," I called out, wondering how he'd missed me.

He stopped dead, his eyes snapping to mine, widening in shock. "Casey?"

I waved awkwardly, and he grinned, breaking away from his group and jogging over to where I was standing. The butterflies in my stomach kicked up.

THE WRONG QUARTERBACK **17**

Before I could say anything, he pulled me into a hug, his arms wrapping around me tightly. It felt good—familiar, comforting.

He pulled back, not letting go completely. His eyes roamed over me, taking his time like he was seeing me for the first time. He traced my body slowly, his gaze getting caught on my chest before he finally made it back to my face. I shifted uncomfortably, kind of feeling like a piece of meat as he took me in.

"Wow," he finally said, stepping back just a little but still keeping me close. "You look . . . different."

"Um, thanks?" I said, trying to sound casual, even though I wasn't sure if that was a good thing. I forced a smile. "It has been a while."

He nodded, but before he could respond, the group of guys he'd been with reached us. I recognized some of them from the photos Gray had posted online over the years.

One of them, a cute brown-haired guy, slapped him on the shoulder. "Who's this?" he asked, his eyebrows moving up and down as he grinned at me.

Gray's arm wrapped around my waist, and he pulled me into his side.

Huh . . . that was . . . different. Everything I wanted, but not what I expected after not seeing him for two years.

"This is Casey," he said, introducing me like I was some sort of prize. His voice was light and casual, but there was something in his tone that felt off.

I glanced up at him, but he wasn't looking at me. He was watching his friends, waiting for their reactions.

One by one, his friends looked me over, and I could feel the sliminess of their stares. They weren't subtle about it, their knowing smiles making my skin crawl. I forced another smile. These were Gray's friends. I wanted them to like me.

There was a brief, awkward pause before Gray cleared his throat, his eyes flicking to my car and then back to me. "So, uh, I assume you have some boxes you need carried in? We've got a frat barbecue at two, so I'll need to get going soon."

I bit down on my bottom lip, trying to hide my disappointment. I'd been hoping we could catch up. Maybe have lunch or something. But I remembered now that he'd told me he'd gotten into a fraternity last year. I knew that was a big deal at Tennessee.

"Oh yeah, of course. It's just a few things," I told him, stepping out of his embrace and moving to open the back.

18   C.R. JANE

Gray glanced in the trunk and raised an eyebrow. "Is that everything?" he asked with a cute grin. "I was expecting more."

"Yep, that's all of it. I think my dorm's right over there," I said, nodding toward the orange brick building in front of us. I, of course, didn't tell him that Mama hadn't bothered going shopping with me before school. And wanting to start over meant that I bought what I could with my meager savings—and it wasn't much.

Gray grabbed the boxes and told the guys he would meet them in a little bit. I waved goodbye to them and then locked my car before following Gray to the dorm, my nerves settling just a little with each step. I was really here.

My dorm building was old, the walls lined with bulletin boards advertising campus events and welcome parties. The air smelled faintly of something industrial, like old carpet cleaner, but I didn't care. Everything was the opposite of where I'd been.

Just what I wanted.

"406?" Gray asked, his breath coming out a bit heavy from the weight of the boxes and the stairs we'd just come up.

"Yep."

We passed a few more rooms, and then we were there in front of an old, nondescript, wooden door. I quickly pulled out the key I'd gotten in my new student packet and swung the door open.

I grinned when I saw inside.

It was small and old, nothing in it but two twin beds on opposite walls, a couple of desks shoved under the single window, and a shared dresser.

But I thought it was glorious.

The walls were bare, the beige cinder block kind that had been featured in every college dorm room since the dawn of time. Maybe some would think it felt a little prisonlike. But after living at home, between those quiet walls the past two years, not being allowed to do anything, and listening to my mom's tears around the clock—this felt like anything *but* a prison.

One of the beds had some suitcases on it, and clothes were already strewn all over, but there wasn't any other sign of my roommate. She'd left me the bed closest to the window, though, with the view of the green just outside—that seemed like a good sign.

Gray set my stuff down and glanced around, rubbing the back of his neck. "Cozy."

I laughed. "Yeah. Cozy."

"I'd forgotten how tiny the dorms are."

THE WRONG QUARTERBACK   19

"Oh, yes, you're the cool guy who lives in the fraternity house now," I teased.

He grinned, and the little butterflies came back.

"You look good," I blurted out before I could stop myself—immediately wishing that there was a way for me to fall through the floor and disappear.

Gray raised an eyebrow, his lips curling into a smirk. "Yeah? You too, Case." His eyes roved up and down my body again. "Very good."

My face heated, and I tucked a strand of hair behind my ear. This wasn't exactly how I imagined it would go. In my head, or maybe in my wildest dreams, we'd pick up right where we left off. Instead, it was awkward, almost like I was a stranger he was trying to pick up.

I almost brought up Ben then, but I stopped myself. From what Gray had said about why he hadn't come home, that was probably the opposite of what he wanted to talk about.

As if he could read my mind, he shrugged, his smile dimming a little. "It's been weird without Ben. I think about him a lot. I imagine that's only going to happen more with you being here."

I swallowed hard, the familiar ache of loss settling back into my chest. "Yeah. I get that."

We stood there in silence for a moment, the weight of Ben's absence hanging between us like a third person.

Gray sighed, running a hand through his hair. "Listen, I know I—we haven't really talked much since I left, but I'm glad you're here, Casey. I really am."

I looked up at him, my heart beating a little faster. "You are?"

"Yeah," he said softly, his eyes meeting mine. "I've thought about you. About us. That night . . ."

I felt my breath catch, memories of the kiss flashing in my mind. "I have, too." My voice came out far too hopeful, but I'd always been shit at hiding how I felt from him.

Gray stepped closer, and for a second, I thought he was going to kiss me again. I tensed in anticipation, my eyes already fluttering closed like I was a heroine in a romance movie.

The kiss never came, though.

Instead, he reached out and squeezed my hand, his thumb brushing over my knuckles. "I've got to get to the house right now, but you should join us for dinner later. You'll like the guys."

I nodded quickly, maybe a little too eagerly. "Yeah, that sounds great."

He smiled, his familiar easy grin making my chest flutter. "Cool. I'll text you the details."

As he walked out, I stood by the door for a moment, watching him go. It kind of felt like we were back in high school, me hovering around trying to get his attention.

But he said he thought about that night—that kiss. That was good, right?

I closed the door and sighed, leaning back against the cold wood as I stared out the window to the green below. There was a group of students tossing a football around, and I studied them for a moment, trying to imagine myself fitting into all of this. It would feel strange for a while, like I was pretending to be someone else—I'd been expecting that. It was like I'd been living in the dark and someone had suddenly flipped on a light—it was normal for it to take a minute to acclimate.

Before I could get too lost in my thoughts, the door burst open, and I went flying forward, stumbling across the floor and barely catching myself before I fell on my face. Turning, I watched as a whirlwind of energy came through the entry in the form of a bubbly blond girl carrying two duffel bags and a stack of hangers.

"Oh my God, hi!" she exclaimed, dropping her bags and rushing over to hug me before I could even stand up. "You must be Casey! I'm Natalie, but everyone calls me Nat. I'm your roommate!"

She pulled back, her blue eyes wide with excitement as she looked me up and down. "I'm so glad you're here! I was hoping I wouldn't be stuck with some total weirdo, you know? Like, what if you were one of those creepy girls who doesn't talk or someone who steals my snacks? And what if I woke up and you were like standing over me and breathing heavily?" She shivered like she was picturing it right then.

I blinked, trying to keep up with her rapid-fire talking, a smile sliding across my lips because she was kind of hilarious. "Uh, yeah. I mean, I promise not to steal your snacks . . . and the other things."

"Thank fuck!" Nat said, dramatically collapsing onto her bed with a loud sigh. "I've been so nervous about this, you have no idea." She unzipped one of her duffels and pulled out a bag of blue Nerds gummies, ripping it open and shoveling some into her mouth as I watched.

That *was* a good snack, though. I made a mental note to get my own.

Nat started pulling clothes out of her duffel bags and throwing them into the piles that were already on her bed from her suitcase, babbling on about how excited she was to decorate the room, what color scheme we should go with, and how she had a Pinterest board full of ideas. I smiled, nodding along as she kept talking, her energy filling the room.

It was very clear that she was the exact opposite of me—loud, talkative, and full of confidence—but maybe that was exactly what I needed.

As I continued to listen to her talk about all the freshman orientation activities we needed to attend and the parties she was going to drag me to, the uncertainty that I'd had started to slip away.

This was what I needed.

This felt like freedom.

CHAPTER 2

PARKER

"Hey, Parkie, I got one for you," Jace said as he threw his helmet on the ground and fixed his man bun.

I felt weird every time I said those words.

I took my time drinking my water because Jace "had one" for me a couple of times a day.

And every time it was awful.

"You can proceed," I told him as I reluctantly put the water bottle down. Matty snorted next to me, and I shot him a grin. One of our favorite things was giving Jace a hard time.

"You two act like I'm not the funniest person on the planet," Jace commented, finally finishing his beauty routine and putting his helmet back on. "But inside, I know that you *pine* for these moments."

"We *pine* for these moments?" Matty drawled as he snapped his own helmet back on. "I can promise you, Thatcher, I've never used the word *pine* before in my life." He side-eyed me. "I bet Parkie-Poo has, though. That big brain of his *loves* the word *pine*."

I huffed out an amused laugh.

"Well, first of all, you just used the word *pine*, and it came off your tongue quite smoothly, so I'm confident you're not a first-timer. But I do agree with you that ole quarterback here probably loves that word. He does have a big brain. I feel good about myself, though. I have a big—"

"Am I interrupting social hour, ladies?" Coach Everett called, mercifully cutting off Jace's sentence as he tossed a football in the air and scowled at us.

"No, sir, Coach, sir," Jace called back as the three of us started jogging over to resume practice.

Coach pretended to snarl at Jace, but it was hard to stay mad at my golden retriever best friend. Mostly because he was one of the best receivers that college football had ever seen, obviously. All of us could do without his bad jokes.

Speaking of jokes . . .

"What did Nala say to Simba in bed?" Jace asked as we lined up to run a play.

"Do we have to?" I groaned.

"Yes, we have to. I'm not going to catch one ball until you listen to me," Jace said seriously.

"But what about his other ball?" Connor, my enormous center, called. Now the whole team was groaning.

"Can we not talk about Parker's balls?" Matty said from down the line.

"I'm still waiting," Jace said, a giant, annoying smile on his face.

"This is chaos," Coach muttered, and I nodded. The best kind.

"Fine. Hurry," I growled as I lined up behind Connor.

"Move fasta," Jace said, and then he began cackling.

It took me a second to get it . . . obviously my *big brain* wasn't working today. Probably because listening to Jace's jokes made me dumber.

"Move fasta. *Mufasa*," Jace emphasized. When not a single player laughed, he scowled. "Y'all need to get a better sense of humor."

"Set . . . hut," I called, and a second later Connor hiked me the ball with a clean, perfect motion, and I dropped back, scanning the field.

Jace cut left, and I launched the ball, watching as it spiraled through the air and fell perfectly into Jace's outstretched arms.

Because I was a god like that.

Jace ran a few steps and then held up the football, shaking his ass at the rest of us as he celebrated the catch.

"How the fuck do we ever win a game?" Coach grunted to Coach Houston, our quarterbacks coach. Coach Houston grinned as Jace came running back and tossed me the football.

"It's 'cause we're awesome, Coach," Jace called as we lined up again.

And so practice went.

This was my third year as the starting quarterback for the Tennessee Tigers, and these crazy, out-of-control idiots around me had become my brothers. Each of these guys would do anything for each other and for me.

We were also the best fucking team in the NCAA.

24   C.R. JANE

Coach Everett blew his whistle, the sharp sound cutting through the shit talk on the field. "Alright, bring it in!" he called, motioning for us to gather.

I jogged over with the rest of the team, everyone forming a tight huddle around him. Sweat dripped down, breaths came heavy, but the energy was high. We could feel it. This was our year.

"Good job today, boys. Even *you*, Thatcher," Coach Everett said, eliciting his usual laugh. Jace rolled his eyes, and Coach grinned. He put his hand out, and we all followed, a sea of hands stacking on top of each other.

"Call it, QB," Coach called.

"On three—one, two, three—TENNESSEE!"

The cheer echoed, settling into my veins as it usually did as we walked off the field toward the locker room.

"Hi, Parker," McKenzie called as we passed by where the cheerleaders had been practicing in the field next to ours.

I pretended not to hear her or the three other girls that also called out our names. I kept my eyes firmly focused in the distance because all of them were the kind of crazy I was not looking for. My dick had once liked cheerleaders, but it had been quickly cured of that.

Jace and Matty had no such issues, waving at their own fans on the team like we were in a fucking parade.

"I think you hurt the poor girl's feelings." Matty smirked once we finally got past the field.

I scoffed, giving him the side-eye. "Can I remind you that she was so desperate to have my babies she tried to put my old cum, that had been sitting in the condom for hours . . . inside of her—while I was *sleeping*."

"So a hot girl tries to have your babies, Davis, cry me a river," said Matty.

I gaped at him.

"No harm, no foul, though, Parkie. All because you listened to me," said Jace, starting to whistle as if it was no big deal that I'd been woken up by McKenzie screaming because her cunt was on fire—thanks to the hot sauce I made sure to pour into every used condom for that reason alone.

Jace had read about some celebrity doing it when we were freshmen. We'd started trying it, as a joke, never thinking it would come in handy.

The relief that I felt as she ran out of the room screaming could not be matched.

"Why are all the crazy ones hot?" Matty muttered, making fun of me as his own personal stalker waved at him from the parking lot.

"Why don't you go over there, Matty? Since crazy, hot girls are no big deal and all," I teased.

THE WRONG QUARTERBACK   25

He flipped me off and jogged off in front of us as his little stalker girl, still nameless to us somehow, stared after him despondently.

"One day one of them is going to crack," Jace muttered as he gave a friendly wave to her. She ducked behind a car, and I snorted because I was pretty sure she still didn't know that we'd noticed her here every day, watching Matty like her life depended on it.

"What the fuck was Cole wearing last night?" Steadman, one of my linebackers, said as we walked into the locker room. He was grinning like a loon as he held up his phone.

And I immediately got why. I gaped at the picture he was showing me.

There was my rockstar brother, Cole, standing on the red carpet, a smug look on his face. He was shirtless, wearing a leather jacket and about twenty necklaces—because apparently that's what rockstars wore.

But that wasn't what everyone in the locker room was cackling about.

It was the fact that his hat, tilted low, had what looked like an owl perched on the brim.

What the fuck.

Being the youngest of three brothers when your oldest brother was a rockstar and the other brother was a superstar NHL goalie wasn't easy. I absolutely jumped on chances like this to make fun of one of them.

Shaking my head, I walked over to my locker and pulled out my phone.

Dang it. Walker had already seen the picture and started the fun without me.

> **Walker:** I'd like to file a formal complaint.

> **Cole:** ?

I quickly typed out a supporting response.

> **Me:** I'm joining.

> **Cole:** Okay, I'll join in too.

> **Walker:** You can't join in. The formal complaint is against you.

> **Cole:** Well, now I just feel attacked.

Me: We're the ones who should feel attacked. You share the same last name as us, and you appeared on national television with a fucking bird on your head.

Cole: Oh, you liked that.

I snorted, and Jace came over to read the conversation over my shoulder.

Walker: What part of this conversation screamed that we liked it?

Cole: It's called fashion.

Me: It's called embarrassing. I wish it had crapped on your head.

"Good one," Jace muttered as I elbowed him for standing practically on top of me.

Cole: It was stuffed!

Walker: Somehow that makes it worse.

Me: . . .

Cole: Hey! None of that rhombus of ridiculousness shit.

Walker: Do you mean Circle of Trust? Because if so, that's blasphemy. If not, what the hell is the rhombus of ridiculousness?

Cole: Tomato, To-may-to.

Me: I don't even know what you're saying right now.

Walker: Me neither.

THE WRONG QUARTERBACK   27

Me: New family rule. No stuffed animals are allowed on national television.

Cole: I can't promise that, Parkie. It's whatever I'm feeling in the moment.

Walker: How about the next time you get that feeling, you let us know, and we'll make sure you "feel" a new last name before you go out in public.

Cole: Rude. My feelings would be hurt if I didn't know that I was awesome.

Walker: . . .

Me: . . .

Me: Awesomely bad.

I was still smiling as I went to put down my phone . . . and then it buzzed in my hand.

My smile instantly died when I saw who the text was from. Martha, Mom's nurse.

Martha: Parker, she's refusing to eat again. We're trying, but . . .

The words made my stomach twist, and whatever leftover buzz I had from practice and making fun of Cole died in an instant.

Matty, noticing my shift, lifted an eyebrow. "Everything okay?"

I tried for a nod, but it didn't feel convincing. "Just my mom again," I muttered, even though everything with my mom the last couple of years had definitely not been *just* a thing.

Matty's brow furrowed, sympathy in his eyes that I didn't want. "Want some company? I can drive over with you."

I shook my head, forcing a smile I didn't feel. "Nah, it's fine. You've got study hall tonight, right? I can handle it."

28   C.R. JANE

He didn't argue with me. He and Jace both knew by now there wasn't any point to doing that. I never wanted them to come with me. The fact that my mother had given up on life wasn't a secret. But it was widely known that I didn't want to talk about it.

Without another word, I changed as fast as I could, grabbing my stuff and heading to my truck. The drive to my mom's place wasn't long, but it was heavy.

She was the reason I'd stayed close to home, why I'd chosen Tennessee over any other school that had offered me a spot—which was literally almost all of them.

Cole was on a world tour with the Sound of Us, and Walker was living his dream in Dallas.

That left me. I was the only one who wasn't as haunted by the memories of our mom—the mom she used to be, when she'd actually wanted to live. I didn't have those, because for as long as I could remember, she'd always been like this. I knew nothing else.

The drive home always felt longer than forty-five minutes. I gripped the steering wheel, trying not to think about what waited for me at the end of the road. Same house. Same silence. Everything I couldn't outrun. The tires crunched on the gravel as I pulled into the driveway, and for a second, I sat there, staring at the front door like I always did.

It looked the same as it had for years. The paint that was chipped, the porch that sagged, and the windows that hadn't been opened in God knows how long. Time hadn't touched this place. Not since Dad. And it wasn't like the three of us hadn't tried. We all had money, especially Cole and Walker. But every time we'd had workmen come over to the house, she'd had a fit. Screaming and crying and scratching herself to the point that she could have been committed.

It hadn't been worth dealing with it.

Thus, the house looked like this.

I sat in my truck for a minute, the drive not long enough for me to put up the walls I needed anytime I dealt with her. And like usual . . . thoughts like that made me feel like a shit son. It wasn't her fault that she'd lost the love of her life unexpectedly. Our family had always had a reputation for falling in love hard. It hadn't happened to me or Cole yet, but I was slightly a believer after seeing how crazy Walker was about his wife Olivia.

It's just that I was pretty sure Walker wouldn't abandon their child—my adorable niece—if something happened to her.

Unlike what my mom had done to the three of us.

THE WRONG QUARTERBACK 29

Taking a deep breath, I finally got out of my truck and walked up the creaky steps to the front door. One more deep breath, and then I unlocked it and stepped inside.

The smell hit me first—stale air and dust, thick enough to taste. The kind of silence that settled in your bones and made everything feel heavier. The nurse was gone for the day, the silence told me that. She was a saint for lasting as long as she did on the days she worked. The fact that she wasn't allowed to dust or move anything around couldn't have been fun.

I got sick every time I thought about the day when she couldn't handle Mom's shit anymore and she left. Who would help me then?

The hardwood creaked under my feet as I walked through the front room. Dust clung to every surface—furniture, picture frames, the old clock on the mantel that hadn't ticked in years. Like the whole house was frozen in the exact moment Dad died, and we'd never bothered to move on.

"Mom?" My voice echoed, too loud in the stillness. No answer, just more silence. My chest tightened.

I found her in her bedroom, sitting in the same chair she always did. It was the last thing Dad had built her before he died.

Her gaze was fixed on something out the window, like she was watching for someone. Like she hadn't figured out he was never coming back.

"Parker, you're here," she said, her voice thin, fragile. She didn't even look at me, though.

"Yeah, I just wanted to check in."

Her hand twitched on the armrest, the only sign she'd even heard me. The nurse had told me that besides not eating, she'd also been agitated today, angry that things were being moved. That they weren't *exactly* where they'd been before. I looked around. But everything looked the same, where it had been for years. The room was a shrine to a life we'd lost. Like everything was waiting for Dad to walk through the front door.

"You hungry? I can make something," I offered, knowing she'd say no.

"I'm fine." She shifted in her seat, a small movement, but enough to kick up a puff of dust from the cushion.

I glanced out the doorway to the kitchen, wondering if it had been stocked recently.

"Have you been taking your meds?" I asked, trying to keep my voice light, casual, even though I already knew the answer.

Her silence was the only confirmation I needed.

"I'm gonna go check the kitchen," I said, more to fill the silence than anything else. "See if there's anything edible in there."

30   C.R. JANE

She didn't stop me.

The fridge door squealed as I pulled it open, and I sighed in relief that Martha had some premade meals in there. Her soup would be a little bit easier to try and cajole down Mom's throat than a PB&J.

Grabbing the container, I shut the door, sneezing as a puff of dust went right into my face.

A tomb.

That's what this place reminded me of.

Leaning against the counter, I rubbed the back of my neck. Sometimes it felt like Dad would be disappointed in me. He'd always treated Mom like a queen. If this had happened while he'd been alive, he would have taken care of her every day without complaint.

Creak. The soft sound of the chair drifted out from the bedroom, and I looked up hopefully. But of course, she didn't appear.

Making a vow to do better, I warmed up the soup in the microwave and slowly walked back to the bedroom, doing my best not to spill.

"Mom, look what I have . . . Martha's zuppa toscana soup. You love this stuff," I told her in a fake, cheery voice as I set the bowl down on the table next to the chair. "And how about I open this window? Get some fresh air in here."

Her head snapped toward me, eyes sharp all of a sudden. "No."

"Mom—"

"I said no!" Her voice cracked, thin as it was, and her arms thrashed around. "I don't want anything." I watched as her elbow hit the soup and it went flying, landing on the pair of Dad's shoes that she'd kept right where he'd left them.

Mom let out an inhuman shriek at the sight of the soiled shoes and launched herself at them. I barely caught her before she hit the ground. "Noooo," she wailed, struggling to get away from me and to the shoes.

My throat felt tight as I held on to her, desperate that she didn't get hurt. "I'll wash them off, Mom. It's okay. Just please stop!"

She didn't stop, though. She didn't stop until she'd worn herself out completely trying to get to the shoes. She didn't stop until I'd let her go, and she'd banged her knees on the wooden floor and cried over the worn leather.

"I'm sorry, Parker," she cried as she fumbled frantically with her dirty pajamas, wiping off the soup with the hem of her shirt. "I'm so sorry."

"I know, Mom," I murmured as I knelt down and helped her.

She didn't stop for hours. Until she passed out right there by the ruined shoes.

When I picked her up to carry her over to the bed, she weighed nothing. She was literally wasting away.

"It's alright, Mom. You rest now," I whispered, that choked, tight feeling still in my chest and throat. I tucked her in, pulling the sheets up to her chin. I could barely remember her doing that for me. And now here I was, long before she was old and gray, doing it for her now.

It fucking sucked.

All of a sudden the room felt smaller, tighter, like the walls were closing in. I glanced at the door, the house feeling like it was pressing down on me. The dust, the memories, the way everything had stopped the moment Dad left. It was suffocating.

I forced myself to leave the shoes, knowing it would just set her off again in the morning if she saw they were gone, and then I strode out of the room, setting the empty bowl in the sink before I hurried toward the door.

After all of that, she still hadn't eaten.

My gaze got caught on the dust-covered frames on the mantel. Photos from a life that felt like it belonged to someone else. The three of us—Walker, Cole, and a tiny me—grinning like idiots next to Dad, all of us clueless about how fast things could change. How everything could stop.

Walker and Cole were lucky.

I got it, I really did. They were older, so the contrast from how Mom was then to how she was now was sharper. Their demons were closer to the surface.

But man, some days, this fucking sucked. That *I* had to be the one who walked into the tomb of a house and faced what was left of her. They didn't have to see the way her eyes glazed over, or how she couldn't remember if she'd eaten that day. Didn't have to deal with the anger or the tears or worse . . . the blankness.

I ran a hand through my hair, trying to shove down the frustration bubbling up inside me. I wasn't supposed to feel like this. I was supposed to understand, to handle it. But sometimes, it was too much.

I stood there for a second longer, waiting for something. Maybe a sign that things could change. But all I heard was my mom whimpering in her sleep.

And that was all I could take for the day.

I turned and walked out, the screen door creaking shut behind me. The weight in my chest stayed, though, clinging to me like the dust that covered everything in this place.

One thing I knew as I drove my truck away from the house like I was being chased . . . ghosts were real.

My mom was one.

CHAPTER 3

CASEY

"I shouldn't have had that third espresso," Nat moaned as we walked across campus, weaving through the steady stream of students heading to their first classes. She was hopping every third step, talking really fast, and she looked a little green . . . but otherwise she looked beautiful. Her blond hair was down in beachy waves I'd never be able to do on myself, and her makeup looked like something out of a magazine.

"How did you drink three that fast?" I asked. I was still holding my mostly full first cup, feeling too nervous to add much caffeine to the mix.

"It all happened so fast," Nat whispered as she brought her fourth espresso up to her lips.

I snorted, glad for the distraction. I hadn't slept at all last night worrying about today. And how it would feel starting classes at the university Ben was supposed to attend.

This was supposed to be *him* walking along this path, *him* grabbing coffee at the Student Center, *him* taking the campus by storm. Knowing Ben, he would have already had tons of friends in the three days of orientation.

It should have been *him* here.

Not me.

"Hey, smile, roomie. I'm the one that's supposed to be puking this morning," Nat teased, nudging me with her elbow. I hadn't told her about Ben yet, but I'm sure it hadn't escaped her notice that I was prone to melancholy. So far, though, she'd been kind enough to ignore it.

"Sorry," I huffed. "Just nervous, I guess."

THE WRONG QUARTERBACK 33

Nat bit her lip as she studied me for a minute. "I think this is going to be a very good year for us, Casey Larsen. I just have a good feeling about it."

I had to grin back.

The morning air was cool, and I was still getting my bearings on the campus layout. I'd been the awkward turtle who had walked my whole class schedule yesterday so that I didn't get lost on my way to class . . . only for Nat to decide to go a completely different direction.

We turned a corner, and I came to a halt when I saw a massive concrete building that looked like it had been plucked from some dystopian movie up ahead. Strange symbols were carved into the stone, giving it a dark, secretive vibe that didn't match anything else around campus.

"Wow. What is that?" I asked, tilting my head as I stared up at the ominous structure.

Nat snorted, shooting a look like she was half-annoyed, half-intrigued. "That? That's the Sphinx."

"The Sphinx?" I repeated. I didn't think that I'd heard of that in any campus tour or catalog.

She nodded. "One of the secret societies on campus. They have chapters at a bunch of colleges around the country, but supposedly they're the most exclusive. Basically every president, every famous athlete, every famous actor . . . all members of the Sphinx during college. I think it started at Darkwood College." She pursed her lips. "Or something like that."

Nat pulled me forward so we were walking again. "Want to hear something weird?"

"What?" I asked curiously.

"They have the biggest water bill in the state."

I raised an eyebrow, looking back at the building. "Why?"

"Good question," Nat said with a shrug. "Nobody has a clue. Part of the mystery, I guess. You've never heard about the campus secret societies before?"

"Nope. Guess the tour left that part out," I murmured, still eyeing the place over my shoulder. Just standing near it gave me chills.

We kept walking, and as we rounded the next corner, all thoughts of the creepy Sphinx building disappeared. A massive banner hung over one of the main campus buildings, and plastered right in the middle was the most gorgeous face that I'd ever freaking seen. The banner said: *This is our year. Are you ready? Parker Davis* was written in block letters at the very top.

I stopped dead in my tracks, just . . . staring.

34   C.R. JANE

Yes. Yes, I was ready.

He was . . . beautiful. Not in the guy-next-door way. He was the kind of pretty that made your jaw drop. Strong jawline, cheekbones sharp enough to cut glass, and a cocky smirk that told you he just knew what to do . . . with his hands.

And those eyes. I mean that had to be Photoshopped, right? There was no way eyes like that existed—blue, piercing, with a line of gold around the pupil and flecks of gold dusted across the blue like stars in a night sky.

Okay . . . he was literally making me wax poetic looking at him.

There was a light shadow of scruff around his jaw that gave him an edge. And his hair . . . I had the sudden, weird craving to drag my fingers through it. The rich brown color was streaked with gold like the sun followed him around.

Something twisted inside me, and there was a strange heat building in my stomach. My reaction was embarrassing. It wasn't like I hadn't seen good-looking guys before. But I'd been wrapped up in Gray for so long that I'd never given someone more than half a glance.

But it was impossible to do that with this guy.

Nat's laugh snapped me out of my lustful trance. She elbowed me, grinning like a madwoman. "Do we need to go back to the dorm . . . get you a change of panties?" she asked innocently.

It took me a second to realize what she was insinuating, and I blushed as soon as I did. "It's just a . . . I mean it's a big—" I glanced at the banner again, my eyes sliding over the huge bulge in his football pants. Definitely Photoshop, right? "It's a big sign," I hurriedly finished, intentionally avoiding her eyes.

She snorted. "Right. It's a big *sign*. I'm just saying . . . it wouldn't be weird if Parker Davis got you going. I'm pretty sure he's every student's fantasy around here. Even the professors get tongue-tied around him."

"And how do you know this already? Do you know him?" I asked casually, feeling strangely . . . jealous that she'd possibly talked to him.

"I wish," she sighed, keeping her gaze on the banner as we walked by. "Alas, all of my knowledge comes from stalking all the fan websites devoted to him before I started school."

"Fan websites? Or fan clubs," I said with a grin.

"I *may* have paid the twenty-dollar membership fee," she said haughtily, a blush now spreading across her cheeks. "But you're not going to be making fun of me when I let you look at the two pictures they send a week."

"How do they have new pictures every week?"

THE WRONG QUARTERBACK **35**

She shrugged. "I mean, I'm sure the whole campus stalks him, so he probably always has cameras taking pictures of him."

My eyes widened. It was hard to imagine being in college and being . . . famous. But I guess that's what he was.

"You can take your own pictures at the game tomorrow," Nat purred, elbowing me like she could see right into my head.

"Casey!" Gray's voice called from nearby, and I heard Nat sigh as I turned to find him walking toward us. I felt . . . guilty. Because for the first time since I'd met him, I wasn't thinking he was the hottest guy I'd ever seen.

"Hi," I said, smiling when he came up and hugged me. I hadn't seen very much of him during orientation. It was rush week for his fraternity. He'd had to cancel our first dinner because of a rush thing that came up. So besides a quick breakfast on one day and one other lunch, I hadn't seen him at all.

"You look pretty," he said, his eyes widening as he looked me up and down. I still never knew what to say when he said it like *that*, almost like he was surprised every time. I couldn't have looked *that* bad before. He had kissed me after all.

Nat huffed next to me again, and I side-eyed her. I was starting to get the feeling that Gray wasn't her favorite person. I'd been really disappointed when he'd canceled dinner on my move-in day, and she'd seemed to hold it against him ever since.

"Thank you. So do you." Crap, this was awkward. I couldn't talk to a guy on a normal day, and that guy being Gray made it even worse.

I could only imagine what I would say if a guy like Parker Davis ever talked to me. Okay . . . not thinking about that.

"Want to have lunch with me after class? What do you have today again?"

My insides sank a little at that. I had sent him my full class schedule as soon as I got it, and I still think he'd asked me that same question at least ten times over text since then. I mean, it was ridiculous to think that he should have to memorize it. But that would have shown he was interested, right? *I'd* memorized his schedule.

In the two times I'd seen him on campus he'd been really touchy-feely, hovering over me so his frat bros didn't get too friendly with me. But I still wasn't sure what *this* was.

"I have History of the Roman Empire and then Calculus II," I told him. He shivered in mock horror, and I grinned. Gray still hadn't declared his major, even though he was a junior this year. At this rate he was going to be on the ten-year college plan if he didn't decide soon.

"We'd better get to class, wouldn't want to be late," Nat said in a sweet, fake voice.

Gray lifted his hat up and ran his hand through his hair. "Alright . . . well, text me when you're done?"

Before I could answer, he swept in . . . and kissed me. It was just once, but it caught me so off-guard, for a second I was afraid I was going to faint. He started walking away, acting like what he'd just done was no big deal.

And then he really did me in.

"Ben would have been proud of you, Case," he called over his shoulder before he just walked away.

My whole body shivered, and I hunched over, wrapping my arms around myself and trying to hold in the tears.

"Casey?" Nat said softly. "Are you okay? Who's Ben?"

"My big brother," I whispered. "He was Gray's best friend. He died in a car crash two years ago. We were both with him."

She didn't ask anything else after that, just wrapped her arm around my shoulders and guided me toward the building where both our first classes were as I moved on autopilot.

Nat walked me all the way to the entrance of my class and turned me to face her, already showing she was a better friend than anyone else I'd ever had in my life.

Besides Ben.

"For the record, I still think this is going to be a great year, Casey Larsen," she said, trying to get me to smile. I reluctantly smiled back, feeling bad I'd gone zombie-girl on her when she'd only known me for a few days.

"I agree," I said softly, and I tried to feel the words in my bones.

For Ben.

CHAPTER 4

PARKER

I was in the front of the lecture hall, flipping through some papers I was going to have to hand out during class, pretending to be interested in what I was doing so I could avoid accidentally locking eyes with any potential stage-five clingers. Being a TA for a freshman history class wasn't exactly thrilling—and I didn't exactly have time for it, but my agent had said it would look good on my résumé. Apparently after the last two years, when the number one draft picks had ended up complete failures thanks to their partying, NFL scouts were wanting to see that prospective players weren't just good at football—they had their shit together too.

So here I was, faking that I did.

My phone buzzed in my pocket, and I pulled it out, hoping it wasn't bad news from Mom's nurse. I really didn't need any bad news today. Not with the first game of the season tomorrow.

I grinned when I saw it was Jace.

> Jace: What does a hot dog use for protection?

> Matty: Please, fuck, no.

> Me: Just let him get it out.

> Jace: How magnanimous of you, QB.

38 C.R. JANE

> Matty: Are you going to tell us?

> Jace: Tell you what?

> Matty: Fucking hell. The answer to the joke.

> Me: I believe it's called a punchline.

> Jace: See, this is why we call you "big brain" behind your back.

> Matty: I've literally never heard anyone call him that before in my life.

> Jace: Maybe they say it behind your back. Maybe they don't want you to get all offended and jealous.

The door opened, and a group of freshman girls filed in, giggling and casting glances my way. There was a reason this class had been the most popular one to get into the last two years—and it wasn't because Professor Hendrick was an enthralling professor.

Spoiler alert. She wasn't.

The professor in question shot me an exasperated glance from behind the desk where she'd been going over her lecture plans. I shrugged, because what could I do? I was worth the hype.

My phone buzzed again, reminding me that a pointless conversation was still taking place.

> Matty: Why would I get jealous of the title "big brain." They call me "big dick" behind my back. Which is much better IMO.

> Jace: 1) Are you too lazy to write out "in my opinion" now. 2) Literally no one calls you "big dick." I literally have an inch on you. So it would be a false statement.

THE WRONG QUARTERBACK   39

> **Matty:** IT'S A QUARTER OF AN INCH, SIR. WHICH STILL MAKES IT HUGE.

> **Me:** So shouty.

I must have laughed because Professor Hendrick coughed and gave me another pointed look. Whoops.

> **Jace:** Thanks, "Big Brain."

> **Me:** Also, I'd like to note that I have the biggest dick out of all of you.

> **Matty:** Since you weren't there the day we measured, we can't be sure of that.

> **Jace:** It's true.

> **Me:** . . .

> **Me:** Class is about to start. Are you ever going to tell us the rest of the joke?

> **Matty:** Was . . . meaning you agree with our assessment.

> **Me:** No.

> **Jace:** . . .

> **Me:** CAN YOU JUST TELL THE FREAKING JOKE?

> **Jace:** QB is a little testy today.

> **Matty:** Okay, Goldilocks.

> **Jace:** Goldilocks?

> **Matty:** Oh, I thought we were just throwing out nicknames.

I glanced up and immediately regretted it. A few of the girls in the front row had intentionally worn skirts, and their legs were spread open like they were a runway waiting for a jet to fly in.

Not that I was comparing my dick to a jet.

Although I hadn't had any complaints yet.

Those freshman girls, though, were never going to have the chance to experience my dick—at least not until they were out of this class. Professor Hendrick had given me a lecture when I'd first started with her that she would ruin my life if she heard I was getting it on with her students.

While she hadn't exactly said that—she had hinted enough about making sure the NFL scouts heard from her about what I'd done to not want to risk it.

My policy was thus very firm that these girls were off limits . . . at least until they were done with the class.

It had worked out for me so far.

My phone buzzed again.

> **Jace:** Okay, let's start this over.

> **Me:** You have thirty seconds.

> **Matty:** Countdown starts now.

> **Jace:** Geez, the pressure.

> **Me:** JACE!

> **Jace:** Okay, okay.

> **Matty:** Could have saved time saying "Ok." Just saying.

> **Jace:** . . .

> **Jace:** As I was just saying . . . what does a hot dog use for protection?

THE WRONG QUARTERBACK **41**

Me: What?

Jace: Condoments.

I snorted, eliciting another glare from the professor. But that one was actually funny. Which almost never happened with Jace's jokes.

Me: Well done.

Matt: I reluctantly concur.

I leaned back, trying to stifle a yawn, when a chair hit the ground hard, the noise slicing through the low murmur of the room. My head snapped up, annoyed at first as my eyes scanned the rows, finding a girl in the back bent over and struggling to pull her chair upright.

I was turning my attention back to my phone when she turned around . . .

Holy fuck.

I stared in awe as she settled into her desk like she wasn't completely blowing my mind. Raven hair that fell in soft waves over her shoulders, dark enough to swallow the light. And her eyes—fuck, were they silver? They looked like it from down here. They glinted in the dim light of the lecture hall as she glanced around, an embarrassed flush to her cheeks.

I needed to see those eyes up close.

I froze, completely forgetting what I was supposed to be doing. It was like a literal goddess had been dropped into the fucking room.

I was losing it.

The Davis family had a curse. Or at least they liked to think they did. Our male family members tended to be *one look and that's all* kind of people. When they found "the one," that was it.

I hadn't believed that it was true—it couldn't be true.

Holy shit.

It couldn't be true . . .

I swallowed hard, my dick feeling like it had become a giant trouser snake in my jeans. It felt like I had been knocked on my head. Like I'd become someone else. I reached down and tried to adjust my dick, but of course that got the attention of the front row because the fucking desk I was sitting at didn't have any protection.

42 C.R. JANE

A redhead literally licked her lips at me, and I flinched like I'd been shot, my gaze jerking back to the beauty in the back because suddenly any girl's attention but hers felt unacceptable.

Alright, Parker. Get your shit together. I stared down at the paper, the words spinning in front of me. A few deep breaths. Nope. That wasn't helping either.

I had to look at her again.

Like she had a magnet attached to her head, my gaze went to hers.

Fuck. She was looking at me.

Something sparked to life inside me. Like I'd had a dead heart all along, and now it was finally beating.

Because of her.

Was this what giddiness felt like? Or was I just about to faint? It felt like the same thing at the moment.

The thud of Professor Hendrick dropping a thick stack of syllabi on the desk had me reluctantly drawing my attention away from the angel I'd just found. The professor's gaze swept the room like she was already disappointed in what she was seeing, and I was a little miffed at the attitude she was giving right then. She had a goddess in her class. She should be behaving accordingly.

"Welcome to History of the Roman Empire," she began, her voice sharp and clear. "If you're here for an easy ride, you might as well leave now."

I glanced frantically at the girl, making sure she wasn't taking that sentence literally. It would be a little embarrassing if I had to jump out of my seat and run after her.

A few students shuffled uncomfortably, but she stayed put.

Thank fuck. I forced myself to focus on Professor Hendrick again. For a second. But then my eyes were drifting once again to . . . her name. What the fuck was her name?

I frantically pulled out the class roster, but of course it didn't have pictures on it. Where was that one? Probably in some email I hadn't bothered to open because before this moment I couldn't have cared less what any of these students' names were. Professor Hendrick frowned at me, probably because I looked as crazy as I was feeling inside. Was I sweating? Yep, I was sweating. My heart was also trying to escape my chest. Maybe I was having a heart attack. This girl was actually making my body have a physical reaction.

Breathe in, breathe out, I coached myself. I wouldn't pull up her picture right now. I could survive without her name for another half an hour.

Maybe.

THE WRONG QUARTERBACK 43

Professor Hendrick started rattling off dates and expectations. Something about midterms, paper deadlines, whatever. I got lost in the way the girl was tapping her fingers on the side of her laptop, like she had a rhythm in her head that only she could hear. It was way more captivating than whatever my boss was saying.

"Mr. Davis, why don't you introduce yourself to the class as our teaching assistant?"

I blinked, and it may have taken me a whole moment to remember that *I* was Mr. Davis. She was talking to me. Everyone's eyes were on me as they waited for me to regain the ability to form words—something I'd never had trouble with before. I stood up, clearing my throat as I glanced at Professor Hendrick. She raised an eyebrow, her lips pressed into a line that said she was unimpressed.

"Uh, yeah, sure," I said, sounding like a complete idiot. "I'm Parker Davis. I'm . . . the teaching assistant for this course." My gaze flickered back to the girl for a second before I forced it away, focusing on the back wall. "My, uh, office hours are posted . . . somewhere." A few chuckles scattered through the room, and my gaze snapped over to see if she was laughing at me too.

She wasn't even looking at me, though. She was staring at her desk, like it held the most interesting thing she'd ever seen. Fuck. This was the worst first impression ever.

Professor Hendrick's frown deepened, but she said nothing, waiting. I took a deep breath, trying to piece together the basics. "You can find me in the department office on Wednesday mornings if you need help with, um, essays or questions. I'm here to assist with anything . . . related to the class."

Good thing I'd at least been able to remember the "related to the class" part of the speech. Although that wouldn't stop the line outside my office from forming with people who wanted help with . . . other things.

My gaze drifted to her again. Wishing there was some way to tell her that she wasn't included in that provision. I would help her with anything . . . literally anything.

I would soon be helping her with *everything* as a matter of fact.

It took me a second to realize that I was just standing there, gaping like a freak. How long had it been since I'd stopped speaking?

I could literally feel Professor Hendrick shooting daggers into the side of my head . . . I just couldn't find it in myself to care.

The professor cleared her throat. "Um, thank you . . . Mr. Davis. And please do use his services if you need help in the class. Mr. Davis got a perfect grade when he took this course, the first to ever do so."

44 C.R. JANE

She'd probably added that last part because of how dumb I'd sounded. My gaze drifted hopefully to the new focus of my existence. Was she impressed?

I just couldn't tell . . . her eyes were still glued to her desk, avoiding my stare like it was something toxic.

There was a blush to her cheeks, though. I was pretty sure she was aware of me.

And now my dick was even harder.

Professor Hendrick cleared her throat loud enough that I snapped back to attention just in time to hear her say, "The Roman Empire was built on ambition, and ambition, as you'll learn, can be both a strength and a downfall."

Ambition. Yeah, I knew something about that. I'd found a new *ambition* in life.

Her.

And like the Romans . . . I wasn't sure yet if she was going to be my downfall.

Casey

I walked into the lecture hall, clutching my bag tighter than necessary as the usual low buzz of conversation filled the room. Hopefully I'd just had my first and only freak-out of the day, and I could start out the school year strong. Scanning the rows, I looked for an empty seat. Ugh. The only ones available were in the very middle of the back of the auditorium. I made my way down the row, apologizing as I went. I'd have to make a note to get here earlier next time.

I'd just gotten to the seat when my eyes caught on something—or rather, someone—and my heart may have stopped.

It was him. The guy from the banner.

Parker Davis, in the flesh, sitting at a long desk next to the professor's lectern. The room seemed to shift, all noise and motion slowing down to a crawl as my pulse thundered in my ears. That banner hadn't been Photoshopped. Not at all. If anything, it hadn't been realistic enough.

He was even more stunning up close. I didn't know that humans actually existed that looked like that. For a second I was worried, like maybe I was having one of those final moments, where your brain conjures up crazy images right before you pass away. Because he was too perfect to be real.

I knocked my chair over.

THE WRONG QUARTERBACK   45

It clattered to the ground with a sound that seemed to cut through the room like a gunshot. Heads turned, eyes darted, and my face felt like I'd somehow gotten sunburned.

Shit.

I quickly bent down to grab the chair and set it upright with trembling hands. Obviously seats needed to be bolted to the floor when I was around.

Great start.

I snuck a peek at Parker Davis, hoping that maybe it hadn't been as loud as I'd thought and he wouldn't have noticed.

But he was looking. And not just looking. His blue eyes were locked onto me, burning straight through to my insides. Was the room spinning? Or was that just me . . . and the fact that I didn't know how to breathe anymore?

Another bolt of heat shot through me, and my fingers went numb for a second.

I frantically dragged my ass into the seat, wincing when I banged my elbow on the little desk attached to it that was somehow supposed to hold my laptop. Could I look up yet? There was no way he was staring anymore . . . right?

I peeked at the front of the room.

Nope. He was still watching me, his expression unreadable but intent. I frantically glanced around. Because I was just imagining this. He had to be looking at someone else. But although there were plenty of students drooling over him, none of them seemed to be having the visceral reaction that you had to have when you caught the attention of a god like Parker Davis. Sweating, pulse exploding . . . underwear suddenly damp . . .

I tried to nonchalantly wipe my mouth. Did I have whipped cream from my drink on my lips? I hadn't been able to eat anything this morning, so it couldn't be food . . . but maybe my lip gloss had smeared?

Okay . . . it didn't feel like I had anything wrong on my face.

I pulled out my laptop, keeping my eyes glued to the screen . . . even though I didn't have anything on it to look at. Somehow . . . I could still feel him staring, though, and every second made my skin tingle with a mixture of dread and anticipation and something I didn't want to name.

The professor, a tall woman with sharp features, began talking, introducing herself as Professor Hendrick. "Welcome to History of the Roman Empire. If you're here for an easy ride, you might as well leave now." Her voice cut through the room, but I barely heard it. All I could feel was the weight of Parker's gaze.

46   C.R. JANE

My pulse thudded in my chest, and it took everything I had to keep my breathing steady. A few other students had noticed, their eyes darting between us with interest, like there was something here they wanted to figure out. I swallowed hard, shifting in my seat and gripping my pen until my knuckles turned white.

I forced myself to listen to the professor, catching snippets of what she was saying about expectations and midterms. But even then, the awareness of him didn't fade. It was like he'd put me in a spotlight, and I couldn't escape it.

I snuck another glance up and found him still watching, his blue eyes locked on me like he was trying to read every thought in my head. My heart did a strange, heavy flip, and I looked away so fast my neck hurt.

The last two years had been lonely. That was the only thing that could explain how I was reacting to a stranger. None of my friends had wanted to deal with the sad girl who had lost her brother. They hadn't known how to talk to me about anything . . . and so they'd just stopped talking to me altogether.

My mother had been so trapped in her grief over the death of her favorite child that her other child . . . the one who was still living . . . disappeared in her mind. We passed each other like shadows in the night, and I could count the conversations that I'd had with her on one hand over the past two years.

And Gray . . . well, I'd lived for his text messages, but if I was honest with myself . . . they'd been few and far between.

That loneliness had to be the explanation for why I was feeling so crazy right now because of a stranger, albeit a hot stranger, eyeing me.

I just wasn't used to it.

"Mr. Davis, why don't you introduce yourself to the class as our teaching assistant?" the professor suddenly said.

And that got my attention.

I peeked up once . . . only to lock eyes with him again . . . and I immediately resumed studying the pencil marks etched into the top of my desk.

Parker started talking . . . and although a lot less articulate than I would have thought he'd be as a guy who probably had to talk in front of crowds all the time . . . his voice . . . fuck. It was deep, rich, a perfect mix of confidence and something rougher that made the air seem heavier. The sound of it vibrated in a way that sank right into my chest, making me feel it more than just hear it. It wasn't just a voice; it was a presence. Low, commanding, with a hint of rasp that made my pulse quicken and my skin flush hot.

His words seemed to brush over my skin and leave a trail of awareness in its wake, heat pooling low in my stomach like a slow burn. It was as if his voice reached across the space between us and pulled me in, locking me in place whether I wanted it or not.

What the hell was wrong with me?

I only caught a few things that Professor Hendrick said for the rest of class . . . which was definitely a problem since I was pretty sure she'd given us our first assignment at the end. All I knew was that the second she said the words "Class dismissed," I was out of my seat, grabbing my bag and hustling down the row as I tried not to trip on everyone else who seemed in no hurry to get out of class.

Maybe it was because they hadn't been stared at all class by the hottest man alive.

It made a difference when you were the one doing the staring, I supposed.

I had made it two steps out the door and had proudly kept my eyes to myself the entire time, when I heard that voice—calling "hey" behind me.

Even though it didn't make sense. I knew Parker Davis was calling after . . . me.

I turned around . . . and it felt a little like my heart might be breaking. Because now that I'd seen him up close, how was anyone, for the rest of my life, supposed to compare?

His lashes were thick and dark, no doubt the envy of every woman who swooned over him. The light from the windows in this hallway was catching on the sharp line of his jaw, the little flecks of gold in those electric-blue eyes. He was devastating, magnetic . . . perfect. The rough shadow of stubble on his face, the way his lips tilted in a half smile—it all sent a wave of heat through me that had me barely able to hold myself together.

"Hey," he said, simple and casual, but his voice carried that same low hum, like it held secrets meant only for me.

It was really bad that I *wanted* those secrets.

"Um—hi?" I managed, the word coming out softer than I wanted . . . and confused. My throat felt tight, like it was suddenly hard to breathe.

His gaze lingered, eyes scanning my face like he was trying to memorize every detail. The world seemed to narrow to just us, the noise of shuffling students and slamming doors fading away. I felt hypeaware of everything— of how close he was—and how he smelled, like clean, masculine energy . . . with a hint of something darker. Or the way his presence seemed to fill every inch of space between us.

I crossed my arms in front of my chest, just in case my suddenly ridiculously hard nipples were poking through my bra and he could see.

"Did you need something?" I finally murmured, when we'd just been standing there gazing at each other for what seemed like an eternity.

He blinked, as if the sound of my voice had broken him out of a trance.

"What's your name?" he asked, and my confusion only grew.

"My name?"

"Yeah, I need it," he answered. His voice was demanding . . . like he felt it was his right to get it from me.

And something inside me definitely wanted to obey.

"Casey," I told him hesitantly.

His responding smile was like the sun coming out from behind the clouds. I wanted to bask in its warmth. I wanted to see it every day for the rest of my life.

Okay, crazy.

"Casey," he repeated, almost to himself, like he was savoring the taste of my name. "I'm Parker." A slightly hysterical-sounding giggle escaped my lips, because he was being so polite in introducing himself, when obviously I knew his name already.

Everyone did.

"There you are." Gray's voice came from behind me, and a second later his arm was slipping around my waist. The unexpected contact made me stiffen, but I forced a smile as he curled himself around my body. What was he doing?

And why did it suddenly feel so wrong when before this morning it was everything I'd ever wanted . . .

Parker's eyes were locked on us, his jaw tightening as he watched. There was a dangerous glint there, almost like he didn't like what he was seeing. The way his gaze burned through me made the air feel heavy, charged.

Gray pressed a kiss to the side of my head, and that snapped me out of whatever daze Parker had me under. I glanced up at him, surprised.

"Ready for lunch?" Gray's voice was low, intimate, and I flushed at the sound of it. At this rate, I was going to look like a tomato for the entire day. He looked at Parker before I could say anything. "Oh, hey," he said, as if he'd just noticed Parker standing there.

Which had to be impossible because I'd never met anyone in my life with such a large presence. Ignoring Parker Davis would be like ignoring a giant naked statue in the middle of a room.

Impossible.

THE WRONG QUARTERBACK   49

"Andrews," Parker said stiffly, lifting his chin. All the warmth he'd had before turned into ice.

The two of them stared at each other, a thick layer of tension building between the three of us.

"Do you two know each other?" Gray asked, his arm still wrapped around me.

"No," I said at the same time that Parker said, "Yes."

Gray shifted behind me, and then his other arm was wrapped around me as well. It felt like he was staking a claim or something.

Which was laughable.

Because in what world would Parker Davis ever be interested in me . . .

And besides, I'd been in love with Gray Andrews forever. How could I be interested in anyone else?

How could I . . .

"Mr. Davis." Professor Hendrick's voice floated out from the lecture hall entrance, disapproving, like she didn't like what she was seeing.

Parker gritted his teeth, turning his attention to me for one more second, all that rapt awareness focused and clear.

"See you later, Casey," he finally said.

And it felt like a promise.

"Bye," I answered, forcing the word out while my pulse thudded in my ears. Parker turned and walked away, and it was all I could do to drag my gaze to Gray.

As Gray unwrapped himself from around me and took my hand, I couldn't help but look back over my shoulder as he led me down the hallway.

I almost tripped when I saw that Parker was paused in the doorway, once again watching me.

And suddenly . . . "bye" felt like the biggest lie I'd ever told.

CHAPTER 5

CASEY

Gray's hand was warm around mine, our fingers laced tight as we walked toward the dining hall. The sun cast everything in a golden light that made the campus look like a picture out of a brochure.

It was hard for me to focus on the view, though. My thoughts kept bouncing from Parker Davis to the fact that Gray's hand was currently tangled around mine.

There was a dissonance in the air between us. I could feel it buzzing beneath the surface.

"So," Gray said after what seemed like forever, his voice casual but forced. "How do you know Parker?"

The question caught me off guard. I glanced at him, his eyes fixed on the path ahead, jaw tight. He wasn't looking at me, but the way he said it—sharp, edged with something I couldn't quite name—it almost sounded like he was . . . jealous.

"I don't," I said slowly. "He's just . . . my TA."

Gray snorted. "So why was your *TA* talking to you in the hallway like that on the first day of class?"

I licked my lips, trying to figure out what to say, because I was as confused as Gray was about what had just happened with Parker back there.

"I'm not sure. Introducing himself, I guess," I finally murmured.

He let out a dry laugh, and I glanced up at his face. He looked anything but amused at the moment. "Right," he muttered. "Just *introducing* himself."

THE WRONG QUARTERBACK **51**

"Are you mad at me?" I asked hesitantly, stopping in my tracks and pulling on my hand so he would let me go.

But he didn't let go. Instead, he pulled me back to him, cradling my hand in both of his as his gaze searched my face. "Casey, Parker Davis runs through girls like they're *nothing*. He's left thousands of miserable women around campus, with no one to pick up the pieces."

Thousands. The words hit me, the significance of them sitting heavy in my chest. I mean, of course a god like that could have absolutely *anyone* that he wanted. But for some reason it *hurt* to think about. I tried to keep my face blank, though, like I didn't care at all about what he was saying—because why should I?

"Why are you telling me this? I don't know him, Gray. He was probably just being nice. I knocked my chair over and made a big scene at the start of class—I'm sure he felt sorry for me," I told him, trying not to remember how Parker's gaze had seemed to caress my skin. And how sparks had spun down my spine at the sound of his voice.

Gray exhaled, the tension in his posture breaking just enough for me to see it. "Because, Case," he said, his voice softer now, "you're . . . you're beautiful. Guys are going to want you. You stand out in every crowd. It's impossible *not* to want you."

My pulse jumped, and I swallowed hard, the unexpected words settling somewhere between my ribs, warm and confusing. "You think I'm beautiful?" I whispered, my cheeks flushing.

A memory rushed back, as vivid as if I were standing in that sun-soaked backyard all over again. I was maybe eight, trailing behind Ben and Gray with that relentless determination only a little sister could muster. They'd been trying to build something—a rickety tree fort or some kind of "boys only" club. I hadn't cared what it was, I just wanted to be part of it, to bask in their laughter and feel like I belonged.

"Casey, stop following us!" Ben's voice had been exasperated, more bark than bite, but I'd ignored him, trudging along, my ponytail bouncing as I struggled to keep up with their longer strides. Gray had glanced back, a grin on his face that always seemed to say *I'm glad you're here*.

"Come on, Ben, let her stay," Gray had said, throwing me a wink. He'd always been the patient one, the one who never made me feel like I was just the annoying kid sister tagging along.

And then my foot had caught on a stray root, and I went down hard, the sting of the fall spreading across my knee, followed by the slow, hot trickle of blood. Tears pricked my eyes, but before I could even let out a cry, Gray was there, dropping to his knees beside me.

"You okay, Case?" His voice had been soft, calm, a balm in itself. He didn't wait for me to answer, gently brushing dirt off my scraped knee and pulling a crumpled bandana from his back pocket. The fabric was warm from being pressed against him, and I watched, wide-eyed, as he tied it around my knee with careful fingers, like I was something fragile.

"There," he'd said, giving me that smile that made everything hurt a little less. "Good as new. Ready to get back at it?"

I'd nodded, sniffling but feeling brave again, like that simple act had mended more than just my skin—it had sealed something in me, too. Gray's eyes, bright with that easy warmth, had lingered a moment longer, and then he'd stood up, offering me a hand to pull me to my feet.

I'd been in love with him from that moment on.

The memory dissolved as quickly as it came, leaving me standing there with the echo of a million memories, of the way his presence had always meant safety. Gray wasn't just some boy in my past. He was a part of me in a way that felt carved into my bones.

Gray suddenly groaned, and his eyes searched mine, intense and a little desperate. "Of course, I think you're fucking beautiful," he admitted, his voice raw and exposed. "I want you, Casey. I think I've *always* wanted you."

The world seemed to tilt, the noise of the campus fading into the background as I stared at him. The way he said it—like he'd been carrying it around for longer than I knew—made something inside me crack open.

"Gray . . ." My voice barely made it past my lips, caught between disbelief and a rush of emotions that swirled around inside me.

"I always kept my distance . . . for Ben," he continued. "And now I feel like a fool, because knowing how much Ben loved you . . . maybe he would have understood. I at least should have tried."

My breath hitched, the weight of his words sinking in, heavy and real. I'd wanted these words for so long . . . I was having trouble believing he was actually saying them.

He moved closer, his hands letting go of mine so they could slide up and cup my face, his thumbs brushing against my cheeks. "I'm probably saying this all wrong," he said, eyes locked on mine. "But I need you to know that it's you, Case. It's *always* been you."

The honesty in his voice, the way he looked at me like I was the only thing that mattered . . . this was it. This was really happening.

THE WRONG QUARTERBACK 53

I let out a shaky breath, the realization that my dreams were actually coming true winding its way into my consciousness, and I nodded. "Okay," I whispered, not sure what else to say.

A small smile tugged at the corner of his lips.

"So are we doing this, Casey? Are you *finally* going to be my girl?" he asked, his voice low, almost shy, like he wasn't sure what my answer would be.

For a brief second, someone else's face flitted through my head. But I pushed it away.

This was real. *This* was what I had always wanted.

"Yes," I whispered, barely able to get the word out before he closed the gap between us, pressing his lips to mine. The world around us faded into a blur, and for a moment, it was just us, tangled in a promise that felt like it had been a long time coming.

Before I could fully melt into it, someone shouted his name from across the lawn. "Gray! Are we eating or not?"

He pulled back immediately, and I looked over his shoulder to see a group of guys and girls approaching.

Gray let his hands drop and he turned, the easy smile he had with his friends slipping back into place as if nothing had happened. "Come on, let's go eat," he said, grabbing my hand and tugging me along.

I followed, but the moment was already fading as he launched into a conversation with one of his friends about the party they were going to after the game tomorrow. Squeezing his hand, I tried not to let the shift bother me, but the way his focus had moved on so fast had the warmth in my chest fading. I felt like I was still standing back there, in the emptiness that he'd left.

And Parker's face was in my head again.

CHAPTER 6

PARKER

Walking away from Casey felt like the hardest thing I'd ever had to do in my life. And that wasn't me being dramatic.

Leaving her with Gray Andrews . . .

Absolutely unacceptable.

Something that was *not* going to happen again.

"Mr. Davis," Professor Hendrick's voice snapped the second I'd forced myself back into the room. The lecture hall had emptied out while I'd been gone, but she was still standing by the lectern, arms crossed over her chest, a look that could have curdled milk aimed straight at me.

"Yes, Professor?" I was glad that my voice was coming out normal. I felt shell-shocked, changed, just from that brief interaction in the hallway.

She raised an eyebrow, the silence stretching just long enough to make my jaw tighten. "Is there something you'd like to share? Something I should be aware of?"

Yeah, I probably shouldn't have been that obvious, basically running after one of her students in front of the whole class. I might as well have put a neon sign over my head that said I was interested.

It was unavoidable, though. If I hadn't gotten her name just now, I might have gone crazy.

Well, crazier than I was already feeling.

"No, ma'am. Nothing to share," I said smoothly, folding my arms and giving her my most practiced, pleasant smile.

Her lips pressed into a thin line, eyes narrowing. "I'd like to remind you, Mr. Davis, of my strict no-fraternization policy between TAs and students. It's not just a guideline; it's non-negotiable."

I nodded, the smile never slipping as I thought about Casey's silver eyes, and the way she'd stared up at me . . . and all the things I was going to do to that tight fucking body.

"Understood, Professor," I replied easily, my voice steady.

But I'd never told a bigger lie.

There was *definitely* going to be fraternizing.

More than she could ever imagine.

And I, for one, couldn't wait for the fraternizing to begin.

I would just have to figure out a way around that rule after the fact.

First steps to becoming a stalker: figuring out everything I could about my girl.

As soon as I left the lecture hall, I slipped into one of the empty, private study rooms that were in most of the academic buildings. These rooms would be almost impossible to get next week when students actually had work to do, but since it was the first day of class, they were all completely empty.

First day of class. It felt weird to think that was all the time that had passed. Today already felt like the longest, most life-changing day of my life. It seemed much more fitting that weeks had gone by, or even months. Not just a couple of fucking hours.

Settling into the chair, the screen's glow reflecting off my face as I navigated through the class roster, my fingers paused when her name popped up. Casey Larsen.

It would sound even better as Casey Davis.

A grin tugged at the corner of my mouth. *Okay, crazy . . .*

I moved to the professor portal. Hendrick had given me access to help with something last year, and I was hoping she hadn't bothered to change the password. I keyed it in and waited, doing an inner fist pump when the screen accepted it.

I typed in her name, and Casey's student profile appeared, neatly organized and full of the usual information: photo ID, major—undecided, of course, since she was a freshman—and home address. My gaze slid over her birthdate and paused at her current schedule. Perfect. A quick screenshot captured it all, and I made a mental note of her roommate's name as well.

56 C.R. JANE

I opened a new tab, fingers typing her name and hometown. I was pleasantly surprised when there were actually a few search results.

She played piano. And she didn't just *play* . . . she was incredible. There were some articles about piano contests she'd been in, bright headlines detailing her wins, her talent. One article even linked to a video on YouTube. I clicked on it, and before I knew it, the soft, rich notes of piano music filled the silent room. She was younger in the video, eyes closed as her fingers danced over the keys, moving with a kind of passion that made it impossible to look away. I sat back, the music winding its way through me, unexpected and sharp. She was talented. Fuck, more than talented. I didn't know much about music, but there was no way she wasn't a prodigy or something.

Wow. Just another tally mark in the goddess column.

I scrolled through a few more search results that weren't relevant before I got to the obituary of a guy named Ben Larsen. Feeling uneasy, I clicked on it, scanning through the page.

Her brother had died. Around two years ago. He'd been about my age. I rubbed at my chest, the sentence *survived by his loving mother, Brenda Larsen, and his younger sister, Casey* making me sick inside.

Fuck.

I got it then. Her eyes had been stunning, yes. And unique. But thinking about them now, I understood why else they had entranced me. Because there was a deepness inside them, a darkness . . . that only came from suffering loss.

I knew that, because the same look was reflected in *my* eyes from the moment my dad had died suddenly and my mom had fallen apart.

I wondered if she felt it too—that emptiness inside of her, like something was missing.

I hoped she did. Because then I could swoop in and fill all the empty parts up.

My phone buzzed with a text, and I groaned when I saw the time. I was supposed to be watching film right now with the rest of the offense.

Matty: Where the fuck are you?

Jace: Blink once if you were kidnapped.

Matty: How the fuck are you going to see a blink through a text?

> Jace: ESP, obviously. I'd be able to sense it through the phone.

> Matty: . . .

Rolling my eyes, I slammed my laptop shut, annoyed for the first time in my life that I had to go to a football practice.

I had so much more stalking to do.

On my way, I typed out as I strode out of the study room and down the hall.

I'd always been a pro at patience in my life. Knowing that if I worked hard, eventually I would get what I wanted. It had worked for football, and I'd make sure it worked with Casey as well.

And I was quite sure that the payoff for this particular patience would be the most rewarding thing I'd earned in my life thus far.

I jolted awake, my eyes searching the darkness of the room, trying to figure out what had woken me up . . . and what had my pulse hammering like an alarm in my chest.

Something was off. The kind of off that prickled the back of my neck and made my muscles tense under the sheets. I sat up slowly, letting my eyes adjust to the slivers of moonlight filtering through the blinds. I didn't see anything.

Swinging my legs over the side of the bed, I reached for a pair of sweatpants on the chair. I pulled them on, the soft fabric clinging to my skin as the cool air hit me. Sleeping naked was my usual thing, but I wasn't going to go investigate the house with my dick out.

Creak. And then another one.

Alright . . . some fucker was definitely in my house. And it better not be Jace or Matty trying to scare me from next door because I wasn't above punching either of them.

I moved as silently as I could to the closet, opening it and grabbing the baseball bat I had in there before I crept to the bedroom door. Cracking it open, I peered into the dark hallway.

Empty.

I took a few steps down the hall, avoiding the floorboards that I knew creaked. This house was older, like all the houses you could rent around campus.

58   C.R. JANE

I was just passing one of the empty bedrooms when a rough burlap bag was suddenly yanked over my head, the thick, scratchy material biting into my neck. "Motherfucker!" I hissed, my body kicking into fight mode before my brain even caught up. I swung, my fist connecting with someone's ribs.

The grunt of pain was satisfying, and I tried again, but it was like ten more people were on me at once, crushing me, pinning my arms to my sides, and forcing me to the ground.

"Hold him, damn it!" a voice hissed.

I jerked and twisted, catching another body with my knee. There were curses, then shuffling feet, and the sound of someone stumbling into the wall. Before I could hit anyone else, my arms were yanked behind me, bound tightly, and my legs tied next. I struggled against the restraints, breath heaving through the stifling bag.

Before I could process my next move, I was lifted and carried away. The hallway turned into the front yard, and then the night air bit at my bare chest. There was a rumble as a car trunk squeaked open, and I was shoved inside. "Fuck," I grunted, the hard metal unforgiving against my spine. The lid slammed shut.

Was this really happening?

I kicked as hard as I could, my feet slamming against the sides, but the only response was the engine roaring to life.

The drive was short, but the minutes seemed to tick by like hours as I continued to kick at the sides and try to get out of the bindings around my wrists. I listened to the tires crunch gravel, and then the car finally stopped, and muffled voices were talking low outside. The trunk popped open, and I didn't wait. I thrashed, twisting my body, trying to kick out at whoever was close enough. My foot connected with something—a knee, maybe—and I heard a curse.

"I'm going to kill you," I snarled, and someone nearby actually laughed.

More hands grabbed at me and lifted me out of the trunk. The bag still covered my face, suffocating, blinding, but I could feel the temperature change. Cooler air, stale. Like we were heading underground.

They took me down steps, my feet bouncing off each one. My shoulders ached from being jerked around.

"Careful with him," a voice said. "He has a game today."

What the fuck? What kind of kidnappers were these guys?

There was a chuckle, and then I was set down on the cold, hard floor. The bag was ripped from my head, and I blinked, squinting against the dim light as I inhaled the smell of wax and damp earth. Flickering candles caught my

THE WRONG QUARTERBACK   59

attention first, casting long shadows that danced along the concrete walls. My pulse raced as I scanned the room, the cold air pressing in from all sides. Candles lined every surface, filling the basement with a strange, almost . . . ceremonial glow. A circle of guys in black masks completed that look. They were standing motionless, watching me with painted, grinning faces.

I shifted, still bound, my wrists aching from the tightness of the ropes. I stared at the masked guys—some of them taller, broader, others leaner, but all dressed in black, blending into the shadows. The masked guy directly in front of me itched his knee, and through the dim light, I saw the bottom of a very familiar tiger tattoo peeking out from beneath his sleeve.

That was definitely Garrett, a senior running back on the team. We'd always given him a hard time about it because the tiger's tail looked like a dick.

I glanced around the room for more clues, and then I saw it—a stone altar on the back wall, carved with the symbol of the Sphinx, unmistakable with its sharp, angular lines and detailed depictions: a scarab at the center, its wings spread wide, surrounded by piercing eyes and Egyptian hieroglyphics. Dark red smears marred the mark on the wall, almost like dried blood, giving it a sinister, creepy edge.

It finally hit me then . . . I was being fucking initiated.

I hadn't ever given the Sphinx or any of the other secret societies on campus much thought. I was firmly of the opinion that I controlled my own destiny. I was going to be the number one pick in the NFL draft, whether I was a part of a secret society or not.

But I guess I wouldn't complain. Only the top students, the most powerful athletes, the ones destined for something more, ever got pulled into the Sphinx.

The guy standing closest to me shifted, stepping closer. His voice came low, muffled by the mask, but I recognized the tone. It was Charlie, the basketball captain. A smirk crept up on my lips, picturing the curly-haired, six-foot-seven, gangly-looking redhead. If this was a real kidnapping, I'd never be able to take them seriously once he pulled off his mask and I saw that face. "Welcome to the Sphinx, Davis," he said, trying to sound commanding and mysterious.

"If this was an invite, you could've skipped the whole 'bag over the head and tie me up' thing. A simple 'you're invited' would have done the trick," I drawled, drawing a few chuckles as someone finally undid the bindings. I gritted my teeth as I massaged my wrists. This was going to be fun for my game today.

60   C.R. JANE

Footsteps echoed against the stone walls behind me. I shifted, glancing over my shoulder, and saw three more inductees being dragged into the room, their heads covered with burlap sacks similar to the one that had been yanked over mine earlier.

The masked figures holding them wore the same masks, and they were all struggling not to get beat up by the guys they were dragging.

One of the guys was putting up quite a fight, jerking against the hands that held him, shouting curses that, even muffled, were unmistakably . . . creative.

"I'm going to kill you, ya back-alley hillbillies. I'll fuck your mom and make you call me daddy! I am not going to be kidnapped by a bunch of wannabe Halloween decorations!"

I snorted. Jace. Only Jace . . .

Did that mean one of the others was . . .

The guys were all dropped to the ground, their bags ripped off, revealing Jace, Matty, and some other guy I'd never seen before.

Jace grinned scarily and pointed a finger at one of the masked figures that had been holding him. "I'm coming for you," he mouthed, and the guy shrank back, hiding behind some of the other Sphinx members. Jace winked at me afterward, like he'd known I'd be here all along.

Matty just looked pissed, glaring around the room like he wanted to burn it all down.

The room suddenly grew completely silent, and the masked men parted, another figure stepping out in front of them all. This one was the leader judging by the fancy, gold-etched mask he was wearing. His voice, amplified by some kind of distortion device he was using, cut through the air with all the resonant authority and mystery that *Charlie* had been going for earlier. I had no idea who this guy was.

"Welcome to the Sphinx," he began, his gaze sweeping over us, the new initiates. "If you make it in, you will gain access to an organization that boasts the most powerful figures in the world. Politicians, captains of industry, even those who move the unseen levers of power—every door will be open to you."

The four of us shifted, his words settling over us. I could feel the change in the air, the anticipation mixed with an underlying current of uncertainty. The promise was definitely alluring.

The leader continued, his voice deep and deliberate. "Over the course of the next year, you will be tested. You'll have to prove that you are worthy of standing in our midst, of bearing the mark of the Sphinx . . .

THE WRONG QUARTERBACK   61

failing any one of these tests would be the single greatest regret of your lives . . ." He paused for dramatic effect, blank green eyes staring at us from behind the mask. "The three tests will happen to each of you at different times, and when you least expect it. Those who complete their tests go on to become full Sphinx members at the end of the year. Good luck, gentlemen."

With that *warm* welcome, he turned and left the room through a side door I hadn't noticed before. Charlie was up again then, this time holding a gold chalice covered with a ton of diamonds and rubies. Those were fake, right? Because that was a *very* expensive-looking cup.

It was the knife he pulled out of his robes, though, that really got my attention. His voice echoed through the chamber. "To prove your commitment, you will offer your blood. Your first sacrifice to the Sphinx."

I watched as he moved to the first initiate, the one I didn't recognize, and handed him the knife. He took it, wincing as he sliced a shallow cut across his palm, crimson drops splattering into the chalice.

I was next, and I took the knife, its hilt cool and heavy in my hand. I glanced down at my palm, flexing my fingers, knowing that any injury there could throw everything off for the game.

Somehow, I didn't think they'd take that as an excuse, though.

I pressed the blade against my chest instead, just below my collarbone. The sting was immediate, a hot line of pain as I dug it into my skin. Blood welled up, warm and sticky, tracing a path down to my ribs.

I tilted forward, letting the blood drip into the chalice. The guy nodded, taking the knife from my hand and moving on to Jace and Matty.

And then it was done.

We were ushered up a set of stairs and out of a door, popping out onto the grass outside the Sphinx like newborn chicks.

"That was fucking weird," Matty grunted as we parted ways with the other initiate and set off toward the street where we all lived. It wasn't that far away. We definitely could have done without the trunk ride.

Or any of it, obviously.

"Very weird," I muttered, extremely annoyed about the fact that the sky was already streaked with the orange of early dawn, and I was going to have to play a game today with minimal sleep.

I was also annoyed that this would be another thing that took away from my plans for Casey. That was unacceptable, actually.

Jace abruptly started to laugh, the sound almost a giggle.

"What's wrong with you?" asked Matty, his patience completely gone.

"You should have seen the chick's face when they came to get me. She probably thinks I died," Jace cackled, stopping and bending over because he was laughing so hard. "She was screaming so loud."

That got a grin out of me . . . and Matty, as we both pictured the scene.

"This won't be so bad, it can't be, right?" Jace asked when he'd finally recovered.

Matty and I glanced at each other, my wariness reflected in his eyes.

I mean how bad could it get . . .

CHAPTER 7

PARKER

Game day.

There was nothing quite like it.

Nothing else could compare to the sheer, electric energy of it—the way the roar of the crowd could shake the ground beneath your feet and rattle the air in your lungs. Walking into that stadium, feeling the weight of one hundred thousand pairs of eyes fixed on you, was like stepping onto a stage where everything was magnified. Every move, every choice, every moment was played out in front of a sea of fans who lived for the highs and lows as much as you did.

There was no middle ground. You were either a god, lifted by chants that echoed your name as if you were untouchable, or a fool, shouldering the blame for everything that had gone wrong. The stakes were brutal and simple—win, and you'd be their hero; lose, and you'd taste the kind of hatred that cut deeper than anything else could.

I'd felt it before, both sides of the coin. The rush of being lifted, riding that wave of glory when everything fell into place and you were invincible, and also the bone-deep sting of screwing up. College football didn't care about yesterday's wins. It was what you did now, today, with the ball in your hands and a stadium holding its breath.

Stepping out onto that field was like a drug, though. The noise swallowed you, the pulse of the crowd synced with yours, and for a moment, it felt like you could do anything. And in that moment, with the stadium chanting, the sweat and adrenaline mixing in your veins, you either became a legend or just another name fading into the background.

I was ready to be a god today.

The locker room was filled with the usual pregame tension, a mix of adrenaline and nerves thick enough to taste. Guys were moving through their routines, headphones in, heads bobbing to silent beats, some of them muttering last-minute mantras to themselves. The air smelled of sweat, leather, and that unique metallic tang of anticipation.

I sat on the bench, lacing up my cleats with deliberate precision, letting the repetitive motion calm the churn in my gut. Game day rituals were supposed to center you, block out everything else except the field and the playbook. But today, my mind wouldn't cooperate.

My phone sat next to me, screen blank. No messages. My jaw clenched as I thought about my mom. It wasn't surprising; last week's visit had been rough. She'd barely acknowledged I was there, and then her fit over the shoes. Still, it was the first season she hadn't managed to send me even a simple *Good luck*. The empty space that absence left gnawed at me.

"Hey, QB," Jace said, throwing himself into the chair next to me and efficiently serving as a distraction. "I've got one for you."

Matty groaned on the other side of me. "He's doing his zone thing. Let him keep zoning."

"What does that even mean?" Jace asked as he pulled his hair back into a ponytail.

"You know what it means. He's getting in his groove. He's doing his thing," Chappie, one of my offensive linemen, said, doing some weird dance that made his entire body jiggle.

"Do me a favor, Chap, my man. Please don't ever do that again," Jace drawled.

"I second that," said Matty.

Chappie bent over, showcasing a large . . . and hairy butt crack, and everyone on my side groaned. "Ya like that, don't you, Jacey? There's more where that came from."

Jace looked a little sick, but the rest of us were laughing.

"Can you say whatever you were going to say before I go bleach my eyes," said Matty, laying his head back against the lockers like Chappie's ass crack had taken the life out of him.

"Alright, this is a good one," said Jace, standing up and starting some high knee stretches as he talked. "What's the difference between a snowman and a snow woman?"

"I have absolutely no fucking idea," I told him as my phone buzzed next to me. I glanced at it, thinking it might be my mom, but it was Walker.

THE WRONG QUARTERBACK   65

"Snowballs," yelled Jace suddenly, his high knee stretches turning into high knee jumps.

There was a beat of silence, and then we were all laughing. "That's two semi-funny ones in a row, Jace-Face. It must be some kind of record for you," called Matty.

Jace grinned smugly, very proud of himself.

I picked up my phone to see what Walker had to say. He'd just started training camp, and Cole was still on his world tour, so my family seats were going to be empty this game.

A thought came to me then, though, one that had a grin spreading across my face, and the disappointment fading.

Casey was probably going to be there. You didn't miss your first football game of your freshman year. And I was quite confident that she would be in those family seats before the season was over.

"Why are you smiling like that?" Matty asked, sounding disturbed.

"Like what?" I asked innocently.

"Like a crazy person," Jace added helpfully.

"This is how I smile now," I told them seriously. "You'll just have to get used to it."

They both gave me heavy side-eye, but my attention returned to my phone.

> Walker: Good luck, Parkie. I'm making the entire team watch the game, so don't fuck up and embarrass me.

> Me: I should have said something like that to you every time you missed a save and lost a game last season :)

> Walker: . . .

> Cole: Can you do my move when you run in for a touchdown this game?

I sighed, rolling my eyes.

> Me: I didn't know you had a move.

> Cole: . . .

> Cole: Did I do that right?

> Me: Walker, can you control him?

> Cole: I just think that the fans would enjoy seeing a Davis original. That's all I'm saying.

> Walker: I literally have no idea what move you're talking about either.

> Cole: This doesn't surprise me at all, Walkie-Poo. You've always been the slow one in the family.

I grunted out a laugh, and Jace once again came over to read my texts over my shoulder—because he was annoying like that.

The next text from Cole was a video of him at a concert doing a hip thrust that made it look like he was dry humping the microphone as he sang. There was a girl in the crowd right in front of him who fell backward.

> Walker: Did she just faint?

> Cole: Smug Sunglasses Emoji

Jace snorted, and I elbowed him because it was rude to be so nosy.

> Me: Why did you write that instead of just sending the emoji?

> Cole: I wanted to make sure you understood what I was saying. Those emojis can be tricky sometimes. What if you think he just looks happy instead of smug? Then you miss the whole point.

> Walker: . . .

THE WRONG QUARTERBACK   67

> **Cole:** Hey . . . that's too much of that.

> **Me:** . . .

> **Cole:** Middle Finger Emoji

> **Walker:** I also think that the emoji would have been just fine for that one. No missing that message.

> **Cole:** Just making sure.

Jace suddenly began jerking next to me, and I glanced over and saw that he was practicing Cole's move in front of the mirror.

"No. Just no," I told him. "I won't throw you a single pass if that's what you're going to do."

"I will intentionally follow you on the field and steal your passes if that's what your plan is," added Matty, looking horrified as he watched.

Jace shrugged and stopped humping the air. "You're right. I imagine my dick is much larger than a rockstar's. Wouldn't want the whole stadium fainting and making the stands collapse."

"Right . . ." drawled Matty. "We'll go with that."

I turned back to my phone.

> **Me:** While I appreciate the suggestion, I think I'll abstain from that particular move and leave that to you.

"Nice word choice," Jace commented, back to reading my texts over my shoulder. "Such a big brain."

I sighed in exasperation.

> **Walker:** Moral of the story, kill it out there, Parkie.

> **Cole:** Exactly. Go. Fight. Win.

68   C.R. JANE

He sent a picture of his head on a cheerleader's body, and with that beautiful sight, it was time for this conversation to end.

The sound of the coach's whistle broke through the room almost the second I'd put my phone away, snapping me back to what was coming. The guys stood up, voices rising as we got ready to hit the tunnel, the roar of the crowd already vibrating through the concrete walls. I took a deep breath, letting the noise fuel me, sharpen me. Game face on.

Let's fucking go.

Casey

The crowd was so loud, the bleachers were literally shaking beneath my feet. I stood there, overwhelmed, trying to take it all in—the sea of orange and white, the Tennessee Tigers flags waving wildly, and the air buzzing with anticipation. I'd never seen anything like this. I'd never made it to any of my high school football games, but there was no way they would have been anything like what was surrounding me.

The stands were packed, shoulder to shoulder, and the energy was insane, like the whole stadium was alive, thrumming with something I couldn't quite explain.

Gray had his arm draped over my shoulder, and I was trying to resist the urge to move out from under it. He and his frat brothers had been drinking since dawn, I was pretty sure, and he was already wasted. I watched as he slurred something to the guy next to him and took another swig of his beer, dribbling some down the front of his orange Tigers shirt.

I'd thought that maybe we would've gotten together last night to talk more about the fact that we were a couple now. But he hadn't even texted me. *Some pledge thing had happened,* he'd told me when I met him in front of the stadium for the game this morning. *Things will be better next semester when the pledge period is done,* he'd continued as he gave me a messy kiss.

Nat had been with me when he'd said that, and her eye roll was so extreme I was a little afraid they were going to get stuck like that.

It will be better next semester, I repeated to myself now as I watched my . . . boyfriend . . . take another drink.

It's just that after two years of barely speaking, it felt like we had a lot to catch up on. I'd once felt like I knew everything about Gray. And now the guy wrapped around me felt like a stranger. Waiting another semester to try and fix that—when we were supposed to be together *right now*—didn't feel like what should be happening.

THE WRONG QUARTERBACK 69

"Want a drink?" he yelled, offering me his beer. I shook my head, thinking that there was no way he wouldn't be blacked out by the end of the game. And I didn't think any of his friends would be any better. I would probably have to make sure he got back to the frat safe, which would be a fun way to start off my freshman football season.

Not.

Suddenly, the crowd got even louder, the noise rattling through my bones as a Jay-Z and Linkin Park mashup blared through the speakers. The players charged onto the field, their orange helmets gleaming under the sun.

And there he was.

Parker Davis led the team out of the tunnel like a king. The stadium lost its mind. His name echoed everywhere, a chant that reverberated off the concrete walls. I tried not to look, I really did, but when his face flashed up on the huge screen, I couldn't stop myself from staring. The camera zoomed in, catching his intense blue eyes, his windblown hair, and the way he carried himself like he knew he was a god among men.

I was mesmerized by how good-looking he was.

I didn't know anything about football. But watching him run out in front of his team, like a commander riding into battle . . . the other team had to have been terrified. Was it just me . . . or was there a spotlight that seemed to follow him as he made his way out on the field?

It wasn't just the way he moved, though—the smooth, confident stride, like the pressure of all those screaming fans couldn't touch him—it was everything. His tan skin, the contrast of his white teeth when he flashed a smile, and those eyes. The kind of blue that wasn't natural, couldn't be. Like the sky on a clear day, piercing and intense. They were the bluest eyes I'd ever seen.

I remembered what they'd been like in person, up close . . . and Gray's arm somehow seemed even heavier.

My breath caught in my throat as the camera zoomed in again. He was tall, towering above most of his teammates, and he was built like he'd been sculpted by someone who hadn't made the rest of us.

I felt a set of eyes on me, and I glanced over to see Nat watching, a knowing smile on her face, like she could read the lustful thoughts running through my head right then. I wrinkled my nose at her, and she laughed before looking back toward the field.

The crowd around me was still losing it, chants for Parker ringing out from every direction, and I found myself staring . . . again. The camera zoomed in and out constantly, flashing him up on the big screen every other minute. He grinned at one point, and I felt a little faint all of a sudden, like his smile held magical powers or something. It was like the entire stadium was held captive by him, me included.

I tried to tear my eyes away, but my gaze kept slipping back to the screen. And the more I watched him, the heavier the guilt sank in. What was I doing? My boyfriend was right next to me, oblivious as he laughed at something, almost spilling his drink on me in the process.

A few bad thoughts were nothing, though, right? As long as you never acted on them . . .

Wasn't there a song about that?

"You excited, babe? Your first college football game. This is gonna be wild," Gray murmured, pulling me in closer, the smell of alcohol heavy on his breath as he kind of made out with my cheek.

I forced a smile, nodding, even though my stomach churned with something else entirely.

The crowd roared louder as Tennessee huddled together, and the cameras showed Parker barking orders to his team. He even looked good when he yelled.

Gray jostled me again, shouting something about how things were about to get crazy. I nodded, not really listening. Parker seemed to glance up at the screen then, those blue eyes flashing as he smirked at the camera, and my stomach did this weird little flip . . . like that smirk was meant for me.

The players lined up to kick off, and I decided it was going to be a long game.

And that maybe I should skip them in the future if this was what my reaction was going to be.

But I could at least enjoy it today.

———

Parker took off down the field, weaving between defenders like they were standing still. The clock was ticking down, the crowd on their feet, the noise a relentless wave crashing through the stadium. My breath caught as he crossed the twenty-yard line, then the ten. And then, like it was the easiest thing in the world, he was in the end zone.

Touchdown.

I screamed, my voice lost in the roar of the crowd. Next to me, Nat jumped up and down, gripping my arm so hard it was a miracle she didn't leave bruises. The energy surged through me, wild and crazy, like I'd stuck my finger in an electrical socket. Gray had ducked out at the end of the third quarter, pale and muttering something about not feeling well, so it had just

THE WRONG QUARTERBACK   71

been me and Nat, glued to every play. Tennessee was already up by two touchdowns before Parker's run, but the crowd was acting like he'd just won the national championship.

"Oh my fucking hell, did you see that?" Nat yelled, eyes wide with exhilaration.

I nodded, my heart racing, eyes locked on Parker as he jogged into the end zone, that grin plastered across his face. And then, my jaw dropped as he turned to the crowd and did an Elvis impression, hips moving with that cocky confidence that made half the stadium scream even louder.

Somewhere down by the field, one of the cheerleaders wobbled and then straight-up dropped, like her knees had decided to give out. I laughed, that dizzy, magical feeling flooding my veins again, like he really was casting a spell across the crowd.

"Am I pregnant? I feel pregnant," Nat said, shaking me as we both watched Parker. "Oh my gosh, *look*. We're up there on the screen. Holy fuck, Casey!" Nat screamed as she took advantage of the screen time to do a sexy little dance that would no doubt stay in some guys' heads for the rest of the day.

I, for my part, stood there awkwardly, counting down the seconds until the camera panned away—something that seemed to take forever.

"What's he doing?" Nat said, eyes still on the screen.

The stadium screen showed Parker staring into the camera then, and as we watched, Parker blew a kiss and then pointed at it.

"Has he ever done that before?" I asked. Nat's family were die-hard Tennessee football fans, and she'd watched every one of Parker's games since the first time he'd started.

"No, never," Nat said, her voice confused. She side-eyed me, a sly little grin spreading across her face. "What if that was for you . . . since you were just on the screen?" she asked, an edge of hysteria in her tone.

I looked at her like she was crazy. I'd mentioned we'd had a strange moment after class, but I hadn't said anything for her to take such a giant leap as that.

"I think the sun is getting to you," I responded, gently pushing on her shoulder as we both glanced down at the chaos on the field as the game ended and the teams combined to shake hands and do postgame interviews. "We should get you some water."

"I'm just saying . . . it's possible," Nat singsonged.

I scoffed, but didn't say anything else.

Because there was no way that's what he'd meant . . . right?

CHAPTER 8

CASEY

I stood in the corner of the room, the bass from the speakers threatening to burst my eardrums. The party whirled around me, people laughing, yelling, dancing, everyone celebrating the game and seeming like they were having the time of their lives.

Except for me.

My gaze cut to Gray across the room, leaning against a pong table with some of his frat brothers, drink in hand . . . surrounded by girls. There were three of them in particular who seemed obsessed with everything he had to say. I'd just left to use the restroom, but Gray didn't seem to be missing me at all.

I squeezed the red cup in my hand, the drink inside barely touched. My eyes narrowed as one of the girls placed a hand on his arm, her laugh a little too loud, a little too close. And he just smiled, completely unaware that I was standing twenty feet away.

Or maybe it was that he just didn't care.

I should go over there, right? Put myself in between those girls, show them who he belongs to . . .

I'd just never thought love would be like that, having to prove that someone is yours.

And when I'd imagined being with Gray . . . I'd never imagined him putting me in a situation where I'd have to do that.

A memory came then . . .

I was sitting on the concrete steps behind the gym, arms wrapped around my knees, fighting the hot tears that refused to stay put. Marcie Evans was such an asshole! She'd called me a big, ugly nerd in front of everyone in the hallway after sixth period, and it had seemed like the whole school was there, laughing and agreeing with her.

"Hey, Case, what are you doing out here?"

I hurriedly wiped the tears from my face, startled to see Gray standing there, hands stuffed into his pockets, eyes narrowed with concern.

"It's nothing," I muttered, looking away.

He didn't move for a second. "Alright, let's go. You're coming with me," he said, nodding toward the parking lot.

"What? Where?" I asked, frowning.

"Doesn't matter. Just get in the car," he said, and his easy smile had me immediately following him.

Just like it always did.

Before I knew it, I was in the passenger seat of his car. Gray turned up the music, some rap song blaring through the speakers as he pulled out of the school lot. He glanced over at me, one eyebrow raised. "So, ice cream or should I throw them in a dumpster? Your call."

A reluctant smile tugged at my lips. "Ice cream."

"Good choice, Case. Much tastier," he said, winking as he turned the wheel sharply, making a dramatic U-turn that had me gripping the seat and laughing despite myself.

The next half hour was filled with him making every ridiculous joke he could think of, from ordering half the menu so we could taste-test all the flavors to making up ridiculous stories about the people who came in while we watched.

By the time I had a spoonful of mint chocolate chip in my mouth, Marcie's words were just a memory.

Gray always had that effect on me.

He was my hero.

I returned to the present as I watched as he gave a pretty girl a huge hug. Where was that guy now?

"Look at that fucking fool."

I jumped, sloshing a bit of my drink over the side. Because I knew that voice. And it was the last voice that I was expecting at the moment. Trying to get a hold of myself, I slowly wiped my hand on my jeans, taking a deep breath before I turned.

Coming face-to-face with Parker Davis.

I opened my mouth to say something, but all my words had disappeared. Awesome.

74   C.R. JANE

It physically hurt to look at him.

He was wearing a tight black Tigers shirt with a dark pair of jeans, and I watched, wide-eyed, as he lifted his arm to push his hair out of his face, revealing a perfect set of abs as he moved.

I blinked a few times to make sure I was really seeing this. Until I realized that I was just gaping at Parker's abs. Right in front of him. I quickly jerked my gaze back up, only to see a knowing smirk on his beautiful face because he knew exactly what I'd been doing.

Fuck. Could a hole open up in the floor, please?

I cleared my throat. "Sorry, did you say something?" I asked, cringing at how raspy my voice came out, like I was a pack-a-day smoker all of a sudden.

He leaned against the wall, his shirt pulling up again.

Don't look at his abs. Don't do it, I coached myself.

"I was saying he's a fucking *fool*," Parker said, his voice deep and low and . . . sensual . . . like his words had the power to wrap around me and hit me right between my legs.

"Who's a fool?" I asked, still confused.

"You're with that guy over there, aren't you? *Gray Andrews*. The one who seems to have forgotten he's supposed to be yours," he drawled, staring daggers at Gray like he'd mortally offended him.

"How did you know that?" I asked, confused about how . . . and why Parker Davis would know anything about me.

Parker's gaze returned to mine. His eyes slowly danced over my skin, like he was trying to take in every detail of my face.

I couldn't help but shiver.

"When I find the girl of my dreams, you can bet your exquisite ass I'm going to find out everything I can about her."

I stared at him, uncomprehending. What had he just said . . . it almost sounded like he'd called me the "girl of his dreams."

He slowly reached over, and his fingers tapped my chin, gently pushing up, so I closed my mouth and stopped gaping at him like some kind of slow-witted fish. I gasped at the feel of his touch.

Was he messing with me right now? He had to be. This must be some cruel prank to take advantage of the naive freshman girl who clearly didn't belong at this party. Maybe this was hazing at its worst.

I searched his face. But his expression was serious, like he meant everything he was saying. If this was all an act right now, there wasn't a better actor that existed on the planet.

THE WRONG QUARTERBACK 75

I took a huge gulp of my drink, needing something to do other than stare at him.

Parker leaned further in, his body so close I could feel the heat radiating off him. One arm braced above my head, fingers splayed against the wall. The space between us shrank, narrowing, leaving just us in this tiny, electrified bubble.

His eyes locked onto mine, intense and unblinking, pulling me in and holding me there, suspended in the moment. I couldn't look away even if I wanted to, not with the way his breath mixed with mine, slow and measured.

The subtle, intoxicating scent of him filled my senses, making my knees feel weak. The world outside blurred, the distant thud of music and chatter fading until all I could hear was the sound of my own heartbeat drumming in my ears and the steady, too-calm way he exhaled.

"Casey," he murmured, his voice low and deliberate, like he was testing how my name felt on his tongue. Each syllable wrapped around me, grounding me to this moment that felt fragile and electric all at once.

"I can't believe you're real, baby girl. You're perfect." His words came out like a groan as his hand, rough but careful, traced the curve of my jaw.

A gasp slipped from my throat before I could stop it. His gaze pinned me, trapping me in this moment that felt as dangerous as it did intoxicating.

"Casey!" The sharp edge in Gray's voice sliced through the air, shattering whatever spell Parker had cast. Before I could react, Gray pushed between us, eyes locked on Parker with an intensity that burned red-hot. "What the fuck are you doing, Davis?" he snarled, his fists clenched at his sides.

Parker didn't flinch. He moved deliberately, a lazy smirk playing on his lips as he shifted back, dragging his hand down the wall and brushing past my side. It felt deliberate, possessive, and I felt the warmth of his touch linger even as Gray's rage grew.

"Just keeping your girl *company*, Andrews," Parker said mockingly, the amusement in his voice cutting deeper. "You seemed . . . distracted." He took his time stepping away, his eyes staying on my face.

Gray's arm was suddenly around my waist, pulling me into him, his touch jealous and grasping. I felt the tight coil of tension in his body, the barely controlled fury that vibrated through him. Parker's gaze turned cold, menacing for just a moment before he smoothed it out, a blank mask slipping back into place. "See you later, Casey," he said, his voice low, filled with promise, as he sauntered off, leaving the space he'd claimed behind.

76 C.R. JANE

Gray's grip on my arm tightened as he spun me toward the exit, dragging me along without a word. My legs moved on autopilot, my mind still reeling from what had happened. The noise of the party faded as we pushed through the door, the cool night air biting into my skin and making me shiver.

He didn't stop until we were outside, away from the thrum of music and voices. Gray turned, eyes blazing. "What the hell was that?" he demanded, his voice raw and accusing. The look in his eyes was a mix of hurt and anger that twisted my insides.

"I don't know!" I cried, the words tumbling out, breathless and desperate. My whole body was trembling, on overload from everything that had just happened.

He growled, and then his lips crashed against mine, bruising and hard. Like almost every kiss we'd had since I'd come here, he tasted of sour alcohol, and I immediately wanted to wash him out of my mouth.

A soft whimper escaped my throat as he pulled back, eyes dark and wild.

"Fuck," he yelled into the night air, the word heavy with frustration as he let go of me. He turned abruptly, fists clenched so tight his knuckles turned white, the muscles in his jaw flexing as he stared out into the dark.

I stood there, my breath heaving, the imprint of his kiss seared into my lips, a strange, miserable feeling swirling in my chest.

"Were you trying to make me jealous?" he finally asked in a strained voice.

"No, of course not. I was coming back from the bathroom, and I saw you with all those girls and . . ."

"What girls?" he asked in a confused voice.

I gaped at him.

"The ones *hanging* all over you," I snapped, anger starting to edge into my voice.

His irritation faded, a smug satisfaction creeping onto his face.

I'd never, in all the time that I'd known him, thought that anything about Gray was ugly.

But that look was.

"Ohhh, so you were jealous. *That's* what that was about."

I opened my mouth to refute what he'd just said, but how did I even explain what had happened with Parker? *I* didn't understand what had happened.

That seemed to be a trend with Parker Davis, actually.

When I find the girl of my dreams . . .

His words echoed in my head, a constant loop that I'd need brain bleach to erase.

THE WRONG QUARTERBACK **77**

Gray was all smooth and charming as he walked back to me, taking my hand and pressing a kiss across my knuckles. "I'm sorry," he said soothingly. "I shouldn't have gotten so mad. You would never betray me like that."

I gulped, wondering how this had all turned on me, when *I* was the one who felt betrayed.

"Ben would be laughing at us right now," he said with a sad smile. "He'd say something stupid that would make us both laugh, and then we never would have had a fight to begin with."

Ben.

I closed my eyes, finding it hard to breathe as a million memories of the three of us spun through my head.

This *was* stupid. Gray and I shouldn't be fighting. I was probably over-reacting, and Gray was *definitely* overreacting.

"Are we good?" he asked, staring down at me with puppy-dog eyes.

I nodded with a slow smile that I had to drag up from deep inside me. "Always," I whispered.

"Let's get back to the party, then," he said, grabbing my hand and pulling me toward the music pouring from the house.

I followed Gray, even though all I wanted was to return to my dorm.

He stopped at the entry and glanced back at me, his eyes cold and serious. "I don't want you to see Parker Davis anymore, alright, Case?"

I gaped at him, but then quickly nodded, not wanting to fight with him anymore.

And once inside, I pretended that I wasn't looking for Parker as I stood behind Gray while he played beer pong with one of his frat brothers.

I also pretended I wasn't disappointed when he seemed to have disappeared.

The good news, though, was by the end of the night, when I helped drag a drunk Gray to his frat house, I was too exhausted and upset to obsess any more over Parker . . . and all the magical, *crazy* things he'd said.

Parker

I stood there in the shadows, arms crossed in front of me as I listened to their conversation. Andrews was smart. He had a trump card in his friendship with her brother, and he knew it. I wasn't worried about him, though. He had so many weaknesses, it was going to be like taking candy from a baby to get him to cross a line he couldn't come back from.

And when he did.

I would be there.

That line was going to come quick, though. He wanted Casey. He wanted her bad. Just seeing him kiss her had me wanting to murder him.

That obviously wouldn't go over well with my girl.

I rolled my neck in a slow circle, feeling the soreness from that sack earlier today. I needed to sleep. Desperately.

I watched as he pulled her back toward the party, even though her body language was screaming she didn't want to go.

Luckily, tomorrow she'd be too busy tutoring to have any time for Gray.

Tutoring me.

CHAPTER 9

PARKER

My phone buzzed as I walked into the student tutoring office. I scoffed as I stared at the text.

> Jace: Send help. I need an IV. I think I might shrivel up and die.

> Matty: WTF is wrong with you?

> Jace: That girl last night was like some kind of vampire. But like one that sucks cocks. I think she sucked all of the cum out of my dick.

> Jace: I'm dying.

I blinked at the phone, unsure of what I was reading.

> Matty: I might be the one dying because now I'm going to have this image in my head until you say the next stupid thing.

> Jace: This is a real-life emergency, Matthew. What would your life be like if I was six feet under? Huh? Think about that before you come at me with your unhelpfulness.

> **Jace:** And you, QB. Who would catch your balls and take care of your balls and make sure your balls were put in the right place.

I almost tripped on air reading that one.

> **Matty:** Why exactly was that so sexual?

> **Jace:** It wasn't. Why is your head in the gutter?

> **Jace:** As I was saying. SOMEONE BRING ME BLUE GATORADE.

> **Matty:** Why not red Gatorade? You don't sound like you're dying to me if you're being picky about the color of your liquid consumption.

> **Me:** Good point, Matty.

My footsteps echoed over the tiled floor as I approached the desk where a nervous, dark-haired girl was staring at me like I was an alien that had just landed in front of her. If I had actually needed help, I could have used any of the team tutors that were on call almost twenty-four-seven. But since I had straight A's, and I didn't want those tutors . . . that wouldn't have been helpful.

Thus I was here.

> **Me:** Sorry, boys, you're by yourselves on this one. Matty, I suggest some orange juice. That usually perks him right up.

I pocketed my phone, ignoring the barrage of texts that followed.

The girl continued to stare at me once I got up to the desk. I smiled at her and her face paled, like she was going to faint.

"Hi," I said, annoyed when she squeaked, got up from her seat, and ran out of sight.

THE WRONG QUARTERBACK   **81**

I glanced at my watch. According to her schedule on the school portal, Casey's first shift as a tutor was still open tonight. I was going to be really displeased if that spot was filled while I was waiting for someone competent to help me out, and I had to figure out that problem as well.

Sometimes being so awesome was really a burden.

Noticing an old-school silver bell on the counter, I banged on it a few times, until finally an ancient-looking woman popped her head around the corner. Speaking of vampires . . . she looked like she'd woken up from the grave and decided to come to work today.

She glared at me, her lips pursed. Yes, this was a woman who could help me. I could tell she'd made up her mind about me before I even opened my mouth. Dumb, muscle guy, here for a quick fix.

Perfect.

I leaned casually against the counter. "I need to get a tutor."

The woman walked over to the desk with a sigh, and I thought about taking a picture of her and sending it to Jace to see if this was who he'd been talking about. She was so pale, I was pretty sure I could see the veins running under her skin.

I smirked at the thought.

"What subject?" she asked sourly.

"Calculus," I said, leaning forward so I could look at the computer with her as she went through names.

She scowled, squinting at the screen as she scrolled, finally stopping on the first calculus tutor available, someone named Hollow Thornley.

"Nope, sorry, she won't work," I insisted quickly. "She hates me. My best friend broke her heart and it brings back bad memories when she sees me."

I had no idea who Hollow Thornley was, but knowing Jace and Matty, it could be the truth.

The lady coughed, shaking her head at my argument. "There's very few available," she growled in a croaky voice.

I pointed to Casey's name on the screen. "What about her?"

The woman leaned closer, going through Casey's information. "She's a freshman, brand new," she warned.

"Perfect," I said quickly, wincing at how eager I sounded.

The woman didn't seem to notice my . . . enthusiasm. "Name?" she droned, her clawlike hands hovering over the keyboard.

"Davis," I said vaguely, hoping I'd read the situation correctly and she had no idea who I was.

82   C.R. JANE

The woman nodded and typed what I'd said before she handed me the appointment details and shuffled away from the desk—probably to go back to her coffin and take a nap.

I was whistling as I left the building, wishing that the day would go faster.

I got to the library twenty minutes early, determined not to miss out on a second with her. To my surprise, Casey was already there, sitting at one of the long wooden tables near the back by the windows. Her head was down, her hand nervously fidgeting with a pencil. I couldn't help but grin as I watched her. How could I not? She made me happy just looking at her.

She just didn't know that yet.

I watched her for a moment, wondering how it was possible for her to make a baggy sweatshirt look better than the sexiest lingerie I'd ever seen. Her hair was down, falling in waves almost to her waist, and she was surrounded by textbooks and notebooks, a feat since school had barely started.

I decided not to even try and wait for my appointment time; the longer I got with her, the better.

People were whispering as I walked through the room, but that wasn't anything new for me. Eventually, she would get used to that too. And realize that it was a very small list of people whose opinion or attention actually mattered.

None of the sheep in this library were on that list.

I pulled out the chair next to her, making sure to brush against her as I sat down. Her eyes darted up, and she froze for a second, staring at me in shock.

"Hey," I murmured. "It must be my lucky day."

Her cheeks immediately flushed, and she literally gulped as she continued to gape at me. I'd always prided myself on self-control, but having those silver eyes on me was literally making my dick ache.

"They forgot your first name," she blurted out.

"Hmm?"

"They just put 'Davis' on the sign-up form online. I—I didn't know it was going to be you," she explained, looking adorably frantic as she began organizing her papers like I was going to have a problem with the fact that they weren't perfectly lined up.

"That's weird," I said casually, scooting my chair even closer to her so my thigh was pressed up against hers.

THE WRONG QUARTERBACK 83

She stared at where we were touching, her eyes darting from my leg to my face, and then back again as she debated asking me to give her some space. There was also the little fact that her *boyfriend* had asked her to stay away from me.

My grin when she didn't say anything felt so wide, I probably resembled one of those scary clowns that had terrified kids since the dawn of time.

I needed to tone it down.

"Umm . . . right. So calculus. You need help with *calculus*." She cleared her throat, peeking at me. "Right?"

I chuckled, taking the opportunity to brush her hair behind her ear. Fuck, it was soft. I was really going to enjoy wrapping it around my fists as I fucked her from behind.

Slow down, Parker.

Casey shivered, inhaling deeply. After a second, I leaned forward, my lips almost brushing hers.

"Breathe," I murmured.

Her breath left her in a sexy gasp, and I inhaled, because I wanted her air inside me.

We stayed like that for a second, just staring at each other, until the *bang* of someone dropping a book nearby made her jump and jerk away.

I had the insane urge to find whoever had dropped that book . . . and *murder* them.

"Alright, Teach." I grinned, leaning back in my chair, even though all I wanted was to scoop her into my arms. "So, you're going to make sure that I don't fail, huh?"

She licked her lips nervously, her fingers tightening around the pencil she was holding. I frowned when I saw her hand start to shake. As soon as she noticed me watching, she dropped the pencil, yanking her trembling hand into her lap.

I filed that away as something I needed to follow up with. If she had an injury, I needed to know how to help her.

I needed to know *everything* about her.

"I'm sure that's not going to happen," she said shyly.

"What?" I asked, realizing I'd missed something she'd said. Unacceptable. Her voice was just a little distracting, like a drug that could make me do anything.

"You're not going to fail."

I propped my chin on my fist and stared at her, amused . . . and a little entranced. "Why do you say that?"

84   C.R. JANE

She flipped through some more papers, clearly trying to distract herself from looking at me. It was so cute, how nervous she was. "You just seem like the kind of guy who's very . . . capable."

"I'm not sure that I've ever been described as 'capable' but I like it." I picked up a strand of her hair and absent-mindedly played with it.

"Do you have any work for me to look at so I can see what you need help with?" she asked, pulling her hair from my fingers and tossing it over her other shoulder and out of reach.

"Yes, right here," I told her, grabbing the calculus assignment I'd brought with me. I was actually in calculus two years ago, so this was an old assignment. But there was no way she'd know that.

She picked up the paper, her brow furrowing as she scanned my answers. I'd intentionally changed a few things, to make it look believable.

"Okay, it looks like you're having trouble here," she mumbled, pointing at a section I'd intentionally messed up. "And this one too. But these are more algebra issues rather than calculus, so that will be easy to fix."

I leaned forward, my arm brushing against hers again, just enough to make her flinch. "I don't know . . . looks pretty hopeless to me," I mused.

Her blush deepened, and she shook her head quickly. "No, it's not . . . you just need to focus more on the structure here."

I watched her closely as she talked, trying to sound professional. She was really struggling, though, her eyes darting up at me every few seconds, constantly fidgeting in her chair. She was doing everything she could to *act* like this was just a normal tutoring session, but she wasn't very good at faking that.

As she worked through my *mistakes*, I glanced over at her notebook. Her own homework was sitting there, half-done. It didn't take long for me to spot some of her answers—ones that were wrong.

"Hold on," she said, suddenly standing. "I'll be right back, I—just need to run to the bathroom." More like she needed a break from the sexual tension between us. But I wouldn't call her out on that.

"Of course," I told her, admiring what must be the world's most perfect ass as she walked away. It was a rare thing when a backside was as good as a frontside. I was a lucky man.

The moment she'd disappeared around the corner, I reached over and grabbed her notebook. It didn't take long to correct her mistakes—just a few quick fixes. I made sure to erase everything thoroughly, so she wouldn't notice anything had been changed.

THE WRONG QUARTERBACK 85

"Hi, Parker." A breathy voice called my name right as I was finishing. I slowly set the pencil down and dramatically sighed in annoyance, just so the witch who had shown up wouldn't miss it.

"McKenzie," I finally said in a bored voice. The fact that she still was trying to get me to fuck her after the hot sauce incident was just another blaring sign that this chick was absolutely insane. There should be a neon sign attached to her head that warned all mankind that they should keep ten feet between their dicks and this girl at all times.

"That was a really good game this weekend. I mean—you were amazing," she gushed, her voice ten times higher-pitched than it normally was. Like I was supposed to be turned on by that.

My eyes widened when I finally looked at her. What was she wearing? It was like a scrap of cloth. I'm surprised nipples weren't showing. She either had a fetish for the library, or she'd known I was in here and purposely showed up.

And then she put her hand on my shoulder.

I immediately stiffened and grabbed her wrist, pushing it off of me. "If you ever touch me again, I'm going to make sure that the whole campus knows what happened that night. Do you understand?"

Her eyes went wide, her lips doing a fake trembling thing. *Fuck*, this was probably turning her on.

"That was just a misunderstanding. I tried to tell you that," she cried.

Before I could respond, Casey came back, her body language stiff and cold as she sat down in her chair, intentionally scooting it over this time so there was space between us.

Fuck. Now I was even more furious.

"Go bother someone else, McKenzie," I said loudly, and she immediately dropped her little act, her cheeks growing red.

"Parker—"

"Now," I growled. Casey shifted in her seat at my tone. *Don't worry, baby, I'd never use that tone on you*, I wanted to tell her.

I turned my head toward Casey, and McKenzie stayed there for another few seconds before realizing she wasn't going to get what she wanted from me. She left with a huff, and the air in the library felt immediately less toxic.

Casey was studying my assignments, her pencil scratching against the paper as she fixed the mistakes. I scooted my chair toward her, erasing the space she'd put between us.

"Sorry about that," I told her, leaning in again, this time letting my hand rest on the table so our pinkies touched.

86 C.R. JANE

"I imagine that happens a lot," she murmured, still not looking at me—but she didn't move her hand.

"I have no interest unless—"

I let the sentence hover, and she finally glanced at me. "Unless what?"

"Unless it's from you," I told her meaningfully.

She snorted, and I grinned.

"None of that . . . *nonsense* during our sessions, Parker Davis," she muttered, her cheeks on fire again.

"It's not *nonsense*, but I like that you didn't outlaw it *outside* of our sessions," I purred, hooking my pinky with hers.

She stared at where our fingers were intertwined for a good thirty seconds before she finally shook her head and yanked her hand away before loudly starting to explain one of the concepts I'd gotten wrong.

I laughed and then pretended to be absorbing what she was teaching me while I lusted after the sound of her voice.

"Thanks for helping me out with this," I said when she'd finally taken a breath. My voice was low, like I was confiding in her. "You're pretty good at this."

She swallowed hard, her eyes flicking to mine. "Thanks."

Her blush deepened again, and I could tell she wasn't used to compliments. Every time I complimented her, every time I touched her, it was like she didn't know how to react.

I frowned. How was that possible? The whole world should be falling at the feet of this beautiful, talented, fucking *incredible* girl.

"Do you think you can try it now?" she asked in a choked voice, pointing to a problem she'd just gone over.

I nodded and reached across her, again letting my fingers graze hers for just a second. She jolted in her seat, but didn't say anything.

"Relax, Casey," I said, smiling softly. "You don't have to be so tense. It's just tutoring."

Her mouth opened, but no words came out. Instead, she nodded, watching while I did the problem exactly correct. Her smile was blinding when she glanced over what I'd done.

"That's perfect," she said excitedly.

"It's only because of you," I told her with a wink, the smile on my face fading as I saw something out of the corner of my eye.

Jace had just strolled into the library, an amused look on his face as he stared around the room, like he'd stumbled into an alien landscape.

THE WRONG QUARTERBACK **87**

I was pretty sure Jace had never been in a library before. Which meant that his presence was because of me. The second he spotted me sitting with Casey, his grin widened. I shot him my best *fuck off* look, but he pretended not to see it.

"Fancy seeing you here, Parkie-Poo. You usually like to study in a more . . . *private* setting," Jace said when he reached the table. His voice was loud enough that a few people at the surrounding tables glared at him, their expressions quickly changing when they realized who he was. Even if you hated football, there was little chance you hadn't seen the huge banner hanging down the English building, complete with his man bun in all of its glory.

He sat down across from Casey and propped his chin up in his hands, batting his eyelashes at her in a way that made me want to kill him. "Thank goodness, you're getting help. I know how much you . . . *struggle* with your classes." He smirked at me mockingly.

If he kept pausing like that, I really was going to reach across and strangle him.

Of course he was referencing the fact that I had straight A's in all of my classes—and I always had. He was also referencing the fact that along with being a Heisman finalist last year, I'd actually been awarded the Academic All-America Team Member of the Year.

But Casey obviously didn't know any of that, and I needed some time to seal the deal before she found that out. At least a *few* more tutoring sessions.

When Casey looked down at the table, I flipped him off, mouthing "Leave" to him frantically.

Jace, however, thrived on pushing my buttons. His grin only grew as he turned to Casey, eyes narrowing slightly as he appraised her. "How come you haven't introduced me to your friend yet . . . your very *pretty* friend, Parkie? I'm Jace, Parker's hotter, *smarter* best friend."

I snorted at that, and he raised his eyebrows at me. "You should tell her, QB, tell her how much smarter I am than you. And hotter too." He wiggled his eyebrows a little more for good measure.

Out of all the things he could try and blackmail me on at the moment, this was what he'd decided to do . . .

What a guy.

"He's much smarter than me," I told her, trying to keep a straight face, although it was really hard. "And as you can see, much hotter," I continued, even though I didn't want her even looking at him.

I only wanted her eyes on me.

88   C.R. JANE

Jace held out a hand toward Casey. "Charmed, I'm sure," he said in an affected English accent.

Before Casey could react, I smacked his hand away, a sharp thwack that had him laughing. "Touchy, Parker," he said, mock innocence dripping from his tone as he wiggled his fingers and shoved his hands in his pockets.

Casey looked between us, wide-eyed, like she was caught in the middle of a conversation she hadn't quite signed up for. "You have a lot of nicknames," she finally told me, and I barked out a laugh as I thought about grabbing her a cup of ice or something to help cool off her face since she hadn't stopped blushing since I'd gotten here.

Jace wasn't done torturing me yet . . . of course.

"I really didn't know you were into libraries," he said, shifting his gaze back to me. "Or . . . extracurriculars." The teasing lilt to his voice was subtle, but it made my jaw tighten.

"Want to hear a joke?" he asked Casey suddenly.

I groaned. "Please, no."

"It's a good one. It will impress her."

I growled at him, and he grinned. Asshole. "You don't need to impress her."

"Ignore him," Jace said to Casey, and my annoyance faded for a second because her smile was so fucking pretty. "He's just jealous because of the whole smarter-and-hotter thing."

Casey laughed, and I reached under the table to try and adjust myself. At this point, maybe I would just die because all the blood in my body had gone to my dick.

"Okay, prepare yourself, because this is a good one," he told her.

Casey nodded, the soft, sweet smile still on her face.

"Why couldn't the lizard get a girlfriend?"

I sighed in exasperation, but like everyone else in this library today, he ignored it.

"Because he had *reptile* dysfunction," Jace finished proudly.

I groaned, but Casey was laughing. Hard.

And now it was definitely time for Jace to go, because I didn't want anyone making her laugh like that—but me.

This was becoming a strange, slightly scary trend in my thoughts. I'd have to examine that closer . . .

When someone else wasn't making her laugh.

"Alright, on that . . . note, I think it's time for you to be leaving. Don't you have that meeting tonight, Jace?" I asked, hoping he could read the *you will die if you don't leave now* in my expression.

THE WRONG QUARTERBACK 89

Jace's lips twitched, but I must have finally looked scary enough that he got the point. "Yeah, that *meeting*. I'd better get going to it," he said in an amused voice, standing up from the table. "It was a very *huge* pleasure to meet you, Casey," Jace continued dramatically before winking and sauntering away.

By the time he was walking out of the library, he'd somehow ended up with a girl under each arm. Which, of course, didn't prevent him from yelling "See ya later, QB" as he left the room.

Casey giggled again, and I sighed in mock annoyance. "Sorry about him," I told her.

Her smile was shy as she finally looked me in the eyes. "He was funny. I liked him," she answered.

"But not more than me, right?" I found myself asking, like a pathetic, insecure fool, as I leaned in closer to her, taking the occasion to play with her hair a little more.

She blinked a few times, studying my face with those gorgeous starry eyes—and yes, I was very well aware that I'd never used that particular descriptor on anything before in my life.

The way I was acting was very new to me.

"Not more than you," she finally whispered, and somehow, it felt like the biggest victory I'd ever won.

We only had ten more minutes left in our session, but I made sure to keep pushing the rest of the time, testing her reactions. Little touches here and there, small compliments that made her blush even deeper. I didn't go too far—just enough to keep her on edge, to make sure she would be thinking about me long after the session was over.

By the time we finished, I could tell she was flustered—and I badly needed to jack off. Casey gathered her things quickly, like she couldn't wait to escape. But I wasn't about to let her go that easily.

"Hey," I said as she stood up, slinging her bag over her shoulder. "Can you put me on your schedule for Thursday, after practice?"

She hesitated, her eyes flicking to mine before she nodded. "Yes, of course," she finally said, taking a step away.

"I'd better get your number, just in case practice runs long or something." I smiled at her innocently, like I didn't have plans to text her constantly. "Wouldn't want to keep you waiting on me."

"Oh, right," she said, way too trustingly, rattling off her phone number for me after I got out my phone. I immediately sent her a text.

"Now you have my number too," I told her, winking. "Feel free to use it anytime . . . and I do mean *anytime*."

90 C.R. JANE

"Oh, I—" she stuttered, and I took advantage of the moment to reach out and pull her into a quick hug, trying not to *come* from how good it felt to finally have her in my arms.

I may have held on for a little too long before I released her.

"Bye," she squeaked, stumbling a few steps away before giving me a cute little wave and all but running out of the library.

I resisted the urge to go after her, promising myself that soon, she wouldn't want to run away at all.

CHAPTER 10

PARKER

> Cole: I knew you were going to use it.

I scoffed at the text from my brother, knowing I'd done this to myself.

> Me: I used a much better version of your move, in fact, I really don't think they're comparable.

> Cole: Let's crowdsource the issue, shall we?

I wrinkled my forehead, leaning back against my pillow as I waited for whatever nonsense he had planned. It had been twenty-four hours since my tutoring session with Casey, and no amount of following her or lifting weights or jacking off could change the fact that I was literally *pining* for her.

It was like Jace had cursed me that day at practice. I'd gone from never even using the word, to pining for someone twenty-four-fucking-seven.

I texted him a *fuck you* for good measure.

Cole sent me a link as soon as I'd finished, and I hesitantly clicked on it, hoping he hadn't sent me blow-up doll porn, like the last time.

Not to yuck on anyone's yum . . . but that shit wasn't for me.

Only Casey was for me, I thought dreamily as I waited for the link to open.

The video that popped up was of Cole and me, side by side. On one side of the screen he was doing his "I want to fuck this microphone" routine and on the other side was my touchdown celebration. Definitely not comparable.

But both *very* popular, apparently.

There were already two hundred thousand views.

> Cole: The consensus is that you're a copycat, Parkie. Look at that pretty poll I made.

I rolled my eyes as I went down to the comments and saw he had, in fact, put a poll up.

> Me: How do I know you're not the one doing all the voting?

> Cole: Like I have time to do that 135,000 times.

> Cole: 155,000 times, I mean. The people are moving fast.

> Me: . . .

> Cole: Hitting me with the . . . you're getting a little edgy in your old age, Parkie.

I grinned when Walker's text popped up.

> Walker: Can we not and say we did. I was trying to sleep.

> Cole: I just lol'd. Every time you say that, it's definitely code for "fuck."

> Walker: Olivia and I were trying to sleep!

I shook my head; it was still hard to believe that Walker had somehow convinced a famous pop star to date him . . . and marry him . . . and then have his baby. He just wasn't that cool.

THE WRONG QUARTERBACK   93

> Me: We'll let you get back to your beauty sleep, Disney.

> Walker: Don't start.

I chuckled, because I could literally hear the growl he'd just given me. So Disney prince–like.

> Cole: Before you go, tell our little brother he definitely used my move.

I waited, knowing exactly what was coming. Because like my two best friends, there was nothing my brothers liked to do more than give me a hard time.

> Walker: It did look suspiciously close, Parker. I'm ashamed you caved to peer pressure.

> Me: 🖕

> Me: Notice how I didn't type that out, Cole.

> Cole: Notice how I didn't get the full intent, Parker.

Before I could answer, I heard a pounding at my front door. Glancing at the clock, I frowned when I saw it was after midnight.

Maybe it was weird that I'd chosen to rent a house by myself, right next to the one that Jace and Matty shared, but I liked my sleep . . . and I liked my privacy. And having someone knock on my door when I was supposed to be sleeping violated both of those things.

I walked to the front door and glanced out the window, not seeing anyone on the porch.

Fuckers.

That was happening more and more often. People finding out where I lived and thinking it would be fun to "prank" the school's quarterback.

94   C.R. JANE

I threw open the door. "Really funny, assholes," I called out to the quiet street. I was about to close the door when I noticed a red envelope on the ground, sealed with a very familiar emblem.

Fuck. It was from the Sphinx.

I grabbed the letter and went back inside, ripping it open as soon as the door closed and reading through the contents, my disbelief growing.

Great, looks like I'd be missing out on another night of dreaming about Casey.

Tonight was Initiation Trial Number One.

———

"Remind me why we're here?" Jace complained as we parked my truck a few blocks away from the cemetery we'd be invading tonight.

I slapped him on the shoulder as I jumped out and opened the back, pulling out the shovels I'd brought for the occasion.

"I just mean, what part of *football player* means *grave robber* to these people?" Jace continued after he'd finally gotten out of the truck and walked over to where I was waiting.

We both stared at Matty still sitting in the truck, staring straight ahead as if he could pretend that we weren't there if he didn't look.

"You have to get him out. This isn't even *our* trial. I'm only doing this because we both know you'll be insufferable if we're Sphinx cool people and you're not," Jace said, crossing his arms and leaning against the truck as he began to whistle.

I needed new best friends.

I walked to the other side of the truck and threw open the door. "Are you coming?" I asked, trying to be nice. It was two o'clock in the morning, and of the three of us, Matty needed the most beauty sleep.

"I can't do it," he said, sounding a bit . . . panicked.

"Sorry?"

"I can't go into that graveyard. Everyone knows that one is haunted."

I blinked at him, trying to figure out if he was kidding or not.

"Alright, well I'll be sure to protect you from any—ghosts—that we see," I said soothingly.

Jace popped his head over my shoulder. "I think he's being serious," he commented unhelpfully.

"Now is not the time to inform us that you're terrified of cemeteries," I snapped, putting all of my team captain's energy behind my voice.

It didn't work. Not even in the slightest.

I waved a hand in front of his face. Nothing.

THE WRONG QUARTERBACK   95

"Maybe offer him a cookie or something. His blood sugar could be low," said Jace . . . beginning to munch on his own cookie that he'd pulled from who the hell knew where.

"Could you be any louder?" I hissed. I didn't know it was possible to eat a cookie like you were working a chainsaw, but Jace was showing me how it was done.

He stuffed the entire thing in his mouth, resembling a man-bunned chipmunk as he grinned at me.

"Sorry, QB," he said in a muffled voice.

I rubbed at my forehead. At this rate, I really could dig up a grave by myself faster than I could with the two of them.

"There's no ghosts," I told Matty. "Jace is way too annoying. They'll get fed up immediately and leave the premises until we're gone."

That had to be the dumbest argument that a person had ever made, but Matty seemed to be considering it, finally turning his head to look at us.

Jace stuffed another cookie in his mouth.

"That's a good point," Matty said, making a face as Jace somehow showered the two of us with cookie crumbs.

I couldn't believe we were really having this conversation.

A dog barked somewhere nearby, and Matty jumped, like that was further evidence to support his ghost argument.

"You didn't even blink when we watched *Silence of the Lambs*," I said incredulously, resisting the urge to hit him over the head with a shovel. Jace and I had been about to wet our pants, and Matty had fallen asleep while a guy wore someone's skin on his face.

"I can *kill* a serial killer. I can't kill a ghost!" Matty snapped back, like that should be obvious to me.

"Matthew Clay Adler, get your fucking ass out of the truck, or I swear, I will find a ghost, and I'm going to sic him on your ass for the rest of eternity!" I growled.

"God bless you, you're an American classic," commented Jace, clapping me on the back.

Matty must have realized I was on my last, tired straw, because he finally dragged himself out of the truck, muttering something about *coming to haunt us if a ghost attacked him.*

"I'll take that chance, buddy," I grumbled back.

I felt like some kind of Bond villain as we crept down the sidewalk . . . with shovels. Trying to stay in the shadows in case anyone had decided to peek out of their windows in the middle of the night.

96   C.R. JANE

"I have to say, when I decided to go to college, this wasn't what I pictured," mused Jace as we got to the cemetery gates.

I humphed in agreement, studying the wrought iron twisted into elaborate almost sinister patterns that were casting jagged shadows across the gravel path. Why the fuck did cemeteries have to be so creepy? If I was ever in charge . . . of cemetery design . . . I was going to make everything look way better. I wasn't sure how. But I was pretty sure I could do it.

"Alright, do you have the bolt cutters?" I asked Jace.

"Yep, and I'm ready," he said, holding them up like a blond Edward Scissorhands.

I took a step away, for safety's sake, and watched as he went to work on the gates, grunting as he cut the metal.

What seemed like an hour later, the chain finally clattered to the ground. I winced, glancing at the houses across the street. But they all seemed to be quiet still.

The hinges squeaked as the wind nudged the gates apart, and we paused, staring out at the headstones that jutted from the earth like rotting teeth. This was one of Tennessee's older cemeteries.

And it showed.

The headstones were covered in moss and cracked by time, and I was a little worried Matty wasn't going to make it through the night.

This place really did look haunted.

"Let me know if you see any ghosts," Jace muttered to Matty, followed by an *oomph* as Matty punched him in the arm. "Or not," Jace grunted, rubbing where he'd been hit.

"Come on," I whispered. "We'll turn on the flashlights when we get further in."

We set off in relative silence, the crunch of gravel beneath our feet and the occasional rustle of wind through the trees the only sounds breaking the thick stillness. The deeper we went into the cemetery, the older the graves became, marked with weathered stone angels and crosses that loomed over us.

I turned on my flashlight at that point, and the beam cut through the mist that had somehow developed, casting pale, shaky circles of light over the uneven ground.

"You know what I was just thinking to myself?" Jace whispered.

I glanced at him over my shoulder.

"I was just thinking that we were missing mist . . . that this place didn't look nearly creepy enough. And now look around us. Mist."

"So, I guess I should blame you for the fact that Matty's about to pass out?" I asked, nodding my head to where Matty was pale-faced as he walked, his shovel out in front of him like he was preparing himself for something to jump out of the shadows.

Jace grinned like I'd said something funny.

We got to a sort of crossroads, two gravel paths going out in opposite directions. I pulled the paper that had been left on my doorstep out of my pocket and examined the map that was included.

"Alright, this way," I told them. "We're almost there."

"Do we even want to be Sphinx people? I mean, I'm not sure that any of us are the kind of psycho that would make someone dig up a grave," commented Jace. Matty jumped at the sound of his voice, like it had surprised him.

I cocked my head as I considered his point. I hadn't exactly told them about my plans for how to get Casey. Those *might* have qualified me as a psycho. I'd have to consult them about that . . . sometime . . . maybe.

"Of course we want to be Sphinx members. Think about all the access we'll get," said Matty grumpily. Jace and I shot each other looks. Matty's family was poor—the kind of poor where there wasn't any food, and he'd had to spend the nights out on the streets more than a few times growing up. He took every endorsement deal he was offered, no matter what it was, because it meant money he could send to his family. Unfortunately, his dad had a gambling addiction, and that money never seemed to go very far. Matty had four younger siblings, and he was always worried about them.

"Okay, so we're going to be Sphinx psychos now. Noted," Jace said supportively, and a shadow of a smile slipped across Matty's lips.

"Where are you, Eleanor?" I muttered, scanning the headstones until my light landed on the name we were looking for. The grave was the only fresh one in the area, a neat mound of dirt heaped over it, flowers wilted and browning at the edges.

"Eleanor Cross," I whispered. According to what we'd been told, her husband had been a higher-up in the Sphinx before betraying them, stealing a ring that held more significance than any of us understood. It had been a symbol of power, something sacred, and Eleanor had worn it even to her grave. Now, it was our task to ensure that the Sphinx reclaimed what was theirs.

Hooray for us.

I dropped my flashlight to the ground and gripped the shovel.

"Holy shit, we're about to become grave robbers," Jace muttered as my shovel sank into the earth with a dull thwack, the sound somehow muffled

98 C.R. JANE

by the oppressive silence of the graveyard. I gripped the handle harder, my palms already sweating despite the cool night air.

"Was that a creak?" Matty asked in a panicked voice, looking around like he half expected a zombie to rise from one of the graves.

"Don't back out now, Mr. Of Course We Want To Be Sphinx Psychos," drawled Jace.

I shot them both a look. "Are you going to help me or not?"

"We're probably getting the raw end of this deal." Jace scowled as he stuck his shovel in the ground. "They definitely would have made it harder for you. We'll probably just be asked to steal, like, a car or something. You know, normal stuff."

"I'd even rob a bank if it meant I didn't have to be out here in a cemetery, digging up someone's grandma," Matty added, looking around again fearfully.

"I'm pretty sure robbing a bank gets you more jail time than grave robbing," I told them.

Jace scoffed. "You would know that, Big Brain."

"Plus, there's adrenaline in bank robbing, you know? *Excitement.* All we get here is the chance of a haunted curse."

Jace and I both gaped at Matty.

"You kind of sound like you might have personal experience with that, buddy. Anything you want to share?" I asked.

Matty rolled his eyes. "All I'm saying is that there better actually be a ring at the end of this little expedition. If all we get is a decomposing corpse, I'm not going to be happy about that."

"You mean a skeleton," Jace corrected as he threw some dirt into the pile we were making next to the grave.

Now it was Matty and I exchanging looks.

"You remember she's only been buried for a week, right?" Matty said slowly.

Jace froze and stared at us in horror. "This was not part of the job description!" he snapped, beginning to freak out. He dropped his shovel on the ground. "I signed up for skeletons, not *Night of the Living Dead* corpses! I want a refund!"

I rolled my eyes and jabbed my shovel deeper into the ground, the sound of metal scraping against the dirt grounding me. "Suck it up, Thatcher. You'll be fine. Just think of it as a really screwed-up scavenger hunt."

"Yeah, a scavenger hunt with dead bodies," Jace muttered, but he resumed digging beside me, his face scrunched up in disgust like he was already touching the corpse.

THE WRONG QUARTERBACK 99

I didn't blame him for being freaked out. If I could pick what would be the worst initiation task, this would have been top of the list—if my brain was even nefarious enough to think about something like this to begin with.

The graveyard was too quiet, the air too still, like it was waiting for something. The moon hung low in the sky, casting long shadows across the tombstones, turning them into twisted, crooked figures in the darkness. I tried not to think about how many bodies were buried beneath our feet or how disrespectful this felt. Luckily, we weren't here to make friends with the dead—a good thing as long as Matty's theories on ghosts weren't real.

"You know," Jace commented, breaking the tense silence, "I bet the old lady in this grave was a total badass when she was alive. I mean, she had to have been to keep the ring until she died. She's probably just waiting for some idiots like us to disturb her eternal slumber, and then she'll take her revenge."

Matty groaned, throwing a handful of dirt at Jace. "Would you shut up? Can you not make this worse?"

Jace just grinned. "Whoops."

We kept digging, the dirt slowly giving way beneath our shovels, revealing the metal casket below. The sound of the metal hitting metal sent a shiver down my spine, but I ignored it, wiping the sweat from my forehead.

"Alright, almost done, boys," I said, tossing my shovel aside and crouching down near the casket. My pulse quickened as I stared at the dark top, realizing this was it. We were about to pop open a casket and steal a ring off a dead woman's finger. If that didn't scream "secret society," I didn't know what did.

For a second, Casey's face popped into my head. I wondered what she would think about this particular situation. I quickly pushed her out of my head. If I thought it was disrespectful to steal from a corpse, it was even worse to do it with an erection.

"You're actually going to open that?" Matty asked, his voice higher than usual as he stepped back, his shovel still in hand like he was ready to run if he saw one finger of hers move.

I glanced up at him. "You want to leave now?"

Jace leaned against his own shovel. "This is your induction thingy. Please proceed with touching the dead body. That falls outside of our job descriptions."

"Of course, it does," I muttered, taking a deep breath as I wedged the tip of the shovel under the edge of the casket's lid. I'd Googled how to unseal

100   C.R. JANE

the rubber gasket they used to seal these things nowadays . . . but actually doing it was a whole other matter.

A few more hits with my shovel, and I heard a pop as the seal broke and the air inside of the casket rushed out.

Along with a terrible smell.

"Help. I'm dying," Jace groaned, staggering back.

I leaned away, bile rising in my throat. The smell of decomposing bodies was way worse than the frogs I'd dissected in seventh grade.

I was going to puke.

I pulled my shirt up over my face, taking deep breaths. Matty and Jace were now several feet away, staring at me in horror.

How helpful. I really wished this was a one-hand kind of job. The smell might end me.

Taking one more covered breath, I dropped my shirt and held out my hand, my nose wrinkled in disgust from the odor assaulting my nostrils.

"Hand me my flashlight," I asked, catching it when Jace threw it over.

Heart pounding, I lifted the lid and shined my light, revealing the body inside. There she was, lying peacefully in her eternal sleep, her face pale and sunken, her hands folded over her chest. And smelly. So very smelly.

"Oh, she doesn't look that bad," Jace commented, cocking his head and covering his nose as he stared down at her over my shoulder. Matty's eyes were firmly trained at the sky.

"This is definitely how you get ghosts," he said roughly.

I kind of agreed with him. This was . . . creepy.

Shining the light over her hands, I breathed a sigh of relief. There it was. The ring.

It glinted in the pale light, the large ruby catching the beam. Etched into the stone was the unmistakable symbol of the Sphinx, intricate lines carved with precision.

I realized then, I had to actually touch her.

"I'm sorry about this," I whispered . . . just in case . . . as I reached for her hand, brushing over the cool, unmoving skin. The ring was snug, but I twisted it gently, heart pounding as it finally slid free.

"There," I said, slipping the ring into my pocket. "We're done."

"We're done?" Matty echoed, his voice filled with disbelief. "We dug up a grave, opened a casket, and robbed a dead woman. And all you have to say is that we're done?"

"Yeah," I said, grabbing my shovel again. "Now, let's cover this back up before someone sees us."

We worked quickly, shoveling the dirt over the casket, tension still thick in the air. The wind picked up, rustling the trees, and for the first time that night, I felt like we weren't alone.

I packed down the last of the dirt, breathing a sigh of relief. "Alright, let's—"

"Wait," Jace whispered, his voice cutting through the night. "Do you hear that?"

I froze, my heart skipping a beat. At first, I thought he was messing with us, but then I heard it, too. Voices. Faint, but growing louder. And then the flashlights—bright beams of light sweeping across the graveyard, cutting through the darkness.

"Shit," I hissed, grabbing Matty's arm. "Let's go."

They didn't need to be told twice. Jace was already scrambling down the gravel path, his eyes wide with panic. "You never told me there would be graveyard security!"

"Why is that something you thought I would know?" I hissed as I took off. My legs moved on autopilot, the sound of my heart pounding in my ears as I sprinted through the rows of tombstones. Matty and Jace were right behind me, their footsteps echoing against the ground, the adrenaline pumping through all of us.

The flashlights were getting closer, and so were the voices. I could hear shouts now, commands being thrown into the night. My lungs burned, but I didn't slow down.

"Fuuuuck!" Jace panted from behind me, but I ignored him, focusing on the tree line up ahead. If we could just make it there, we could disappear into the woods, lose them in the darkness.

"Keep going," I growled, pushing myself harder.

The flashlights cut through the tombstones like searchlights, getting closer and closer with every second. The shouts were louder now, more frantic.

Just as I reached the edge of the graveyard, I heard a shout from behind. I didn't stop to look back. I dove into the tree line, the branches scratching at my skin as I pushed through the underbrush, my heart still racing.

We kept running until the flashlights were gone, until the voices faded into the distance, until the only sound was the ragged gasps of our breath and the wind rustling the leaves.

When we finally stopped, I leaned against a tree, trying to catch my breath. My hands were shaking, my heart still pounding in my chest. But we'd done it. We'd gotten the ring, and we hadn't been caught.

102   C.R. JANE

"Holy shit. Holy shit. Holy shit," Matty groaned, collapsing onto the ground. "That was . . . insane."

"Insane? That's all you're calling it?" Jace started frantically patting his body all over.

"What are you doing?" I panted, because that was all I was capable of at the moment.

I stood up, my breath still coming out in gasps. I thought I was in great shape, but evidently a thousand-yard sprint was beyond my cardio abilities.

"Making sure all my limbs are attached. I'm numb and tingly, and we just ran for our fucking lives!" Jace said indignantly, giving his leg one last pat before he stood up too.

I grinned as I pulled out the ring, holding it up as my head spun from the adrenaline of what had just happened. "We did it, though. We fucking got the ring."

"Yeah," Matty muttered, staring up at the sky from where he'd collapsed. "But that woman is probably going to haunt us for the rest of our lives."

Jace frowned at him and shuddered.

I slipped the ring back into my pocket, a small smirk tugging at my lips. "One step closer to the Sphinx, boys."

I slapped Jace on the ass before I held out a hand to help Matty off the ground.

We stumbled our way back to the truck, exhausted and exhilarated all at the same time.

And yes, a little afraid Eleanor was going to start haunting us.

CHAPTER 11

CASEY

It had been a long freaking day. I'd known college was going to be hard, but the class load was more than I anticipated.

I was exhausted.

And honestly . . . a little lonely.

Besides Nat, I hadn't made any friends. And Gray . . . well, I didn't want to think about Gray at the moment.

I was having trouble finding the boy that I'd loved in the man I was supposed to be dating. And maybe he was regretting me, as well. We certainly hadn't spent enough time together for him to find any redeeming qualities in me.

I stared down at the latest text he'd sent me, that he had a pledge event he was in charge of tonight, and he'd see me tomorrow. Another dinner canceled. Another dinner that I'd eat alone.

Walking down the hall, my bag slung over my shoulder, I was wondering for the first time if maybe I'd made a mistake coming here.

The building was nearly empty, the muffled echo of my footsteps the only sound around me. As I passed by one of the open doors, something caught my eye. A piano. It sat there, black and gleaming under the dull fluorescent lights, almost out of place in the sterile, academic setting of the building. I stopped, my feet freezing in place. Seeing it pulled at me; it made my chest ache in a way I couldn't quite explain.

For a moment, I stood there, staring at it through the open doorway. The room was empty, quiet. No one would know if I went in.

104   C.R. JANE

My hand tightened around the strap of my bag. I hadn't played in a long time. Not since I'd stopped being able to get through an entire song, and I'd given up on my hand ever cooperating.

For most of my life, playing had been an escape, one of the few things I was better at than everyone else. One of the only things that ever got the attention of Mama. Losing it on top of losing my brother had been . . . devastating. For weeks I'd thought about killing myself—something I'd never admit to anyone else. It was all I could do to claw myself out of depression.

I hovered for one more second and then stepped inside before I could talk myself out of it. The door clicked softly shut behind me. The sound echoed in the small room, and my heart was pounding in my chest as I approached the piano. Which was dumb. Something that used to be as easy as breathing shouldn't make me feel that way.

Dropping my bag to the floor, I sat down at the bench, my fingers hovering above the keys. The cool, smooth surface beneath my fingertips felt foreign, yet familiar, like a memory I hadn't quite forgotten but was afraid to touch. I closed my eyes, drawing in a shaky breath.

I could do this.

My fingers grazed the keys lightly, and the sound that followed was soft, hesitant. It wavered in the air like a fragile whisper, the kind that could break if I wasn't careful. I let my fingers move, playing a few notes, something simple, something I didn't have to think about too much.

But then I started to play for real.

The music came slowly at first, hesitant, like it had to find its way back to me. And then it flowed. My hands moved across the keys, and for a few precious moments, I forgot about everything. The ache in my chest, the confusion, the fear—none of it mattered when I played. The sound wrapped around me, filling the empty room, each note pulling me deeper into a place I hadn't let myself go in so long.

But then it happened.

The familiar pain shot through my hand, sharp and unforgiving. My fingers cramped up, seizing mid-note. I stopped, my heart lurching in my chest as I stared down at my hand, watching it tremble, useless. The room seemed to close in around me, the silence swallowing up the music like it had never existed.

My chest tightened, and before I could stop myself, tears welled up in my eyes. They blurred my vision, but I didn't care. I couldn't play. I couldn't even make it through a single song without my hand betraying me, reminding me of everything I'd lost, everything that was still broken inside me.

THE WRONG QUARTERBACK 105

I pressed my hand against the keys, the notes clashing in an ugly, jarring sound, and that's when the tears started falling for real. Silent at first, then shaking, sobs racking my body as I sat there, helpless. My head dropped forward, my forehead brushing the cold, smooth surface of the piano as I wept.

The grief, the anger, the frustration of everything I'd been holding inside, everything I hadn't allowed myself to feel—it all spilled out in that moment, crashing over me like a wave I couldn't fight.

I hated this. I hated that something so small, so stupid, could break me like this. I hated that no matter what I did, I couldn't fix it. I couldn't fix myself. And no matter how much I wanted to, nothing would ever be the same again.

But what I hated worst of all . . . was that my inability to play the piano . . . it reminded me I'd never see Ben again.

Parker

I stood outside the building, leaning against the wall, scrolling aimlessly through my phone as I waited for Casey. I knew her class was supposed to be done by now, but the minutes kept ticking by and she hadn't come out. Checking her class schedule again, I made sure I hadn't messed up where she was supposed to be.

Nope, she'd definitely just finished her freshman writing class.

So where was she?

My phone buzzed.

> Cole: You're a fucking wall, little brother.

> Cole: Did I do that right . . .

Quarterbacks were definitely not supposed to be walls, so I waited for Walker to respond as I kept my eye on the door.

A few seconds later he did.

> Walker: Just doesn't have quite the same ring to it when it's not Lincoln saying it Cole-Bear.

> Cole: You're way too obsessed with that guy.

106   C.R. JANE

I decided to jump in at that point because Lincoln Daniels was a god, and there was nothing you could say to convince me otherwise.

> Me: Can you blame him?

Glancing up, I noticed that the students around me had started to thin out, and still, no Casey. I guess there was a chance that she'd gotten out thirty minutes early, but it wasn't likely. My jaw clenched imagining some guy trying to talk to her inside. Pushing off the wall, I slid my phone into my pocket and walked toward the doors.

I moved through the building, the sound of my footsteps echoing in the near-empty hallway. Every classroom I passed, I glanced in, trying not to seem too obvious, but scanning nonetheless. Where was she?

And then I heard it. The soft strains of piano music. Like there was a string leading me, I followed the music until I was outside one of the music practice rooms. I peered through the narrow window in the door, a sense of relief flooding my veins when I saw her.

Casey was sitting at a bench, her posture straight, fingers gliding over the keys as the music came alive around her.

It was the expression on her face that got me, though, soft, distant, like she was in some kind of dream world entirely, a place where nothing else could touch her.

I wanted to be there with her too. I turned and leaned against the door and listened, letting Casey's music fill the spaces I didn't even know I needed filled.

The music stopped with a harsh clang that jarred the quiet hallway. I straightened and spun around, peering through the window to see what was happening.

Casey was slumped over the keys, her shoulders shaking, muffled sobs breaking the stillness. One hand clutched her other, fingers trembling and tight, like she was trying to stop some unseen pain.

What the fuck?

I didn't bother knocking, I just pushed the door open and stepped inside. Her head snapped up, her eyes wide and red from crying, her hands trembling as she frantically wiped at her face. "Parker?"

I closed the door softly behind me, locking her into this space with me.

"What are you doing here?" she sniffed.

"Oh, baby," I said, feeling like my heart was breaking because hers obviously was. "Tell me what hurts?"

THE WRONG QUARTERBACK   **107**

She stared up at me, silent tears sliding down her face.

"I was passing by and saw you through the window," I murmured. I nodded to the glass on the door, making it seem like pure coincidence. Her eyes flickered to it, still red, still raw.

"I've never heard anything like that. You're beautiful," I told her in a choked voice. "Everything about you."

Casey swallowed hard, her lips pressing into a thin line before she spoke. "Please don't say that," she whispered.

I stepped forward, the sound of my footsteps muffled by the carpeted floor, not stopping until I was standing in front of her. "Why are you crying, baby?"

She hesitated, her eyes dropping to the keys, her fingers twitching slightly. And then she sighed, the words tumbling out before she could stop them.

"I was going to be a concert pianist." Her voice was small, broken. "And then I was in an accident . . . and I hurt my hand."

I didn't move, didn't say anything for a moment. I let the weight of her confession settle between us.

"What happened?" I asked quietly, thinking of her hand trembling during our tutoring session. Was that what she'd been talking about?

Her eyes flicked to mine, searching for something. But then, slowly, she turned back to the piano, her fingers hovering above the keys. She pressed down gently, and her left hand moved effortlessly. But her right hand . . . it shook, the notes coming out stilted, off-rhythm. She flinched, her fingers locking up as the shaking got worse.

I didn't say anything. Instead, I sat down and reached out, placing my hand gently on top of hers. "Let me help you," I told her. She stiffened for a second, her breath catching in her throat, but she didn't pull away. She moved her fingers, and every time the trembling started, I would press her fingers down against the keys, steadying her, until the tension in her hand slipped away.

"Keep going," I whispered, my voice low.

She let me help her, her body relaxing long enough that we were moving as one. The music was slow, soft, and for a moment, everything else seemed to fade away. It was just us.

After a minute, she stopped, her breath coming out shaky, her eyes meeting mine.

Fuck. She was unreal.

Her starry eyes.

Her perfect pink lips.

I needed her.

There was something in her gaze, like I'd unlocked something inside of her, and she didn't know what to do with herself now.

Leave it all to me, I wanted to tell her.

I'll take care of everything.

I slowly moved my hand to her cheek, trying not to make any sudden movements that would make her skitter and run.

Her skin was so fucking soft.

I softly stroked her cheek, savoring the gasp that slipped from her mouth.

Before she could move away, I leaned in . . . and kissed her cheek as she quickly turned her head.

Sighing against her skin, I couldn't help myself. "I know you feel this. Like something has happened to my fucking soul. Like I can't breathe without you anymore. Tell me it's not just me who's gone crazy. Tell me you're right there with me," I begged roughly.

Tangling my hands in her hair, I gently turned her head so she had to face me.

"I'm sorry, I can't," she whispered, pulling from my touch and practically sprinting from the room.

I stared at the book bag she'd left on the floor feeling strangely . . . invigorated. The idea of us had become a concrete thing in my mind. I could already see it, what our future would be like, how we were going to be so incredibly happy.

I'd be there for her, in whatever way she needed me.

I could tell she thought she was broken.

But I'd help change her mind about that.

Get ready, baby. I'm coming for you.

CHAPTER 12

CASEY

The sky was gray and heavy, like it was about to downpour. I walked up the small hill, my boots crunching against the dead leaves and dried grass. Mama had picked this place because it overlooked a lake, and Ben had always spent most of his summers out in the water.

At first I'd come here every day after we'd buried him. I'd sit by his grave and talk. About nothing. About everything. The words would just come out.

After a while, though, the visits turned weekly . . . and then monthly. And then finally, I hadn't come here at all.

Maybe it was because I'd stopped having anything to say, since every day at home felt like I was trapped in a mausoleum.

Today I needed to see him, though. I needed to remember. I'd driven here as soon as I'd gotten out of class.

I finally reached his plot. The headstone was simple and straightforward, not nearly enough to capture the spark of light that Ben had been in real life. I stood there, swallowing that knot in my throat, feeling that familiar ache creep up.

"Hey, Ben," I murmured, my voice rough and miserable. "It's been a while. I'm sorry about that." The words hung in the air, swallowing the quiet around me. I hated that it felt so awkward.

But I also hated that I had to be here to talk to him at all.

I slid to the ground, my arms wrapping around my knees as the wind stirred the leaves around me. "I wonder when this will get easier. People always say that time heals all wounds, but I'm pretty sure they're full of shit."

110 C.R. JANE

I laid my head on my legs as a fresh beat of pain arched through me—because he would always laugh at how goofy I sounded when I tried to curse.

"Gray said something to me, you know," I said, kicking at the grass with the toe of my shoe. "He said . . . he thinks you'd want us to be together. Me and him. But I'm not so sure that's true." A tear rolled down my face. "I don't know what you'd want. I just know that I miss you."

Another tear fell down my skin. And then another.

"I feel like I'm forgetting you," I whispered. "I can't hear your laugh anymore. The way that you smiled is fading from my memories unless I look at a photograph." A hiccuped sob lurched from my mouth. "And I'm so afraid of the day that it's all gone, you know? Because you deserve to be remembered, Ben. I wish the whole world could have known you, how special you were. It feels like I'm letting you down every day that goes by." I picked at a piece of the grass in front of his headstone. "I'm angry that grass has grown here. I'm angry that so much time has passed that when I left home, there was even dust covering your bed. What happens one day when I wake up and I can't remember you anymore? What's going to happen then?"

The wind sighed past my cheek, and I leaned into it, wanting it to be a sign from him.

But it was just wind.

It's always *just* wind.

"And it kind of feels like I'm trying to live your life . . . and I'm messing it all up. You would have done all of this so much better than me. You would have already had a million friends. You would have been making the most of every opportunity that came your way. You would have lived so much better than what I'm doing . . ."

It was hard saying those words out loud. I was ashamed of them. I'd promised myself I'd try and live this big life in honor of Ben . . . and here I was, failing at it miserably.

It hurt to admit that he would have done it better.

I traced the letters on the stone, lingering on his name as I tried to summon up some of the sunny memories I had with him, the ones laced with so much light that they could actually drown out the dark. Like when he taught me to swim or how he ate his Oreos so painfully slow because he considered them to be a superior food group.

Or how his hugs felt.

A smile sprung to my lips. "There you are," I murmured as I soaked in the warm feeling I could still get from those memories.

THE WRONG QUARTERBACK   111

I tapped the headstone as I stood up, the smile still on my lips. "Bye, Ben."

The first raindrop landed on my cheek, cold and stinging. I swiped it away, but more followed, dotting the stone, turning the gray even darker. It felt like the sky was crying with me, like it understood that today was a day of mourning.

I walked away, and despite the good memories I'd been able to conjure up, it still felt like I was leaving him all alone.

And that maybe . . . I should be in the ground with him.

———————

Rain soaked through my hair, dripping cold down the back of my neck and plastering my clothes to my skin as I stood shivering on the stone steps of Gray's frat house. The thud of bass-heavy music leaked through the walls, muffled shouts and laughter hinting at the chaos inside. I clenched my phone tighter in my hand, the screen dark. He hadn't answered any of my calls, and for some reason it had seemed like a great idea for me to come here to try and talk to him.

I was pretty sure I was a fool.

I raised my fist and knocked, the sound barely cutting through the noise. It was freezing out here. Way colder than Tennessee falls were supposed to be. My breath came out in shaky bursts, steam rising into the night air as the cold gnawed at my skin.

The door finally swung open, and a shirtless guy with a name tag with the word *Pledge* slapped across his hairy chest stumbled forward, bleary-eyed and reeking of beer. "Hey, there," he slurred, swaying on his feet. The smirk on his face sent a shiver of disgust crawling up my spine, and I felt the urge to go take a shower and wash that smile off of me.

"Can you get Gray, please? Gray Andrews. I'm his girlfriend," I quickly added. My voice was somehow steady, which was good. I didn't want to cry in front of this idiot.

He raised an eyebrow, his smile growing as if what I'd said was funny. "Yeah, sure thing," he said, turning and weaving his way back inside. The door hung open for a second, letting out a blast of humid, alcohol-saturated air before it creaked shut, leaving me alone again in the storm.

Water pooled around my feet, and I wrapped my arms tighter around myself, teeth chattering. It was literally a downpour out here tonight.

And with each minute that passed it felt more and more like I'd made a mistake.

112   C.R. JANE

I finally turned to go, but the door opened, and Gray stumbled out. His hair was mussed, eyes glassy, but they softened when he saw me. The concern that flared up in them made my chest constrict.

"Case?" His voice was hoarse, tinged with confusion and the edges of a night spent drinking. He took a step closer, brows drawing together as he took in my drenched state. "What the hell are you doing out here?"

"I went to Ben's grave today," I whispered, my voice barely holding together. It felt like the rain and cold had seeped all the way through to my bones. "I—I'm feeling weak. I just need to be around someone who loved him the way I did, you know? Sometimes . . . sometimes it just feels like too much."

His face fell, and he reached for me, fingertips brushing my arm like he wasn't sure if touching me would hold me together or break me apart.

"Case, I'm—" His words tangled on his tongue, the sadness in his eyes cutting through me. Before he could say more, another voice called out from the doorway.

"Gray! We need you in here, man!" A guy, just as drunk and oblivious as the first one who had opened the door, poked his head out, looking annoyed before noticing me and raising an eyebrow.

Gray's jaw tightened. "Come inside," he told me. "We can go to my room, and you can get dried off in there while I finish up."

I hesitated, pulling away from him. "It's okay, I can just go—"

"Just come inside, Case. Everything's going to be alright."

I wanted to believe him. I wanted to believe *in* him.

Gray took my hand, his fingers warm against my frozen ones, and led me inside. The heat of the house was immediate, pressing against my wet skin and making my clothes stick uncomfortably.

It also smelled really bad.

There was nothing like the smell that came from a large group of drunk people confined in a small space.

I barely registered the chaos of the room we passed through—shirtless guys with pledge name tags standing in a line, a kiddie pool set up in front of them. One of them was guzzling something while the others cheered, but Gray didn't pause long enough for me to make sense of it. He tugged me up a set of creaking stairs, the noise from below fading into a muffled roar as we turned the corner and entered his room.

The door clicked shut behind us, and the quiet was almost startling. I glanced around; Gray's room was cluttered, but some of it reminded me of his room growing up. There was still the scent of old cologne and the faint

THE WRONG QUARTERBACK   113

musk of laundry that needed washing. Posters of football and basketball legends covered the walls, faded and tacked up. A bookshelf in the corner leaned under the weight of scattered notebooks. His bed was unmade, navy sheets twisted and rumpled, one pillow teetering on the edge like it might fall at any second. A Tennessee Tigers flag hung crooked above the headboard, and a small lamp glowed dimly, casting soft shadows.

Gray disappeared into the small bathroom connected to his room and returned with a towel. He handed it to me, his eyes lingering, searching my face like he could read all the words I hadn't said. "Here," he said, his voice still gentle and everything that I needed at the moment. I was so wet that I was literally leaving a puddle on his wooden floor. I quickly wrapped the towel around my hair and squeezed, trying to stop it from dripping anymore.

He laughed softly and turned to his dresser, rummaging through it before pulling out a pair of sweats and a faded gray T-shirt. "These are going to drown you, but at least they're dry," he said, holding them out. "I need to give you a drawer if you're going to make this a habit, though," he tried to tease.

"Thanks," I whispered, my voice wavering. The warmth of the room was starting to seep into my skin, but it didn't touch the chill that sat heavy inside me. The silence stretched between us, almost awkward but laced with something deeper—grief and unspoken words . . . and the past.

"You should have told me you were going to the cemetery. I would have come with you," he finally said, sliding his hands into his pockets as he leaned against the door. "That's what, a two-hour drive just to get back there?"

"Yeah," I answered, staring at the blue tinge of my fingertips. "It was a long afternoon." I glanced up at him. "When was the last time you went?"

He looked torn at my question . . . and ashamed. "Not since the funeral," he finally muttered.

I nodded, wishing I hadn't asked at all. Gray stared at the floor for a long moment before he walked over to his desk and picked up a photo frame that I hadn't noticed before.

It was us. Gray, Ben, and me. We were standing on the dock, and Ben and Gray were both holding up big fish that they'd caught, both of them looking so proud. Meanwhile, I had my arms crossed and a scowl on my face because I hadn't caught anything yet.

I smiled, remembering that day.

Both boys had finally gotten sick of my bitching and spent the rest of the afternoon helping me to catch my first fish. And when I'd finally gotten a bite on my line . . . it had been a fish about the size of my hand.

114   C.R. JANE

I'd still been so proud of myself. Even though Ben was the one who'd actually put the worm on the hook, and Gray had been the one to pull the fish in.

"The Three Musketeers," he said quietly as he stared at the picture.

I had the strong urge to burst into hysterics again, but I held it in.

A knock pounded on the door and we both jumped, the frame falling from Gray's hands and landing with a thump on the floor. "Gray, get the hell downstairs. You're supposed to be managing this," a drunken voice called.

"Shit," Gray cursed, crouching down and picking up the frame. It was cracked, and this time, I couldn't stop the tear that slid down my face.

Why did that crack feel so symbolic?

Gray looked just as devastated when he finally straightened and set the cracked picture back on his desk.

"I've got to get back down there. Just get changed and crawl into my bed." He winced, looking at his unmade covers. "I promise they've been cleaned . . . recently."

I nodded, biting down on my lip as I stared at him, wishing he would stay . . .

"I'll just handle this and then we'll talk. I promise." He crossed the room and pulled me into his arms, giving me a soft kiss that for some reason felt . . . heartbreaking.

"Love you, Case," he whispered, and I blinked up at him, in disbelief that the words had come out of his mouth.

I opened my mouth to say it back to him, but another knock on the door cut the words from my tongue.

"I'm sorry, I'll be right back," he promised, pressing a hasty kiss to my mouth and then walking to the door. "Right back," he repeated . . . like he was trying to convince himself.

I stood in the room awkwardly for a minute before deciding to get dry.

A shower later, I slipped into his sweats and used his brush to get the snarls out of my hair.

And then I sat on his bed to wait.

I looked at that picture again, trying to ignore the crack across the glass, trying to remember how the sun had felt as it had roasted our skin that day. I tried to remember the sound of Ben's jokes and the water licking against the wooden dock, and the way Mama had brought out lemonade, a fond smile on her lips as she'd looked at the three of us.

It was another memory that was fading, just like all the others. It didn't help that my thoughts were constantly disturbed by yells and cheers from downstairs as the fraternity members did . . . whatever they were doing.

THE WRONG QUARTERBACK   115

Gray had said he'd be right back.

I waited.

And waited.

Finally falling asleep when it was close to two o'clock, the feeling that I was pathetic floating through my soul.

———————

Dawn broke through the thin slats of the blinds, streaks of pale light filtering into the room and casting it in a tired glow. Gray's arm was heavy around my waist, his breath warm against the back of my neck, the unmistakable stench of alcohol clinging to him.

I sighed, careful not to wake him as I shifted and untangled myself from the sheets. He stirred, murmuring my name in a slurred, half-conscious voice that made my chest tighten and ache all at once. I pulled the covers up over his shoulders, pausing for a moment as I stared down at him. His face was peaceful in sleep, the tension gone, leaving only the boy I used to know.

The floor creaked as I moved, and I winced, holding my breath until he settled again, snoring lightly. I slipped my shoes on and stepped into the hall. The house was eerily quiet now, the wild energy from before completely snuffed out.

When I reached the large room I'd passed last night, I hesitated. Guys were sprawled out on the floor, limbs tangled and twisted in awkward angles, the sour smell of vomit heavy in the air. I would never get why Gray loved this place so much.

I wrapped my arms around myself as I slipped through the front door, the morning air biting against my skin and waking me up. The first rays of sunlight cut across the sky, no sign of the storm that had pelted the campus last night. I sighed, because I was exhausted, and the sky felt too happy for what I was feeling.

I stood there for a moment, eyes closed, breathing in the cool, damp air, trying to muster the energy for another day of classes, of pretending everything was fine. But as I walked away from the house, the fatigue pressing down on me, a strange thought surfaced, uninvited and sharp.

For the first time, I hoped I wouldn't see Gray that day.

CHAPTER 13

PARKER

I spotted her sitting on the bench outside the building, wrapped up in her thoughts and looking like she hadn't slept in days. Her eyes were shadowed as she stared blankly at the book in her lap, their usual brightness dulled by exhaustion. I rubbed at my chest, realizing that more and more I was affected by her moods. If she was unhappy, or sad, or tired... there was no way for me to be okay. I shifted the coffee cup in my hand, nervous as usual because I was about to talk to her.

I'd never had this much on the line before as I did with this girl.

"Hi," I told her, amused at how surprised she looked every time I talked to her. If she knew how much I'd been watching her this week, she maybe wouldn't have been so surprised.

She probably would have been creeped out, though.

"Oh, hi," she said, a blush immediately creeping up on her cheeks. She started frantically brushing her hair back and adjusting her clothes, like there was any way that I could think she looked less than the most beautiful girl who had ever walked the planet.

"For you, my lady," I told her, handing her the cup before sitting down next to her on the bench.

"Thank—thank you," she said gratefully, immediately taking a sip, only to jerk back in surprise. "How did you know?"

I bit down on my lip, fighting the stupid grin that would give me away. The rush that came from making her happy was better than winning any championship game. "You had it written on your cup the other day," I said, shrugging like it was no big deal, and I hadn't taken a photo of her cup in her hand so I could make sure to remember it always. I also was obviously not going to tell her that I had gotten that exact drink every day, just in case she looked like she needed it. Peppermint mocha with extra whip and a shot of espresso was, in fact, not my favorite drink.

She stared at me, the exhaustion in her gaze replaced with something that made my pulse start to race. "Thank you," she said again, softer this time, like the words were for more than just the coffee.

I cleared my throat, suddenly aware of the heat climbing my neck. "Listen, I'm not going to be able to talk to you in class today. The professor has a stupid rule I'm working to get rid of," I said, glancing toward the building, where Professor Hendrick's no-nonsense face loomed in my mind. "But just so you know, I'll be thinking about you the entire time."

Her eyes widened, and she glanced down, a nervous laugh escaping her. "Don't talk like that," she said, but there was a hint of something in her voice, a waver that told me I'd hit the mark.

I shrugged, not bothering to hide my smirk. "Can't help it," I said, meeting her silver eyes straight on. "I'm obsessed."

She snorted, and I grinned. She thought I was joking . . .

"How about we have a sign?" I told her.

"A sign?" she asked hesitantly, taking another long draw from her cup.

"Yeah. Every time I'm thinking of you, I'll turn my hat backward," I said, gesturing to the Tigers ball cap I was currently wearing forward facing.

She looked amused. "I mean that could work, except you could forget, and then I would get confused about whether you were thinking about me or not."

I nodded, pretending to think about it seriously. "That works for me," I told her, backing away since I needed to get to class a few minutes before the students started to arrive.

She gaped at me as I walked away, and I winked before finally turning to watch where I was going.

I did sneak one more glance at her, though—because how could I not— and her eyes were *definitely* trained on my ass.

"Like what you see?" I called out over my shoulder, laughing as she jerked her gaze away, pretending to look at the grass beneath her feet as her blush deepened, and she gave a little scoff.

"That's okay, keep looking, baby, just know I do the same thing every time too," I told her, watching, entranced, as the faintest smile played on her lips.

118   C.R. JANE

Casey took another sip of her coffee, and I knew I'd gotten one step closer to my goal . . .

Winning her heart.

In class, I leaned back in my chair, watching as the students filed in. The room was loud with the usual chatter as students settled in their seats, flipping open notebooks and pulling out laptops. My attention was glued on the door, though, waiting. When Casey walked in, still clutching the coffee I'd given her, my pulse immediately picked up in anticipation, a thrum that made the corners of my mouth tilt up.

I stared as she settled into her seat, opting for one in the back toward the side this time. She finally glanced my way, trying to be discreet, but the way her eyes softened and her cheeks flushed gave her away. I didn't waste a second and reached up, making a show of turning my hat backward with a slow, deliberate movement, eyes locked on hers the entire time. Her mouth dropped, and I grinned, winking before I quickly dragged my gaze away, realizing that I was not being nearly discreet enough. I planned on handling the issues Professor Hendrick was going to have with Casey and me, but that was another step in my plan—not something I wanted to deal with today.

Professor Hendrick started talking, her voice droning on about the intricacies of Roman governance or some other details that may have been interesting to me the first time I'd heard them, but were definitely not interesting to me now. Every time Casey's gaze drifted back toward me, I caught her, a smile playing on my lips as I tapped my hat, a silent message: *I haven't forgotten.*

She shifted in her seat, biting her lip and casting her eyes down, the pink in her cheeks spreading. I loved how easily she blushed; there was no way for her to hide how she was feeling from me. It also made the long, boring class feel like a game, with me trying to see how many times I could make that pretty flush appear. Every time I caught her staring, I would tap my hat, and every time, she acted like it was the most shocking thing she'd ever seen.

I wasn't surprised when she fled the moment Professor Hendrick ended class. I let her go, knowing she had another class to get to, and besides . . . I had plans of my own.

"Something wrong with your hat?" Professor Hendrick commented as I gathered up my stuff to leave.

"Pardon?" I asked, pretending to be thoroughly confused by her question. The woman was as observant as a cat.

THE WRONG QUARTERBACK 119

"I've just never seen you so distracted by a ball cap before, Mr. Davis."

"Having a bad hair day," I told her, flashing her a charming grin as she peered at me over the spectacles she was wearing today, like some kind of witch trying to see my brain.

"Have a good day," I called to her before hustling out of the room, and I felt her eyes on me the entire way . . .

———

I walked into Casey's dorm building, knowing that she was in another class for the next two hours and that her roommate was with her. It had been a minute since I'd been in the dorms. This was a newer building than where I'd lived freshman year. It still sucked, though. I couldn't wait to move Casey out of here and in with me.

I could faintly hear the low hum of conversation and music filtering in from down the hall. The girl at the front desk barely glanced up at first, too absorbed in whatever TikTok dance was playing on her phone. Perfect. I cleared my throat, leaning against the counter just enough to catch her attention.

"Hey there," I said, flashing a smile that I knew worked every time to get me what I wanted. Her eyes snapped up, widening a bit as she registered who I was. She practically threw her phone down, leaping up from her chair.

"Oh, hi! Um . . . can I help you?" she stuttered, straightening up and beginning to play with her hair.

"Yeah, you can," I said, keeping my voice low, like we were in on some kind of secret. "My buddy, Jace, left something in a girl's room, and he sent me to pick it up since I was passing by."

"Jace Thatcher?" she asked breathlessly, and I held in my eye roll. Jace would be eating this shit up right now. He never got tired of the attention we got.

"Yep. Marbella Frank's room. He left his lucky socks in there, and tomorrow's a big game. He can't play without them."

Lies. All lies. Jace's lucky thing was his hair, the reason he had long, flowy locks that we gave him shit about all the time. He believed he would have a Samson moment if his hair was cut. Definitely no lucky socks existed. And although Jace *had* hooked up with Marbella, it was last year, and he wouldn't even remember doing it if you asked him. I just remembered because she'd tried to sleep with me right after by walking into my room naked in the middle of the night.

It was unfortunate that she was the only person I knew who was living in the same dorm as Casey, but at least I could use her name.

Her face shifted from awestruck to conflicted, the rules clearly warring with whatever flustered thoughts were running through her head. "I . . . I don't think I'm supposed to give out room numbers. It's, um, against policy."

I leaned in a little closer, watching as her pupils widened and her breath hitched. "I get it, really. And I wouldn't ask if it wasn't so important. Could you maybe make an exception? Just this once. It will be our little . . . secret." Her eyes lit up at that idea. I glanced at my watch, annoyed that my minutes were ticking down while I was having this conversation.

She hesitated again, biting her lip and then glancing around, as if someone from Admin was lurking in the shadows. "Okay . . . but just this once," she whispered, her fingers tapping nervously on the keyboard as she searched for the room number.

While she was focused on the screen, my eyes flicked to the set of three keys on the hook behind the counter. One of those had to be the new universal key the college had added to the dorms over the summer after a few too many "accidental" lockouts.

I reached over casually, fingers brushing the keys while the girl kept typing, completely oblivious. I slipped it into my pocket just as she turned back to me, eyes wide with guilt.

"She's in room 314," she said, almost whispering. "Please don't tell anyone I told you."

I grinned, giving her a wink that made her blush deepen. "Your secret's safe with me." I turned, heading for the stairs, my heart picking up speed as I climbed.

Room 314. Not where I was actually headed.

When I reached Casey's door, I took a deep breath before sliding the key into the lock, the soft click echoing in the quiet hallway.

And then, I was inside.

I stepped into the room, closing the door behind me and letting the silence settle around me. Taking a deep inhale, I could faintly smell the vanilla and cherry perfume that she wore. My dick began to get hard just from that.

Looking around, it didn't take long to figure out which side was Casey's. The sweatshirt she'd been wearing yesterday, now neatly folded at the end of the bed, caught my eye immediately. The rest of the bed was unmade, sheets rumpled like she'd bolted out of bed this morning, probably running late.

I walked over to her desk, glancing at the books stacked haphazardly, some open with sticky notes marking pages. History, music theory, a novel with the spine cracked from too much reading. She didn't just skim; she dove deep.

THE WRONG QUARTERBACK **121**

There was a framed photo beside the books, slightly askew, like she'd touched it recently. It was her and the guy I recognized from the obituary I'd seen online. Her brother. Dark hair, the same intense eyes, except his smile was broader, more carefree. Her arm was looped around him, and they were leaning into each other. It was obvious that they had been close. My heart ached thinking about her losing him. I couldn't imagine losing my brothers.

I wonder if her heart would hurt for me like this when I inevitably lost my mom.

Don't think about that.

I set the picture down and moved to her bedside table, noticing the small details. A bracelet, delicate and a little tarnished, half-hidden by a book. It was a romance book, or *romantasy* . . . I think that's what people called it, with a birdcage on it that looked like gold liquid was coming out of it. *Gild.* I wondered if there was some hidden meaning there, and Casey also felt like she was trapped in a cage.

If so, I couldn't wait to help free her.

There was a worn-out music sheet sitting next to the journal. The notes were smudged in places, the paper creased as if it had been handled over and over. Obviously I knew she played piano, but judging by this, it looked like she had been writing her own music at some point in time as well.

I really wanted to hear her play it.

My gaze drifted back to her bed, spotting a pair of underwear still tangled in the shorts set I assumed she'd worn to sleep.

Hesitating, I stared at it, trying to control myself and the fact that my dick was aching. This was just supposed to be a fact-finding mission, a way for me to find out more about her to help with making her mine . . .

I lost my internal battle and walked over, pulling out the underwear and bringing it to my face, moaning as I inhaled her sweet scent.

I wanted her cunt so bad.

I needed it.

Just a little longer, I told myself.

I glanced at the bed and then my watch, knowing I was running out of time. But I couldn't help it. I slid into the bed, falling face-first into her pillow so I could breathe in her scent.

Fuck. My dick was so hard, I couldn't stop myself. I rutted into the bed, thinking about sinking into her. Abruptly rolling over, my chest heaving because I was so out of control . . . . I pulled down my joggers so I could free my aching cock.

The head was already shiny and red, cum seeping out of it because I'd never been this turned on in my life. I wrapped her underwear around my dick, gripping it as tightly as I imagined her pussy would be.

And then I fucked my hand.

Over and over again, a porno flashing through my mind of all the ways I was going to take her. How I was going to shove my dick down her throat and choke her with my cock. How I was going to fill her pretty pink pussy with my cum after I fucked her holes with my tongue. How I would push her tits around my dick and fuck them, covering her neck and face when I came. How I would eventually take her ass, over and over again before I pulled out and sprayed my seed all over her back.

I was going to fucking ruin her.

Just like she'd already ruined me.

I climaxed hard, spots of black clouding my vision as my cum spilled out, the orgasm better than anything I'd ever felt.

I was shocked as I came down, feeling like I'd just had an otherworldly experience.

If this was what it was like orgasming just from the thought of her, I could only imagine how good it was going to be to come inside her.

A brief image of Casey round with my child hit my brain . . . and my dick was suddenly hard all over again.

For fuck's sake, Parker. Give her a few years.

At this rate my cock was going to fall off. I'd never in my life had to masturbate as much as I had since finding Casey.

I sighed, turning my head so I could breathe her in while I thought about what I had planned for tomorrow night. Her roommate had taken the bait, eagerly saying she'd go to the party and bring her roommate with her. Jace didn't know why he'd been inviting a random freshman to his house, but he'd thought Natalie was hot, so he hadn't complained. I'd also made sure that an invitation was extended to Andrews's frat.

Glancing at my watch again, I knew it was time to go. They'd be coming back anytime now. Studying some of the cum that had escaped her panties and ended up on my hand, I wiped it on her pillow.

I stared at it proudly as I slid out of the bed, adjusting the covers back to where they'd been. There, now her bed would smell like me too.

I was whistling as I walked out and locked the door. The girl at the desk was pretending not to be watching for me as I came back out into the lobby, and I shot her a little salute, pointing to my bulging pocket like I'd secured the socks.

Even though I'd actually taken Casey's thong, and it was what was in my pocket at that moment.

No socks to be found.

I mimed zipping my mouth shut, and she giggled, giving me a flirty wave as I left.

I was ecstatic as I walked out of the door, eager for the night to come, and the party I was about to prep for.

CHAPTER 14

CASEY

Natalie stood in front of me, hands on her hips, a wicked grin lighting up her face. "Roomie, we're going to this party if I have to drag you there myself."

I yawned. It was a freaking Wednesday. I didn't know if I had it in me to party on a Wednesday.

Especially after how little sleep I'd gotten last night.

Nat dropped to her knees, clasping her hands in front of her. "Please, please, please," she begged. "We need some bonding time. Don't make me go with the weirdos down the hall. They smell like cheese."

I snorted and shook my head in mock exasperation. I was positive that the girls down the hall—who were cheerleaders—did not smell like cheese. But it did make me feel like she really wanted me to go.

Natalie must have smelled victory because she leapt to her feet and started frantically rifling through her makeup bag, humming some pop song under her breath. Before I knew it, she'd pulled me in front of the tiny dorm mirror and was inspecting my face like it was a canvas.

"Okay, first things first. Close your eyes."

I obeyed, feeling the light dusting of a brush sweep across my eyes. Natalie's chatter filled the silence, a constant stream of comments and stories that were all incredibly amusing.

"How did you hear about this party again?" I interjected as she started on my eyeliner.

"I'll never forget it until the day I die," she swooned dramatically. I popped open an eye, and she bopped me on the nose. "Keep your eyes closed."

THE WRONG QUARTERBACK   125

"Yes, ma'am," I sighed.

"Anyways . . . as I was *saying*. I was eating some pizza in the dining hall, when all of a sudden, Jace Thatcher, the star wide receiver from the Tigers, sits down across from me and starts talking."

My eyes flew open at that, and she almost stabbed me with the eyeliner stick. Jace Thatcher had been that guy in the library who was friends with Parker. There's no way Parker had asked him to invite my roommate so I would come . . . right?

I snorted as Nat freaked out about almost blinding me for life. There's no way that was what happened.

"Sorry, continue," I told her.

She humphed as she finished my eyeliner a little aggressively.

"You have no idea how lucky you are, Casey," she said, leaning in closer as she added mascara with a steady hand. "These cheekbones, this skin—fuck, if I didn't love you already, I'd be jealous."

I blinked at her reflection, surprised. Compliments weren't something I was used to. "Thanks," I mumbled, my voice coming out shy and awkward.

"Okay, but you were saying, about Jace," I prodded, pretending I didn't see her knowing grin.

"He just talked to me for like ten minutes about how school was going and where I was from . . . and then he invited me to the party he and his teammate are throwing tonight and told me to bring a friend." She clapped her hands together, powder flying off her brush.

"Who's his friend?" I asked.

"Matty Adler, the Tigers' star tight end."

I nodded, pretending that I knew who she was talking about.

"I'm going to point out all these guys tonight, or at the next game if some of them aren't there," she told me, grinning as she stepped back to admire her work before tilting her head thoughtfully. "Oh, you're going to break hearts tonight," she declared, swiping on a last touch of lip gloss. "Trust me, by the end of the night, you're going to have *lots* of names to remember."

A nervous laugh bubbled up out of me. I'd never done this before—never sat with a girlfriend and shared makeup, never had someone fuss over my appearance with that kind of affection. It felt . . . nice. It had been something I'd hoped I'd experience someday, but I hadn't thought it would happen.

Natalie turned to grab her own lipstick, chattering on about who would probably be at the party and who to avoid. "Parker Davis will probably be there," she added, raising an eyebrow at me with a teasing, knowing smirk.

126 C.R. JANE

My stomach flipped at the mention of him, and I felt my cheeks heat up. "Gray and his friends are also going to be there," I said, pretending that Parker's name didn't do anything for me.

I was half convinced Parker wasn't real.

There was no way that someone existed that hot . . . and that sweet. There was no way how he'd been acting was real. Or at least that's what I was telling myself.

"Casey, please," she said, rolling her eyes dramatically. "I say this as your new best friend and the girl you're going to be stuck with for the rest of your life. Are you sure that Gray's what you want?"

I blinked at her, surprised she would come out and say it like that. "Gray's just been busy with the pledge term," I told her. "You'll like him when you see what he's really like."

"You mean when he's not drunk all the time and ditching you every time you make plans."

I flushed at that comment . . . because it wasn't *not* true.

"You'll see. It will be different," I finally said, not sure who I was trying to convince. Gray had called and apologized this morning after he'd woken up and I'd been gone. But it seemed like all he'd been doing since I'd gotten to campus was apologizing, didn't it?

She frowned, but didn't say anything else, and we finished getting ready for the party in relative silence.

"I'm sorry," she finally blurted out as we were getting ready to leave the room.

"For what?" I asked, confused.

"For not being supportive about Gray. I'll—try harder. For your sake," she added.

I surprised myself by giving her a quick hug. "I've never really had a good friend, Nat," I told her honestly. "I'm thinking I finally have one."

Natalie's eyes welled up, and her lower lip trembled . . . like she was going to cry. "I think I got one, too."

I smiled, and she huffed at me, waving her hand at her eyes. "Now enough of this mushy stuff. We are *not* messing up our makeup. We are going to this party. And we are going to slay!"

"Did you just say *slay*?" I asked, raising an eyebrow as she literally pushed me out of our room.

"I did, and feel free to adopt it. It's what all the cool kids say." She winked.

THE WRONG QUARTERBACK **127**

As we walked down the street, I realized I was actually feeling . . . anticipation. Maybe this party wouldn't be so bad after all.

The music pounded through the house, loud enough to make the walls vibrate and people shout over it just to be heard. The party smelled like spilled beer, sweat, and a hint of someone's cologne that was way too strong. I leaned against the wall, taking small sips from the red cup Nat had handed me . . . trying not to look as out of place as I felt.

Beside me, Nat was buzzing with energy, her eyes scanning the room like a hunter looking for her next target. Then, out of nowhere, she elbowed me, her eyes wide and gleaming.

"I want him," Nat announced, practically bouncing on her toes.

I glanced over to the kitchen where she was staring lustfully, expecting it to be some smooth frat boy like the one she'd hooked up with during orientation . . .

But it was not.

Instead, my eyes landed on a massive guy, one of the football team's offensive linemen by the looks of it. The guy was easily over six feet tall and built like a mountain. He had on a ratty cutoff shirt that barely covered his enormous, hairy belly, which peeked out from underneath.

"Him?" I asked, half laughing, half choking on my drink.

Nat nodded, completely serious. "Yes. I want to *climb* him."

I stared at her, trying to decide if she was joking. But Nat was already smoothing down her skirt and adjusting her bandeau top, eyes locked on her target like she was about to go win a prize.

"Where are you going?" I asked as she started strutting across the room with all the confidence in the world, her sights set on the human mountain who looked like he could bench-press a truck.

"Wish me luck," she called over her shoulder.

Nat wove her way through the crowd like she owned the room. The giant offensive lineman was mid-laugh, holding a can of cheap beer. I watched as she sidled up to him, all smiles and hair flips, and he looked down at her, eyebrows shooting up in surprise before breaking into a wide grin.

She said something to him that made his smile falter for a split second before turning into a broad, surprised smile. From where I was standing, I could swear her lips formed the words "Hey, big bear, I want to climb you like a tree."

128 C.R. JANE

My eyes went wide. There was no way she'd said that . . .

The lineman set his beer down so fast it wobbled on the table, and without missing a beat, he held his massive arms out. Nat didn't hesitate. She jumped, wrapping her legs around his waist as he caught her effortlessly. The room erupted in laughter, hoots, and cheers as they started making out feverishly. Nat was indeed literally trying to climb him as he grabbed her ass with both hands.

I choked on my drink, half laughing, half in shock.

I wondered what it would be like to be that confident in yourself, to see something you wanted, and actually go after it.

Natalie was pretty freaking awesome.

With the exception that I was now at this party by myself . . .

I'd just pulled out my phone to see where Gray was when his arms slid around my waist. "Case," he murmured, pressing a kiss against my neck that had me squirming uncomfortably.

Because based on what I was smelling . . . he was already drunk.

"Hi," he said, grinning handsomely at me when I turned around to face him.

I didn't want to be the nag who got mad at her boyfriend every single day, so I just pressed a kiss against his lips and didn't mention his bloodshot eyes.

"Hi, yourself," I told him with a soft grin.

His eyes raked up and down my body. "I'm the luckiest guy at this fucking school," he said, his hands sliding up my sides.

I closed my eyes, trying to enjoy it, Gray's lips pressed against mine, messy and eager, his breath hot and tinged with beer and whatever else he'd pregamed before he'd come here. His hands gripped my waist, pulling me closer. The room was a blur of pulsing lights and sweaty bodies, music thumping hard enough to rattle in my chest, drowning out coherent thought.

But then, I opened my eyes . . .

Parker stood across the room, half in the shadows, his face carved into an expression I hadn't seen before. His jaw was tight, muscles flexed under the sharp lines of his cheekbones. His eyes . . . they were burning holes through me. It was more than anger; it was fury tempered with something darker, something that made my pulse stutter.

For a moment, the noise around me muted, the thrum of the bass and chatter dimming to nothing. It was just Parker and that look, the heat in his gaze pinning me in place, making my skin flush and prickle under the

THE WRONG QUARTERBACK   129

intensity as Gray kissed down my neck and my chest. Parker didn't move, he didn't blink, he just watched me.

Gray shifted, pulling back to mumble something against my lips, oblivious to the shift in the air, but I couldn't focus on him. I couldn't focus on anything but Parker, standing there, as if he was daring me to look away first, to pretend this moment hadn't just shifted the entire room off its axis. I could read his mind from here.

What are you doing?

How could you kiss him?

And worst of all . . . *You belong to me.*

"I have to go to the bathroom," I said suddenly, pushing away from Gray. I needed a break, a moment to get myself under control, a moment away from Gray . . . and Parker.

"Hurry back," he told me, for the first time since I'd come to school not seeming like he wanted to get away from me and be with his friends.

Which was just another reason that I couldn't look at Parker.

The room spun with heat and the aftermath of too many eyes, Parker's gaze still burning into my skin even as I wove through the crowd.

I made it out of the living room, but a line of impatient girls were waiting for the bathroom, stretched down the entire hallway.

"You can use mine." A voice cut through the noise, low and smooth. I turned, startled, and found myself staring at Parker's friend from the library, Jace. He leaned against the wall, freakishly hot looking, a smug smile on his lips like he knew something I didn't.

"Oh, um—" I stammered.

He leaned a little closer, that easy grin not faltering. "Don't worry, it's just down the hall. No line, and I promise, I don't bite." He cocked his head, mischief flickering in his expression.

"Can *I* use your restroom?" a girl asked, stumbling into me as she tried to get Jace's attention.

"No, sorry, only Inner Sanctum members are allowed," he told her with a charming smile.

"Huh?" she asked, but he was already pushing me past the hallway and leaving her behind.

"What's the Inner Sanctum?" I asked, confused.

"Is that one not doing it for you? Do you like the Loyalty League more . . . or the Silent Syndicate? Oooh, what about the No Drama Llamas?" he asked innocently.

"Ummm. I'm not sure I'm qualified to make this decision for you. Who exactly is in the . . . No Drama Llamas?"

"You're right. That one sounds ridiculous," Jace said, fixing the bun on top of his head.

I'd never been a fan of long hair on guys, but I didn't think a world existed where Jace Thatcher wasn't considered hot.

Not Parker Davis hot, obviously.

But still hot.

Oh, shit. I definitely shouldn't be thinking that.

"Well, it's Parker, Matty, me of course . . . and hear me out on this, I'm thinking . . . *you*," Jace commented, pulling me out of my inner freak-out.

"Wait . . . what about me?" I asked as we got to a door at the end of the hallway.

Jace was whistling as he took a key out of his pocket and then unlocked the door.

"Just lock it behind you right now, and then lock it again when you leave, and come find me if you need to use it later," he told me, throwing open the door with a flourish and beginning to head back down the hallway.

"Thanks," I said, still really confused by what he said.

"And I'll keep brainstorming our team name," he called to me.

"Okay," I said softly, watching him for a moment before some girls noticed the open door and started to head my way.

I slammed the door shut with a thud, and locked it . . . right before someone tried the door handle.

Leaning my forehead against the door, I took a few deep breaths. I'd go to the bathroom, get my head on straight . . . and then get back to my boyfriend.

Everything was going to be okay.

CHAPTER 15

PARKER

"Looks like you need a refill," I said casually, passing where Andrews was talking to his friends and holding out a red Solo cup to him. He immediately took it from me, his eyes glassy from how much he'd already drunk. His friends all stared at me eagerly, launching into how great that first game was, and all the bullshit that comes with people wanting to suck up to me.

Andrews had evidently forgotten how threatened he'd been feeling about me and his girlfriend, and I watched as he downed half of the drink in one go. Idiot.

Although it probably had never crossed his mind—sober or drunk—that I would drug him to get his girl.

I hadn't ever seen myself doing that either.

But desperate men obviously did desperate things.

Giving the group a few claps on the back so they would feel good about themselves, I told them I would see them later and then left for the other side of the room.

The music pounded, drowning out most conversations, but I spotted the girl I needed—Bethany, or something like that. Matty had once made the mistake of fucking her, and she'd tried to move into the house the next day. She was just what I needed for this next step. A social-climbing, stage-five clinger.

She was also a few drinks deep, swaying on her feet. Perfect.

I approached her, offering a charming smile. "Hey, one of my friends over there has been dying to meet you all night."

She nodded, blinking slowly as she stared up at me, dollar signs practically visible in her eyeballs.

"You should definitely go talk to him. He's that guy in the orange polo over there," I continued, pointing out where Gray was standing.

The girl stuck out her lips at me in a weird fish face. "But I've been *dying* to meet you," she whined, reaching out to touch my chest.

I quickly stepped back so she couldn't touch me. "Sorry, I'm taken," I told her. "But my friend over there is a *big* deal in his fraternity. He'll be able to get you into all the Beta Omega parties. And the football team goes to those parties all the time."

"Oh," she said hopefully, like I'd just offered her a seat on my dick at a future date. "I'll go over there."

"He likes aggressive girls," I called after her, and she grinned over her shoulder, because we both knew *aggressive* was her particular specialty.

I watched as she walked toward Andrews, all of a sudden adopting a weird swaying motion where it looked like she was trying to push her hips out of socket.

Gray had already been drunk when I'd handed him that drink, but now his eyes were *really* messed up, his lids heavy, like he was staring through a fog he couldn't shake. His movements were slower—his coordination dulled to a dazed, clumsy shuffle as he leaned back against the wall, looking almost like he was trying to steady himself but wasn't quite aware enough to care.

When Bethany, or whatever her name was, approached him, pushing through his fraternity bros to get to him, he barely registered it, his gaze drifting over her like she was just another blur in the crowd. She gave him a sultry smile, trailing her fingers along his arm until she had his full, hazy attention. And then, without hesitation, she latched onto his lips, pulling him into a messy, uncoordinated kiss. His arms moved, half-heartedly, resting awkwardly on her shoulders like he was trying to figure out where they were supposed to go.

He kissed her back, but it was sloppy, his lips moving with no rhythm, no purpose, just a slow, confused response. It was obvious he wasn't fully processing what he was doing, each move heavy and clumsy, like he was trying to remember what came next and failing. His eyes stayed half-open, his expression distant, almost like he was sleepwalking through the whole thing.

I took a sip of my drink and leaned against the wall with a smile, ready to watch the show.

There was no part of me that wanted Casey to be hurt. But I couldn't take another day of seeing him with her.

THE WRONG QUARTERBACK 133

I would make it up to her after this, though; I'd make her life so happy that this would just be a blip in the radar of our long, amazing life together.

Casey came around the corner then, stopping dead in her tracks when she saw them—Gray pressed against the wall, lips locked with another girl. The look on Casey's face was exactly what I'd been after. Shock. Pain. Betrayal. Their relationship crumbling right in front of her.

She obviously hadn't noticed that Gray was out of his mind, that he had no idea what he was doing. He probably wouldn't even remember that this had happened when he woke up in the morning.

But she would.

She stood there for a second, frozen, like she couldn't process what she was seeing. Then she turned and bolted, rushing past the crowd and out the back door.

I waited, giving her a few moments to fall apart. Then, I followed her.

The door screeched as I pushed it open, and there she was, standing at the edge of the yard, her arms wrapped around herself like she was holding on for dear life. Her shoulders shook, but she wasn't crying—not yet. I could see it, though. She was breaking.

I approached slowly, making sure my footsteps were quiet, careful. "Casey?"

She flinched but didn't turn around. Her voice was barely above a whisper. "I don't want to talk right now, Parker."

"I saw what happened," I said, keeping my tone low, soft. "He's the biggest fucking idiot in the world."

She stiffened at my words, and I stepped closer, just enough to show I was there, but not enough to push. Not yet.

"I don't get it," she whispered, her voice trembling. "Why would he do that? After everything . . ." She glanced up at me, tears gathering in her silver eyes. "What did I do wrong?"

Fuck. That question hit me right in the chest. That she would even think that.

"Are you kidding me? The only person who did anything wrong in this situation was that asshole. If you were my girl . . ."

She was still staring up at me, vulnerability radiating off her.

I took a step closer.

"If you were my girl, you would be the only thing that I would see. I would spend *every* day proving to you how fucking perfect you are for me. There would never be a day that you would doubt it," I murmured, catching one of her tears on my finger.

134   C.R. JANE

"Why couldn't he?" she finally whispered, before she turned and once again . . . ran away.

Casey

I turned the corner, pushing through the thick crowd, the noise and heat pressing in on me, a hazy quality to the air.

And then I saw him—Gray, his back against the wall, his arms wrapped around someone who wasn't me. My heart stopped, a hollow, aching pause that made the air catch in my throat.

He was making out with her, his lips tangled with hers, hands drifting to her waist like it was the most natural thing in the world. Like I didn't exist. My stomach twisted, an icy, dead feeling spreading through my chest as I stood there, frozen, watching my worst nightmare unfold right in front of me.

I wanted to look away, to pretend it wasn't real, but I couldn't.

This was Gray—my Gray, the boy who had been there through everything, who had promised me a thousand things—wrapped around another girl like I meant nothing.

I couldn't breathe. All I could think about were his words, the ones that had pulled me in, that had made me feel like we were building something real. He'd said he thought Ben would have understood, that he would have wanted this for us. That he would've been okay with us being together. But this? Ben would never have supported this. My brother would never have wanted me to feel this kind of betrayal, this sick, hollow ache that crept through my chest and made it hard to breathe.

Gray had promised me something—something sacred—and he'd thrown it away like it was nothing.

"Casey!"

I woke up with a gasp, tears streaming down my cheeks. Natalie's concerned face was hovering over me.

"You were crying out in your sleep," she murmured, sitting down on the edge of my bed. Her lower lip suddenly trembled, and she threw herself on me. "I'm so fucking sorry, babe. He's the worst. The absolute worst."

"Who told you?" I croaked out.

She squeezed me for one more second before she pulled away. "Parker came and got me and sent me after you. He was really worried about you," she said softly.

Parker. I couldn't think about him right now.

THE WRONG QUARTERBACK **135**

If my heart could be broken by a guy like Gray . . . I had a feeling that it would be absolutely demolished by someone like Parker.

"I just can't believe he did that," I whispered. She scooted back so I could sit up.

Glancing out the window, it was still dark outside. Maybe that was a good thing. Because what was I supposed to do after this, when I inevitably saw Gray? What was I even supposed to say to him?

"Want me to kill him?" Natalie asked, and I stared at her in shock, noticing for the first time she was still in her party clothes, her eyeliner smudged underneath her eyes. "Well, I wouldn't *personally* kill him. We could just find a hit man or something. You can find anything online these days." Her face was completely serious.

"No, that's alright," I said slowly, trying to smile, but finding myself incapable of it at the moment. I brought my legs to my chest and laid my cheek on my knees, looking at her. "I just didn't think he was capable of hurting me like that, you know? Breaking up with me, yes. But to cheat on me, in *front* of me. I—I feel like everything I knew about him was wrong." More tears slid down my face and wet my sheets.

"I'm so sorry, sweetie," she murmured, rubbing my back. I'd told her about Ben and how he and Gray had been best friends. And how I'd thought I'd been in love with him since the day he'd first walked through our door.

"This won't make you feel better . . . but he did seem really out of it. He'd definitely drunk too much."

"No, it doesn't make me feel better," I said, turning to bury my face against my knees for a moment. "He's been drinking a lot this whole time, but I guess I just assumed there was a line, you know. When he would stop." A sob slipped from my mouth, and I was mad about it, because it wasn't a sob he deserved. "When you love someone, you should have a line."

We sat there in silence for a long time. She would rub my back every time I cried and tell me she was so sorry I'd been hurt.

"Thank you for being here," I finally told her hoarsely as the sun was starting to light up the horizon. "It's nice not to feel so alone."

She grabbed my shoulders and gave me a gentle squeeze.

"I'm still feeling good things," she said quietly, and I let out a quiet huff. Because I wasn't, not at all.

I eventually forced myself out of bed, even though Natalie thought I should take the day off. I didn't want to stay in our room, though, going

136   C.R. JANE

over everything again and again. Every time I closed my eyes I saw him kissing her.

Hopefully class would distract me . . . a little.

The ache of last night sat heavy in my chest as I washed my face and threw on clothes. Staring in the mirror, I inwardly groaned. I looked like my heart hadn't just been ripped out, but stomped on too.

No revenge look was going on here.

Natalie walked with me out into the hallway, her usual bubbly energy dialed down to something softer, more understanding. She didn't ask any questions, just fell into step beside me, her quiet presence a reminder that I wasn't completely alone.

We'd made it to my building before he appeared, as if summoned by my worst thoughts.

Gray.

If I thought I looked bad . . . he looked worse. His face was pale, eyes rimmed with dark circles, and there was a green pallor to his skin, like he was going to be sick at any moment. He looked awful, like he was barely holding it together.

A part of me, the one that had always loved him, felt bad for how horrible he looked. He was clearly suffering, and I had always just wanted him to be happy. I'd always thought that *I* could do that for him.

But I needed to stop thinking that way.

"Casey," he said, stumbling off the wall he'd been leaning against, his voice thick, the desperation clear. "I don't know what happened last night. I don't remember . . . any of it. I swear." He shook his head, his eyes pleading, reaching for something in me. "I'm so sorry. I would never—"

I stared at him, the sting of tears threatening, my throat burning with everything I wanted to say but couldn't. *Sorry.* As if sorry could erase the image of him tangled with someone else, of every promise he'd broken. As if it could take away the betrayal that still clawed at my chest, raw and unhealed.

"No," I whispered, my voice trembling. "I don't care what happened, Gray. I *never* want to see you again."

He fell back a step, like I'd physically struck him, his whole face shocked and disbelieving. "Casey, I don't even remember anything. I would never have done that to you. Ever. I love you!"

Now I was the one who felt like I'd been slapped, because that word . . . *love.*

It couldn't possibly make me feel like this.

THE WRONG QUARTERBACK   137

I looked away, refusing to let him see the tears that were already gathering in my eyes.

Natalie touched my arm gently. "Let's go. You're going to be late," she murmured, shooting Gray a dirty look.

Without another word, she looped her arm in mine and led me toward the entrance to where my class was. Thank goodness she knew where we were going; my autopilot wasn't working at the moment.

"Casey! I'm going to prove it to you. We're not done!" Gray yelled after us, but I didn't look back.

I held my head high, even as my heart shattered with every step. And I didn't let the tears come until we were out of his sight. I may have sobbed after that, but at least I hadn't done it in front of him.

Because he didn't deserve my tears.

CHAPTER 16

PARKER

"You're in a chipper chapper mood," Jace commented as I threw him the ball. We were doing a few warm-up passes before drills started, and he was wincing every time he caught the ball from how hard I was throwing.

I couldn't help it, though. It felt like last night had been this huge turning point, and I couldn't wait to start the next step.

"Just really excited about life right now, Thatcher," I told him as he broke left, and I launched the ball. Jace reached up and caught it midair over his shoulder.

And that's why he was the best.

Jace was grinning as he jogged back toward me.

"Sure it doesn't have to do with a *certain* girl? And the fact that her *certain* boyfriend fucked up big-time last night?" asked Jace, fluttering his eyelashes at me obnoxiously.

"Why do you keep on saying 'certain' like that?" asked Matty.

"Or is it the fact that you were the one who made the boyfriend fuck up in the first place?" Jace continued, ignoring Matty completely.

I huffed out a laugh. Jace's brother was basically a pharmaceutical company unto himself, so I'd had my pick of drugs to choose from. Unfortunately, that meant Jace knew all about my plan. Which led to Matty being told as well.

Good thing I trusted these guys with my life.

"So that's it, we're just crazy now?" Matty asked, grabbing the football from me and beginning to toss it in the air. "We're just talking about this like it's nothing?"

THE WRONG QUARTERBACK   139

Jace stole the football from him. "It's called true love, *Matthew*. Just wait, you're going to crack one of these days over Ms. Stalker, and it's all going to be over. You're going to be insufferable."

The three of us glanced over to where the blonde was sitting in her car, watching us closely.

Matty growled when she ducked down in her car, and Jace grinned because one of his favorite activities in life was annoying him.

"Ooh, I have a good one. It perfectly fits this situation," Jace said, right as Coach blew on his whistle.

"What?" I asked as we began to jog over to where the team was gathering.

"How does a wiener go camping?"

"How does this have anything to do with Parker literally stealing someone's girlfriend?" Matty complained.

"You can't steal something that belongs to you," I told them, and they both blinked at me . . . looking concerned.

"The delusion is setting in. We'd better call a doctor," Jace whisper-yelled.

"We can't. They would lock him up," added Matty.

"Are you going to finish the joke or what?" I asked.

"In a Wiener-bago," Jace said quickly.

We both stared at him.

"It's not funny because you ruined it with all your talking. But I'll forgive you this time. What I really want to know is how exactly are you going to make her *your* girl? I know what happens in these situations. She's going to be telling herself that all men are ogres. And you, my friend, are going to be the ogre-est."

"Ogre-est. That's definitely not a word," I told him.

"He has a big brain, he would know," said Matty.

"Can you answer the question?" Jace sighed.

I grinned.

"Is that . . . a dick reference . . . when you smile like that?" Matty asked. "Because it's a little creepy."

"I'm glad someone said it," Jace commented.

Coach's whistle pierced the air again, cutting through the scattered chatter on the field. "Quit your fucking yapping and start drills, gentlemen! Hustle up—let's see if any of you can actually move today."

Jace shot me a look, rolling his eyes. "This isn't over. If you've got a master plan, I want to hear it, Davis."

I chuckled and winked before lining up as Coach Everett barked out the next set. "Sprints first! I want to see speed—down and back in under twelve seconds. If you're late, we're doing it again."

We took off at the whistle, feet pounding against the turf, the steady rhythm broken only by the slap of cleats and heavy breaths. I kept my pace, pushing hard, glancing around to clock who was dragging behind. Jace was keeping up, stride for stride, his eyes narrowed, challenging me with every step.

As we crossed the line, Coach's voice boomed again. "Good, now we're going through passing drills! Davis, take lead. Receivers—run those routes clean, or we're starting over."

I nodded, grabbing a ball and huddling with the receivers. "Alright, quick slants to start. I want those cuts sharp. No sloppy routes, or Coach is gonna have us doing burpees till tomorrow."

The receivers grumbled but nodded, spreading out as I lined up. Jace was first, lining up on the left. He took off at the snap, darting inside, making a tight, precise cut, and I fired the ball right into his chest. He caught it clean, tucking it in and turning upfield before sprinting back, giving me a quick nod.

And so the drills continued, each one faster than the last, Coach's voice keeping us in line.

When he finally whistled that practice was over, I was the first one off the field.

After all . . . I couldn't be late. I had a tutoring session to get to.

I'd been a little afraid Casey was going to ghost me tonight, and I would have to track her down. But there she was, sitting at the same table by the window, where the light softened everything, and she looked like an angel I didn't deserve.

Good thing I didn't care about things like what I deserved—I'd always been more of the make-your-own-fate kind of guy.

Casey looked up from her notes as I slid into the seat next to her. I flashed her my best smile and considered it a win when she still blushed after everything that had happened last night, even if she did eye me warily while doing it. I made a show of pulling out my math textbook. I'd already doctored my answers so I could keep her busy for a long time trying to teach me all the things I already knew.

"Hey," I said, nodding at her pile of notes. "Hope you're ready to help me out again. I've half convinced my professor I'm not an idiot."

At least I could say it wasn't the worst lie that I'd told her, right?

THE WRONG QUARTERBACK **141**

A small laugh fell from her lips, and I soaked in the sound like a druggie finally getting his next fix.

I loved everything about her. Her smile, her laugh, the way her eyes crinkled when she thought something was funny. Sometimes it hurt being this close to her because all I wanted was for her to be mine. I wanted to latch myself onto her and stitch her to my side so we were never apart.

That sounded creepy, but I obviously meant it in the most obsessed, deranged, lovestruck way, of course.

"I thought we went over this concept last time. You're going to fire me as a tutor soon," she huffed, biting down on her lip as she glanced over the problems.

I didn't miss the way she stiffened as I moved closer to her—close enough that every inhale gave me her scent.

"No, I don't think we covered that. You helped me with exponential functions, and look at this grade. Best teacher ever," I told her, nudging her shoulder as I showed her the $A+$ on the two-year-old worksheet I could have done in my sleep.

Her pretty eyes widened, and I got a little lost staring at the blue ring around the silver. "Wow, I don't think *I* could even get that high of a grade," she murmured, a frown staining her lips.

Shit. I should have changed it to a B.

"It's only because of you, I could even get that grade. But I still have a long way to go to keep up in this class. We'll have to keep working hard."

She nodded, dragging her gaze from the paper to my face, her pupils expanding as she stared at me.

Quit fighting this so hard, Silver, I cajoled in my head, doing everything I could not to lean forward and taste those lips.

We went to work, me pretending to nod and listen to what she was saying as I daydreamed that we were fucking against the stacks.

My dick was so hard and out of control, I was afraid that I was going to pass out. My gaze kept darting from her to the shelves . . . and finally I couldn't stop myself anymore.

"How are you doing?" I asked, and she stiffened.

"I don't really want to talk about it," she finally answered.

"You know, I've been told I'm a very good listener."

Casey set the pencil down, and I got a little lost for a minute. Her hair was down, framing her face with untamed waves. It didn't look like she was wearing any makeup, but her skin was so smooth looking I kind of wanted to rub it to make sure.

142   C.R. JANE

Because no one could be that perfect, right?

"I don't think you want to hear anything I have to say right now," she said, and I blinked because I realized I'd gone into some kind of trance staring at her.

"I want to hear everything," I quickly sputtered out.

She sighed and hung her head, and when she finally glanced back at me, I knew what she was about to say wasn't going to be good.

"Stop playing games with me," she said in a choked voice, her eyes growing wild. "I'm not some stupid toy for you to play with!"

I gaped at her. I guess this is what Jace had meant when he said she was going to think I was the ogre-est.

"Why do you think I'm playing games with you?" I asked, sitting back in my seat.

She blinked at me, like she'd expected me to admit it and now I was shocking her.

"Well, I—" she stuttered.

"Tell me, baby, what about me says that I'm playing games? Is it because your asshole ex was just that lame, and now you're having trouble believing that someone as awesome as me would want you?" I raised an eyebrow and watched as she dropped her eyes.

Clearly, I'd hit it right on the head.

I tipped up her chin, forcing her to look at me. "You blow my mind every time I see you. You're the one who's out of *my* league."

She blinked, her lips parting as she stared at me, surprised, and completely taken aback. "What?" she murmured, a hint of confusion mixed with disbelief in her voice.

I shrugged, unable to hold back a smile. "I'm just trying to keep myself in the game, baby, before you realize that you're too good for me. You're too good for anyone . . ."

"You're out of your mind, Parker Davis," she finally said, picking up her pencil and pretending I couldn't see the way her pulse was going out of control in her neck.

"I *am* out of my mind, Casey Larsen. I'm glad you finally noticed."

I closed the textbook in front of me. "You know, I've got to track down this one book, and I have no idea where to look. Want to help me find it?"

She looked relieved, like this was going to be a break from everything I'd been saying.

"Sure," she said, pushing away from the table. "Which one is it?"

THE WRONG QUARTERBACK   143

I rattled off a title that I was pretty sure didn't exist, knowing she wouldn't question it. I led her deeper into the stacks, weaving through the narrow rows and heading down the stairs to the rooms that no one was ever in. The noise of the main library faded, replaced by the kind of quiet that I was looking for.

"Bet you haven't been down here before?" I said, watching her admire all the old books. I bet she was a girl who wanted one of those libraries with the ladder that moved along the walls like the girl in *Beauty and the Beast*.

I would definitely have to make that happen for her.

"I just started here, *of course* I haven't been down here yet," she murmured. "I didn't even know about this level."

I had been down here only once, when Matty got drunk and hooked up with some girl in one of these stacks. He'd passed out on the floor, and when Jace had realized he hadn't come home and practice was about to start . . . I'd been dragged down here to save our best friend.

Did I mention that Jace only knew where he was because he'd added both of us to his Find My Friends app without asking permission . . . because apparently stalking was our thing?

I leaned against one of the shelves, watching her peruse the books with an awestruck look in her eyes.

I wanted her to look at *me* like that.

"You want to know something that's guaranteed to make you feel better?" I told her after my dick could no longer keep his distance.

"What?" she asked, frowning when she saw I was staring at her.

"It's simple, really," I said as I began to stalk over to where she was standing.

She stared at me wide-eyed, not blinking until I was right in front of her, cornering her against the books, caging her in with my arms above her head so she couldn't run away.

"The best way to get over someone is to get under someone new," I murmured in her ear, making sure that my lips brushed against her skin with every word.

Casey went very still, and I waited patiently. I needed her to make this move. I needed her to break through whatever barriers she'd put up in her brain because I knew if I could just get her to give in by even an inch . . .

I'd be able to keep her forever.

"Who exactly says that?" she finally whispered, and I could see it, there in her silver gaze . . . she was close.

"Everyone," I told her, my lips now brushing her cheek. "Absolutely everyone."

"Sounds like I should find someone to help me with that, then."

I grinned, pulling away so I could look at her, and I growled. "Except I'm not about to let anyone else have that fucking privilege."

CHAPTER 17

CASEY

I don't know why I did it. Maybe later I'd claim temporary insanity, but right then, I couldn't stop myself.

I had to kiss him.

Parker was bent over, already eye level. Between the lock of hair falling across his forehead and the fact that his face was the most gorgeous thing I'd ever seen . . .

And the fact that I was now single . . . and heartbroken . . .

I couldn't be blamed for leaning forward and softly grazing his lips. Just one kiss—to cure this fire that had been burning inside me since the second I saw him . . . one kiss.

Except he wasn't satisfied with only that.

"Finally," he murmured, his hands coming up to tangle in my hair. He brushed his lips against mine again, softly moaning like just that light touch was going to be the end of him.

This . . . this was what a kiss was supposed to be like.

Like a whisper turning into a shout. Like colors filling an empty canvas. Like a song coming to life under my fingertips.

This was what a kiss was supposed to spark.

It was supposed to make you feel alive.

Parker gently coaxed my lips apart, his tongue slipping into my mouth, tasting me.

"Fuck," he growled. "I knew it. I knew it would be like this."

His kiss turned aggressive, his deep, long licks into my mouth desperate and dominant.

146   C.R. JANE

Every time his tongue slid over mine, a surge of lust sped through my veins.

"Parker," I whimpered as his lips owned me.

"You taste so good, baby," he said between wild kisses. "I'm done. Ruined. I need this, every day. Fuck."

Keeping one hand threaded through my hair, moving me exactly how he wanted, his other hand slid down, pulling me against him so I could feel every inch of him, including what felt like a baseball bat pressing against my stomach.

Holy fuck, his dick was huge.

"Stop thinking, Casey," he whispered, his hand on my lower back yanking me even closer, so my breasts were smashed against his sculpted chest. He sucked on my tongue, groaning as his hand slid further down and gripped my ass.

"Are you going to be a good girl and let me eat that perfect pussy?" he asked roughly, as his lips slid down my neck, licking and biting in a way that was sure to mark me.

I realized I wanted that. Even though this was only for tonight . . . for this moment . . . I wanted physical proof that Parker had been here.

"I want your words, baby," Parker pressed, and all I could do was moan in response. "Say it, Casey. Tell me you want me to lick that pretty cunt." He bit down in the space between my neck and my shoulder and I cried out again. "I want you to beg for it," he growled.

"Please," I gasped. "Please, please, please."

His hand came between us, gently massaging my breast as his lips went back to mine. He swallowed my whimpers and moans as he pinched my nipple, my shirt and bra doing nothing to dull the sensation. Parker switched to the other one, and my head fell back.

"Look at you, so responsive. My perfect little fuck toy. But I need more," he rasped, pushing my shirt up and snapping my bra with one hard tug. My breasts tumbled out, and he lifted and squeezed them together as he stared at them. He touched his thumbs to my nipples, softly rolling them around until pleasure was building in my spine, and I wanted to cry because they felt so sensitive.

My breasts were out . . . in a public place.

And I thought I might die if he decided to stop right now.

"Do you want me to suck on these sweet little nipples, baby?"

Parker continued the slow roll of his thumbs while he licked a long line up my chest, until his tongue was circling my pulse. He bit down, pinching my nipples at the same time.

THE WRONG QUARTERBACK   147

"Please," I all but sobbed.

I felt the heat of his mouth, and then it was closing around my nipple, sucking and biting at my tip.

My fingers wound through his hair, holding him there as he scraped his teeth across my skin, soothing away the sting with the slide of his tongue.

He groaned as he switched sides, giving my other breast the same sweet torture. My panties were soaked, pleasure pulsing between my legs.

"Fuck, I need more," he said, a deep moan tearing from this throat as he released my nipple with a *pop* and then sank to his knees.

My eyes were wide as I stared down at the god in front of me. His deep blue eyes seemed to glitter and burn as he pulled on my leggings, pushing them down until I was standing there in nothing but my skimpy panties.

"Yes," he murmured, pushing his nose against my core and breathing in deeply. He growled and then turned his head, biting down on my thigh until I cried out.

"Wait," I said suddenly, my clit pulsing between my thighs.

He licked at the indention in my legs before sitting back, his pupils blown out as he glanced up at me, his hair a complete mess from my hands pulling at it.

"What is it, baby? I'll give you anything," he rasped. "But I *have* to eat this fucking *perfect* pussy."

I'd never seen anything hotter. This big, strong, *perfect* specimen of a male, on his knees . . . for me.

"I—I've never done this. I've never done anything," I told him. "I just . . . wanted you to know." My breath was coming out in gasps as I watched a slow, sexy grin spread across his face.

His eyes were gleaming in the dim light down here, and there was a heat in his gaze that promised me that I was about to take a wild ride.

And I couldn't wait.

"Good, then I'll be your *first* and your last, Casey Larsen, and I'll get to ruin you, baby, starting right fucking now."

My thong was gone the next second, and his hot tongue slowly licked up my slit, like he was trying to taste every single inch of me. I fell back against the bookshelf, the edge biting into my skin.

"Parker," I cried as he grabbed my leg and pulled it over his shoulder, so I was spread out before him . . . waiting for him to feast. He pressed me further into the shelf so that I couldn't move, growling against my core as he licked up to my clit and then circled it slowly.

148   C.R. JANE

"Mine," he snarled, sounding half-crazed as he sucked my clit into his mouth.

Two fingers slid through my wetness before he slowly pushed them inside me.

My cries were echoing in the air as his fingers thrust in and out, his tongue sucking and feasting on my clit.

He pushed my leg out wider as his fingers curled, rubbing up against some magic place inside of me.

I sobbed as he continued to feast on me like he was obsessed, like I was some magical nirvana he'd been waiting his whole life to taste.

Obviously, I wasn't experienced, but I'd heard enough girls talking about it over the years to know it wasn't usually like this. Where it felt like the guy was eating you like he was born to do it.

Like he loved it.

Parker slid in another finger, and I cried out again, the sensation of fullness almost too much. My head thrashed around as I tried to center myself, and he laughed softly, sucking my clit even harder as his fingers moved in and out.

"That's it, baby," he said in between licks. "Give it to me."

He slid his tongue through my folds before returning to my clit.

My core tightened, and I whined, crying out as pleasure tore through me. I was belatedly aware of my hips thrusting against his face, but I couldn't help it. His fingers and mouth continued, pushing me into my first orgasm. It tore through me, so good that I wasn't sure I'd ever be the same.

"Yes, yes, yes," I chanted as I rode his face, the stubble on his jaw scratching my inner thighs.

"That's one," he said as he lifted his face from between my legs. There was a triumphant smile on his beautiful lips, now shiny and wet from my cum.

"One?" I gasped, not sure I could actually take another.

But then his tongue was pressing into my core as his hands massaged my ass and brought me closer to him.

"Never tasted anything so good, baby," he growled . . . right before his fingers slipped between my cheeks, and he was suddenly massaging my asshole.

Fuck. Fuck. Fuck.

The tip of his finger pressed against my hole as his tongue fucked in and out of me . . . and that was it. I was coming again, sparks seeming to explode in my vision as my senses went into overload.

THE WRONG QUARTERBACK   149

I was faintly aware that I was pleading with him, my fingers digging into his shoulders as my pussy clenched around his tongue.

My legs gave out, and he caught me, easily holding my body up as his tongue lazily licked through my folds.

All I could do was blink at him as he pulled back and stared up at me. His hair was mussed, his eyes almost feral looking as he slowly lowered my legs and stood up, holding on to me the entire time so I didn't collapse.

"That was two," I whispered, almost blinded by his answering smile.

He kissed me, and I could taste . . . myself. I didn't know how much I would love it, tasting both of us on his tongue . . . like part of me was now inside him . . . and would stay there . . . even after this night was done.

Parker pulled away, and the look on his face was so smug, I almost wanted to laugh—if I was capable of that at the moment. I was still in a daze from the magic of his mouth. "You're very proud of yourself, aren't you?" I finally got out, my voice hoarse from all the noise I'd been making.

Shit. I glanced around, kind of shocked that no one had come down here to see what all the noise was. It must have been pretty soundproof, but still, I was standing here in the library . . . with my pants down. Who the fuck was I?

"Proud that I convinced you to let me taste the most delicious pussy on the planet . . . yeah, I'm pretty proud of that," he growled, leaning in for another bruising kiss.

I pulled away, frantically grabbing at my leggings to pull them up. I was bare-assed against a bookshelf . . . how long had we been gone? There was no way that it hadn't been a while. There was no one in the library that wasn't aware of Parker's presence tonight. Which meant that they were also going to be aware of exactly how long he'd been gone from that table and in the stacks.

With me.

"I need to go," I said, desperately trying to tie the front of my bra together since he'd snapped it open. Fuck. It wasn't working.

"Hey," he said, stilling my frantic hands. "It's okay."

"No, it's not okay," I snapped, patting at my hair because I was sure it was a mess. "Why did I pick the most popular guy in Tennessee for my rebound?"

Parker growled, and then his hand was gripping my throat, holding me in place so I would stop freaking out. His thumb gently pressed on my pulse and a deep, hiccuped breath burst out of my mouth. He pressed against me, his hard length a huge reminder that only one of us had an orgasm tonight.

"I don't want to ever hear you call me that again," he murmured in an almost *scary* voice, each word clipped and steady. His fingers tightened, just slightly, grounding me while my mind spun.

"Call you what?" I whispered.

"A rebound."

"Isn't that what you are?" I said, knowing that I sounded like a brat.

He shook his head. "I'm not some temporary Band-Aid, Casey. And I'm definitely not some fuckboy you're allowed to forget."

"I need to go," I told him, pushing on his arm.

"You don't get to regret this. You don't get to regret *me*. I'll let you run tonight, but get ready for me, baby. It's go time tomorrow. You let me taste you. There's no ending to this story where I don't get it all."

I gaped at him, because he sounded so serious.

"I'm still—I literally just broke up with someone."

"Bullshit. You and I both know this was inevitable, the kind of inevitable that gets tattooed on your skin until the day you die. I'm not going to be your rebound, Casey Larsen. I'm your endgame."

"Endgame." I breathed, trying to ignore the part in my soul that wanted so badly to believe him. That was just the desperate girl inside me who had lost the one person who'd ever cared about her, and who'd been betrayed by someone she'd loved after that.

That's all this was.

He released me, stepping back and allowing me to fix my clothes.

I stalked off toward the stairs, and he grabbed my hand before I could go far.

"What are you doing?" I asked as he led me forward, keeping my hand firmly grasped in his.

"Showing you how it's going to be from now on," he said in a calm, level voice as he led me down one row and then another, before we got to the stairs.

"Everyone's going to be looking," I said quietly, and he grinned back at me over his shoulder.

"That's what I'm counting on, Casey," he responded.

And I didn't have anything to say after that.

Parker held my hand the entire way back to the table, smiling and saying hello to people as if this was all normal. They gaped at us, their eyes locked on where he was gripping my hand. He briefly let me go so I could gather up my things, and then he grabbed my bag, hoisting it over his shoulders as he took my hand once again.

THE WRONG QUARTERBACK **151**

He didn't try to talk to me as he walked me to my dorm. He led me straight to my door, where he watched as I got out my key and unlocked the door as quietly as I could. Nat had texted me she was going to bed, as it had gotten late.

"I'll see you first thing in the morning, baby," he purred, all smiles and hotness as he cradled my face and gave me the kind of kiss that had me wanting him on his knees once again.

It was only later, when I was in bed, reliving every touch, every kiss, everything—as Nat snored softly across the room—that I realized I'd never told him where my dorm room was.

That thought quickly faded, though, in the face of everything that had happened that day, and I slipped into sleep with an actual smile on my lips.

I didn't think of Gray even once.

Parker

The door closed behind Casey as she slipped into her room, and I stood there for a couple of minutes afterward, just staring at the door. Like if I stared long enough, she'd open it back up.

It was all I could do to force myself to eventually start walking down the hallway . . . to force myself to walk home. It felt wrong to be anywhere without her.

I'd never thought of myself as having an addictive personality, but it was official. I was addicted to Casey Larsen.

I was also . . . probably never going to wash my face again.

Breathing in, my eyes rolled back as I caught her smell. I used to think it was ridiculous when guys talked about a girl tasting good. I didn't mind going down on a chick, but I'd never considered it a *good time*. It had always been a means to an end in order to get what I wanted.

But I got the hype now. I fucking got the hype.

I was convinced that there was nothing on Earth that tasted as good as Casey's cunt.

The second I stepped out of her dorm, I couldn't hold it in. I let out a loud whoop, throwing my fist up in the air, not caring who might be watching. Let them look. I felt deranged . . . insane, and I didn't care one bit. The grin on my face stretched wide, muscles aching with the kind of happiness I didn't know you could feel.

This was it. This was what I'd been obsessing about since the moment I'd first seen her in class.

152 C.R. JANE

And now I wanted more. I wanted her by my side, in my truck, in my jersey, in my bed, on my dick . . . I wanted to never be without her. The logistics of that would be difficult, but I'd always liked a challenge.

Every little thing about her was under my skin, from that shy smile to the way her eyes told me everything she was feeling. Fuck. I couldn't think of anything else that mattered anymore. Everything I did was a means to an end to make her happy, to help build this thing I wanted more than anything else. Every step I took was light, charged, like I had a live wire running through me. I wanted to text her already, just to keep some connection going, as if being with her for hours today wasn't enough.

I plotted out my day tomorrow, groaning when I remembered practice—the last one before Saturday's game.

That was another thing I had to plan, making sure Casey was front and center in the stands.

I didn't want to have to wonder where she was in the crowd. I wanted to be able to look over and see her, to make sure she would know that every great play was because of her.

My dick was still aching, like I hadn't even orgasmed. She hadn't noticed that I'd come in my pants—thanks to the performance leggings I was wearing under my black sweats.

I'd never done that before. I'd always had self-control like a fucking king. One taste of her, though, and my cock was exploding.

It was the *Casey Effect*, I decided, and I wasn't mad about it.

I'd bring her coffee first thing in the morning. I'd be there after class and for lunch. I'd stick to her side until practice, making sure she didn't have a moment alone to second-guess this anymore than she already was.

And the second I could, I'd get another taste of her.

Casey Larsen, you're *mine*.

CHAPTER 18

CASEY

It was a fact that I was fucked in the head. My brain was incapable of believing that someone like Parker Davis could really be interested in someone like *me*. So when I walked out of my dorm, still rubbing the sleep from my eyes, I completely froze.

Parker was the most beautiful man on the planet. It was a fact, undisputable in every way.

His shirt was tight, accentuating every one of his muscles and fuck . . . it wasn't fair to the rest of us that he could look like that. I had the urge to glance behind me, because I still wasn't convinced that the smile curving on his lips was actually for me.

Everyone who walked by was staring at him, and who could blame them? It would have been weird if they didn't. He had this larger-than-life magnetism that made you want to fall to your knees and worship him.

"Good morning, baby," he said, holding out a coffee. One that I would bet was my favorite, once again.

I took it, still stunned. Before I could get my words together, he leaned in close, his voice dropping to that low, steady tone that did things to my insides. "One thing you should know about me," he murmured, his eyes locked on mine, "I *always* keep my promises."

The words lingered in the air between us, and I just stared at him, speechless. He straightened, his easy confidence in place, and grabbed my hand, pressing a kiss against my skin.

Of course, I blushed, because I couldn't help but think of where those lips had been just the night before . . .

154   C.R. JANE

I fell into step beside him, warmth from the coffee and his touch seeping through my veins.

"I have practice this afternoon," he said, his tone apologetic, like it was something he needed forgiveness for.

There was another home game tomorrow, I remembered.

"Who are you playing?"

He smiled like he thought it was cute that I hadn't memorized his entire football schedule. When he looked at me like that he made me want to, even though last week had been the first football game I'd ever watched in my life.

"Vanderbilt. They're not looking that great this year, but it's a rivalry game, so they'll be gunning for us." He glanced at me as we walked.

"You're going to come, right?"

Before I could answer, the group of students in front of us thinned, and I spotted him—Gray, standing just outside. Since I knew his class wasn't anywhere near here, it was obvious that he was waiting for me.

At least he didn't look hungover today.

My breath caught, the now familiar mix of sadness and anger twisting in my chest. But before I could process it, Parker's arm slid around my waist, his hand settling there like it was where it belonged. I glanced up at him, wondering what he was thinking, but he wasn't looking at me; his gaze was set firmly on Gray, a clear threat in his eyes.

Gray's eyes were wild as he stalked toward me, his shoulders tense, jaw set tight. He stopped just inches away, his gaze locked to where Parker's arm was still firmly around my waist. His face twisted, hurt and accusation clashing in his expression.

"Are you for real right now, Case?" he said, voice thick with disbelief. "I heard rumors last night, but I didn't want to believe them. I thought . . . I thought they couldn't be true." He shook his head, his face paling as he searched my eyes. "You lied to me. You made me think *I* was the one messing up. And look at you, fucking around with him the entire time."

His eyes welled up with tears, and I wanted to die, because I'd never wanted to see him like that.

"Whore," he whispered, the words sharp and venomous.

My stomach twisted, and I opened my mouth, but no words came out.

Parker moved faster than I thought was possible. One second he was standing beside me, his body tense, and the next his fist was crashing into Gray's face with a sickening crack. I cried out as Gray stumbled back, his hand flying to his nose as a rush of blood poured out, bright and startling against his pale skin.

"Say that again and I'll fucking kill you," Parker growled, his voice low and dangerous. His entire body radiating fury, his chest heaving as he stared Gray down.

Gray stumbled back, wiping at his face, smearing the blood across his cheeks. Giving me one last look that showed how absolutely betrayed he was feeling, he spun around and walked away, his back rigid as he disappeared down the hall.

For a moment, I just stood there, numb. The world felt blurry, the edges of everything dull and muted.

"He didn't mean it," I whispered, like I was trying to convince myself.

"I *will* kill him." Parker's voice was calm in a scary way that would have made me shiver if I hadn't felt so numb. He gripped my waist, and he turned me to him as my chest ached with a disarray of guilt and confusion. "You did *not* do anything wrong," Parker said firmly, his voice steady, like he could see everything unraveling inside me and was determined to pull me back together. "This? Us? It was *always* going to happen."

I laughed, a harsh, bitter sound that didn't feel like mine. "Gray's right," I admitted, my voice barely above a whisper. "I wanted you from the moment I saw you. I couldn't get you out of my head."

Parker's grin spread, slow and satisfied, as if I'd just given him the best news of his life. "Well," he murmured, his voice dropping low, "at least you're *admitting* it."

Before I could react, he pulled me in, his mouth capturing mine in a kiss that was anything but gentle. His hand slid up my back, anchoring me, and I lost myself in the heat of it, in the intensity that left me pulling at his shirt, wanting him closer, wanting him more. When he finally pulled back, my heart was pounding, and my legs were unsteady.

Parker smirked, brushing a thumb over my cheek. "Come on, let's get you to class," he said, like nothing had happened. With his arm still around me, he led me down the hall.

I was a mess of confusion, though, with the agony in Gray's eyes echoing in my mind.

Parker

"He's getting his dick sucked."

Jace's voice cut through the daydream I'd been having about Casey, and I glared at him.

"What did you just say?" I asked, a threat clear in my voice.

156 C.R. JANE

He held up his hands, already dressed for the game. Matty was also watching me with a frown, like he didn't recognize who I was.

"I'm just saying, where are you? Because it looked like you were thinking about getting your dick sucked," Jace continued.

"I wasn't thinking about that," I griped, working to get my shoulder pads on since I'd been sitting here spaced out for who knows how long . . .

Because I'd been thinking of getting my dick sucked.

Casey on her knees was my wildest fantasy at the moment, and something I really wanted to happen . . . soon.

I tried to will my erection down, thankful I was already wearing my football pants and it wasn't as obvious . . . even though my dick was trying to pop out of them.

Jace would never have let me off for having a woody right before the game.

I got the rest of my uniform on, working on self-visualizing and manifesting plays and touchdowns—all the things that our sports psychologist went over with us regularly.

They were just more *interesting* manifestations today. Because every time I imagined myself passing or running into the end zone . . . the play ended with a blow job.

I needed to get my shit together. As long as Casey's roommate did her job, Casey was going to be front row, right behind the end zone. If I wanted to get into that end zone, I needed to actually think about football without it ending in an imaginary orgasm.

I'd thought about her after every play last game, wondering if she was in the crowd . . . if she was watching me.

And then when I'd looked up and saw her on the screen . . . well, I'm sure she didn't connect that the blown kiss had been for her.

But it *was* for her. Everything was for her.

"Alright, this is getting serious, Davis. Which animal has the largest chest?"

I gaped at him. "Why do you think *that's* going to help with my focus?"

"Because you'll be at least thinking how clever and witty I am rather than how you want your dick massaged," Jace snapped, sounding very confident in his idea.

"Can we stop talking about Parker's dick?" Matty complained, rolling his head back as he stretched his arms.

"Almost sounds like you're jealous, Matty," I told him.

"That inch really stays with you, doesn't it?" Chappie called out from across the room.

THE WRONG QUARTERBACK **157**

"Parker's dick wasn't even there that day! It could be smaller for all I know!" Matty said indignantly.

"Really, Matthew. Are you pretending you haven't seen Parker's dick?" drawled Jace. "It's like a monster had a baby with a blue whale and settled between his legs for a party."

"That was . . . oddly specific." I frowned. Although he wasn't wrong . . .

"CAN WE STOP TALKING ABOUT PARKER'S DICK!" Matty roared.

The whole locker room burst into laughter, and Matty flipped us all off. "I hate you all," he hissed.

Well, at least I was distracted now.

"Oh, what's the answer, Thatcher?" Collins, our kicker, called out.

"Well, since you asked so nicely . . . to remind you—since y'all mother-fuckers interrupt me every single time—the joke was, 'which animal has the largest chest,'" Jace began.

I resisted the urge to interrupt him.

"A Z-bra," Jace finished . . . right as Coach Everett came into the locker room.

That didn't stop us from groaning and throwing things at Jace—because we were professionals like that.

"Fucking hell. Get your heads on straight," Coach barked, along with some other choice words, as we got ready to run down the tunnel.

"You feeling good, QB?" Jace shouted, jumping up and down.

I grinned, rolling back my shoulders. "I'm always good, Thatcher."

He snorted and shook his head.

We ran down the tunnel, and the noise of the crowd rolled over us, the stadium roaring with excitement. The bright stadium lights made everything come alive, the air charged with the energy of thousands of people. My heart pounded in my chest, but not just from the anticipation of the game. I scanned the stands, searching for *her*.

And there she was.

Sitting in the front row, right where I wanted her.

And fuck . . . I was getting hard again. She was wearing the jersey I'd had delivered to her room—the one with my name on the back—looking a little nervous as she stared around, like she wasn't sure how she'd ended up there.

Her roommate was beside her, talking a mile a minute judging by how many times she was opening her mouth, but Casey's eyes . . . they were on me. I couldn't help the smile that spread across my face.

158   C.R. JANE

Perfect.

I locked eyes with her for just a second before I tugged my helmet on, and I turned back to the field. That was all I needed. She was here. She was watching. Now it was time to give her a show.

The game started fast, Vanderbilt coming at us hard like they always did, but I didn't let it faze me.

I lived for games like this.

Jace's worries about where my head was were in vain. There was no way I wasn't playing like I was fucking Superman with Casey watching. Thinking of her sitting just yards away, taking in my every move, every pass, every play . . . it pushed me, made me sharper, faster. I wanted her to see me at my best.

The snap, and I took the ball, feeling the weight of it settle into my grip. I dropped back, scanning the field. Matty was already cutting across, weaving through Vanderbilt's defensive line like it was easy. I launched the ball, a tight spiral, and watched as he snatched it out of the air, gaining us a good fifteen yards.

The crowd roared, but I barely heard it, already lining up for the next play. Hurry-up offense was my preference, and I grinned as Vanderbilt scrambled to get to the line. I did a quick handoff to Griffin, our running back, and he barreled forward, muscling through, dragging two defenders with him until he was finally brought down, but not before we'd clawed our way another ten yards closer to the end zone.

"Let's keep it moving," Coach yelled from the sidelines, his voice urgent as he motioned for us to line up fast. I called the next play, eyes scanning the defense, watching as they shifted, their safeties moving up, ready to blitz.

On the snap, I took off, running to the right with the ball tucked tight against my side. The defense shifted, leaving a gap just wide enough for me to exploit and allow me to sprint down the field. The crowd was going nuts, the sound shaking the ground under my feet, but all I could think about was getting to the end zone. Getting to her.

I faked left, then darted right, slipping past one defender and narrowly dodging another. With every step, I closed in on that end zone, and I could feel the anticipation thrumming through my veins. There was just one guy left between me and the goal line, his eyes locked on me, ready to take me down.

THE WRONG QUARTERBACK   159

Normally I'd run out of bounds, but today, with Casey's eyes on me, I felt invincible. He dove forward, and I launched myself in the air, hurdling over him in one clean motion.

For a heartbeat, time froze, the world blurring around me as I sailed over his back. And then, with a thud, my feet hit the turf. The crowd erupted.

Touchdown!

I straightened, holding the ball high, my chest heaving. This—this was why I played this game.

My adrenaline was spiking as I glanced back at my teammates running to celebrate with me. But I wasn't done. Not yet.

I jogged toward where Casey was sitting, my heart hammering with anticipation. The crowd was still going wild, the cheers echoing in my ears, but my focus was on one thing. One person.

Her.

Ripping my helmet off and throwing it on the ground, I hoisted myself up onto the railing, my eyes locked on hers. For a split second, I saw the surprise flicker across her face.

I didn't give her time to think.

Without a word, I wrapped my hand in her hair, leaning in and kissing her, the noise of the crowd fading into the background as I tasted her, licking deep into her mouth like I'd licked her pussy just the other night. She whimpered against my lips, and my kiss turned rougher, more desperate. I made it last, even with the roar of the crowd around us. I wanted her to know exactly what this was. I wanted him to see this, somewhere in the stadium. I wanted him to watch this on the screen and know . . .

This girl was mine.

When I pulled back, I grinned, pressing the football into her hands. "This is for you, my lady," I said, my voice low enough that only she could hear.

Her eyes were wide, her breath coming out in cute little gasps as she stared at me, still processing what had happened. I gave her one more kiss, and then I jumped down, becoming aware of just how loud the crowd had gotten, that the ref was blowing his whistle . . . and that Coach was literally losing his motherfucking mind.

I smirked and waved at the crowd before grabbing my helmet and jogging over to the team. But I couldn't help glancing back at her one last time.

She was still watching me, clutching the football like it was some kind of lifeline, her expression a mix of confusion, excitement, and something else. Something that told me I'd gotten a little bit closer to getting her.

The game wasn't over, but in my mind, I'd already won.

160   C.R. JANE

"Knew you were still thinking about getting your dick sucked," Jace mentioned as I made it back to the sidelines, elbowing me with a huge, goofy grin on his face.

"Go fix your hair," I scoffed. But I was grinning back.

This was just another reason why Casey was *everything*. She made everything better. Even the game I'd loved my whole life.

Casey

"I can't breathe," Nat squealed, grabbing my arm and literally shaking me.

"You can't breathe? He just did that in front of everyone . . . ESPN is at this game!" I gasped, feeling a little light-headed because I was still hyperventilating over what had happened.

I would think I was just dreaming if it weren't for the fact that Nat was rattling my brain with her excitement. Pretty sure my dream wouldn't be creative enough for that.

"You're the luckiest daughter of a bitch I've ever met, Casey Larsen. And also, I'm pretty sure that I have telepathic skills . . . because who told you this was going to be your year? This girl," she said, finally releasing me to point at herself with two thumbs.

"Did you just say 'daughter of a bitch'?" I asked, trying to ignore the people around us that were now all staring and talking about me.

"It felt more girl-powerish," Nat replied primly, before she started jumping up and down and shaking me again. "Parker is in *luvvv* with you. Parker is in *luvvv* with you."

"Sit down," I hissed, my face bright red. Of course, that didn't stop me from watching him like it was my job. Taking in every detail as I watched him joke around with Jace.

"Pinch me," I suddenly demanded . . . just in case.

Nat snickered at me and obediently pinched my arm . . . hard.

"Ow," I said, gazing around. Nope, I was still here. This had really happened.

I watched as Parker ran back out on the field. "Nat," I said, feeling strangely sad as I watched him play like some kind of football god. Because this felt so big, I wasn't sure how it was possible for me to survive it. "What do I do?"

She grabbed my chin and forced me to look at her. "Girl, you hold on fucking tight and enjoy the ride."

THE WRONG QUARTERBACK   161

Nat released me and my eyes snapped back to the field.

"Enjoy the ride," I murmured to myself, listening to the crowd scream as Parker threw another completed pass.

I really wanted to try.

CHAPTER 19

CASEY

"Why are we doing this again?" I moaned once we were back in our dorm, and Nat had forced me to start getting ready for the party the football team was throwing tonight. Parker had a bunch of post-win interviews to give and had asked Nat to watch out for me until he was through.

Because evidently I needed to be watched out for now.

Although comparing it to Gray ditching me the first game because he was drunk and feeling sick, having someone go out of his way to make sure I made it home safe was certainly a different experience.

Something I didn't want to examine too closely because it was another mark in the "Parker Davis May Be Perfect" column . . . and I wasn't sure I was ready to believe that yet.

"Because you're dating the star quarterback on the team, and he's going to show you what a college party is *supposed* to be like. The exact opposite of that fuckwad," she said, a little growl at the end of her sentence when she referenced Gray.

I bit down on my lip, dread and anticipation both flooding through my veins.

Nat giggled as she looked at her phone.

"And who are you texting?" I asked, setting down my brush and grinning at how twitterpated she looked just then.

"Hunter," she sighed, clutching her phone to her chest. She and the lineman had been hot and heavy since that fateful party.

The one that I didn't want to think about because it still made me cry . . .

"Maybe I should stay in. I think I've proven that parties and me just don't go together," I pressed when she turned to look at me.

Nat threw her phone down, her blond hair flying behind her as she rushed toward me and tackled me back on my bed.

"Listen, ma'am. We are going to this party. You are going to have fun. We are going to get drunk. And your smoking-hot new boyfriend is going to show you the good side of life. Got it?" she said, waving her finger in my face.

"Get off me," I humphed, pushing on her shoulders. She was a strong little thing.

"Say, 'Natalie, I'm going to let my gorgeous new boyfriend screw me silly,' and I'll get off," she said, raising her eyebrows up and down lecherously.

"What? No! And he's not my boyfriend. I had a boyfriend, and I just dumped him for cheating on me. I can't have a new boyfriend just a few days later!"

"Oh, girl. You're in denial. Parker Davis is *definitely* your boyfriend," she said, smirking at me as she finally jumped off.

"This can't be real, Nat. It happened too fast. Nothing this fast can last," I whispered. "I had years to build something with Gray. To build a foundation that I thought could last forever once we finally happened." I stared out the window.

Natalie's smirk faded, and she sat down next to me.

"I'm sorry he hurt you. I want to kill him for doing that."

I kicked my foot out, staring at the pink polish on my toes.

"I think a part of me wonders what Ben would think about all of this, too. If he would be ashamed because I gave up on Gray so easily."

Nat was quiet for a long moment.

"Obviously I never met your brother, but I feel like I've gotten a pretty good idea of who he was from what you've told me. And the kind of guy who loves his sister like that . . . he'd never be okay with a man treating her badly—his best friend or not."

I opened my mouth to object. To say that maybe I hadn't taken enough time to listen to Gray. Maybe he needed help with a drinking problem, and I'd turned my back on him when he needed me the most. Maybe I hadn't been a good enough girlfriend . . .

It was like she could read my mind.

"You are *not* responsible for a man's bad behavior, Casey. Now repeat that for me, right the fuck now."

"I am not responsible for a man's bad behavior," I repeated obediently.

164 C.R. JANE

"Good girl," she said, giving me a high five. "Now, get off this bed and start getting ready. We have a party and more orgasms to get to. Emphasis on the *more orgasms*, of course."

I bit down on my lip, trying not to think about Parker's capacity to give me *more* orgasms.

It was a losing endeavor, though.

So, I got ready for the party.

Nat opened the door, barely getting out a "Hey" before Parker brushed past her, his eyes zeroed in on me like he couldn't see anything else. In two strides, he was there, his hands sliding around my waist as he pulled me in, his mouth on mine before I could even blink. He kissed me like he'd been holding his breath the entire time we'd been apart, and I melted, my hands gripping his shoulders, the world narrowing to the taste of him, and the feel of his heartbeat pounding against me.

We stayed like that until Nat began clearing her throat . . . loudly. Parker pulled back just enough to look at me, his lips curving into that irresistible smirk. "You look amazing, by the way." His hand lingered at my waist, fingers brushing the fabric like he couldn't stand not touching me. Nat and I had decided to stay in our jerseys and miniskirts, and judging by the way Parker was looking at me—like he wanted to eat me—he was very happy about that decision.

"Don't mind me," Nat muttered across the room. "I'll just be over here wishing it wasn't socially unacceptable for me to pull out my vibrator right now. The two of you are HOT!"

Parker scoffed, and I laughed, but neither of us looked at her. We were both trapped in our own little world, a world I still didn't understand how I'd ended up in.

"I don't want to go," he growled. "I just want to take you away and keep you to myself. Everyone is going to be looking at you." He kissed me again like it was impossible to stop.

"No, sir," Nat interjected. "Our girl is going to this party, and you are going to show her a good time."

"*Our* girl?" he asked, a weird, silkily dangerous undertone to his voice.

Nat gulped dramatically. "Sorry, sir . . . Daddy. I meant—your girl. Definitely *your* girl."

I started laughing, and I couldn't stop. Tears were streaming down my face as I bent over. When I finally stood up, Parker was staring at me . . . that awestruck look that I'd never understand there in his gaze.

"What?" I asked, wiping at my face and suddenly feeling self-conscious.

"I love the sound of your laugh, baby," he murmured, and I flushed, because the way he said that sounded so . . . intimate. Like we were tangled together in bed.

Or maybe that was just wishful thinking . . .

Nat cleared her throat loudly. "Unless you want me to combust spontaneously into flames because of the sexual energy the two of you are giving off right now . . . you should probably go. But don't worry, I'm happy to report she does not have a curfew. So feel free to keep her out as late as you want." She grinned almost evilly. "And I do mean as late as you want."

Parker looked faintly amused, and he sighed dramatically. "If we must," he groaned, giving me one more kiss before he took my hand and started to lead me out of the room.

"Are you coming with us?" I asked, pulling on Parker's hand so he would stop.

Nat grinned and did a little shimmy, holding up her phone. "Hunter just texted me that he wants . . . a little *treat* before the party," she said, her eyes gleaming. "So, I'll meet you there."

Parker snorted, wrapping an arm around my waist as he buried his face in my neck. I shivered as his tongue licked along my skin.

"Okay," I said in a weird, high voice. "I'll see you there."

Parker dragged me out into the hallway. I pretended not to notice how . . . busy it suddenly was. Like word had gotten out that Parker Davis was here, and all the girls who lived in the dorm were out to present themselves. Some girls were walking around in skimpy towels, even though I was quite sure they hadn't just taken a shower judging by the full face of makeup they were wearing.

But it was like Parker didn't even see them. He didn't respond to their waves or when they called his name. He just kissed the side of my head and walked me past them all.

What did he see in me? That's all I could think as we walked. Even if this faded or burned out in a week . . . or tomorrow . . . for the rest of my life, I'd never understand what was going through his head right now.

Parker's huge black truck was parked right in front of the building, in a clear no-parking zone. But there were no parking tickets on the dash. Even though usually the campus police had a ticket written if you even idled out front.

The rules were just different when you were a god, apparently.

He helped me into his truck and then walked around the front and got in. And I stared at him, finally having a chance to take him in, in all of his glory.

Parker leaned back in the driver's seat, one hand gripping the wheel, his other arm draped around my shoulders as he pulled away from the curb. He was wearing a white V-neck shirt that clung to his chest and arms in all the right ways, the sleeves tight enough to show off the muscle underneath. The shirt brought out the depth of his tan, a rich warmth that contrasted with the light fabric, and I couldn't help but stare as he shifted, his fingers absently tapping along my shoulder.

His gray sweatpants were dangerously low on his hips, and every time he shifted, his shirt lifted just enough to reveal the hard cut of his Adonis lines, those sharp grooves that disappeared below his waistband. He was wearing a backward cap, strands of his brown hair just barely brushing against his forehead. As if that wasn't enough . . . he was wearing a chain—silver, simple, resting just above the collar of his shirt, catching the light and drawing my eyes to the line of his neck, his jaw, the stubble that he hadn't bothered to shave.

He'd probably thrown that on without a thought, completely oblivious to the fact that he looked like he'd stepped out of some daydream.

"Keep looking at me like that and see what happens," he rasped suddenly, grabbing my hand and placing it on his lap . . . and not just on his lap . . . on his enormous, rigid dick that was stretched down his thigh.

I almost fainted. It was a fact. My panties were completely soaked, and I was trying to count backward to get a hold of myself. But then . . . as if my hand had a mind of its own . . . I squeezed.

"Fuck," he growled, and the truck jerked, swerving up onto the curb with a hard jolt that threw us both forward. Parker's hands flew to the wheel, steadying us as we narrowly missed a tree, the tires squealing as he got back on the road. He came to a stop, his chest heaving, hands gripping the wheel so hard his knuckles were turning white.

He turned to me, eyes dark and intense, his breathing ragged. "You don't understand," he said, his voice low, thick with something raw. "Everything with you is . . . more. All I want is for your hands to be all over me, every second. But, damn, you gotta give a guy a warning, baby. I'd like to make it to the house in one piece."

Before I could answer, his hand slid up, threading through my hair, his fingers gripping as his lips crashed against mine, fierce and urgent, like he'd been holding back everything until now. He kissed me like he was starving, like he couldn't get close enough, his fingers tightening as if he was afraid that I'd run away.

Parker pulled away, looking torn, like he was on the precipice of some major decision.

"Just one taste," he muttered suddenly, as if he was talking to himself.

A second later his seatbelt was off, and he was lunging toward me, his hand sliding up my thigh, pushing up my skirt. He traced the edge of my panties for a second and then slipped past the material, teasing my slit with his fingertips before he shoved two fingers deep inside my core.

"Parker!" I gasped, my head falling back on the seat.

"You're so fucking wet for me, baby," he murmured. "You're such a good girl."

I whimpered, the praise soaking into my skin.

"Do you want me to finger fuck you, baby, give us both what we need?"

I gasped in response, and his answering sexy laugh almost made me come right then.

"Give me your words," he ordered, sliding his mouth against mine, his tongue lazily slipping inside for a second before he pulled away to look at me.

"Fuck me with your fingers, Parker. I want it," I whispered, dying a little as he immediately started pumping his fingers in and out, the corded muscles of his arm flexing as he moved.

"Yes. Please. Please. *Please*," I begged.

"Kiss me," Parker said roughly, his eyes glittering in the dim light as he watched my reactions.

I whimpered, and his mouth moved against mine, my lips sucking on his tongue as he forced a third finger inside.

"You're going to choke my dick, baby. Aren't you? Your pussy is so greedy, squeezing my fingers so tight." He laughed when I cried out again. "I know you want more," he soothed. "I'm going to give you more tonight."

He pressed his forehead against mine, forcing me to look at him as my muscles trembled, and I began to fall apart.

"That's it. That's my sexy, perfect girl. Come for me. *Now*."

He swallowed my cry as I fell into an orgasm, hot waves of pleasure pulsing through my insides. His face was tense as I clenched around the slow, smooth movement of his fingers as he fucked me through the ecstasy.

I watched as Parker pulled his fingers from my core and brought them to his mouth, his fingertips glistening with my cum . . . and then he licked them off like I was his favorite flavor of ice cream.

"My sweet girl, giving me exactly what I want," he purred. He sucked on his finger for one more second, before he kissed me softly. Tenderly. His lips slowly dragged over mine, and I once again moaned at the taste of . . . us.

168 C.R. JANE

"You're so fucking beautiful," he murmured as he pulled back, his gaze darting over my features like he was trying to memorize them.

"Fuck," he groaned as he sat back in his seat and put the truck in drive. "I'm not sure that will be enough to get me through the night."

His face was pained as he reached down and adjusted his dick, which was now like a living, breathing monster trying to escape his sweatpants.

"Do—do you want me to help you with that?" I asked shyly, reaching for his cock. He grabbed my hand and placed it on my leg, preventing me from touching what I really wanted.

"We're never going to get to the party if you get anywhere near him right now. I'm riding the edge, baby. Let's not try to kill me. I haven't even felt your perfect cunt yet."

I blushed and looked back at the road, ignoring his smug glance as I fidgeted in my seat like I hadn't just had an orgasm.

"You meant 'it,' right?" I finally asked after a second, gesturing to his dick.

Parker grinned, the effect so stunningly sexy that I forgot what I'd been talking about for a moment.

"No. My dick is definitely a 'he' and has his own free will. I've always thought I had control . . . but since I met you"—he winked at me—"I've stopped trying to hold him back. I'm pretty sure I've had a nonstop erection since the moment I saw you."

I gaped at him and then stared down at his *still* very hard dick.

He put an arm in front of it. "Give him some space, baby. He can only take so much."

I snorted, squirming around once again, trying to relieve the ache I felt every time he opened his mouth . . . or I looked at him . . . or basically anything happened with Parker Davis.

"Tell me something real about you," I suddenly blurted out, when the sexual tension in the truck felt like too much. "Tell me something that I can't read online or hear about you around campus."

He glanced at me and then looked back at the road, tilting his head as if he was thinking hard. Another slow grin graced his lips.

"My family believes in love at first sight," he finally said softly, as if he knew the words would freak me out.

Because that word . . . it shouldn't be anywhere near us right now.

But I guess I had asked him for something.

"Every male in my family, for as long as I'm aware of, has known with one look that their girl was the one. I never thought it applied to me. Imagine my surprise . . ."

THE WRONG QUARTERBACK   169

His words died off . . . and judging by the laughter in his blue gaze, he was waiting for me to ask him to finish.

But I didn't, ignoring his chuckle and remaining quiet for the rest of the ride until we pulled into the driveway of the house next to where the party was.

"This is my place," he said, gesturing to the small white house.

"You live alone?" I asked, surprised. I guess I had assumed he lived with Jace and Matty.

"I like my space, and they don't always keep the best track of the girls they bring home," he said. "I'll give you a tour later. I don't want Jace to decide to hunt us down. He's texted me twelve times telling me to hurry up."

I moved to open the door, and he growled. Literally growled. "Stay right there," he ordered, hopping out of the truck, and then jogging around to help me out.

"Are you trying to kill me?" I asked, repeating his earlier words back to him. He kissed me again . . . like he couldn't help himself, and then leaned in, so his lips were brushing my ear.

"I'm trying to make you fall in love with me."

With that announcement, he grabbed my hand and led me next door to where music was blaring out from the open front door, and Jace was leaning against the threshold, staring at his watch dramatically.

"Welcome, fellow Inner Sanctum members," he said, throwing his arms around both of our shoulders. "We've been waiting for you."

"What did you just call us?" Parker asked, sliding Jace's arm off my shoulder so that he wasn't touching me anymore.

Jace snorted and glanced at me. "Do you think he would like *Core Crew* or the *Loyalty League* better?"

"I was more fond of *No Drama Llamas*, actually," I said with a smile.

Parker frowned, like he didn't like that we had an inside joke.

"I like her," Jace announced to Parker as he led us into the house. "I say we keep her."

"That's the plan," Parker whispered in my ear, and I must have been crazy because I could have sworn I heard one more word after that. It sounded an awful lot like . . . *forever*.

This party was completely different from the others. As soon as we stepped through the door, a guy in a jersey handed Parker a beer, nodding at him respectfully, and, to my surprise, he handed me a mixed drink, like we'd just stepped into some exclusive club.

170   C.R. JANE

Parker stayed close, one arm wrapped around my waist, guiding me through the crowd, his touch firm and steady. People flocked to him the second we walked in, like he had some kind of magnetic pull. It was a stream of handshakes, pats on the back, and knowing grins thrown his way, but his focus never wavered. Every time someone tried to drag him into a conversation or grab his attention, he'd pull me closer. If he did decide to talk to someone, he didn't let go, his fingers tracing slow, absent-minded circles on my side, like he was marking his territory while he spoke. He played with my hair, his fingers brushing my shoulder. He also made sure to include me in every conversation, even if it was something he had to have known I wouldn't have a clue about . . . like football.

I didn't want to keep comparing them, but I couldn't help it. Gray had treated me as an afterthought at the two parties we'd gone to together, like he was doing me a favor when he paid attention to me instead of his friends. Parker treated me like I was the center of everything. Like I was the reason he was at the party to begin with.

Girls looked over with wide eyes, whispering to each other, a few of them bold enough to try and touch his arm, brushing against him as they passed. But Parker shifted subtly, every time, occasionally pushing their arms away when they didn't get the hint.

And I kept thinking . . . *there's got to be a catch to this*.

Parker was talking to some of the players on his team, when I tapped him on the arm. He immediately leaned over mid-sentence to see what I wanted.

"What's up, baby?"

"I'm going to go to the bathroom," I murmured to him.

He nodded, looking around. "Okay, let me get the key from Jace or Matty."

"I can just wait in line," I whispered, and he shot me an incredulous look before glancing around again and spotting Matty.

"Yo, Matty. I need a key," he called, and his dark-haired other best friend nodded from the kitchen and headed our way.

Did they have to apply to be a part of this friend group? Because if the criteria for the Loyalty League was this kind of beauty . . . there was no way that they'd even look at my application.

Matty was the same kind of gorgeous as Jace and Parker, the kind that turned heads every time they walked into a room. His black hair fell just past his ears in a perfectly tousled, effortless style. His eyes were a light,

Caribbean blue, the kind that seemed almost unreal against his tan skin. They were piercing, intense as they studied me, making me nervous, like he could see right through me, and he knew I didn't belong. Like Parker, his body was a work of art, strong but lean, and even his movements had this easy confidence, like he was never in a hurry but always in control.

The three of them were unreal.

"What's up, Parkie-Poo?" Matty said with a grin, and I watched as they did some kind of male friendship handshake—or at least that's how I would describe it.

"I need the key to your room. Casey needs to go to the bathroom," Parker told him.

Matty studied me again. "Are you going to introduce me? It feels like we're moving a little fast—my toilet is a very sacred thing, as you know."

Parker scoffed, and Matty grinned. The two of them . . . were a lot together. And it just got worse when Jace appeared, pushing his way between Parker and Matty so he was front and center.

I gaped at the three of them, feeling a little bit . . . light-headed.

"Ooh, are we doing introductions? I can do them," Jace said excitedly, gripping Matty's neck and shaking him a little like some kind of really hot puppy.

"Casey, this is Matthew aka Matty aka Sir-Grouch-A-Kins aka The Third Amigo," Jace said before anyone could get a word in. "Sir-Grouch-A-Kins, this is Casey aka the love of Parker's life aka the fourth Inner Sanctum member."

I was speechless, waiting for Parker to say something—to dispute what Jace had said and tell them we were just getting to know each other. But Parker said nothing. Literally nothing. He just grinned . . . almost proudly . . . like that's exactly how he would have described me himself.

Matty reached out to shake my hand, and Parker smacked it away. "No touching," he growled, and Matty and Jace looked at him amused, before they both burst into laughter.

"No touching," Jace repeated, in a sort of Cookie Monster voice as he continued to laugh hysterically.

Parker sighed in mock exasperation and held out his hand. "Can you give me the key?"

Matty made a big show of getting it out of his pocket and presenting it to him like it was the Holy Grail.

And now I was a little nervous to use it, actually. I had a feeling Matty didn't miss much. What if I forgot to flush or something?

"Thank you, Sir-Grouch-A-Kins," Parker said, and Matty scowled at him.

"Can we please not make that a thing?" he groaned. "We can't encourage him like that."

"Ooh, speaking of encouragement," Jace began. "One thing before you go. Casey, what's the difference between peanut butter and jam?"

Parker and Matty sighed almost simultaneously. "Just tell him you don't know so we can get this over with," Parker whispered—loudly—to me.

"Um . . . I don't know," I replied obediently, and Parker's hand slid from my waist to my ass as if that had turned him on.

"Only one has nuts," Jace crowed, throwing his arms in the air and pumping his fists up and down . . . similar to the touchdown celebration he'd done on Saturday.

I giggled, and Jace grinned.

"Alright, let's get you to the bathroom," said Parker . . . sounding grumpy.

Jace's grin only grew wider, and I was a little afraid of the mischief he was plotting right at that moment.

Parker led me away from his friends, holding my hand the entire time down the hall, not releasing it even as he unlocked Matty's door.

"You can't go in with me to the bathroom," I told him . . . and a hint of a blush appeared on his cheeks.

"I know that," he scoffed.

I raised an eyebrow . . . because did he?

"I'll wait right here," he said dramatically . . . as if it was a hardship.

And there went my stupid heart again. Because why did he have to say the cutest things?

I used Matty's very clean bathroom—making sure I flushed and left everything exactly as I found it—and went back out to the hallway. Parker was further down the hall, a few of his teammates talking to him. A bottleneck of people had formed around them, and I sighed, wondering how I was going to get back to Parker.

I locked eyes with Parker, and he said something to his teammates before moving to push his way toward me. I was about to try and push through, too, when my attention snagged on two girls right in front of me, their voices carrying over the noise.

"She's such an idiot," one of them muttered, rolling her eyes as she watched Parker. "I mean, seriously, does she really think she's special? Everyone knows Parker isn't a one-woman guy."

THE WRONG QUARTERBACK   **173**

My stomach twisted, an icy prickle spreading up my spine. I shifted back, hoping they'd move, but they just kept talking, voices low and smug.

"Didn't you hook up with him?" the other girl asked, her eyes wide with curiosity.

The first girl tossed her strawberry-blond hair over her shoulder, a satisfied smirk spreading across her very pretty face. "Yeah, right before school started. I have his number too. I think I might shoot him a text tonight, you know, see if he's down for a repeat. He was so fucking good. His dick is huuuge . . . and he knows how to use it."

The second girl laughed, nudging her. "Maybe I can come along. They say Parker can go all night."

Their laughter grated, every word hitting like a fresh wound, the confidence in their voices sinking into me like ice water. I fought to keep my expression neutral, but inside, my chest was *aching*.

Parker was suddenly there, his easy smile stunning me as I gazed at him. The girls were now looking at me, too, twin smiles on both of their faces because they'd realized I'd overheard.

I let Parker take my hand, and he led us out of the hallway and back into the main room, which seemed to have gotten three times as crowded while I'd peed. He led me to where Jace and Matty were, and I glanced around the room, stiffening when I caught sight of Hunter on the couch—Nat nowhere to be seen. There was a girl on either side of him, and he was taking turns making out with each one, his hand feeling up their breasts right in front of everyone.

I quickly pulled out my phone, texting Nat to ask where she was. She had told me she and Hunter had decided to be exclusive. Had something happened when he'd stopped by . . . because this wasn't looking exclusive . . .

> Nat: Ugh. My cramps started, and I'm crampy and crabby and miserable. Have fun without me, though, and tell Hunter I love his dick.

The text made me sick . . . for more reasons than one.

I snapped a picture of Hunter and sent it to Nat, because she needed to know.

I couldn't help but watch Hunter some more as I waited for Nat to answer . . . and I also couldn't help but think . . . if one of the offensive linemen was like this . . . then what was the star quarterback like?

I stood there, panicking, noticing again all the women who were staring at Parker, Jace, and Matty like they would do anything to have them. Like their life's purpose was to get into bed with them.

Was this stupid . . . to think that Parker may be serious about us? To think he might be—mine . . .

He'd seemed to know right where he wanted to go in the library. Was that his usual spot? Did the passenger seat in his truck usually have a girl writhing on it? Had he kissed a girl on national television in the past . . .

"Hey, what's going on? I can feel you freaking out," Parker murmured, concerned, as he tipped my chin up to look at him.

I bit my lip, having trouble meeting his eyes. "How many of the girls here have you hooked up with?" I asked, the words rolling out of me before I could stop them.

Parker's eyes grew wide. "Why are you asking that?"

"I mean . . . it's a lot, right? I'm over here a virgin, and you've been the biggest manwhore on campus. Haven't you?" There was a feral panic to my voice, like I was unraveling.

Parker nodded at Jace and Matty, and they stepped away, taking the crowd of people that had gathered with them.

I glanced over at Hunter again, and Parker's gaze followed. "Fucking hell," he growled, his eyes shooting daggers at his teammate.

Before he could answer anything, there was a commotion by the front door, and Nat stormed in, eyes blazing, her feet stomping against the floor like war drums.

She must have sprinted the entire way to get here that fast.

A murmur rippled through the room, but Nat didn't slow down, her gaze locked onto her target: Hunter.

"You fucking asshole!" she screamed, her voice cutting through the noise. Without a second of hesitation, she stomped over and launched herself onto his lap.

Hunter's eyes widened, clearly caught off guard, but he didn't have time to say a word. Nat's fist shot out, landing a solid punch to his nose with a force that echoed in the room. He barely blinked before she hit him again, the second punch landing right on his cheekbone.

"Get it, girl!" I thought I heard Jace yell.

Blood trickled from Hunter's nose, a crimson streak cutting down his face as he tried to steady himself, looking at Nat with surprise. Before he could respond, two guys jumped in, grabbing Nat by the arms and hauling

THE WRONG QUARTERBACK   175

her back, though she was still writhing in their grip, spitting every curse word she could think of.

"You arrogant, lying son of a fuckwad!" She kicked out, trying to land another hit, her eyes blazing as she twisted against the guys holding her.

I broke free of Parker's grip, rushing over to her side. Nat's face was pale, her chest heaving, but she wasn't crying. There was just a fierce, unfiltered anger radiating from her, like she was holding herself together through sheer fury alone.

"Nat," I said softly, reaching for her hand as she finally stopped struggling. She looked over at me, her breathing rough, but she let out a small, sharp breath, her shoulders dropping just a fraction.

"I'm fine," she muttered, her voice thick with frustration, eyes darting to where Hunter was in the kitchen now, trying to clean up the blood dribbling from his nose. "Can we go back to the room?"

"Of course," I told her.

Parker was right by us then, a tic in his cheek when I told him I was leaving. "We need to talk," he said as he walked with us out of the house to drive us back home.

"We'll talk . . . later," I told him, my arm wrapped around Nat. She shot me a questioning look but didn't say anything.

Parker and I stayed quiet the short drive back to the dorm, but Parker kept looking at me every few seconds, as if he was willing me to talk.

We got to the dorm, and Nat and I got out. "I have practice in the morning," he said to me frustratedly. "We really should talk tonight."

"I need to be there for Nat," I told him, even though with the weird hand gestures she was making, she was encouraging me to talk to Parker.

He nodded stiffly and went to get back in the truck, pausing at the door for a moment before he turned and suddenly grabbed me.

"You're not allowed to second-guess me either, Casey. Add that to the list," he growled before his lips devoured me like he was trying to take my soul as well as my heart.

When he released me, my breath was coming out in gasps.

"See you tomorrow," he murmured, watching me as I walked with Nat into the dorm.

"He's intense." Nat giggled, and I nodded, leaning against the door for a second as I willed my legs to move. "He also gives me hope," she said. "I didn't trust my instincts with Hunter, but I'm not wrong about Parker. He's craaazy about you."

"I hope you're right," I told her, deciding not to tell her about my freak-out since I was the one who was supposed to be there for her tonight.

"I'm always right," she answered as she pushed me toward the stairs.

I glanced over my shoulder to where Parker was still sitting in his truck, staring at the dorm door like he wanted to beat it down. We locked eyes through the glass, and I sent him a wish right before I turned the corner.

Don't hurt me.

I don't think I can survive you.

I didn't see what his response was.

CHAPTER 20

PARKER

I was lying in my bed, miserable because all I wanted was to go kidnap Casey out of her dorm and make her talk to me. If I could somehow force her to live with me so I didn't have to sleep without her anymore . . . that would have been great as well.

But unfortunately, pretending you weren't a psycho meant you couldn't do things like that—yet.

My phone buzzed, and I grabbed it on the off chance that Casey had texted me, doubtful since it was three in the morning.

It was not her.

> Cole: I think you're in the wrong profession, Parkie.

I sighed, the normal smile I would have at this point nowhere to be found.

> Me: It's 3 a.m.—why are you texting me right now?

> Cole: Because now I know—you've got a little rockstar in you. So, of course, you'd be up.

> Me: What makes you say that?

178   C.R. JANE

> Cole: Making out with a girl in the stands after you score . . . very rockstarish of you.

> Walker: It's fucking 3 a.m. Why the fuck are you texting right now?

> Cole: Whoops. Didn't mean to include you, Disney. You're definitely not rockstar material.

A ghost of a smile slid across my lips.

> Walker: 👆

Before I could read another text, there was a heavy pounding at my door. I sat up, blinking in the dark, the sound echoing through my place.

Who the fuck was it?

I threw on a shirt, rubbing my very tired eyes as I made my way to the door. The pounding continued, echoing louder with every step. I swung the door open, prepared to rain hell on whoever was at the door—but my planned *fuck you* faded on my tongue right away. Two officers stood on my front porch, their faces set and serious, the cold gleam of their badges reflecting under the porch light.

One of the officers, the taller of the duo, stepped forward, his eyes hard and cold. "Parker Davis?"

"Yeah?" I answered, my voice coming out more uncertain than I liked.

"You're under arrest," he said in a steady voice, "for grave robbing and desecration of a gravesite."

Oh shit.

Before I could say a word, the officers moved in, one of them yanking my arms behind my back as the cold metal of the handcuffs bit into my wrists. I barely had time to register what was happening before they dragged me forward, out of the house. My pulse hammered, every instinct screaming at me to fight, to resist, but I forced myself to keep it together.

The night was quiet, traffic on the street nonexistent. A twisted kind of relief flickered in me—at least no one was around to see this. But then another realization hit just as hard: my phone was sitting on my bed. I'd walked out without it, never thinking I'd need it.

THE WRONG QUARTERBACK   179

They shoved me into the back of the squad car, the door slamming shut with a heavy thud. The confined space felt suffocating, the reality of it closing in fast. One of the officers turned around in his seat, his voice steady and impersonal as he started to read my rights.

"You have the right to remain silent. Anything you say can and will be used against you in a court of law . . ."

The car pulled away from the curb, and we took off.

This was actually happening. How the fuck was I going to get out of this? How long would it take for this to make the news? What was going to happen to my career? Did the Sphinx have some kind of legal counsel for the shit they asked inductees to do? I needed to call Walker or Cole.

Fuck.

Casey's face appeared in my head. She was going to freak out.

The officer driving looked at me in the rearview mirror, a twisted smile on his face.

"So, you're the big shot who thought it'd be fun to dig up a dead woman." He scoffed. "Did you get a thrill out of that, Davis? Pulling open someone's grave like some sick fuck?"

I kept my expression blank, staring straight ahead, refusing to give them any reaction.

"What were you after, Davis? Some sort of sick trophy? Not getting enough pussy on campus?"

Alright . . . that was disgusting.

I kept my face impassive, my jaw tight, staring out the window at the blur of city lights, trying to block out their words. They were fishing, desperate to get a rise out of me, but I wasn't giving in.

"What's the matter?" the cop in the passenger seat taunted, his voice dripping with sarcasm. "Big man goes silent when he gets caught, huh? Thought you'd be bragging about it, Davis. Thought you'd be proud of what you did."

The cuffs bit into my wrists as the officers led me out of the car, dragging me through a back door into a nondescript building I assumed was the police station. My brain was reeling. This was a nightmare, a screwed-up, surreal *nightmare*.

They shoved me into a cold, cramped room, a single light flickering overhead. A table sat in the center of it, two chairs on either side, like something straight out of every cop movie I'd ever seen.

The officers smirked, practically shoving me down into the chair.

One of them leaned in close, a smirk on his face. "Think you're hot stuff, don't you, Davis? The golden boy, everyone's favorite football star?" He

180   C.R. JANE

chuckled, low and mocking. "You're nothing but a little punk in cuffs now. Can't throw a pass to save yourself from this."

I clenched my fists, forcing myself to keep calm, keep cool. If I showed even a hint of nerves, they'd pounce. "I don't know why I'm here, Officer. This seems like a mistake you're going to regret," I said evenly.

Another officer, the one who looked like he was enjoying this way too much, crossed his arms and leaned against the wall. "Grave robbing, Davis. Desecration of a gravesite. You really think you're gonna come out of this one clean? We know you did it, so why don't you save us all a little time and confess?"

I blinked, keeping my face blank. "I'm just as shocked as you are, gentlemen . . ." I let out a half scoff, shaking my head. "Why would I—"

"Why?" he interrupted, eyes narrowing. "Don't play dumb, Davis. We know about the Sphinx. We know about the little hazing ritual, and we know that you're up for induction. All we want is for you to say it." He leaned closer, voice dropping to a low whisper. "Just say it was the Sphinx. You admit to that, and we'll call it a stupid hazing prank. You can save your precious career, maybe even walk away with nothing but a slap on the wrist."

I stared straight ahead, letting his words wash over me. They didn't have proof. If they had evidence, they'd be throwing it in my face by now. All they had was a hunch, rumors. And I didn't believe for one second that me saying anything would fix this.

I forced myself to stay calm, even though my heart was attempting to beat its way out of my chest. "I don't know what you're talking about," I said flatly, meeting his gaze head-on. "Sphinx? Hazing? I don't know anything about that."

The officer's mouth twisted, his jaw tightening. "You're really going to play this game, aren't you?"

I shrugged, feigning indifference. "I'm not playing anything. You're accusing me of something I didn't do. I have no idea why you'd think I'd be involved in something like that."

The officer scoffed, crossing his arms. "Come on, Davis. Everyone knows you'd do anything for that damn football career of yours. Think about it. A little confession, and this all goes away. You'll be back on the field before you know it."

I bit down, every muscle in my body tense. "I'm not admitting to something I didn't do."

"Fine," he sneered, pacing in front of me. "But think about this: we leak this story. All those scouts, every single NFL team? They're gonna hear all about the golden boy grave robber. Your face will be plastered on every news channel. You'll be ruined."

Ruined. I wasn't a big fan of that word at the moment.

His partner leaned in, joining the act. "Last chance, Davis. Tell us what happened. Call it hazing, say it was just some Sphinx stunt, and maybe, just maybe, we'll let you keep your dreams." He let out a slow, mocking chuckle. "Otherwise? Well, good luck trying to throw touchdowns in jail."

I swallowed, keeping my breathing steady. The last thing I would do was give them what they wanted. If I cracked now, it was over. I held my gaze steady, refusing to flinch under their scrutiny.

"Sorry," I said, my voice cold and calm. "But I have no idea what you're talking about. And since you don't seem to have any real evidence, I think I'll be wanting my one phone call now."

I didn't get my phone call.

Instead, the hours dragged on in a haze of questions, accusations, and threats. Every time they left, I thought maybe, just maybe, it was about to be over. But then the door would open, and another round would start—questions about the Sphinx, demands that I just admit to the crime, taunts about how I was ruined. They even threw in details about the woman's family and how they wanted to see me punished to the fullest extent of the law. Evidently, grave robbing was a Class E felony in Tennessee, and I could look forward to at least four years in prison for my future.

Sometimes they would try the "nice guy" routine, where one of them would pretend to be sympathetic about my situation. Say that he understood what the Sphinx represented, and he could understand how I would be tempted.

"It's a lot of pressure, isn't it, looking after your mom?" the tall one said. I stiffened, resisting the urge to jump over the table and drop-kick him. "And those famous brothers of yours. That's a lot of pressure, too, living up to that?" he continued, because I think of the two of us, he was the one who liked digging a grave. "What's going to happen to your mom when you're in prison, Davis? Who's going to watch over her then?"

I bit my lip so hard it started to bleed. What *was* going to happen? My brothers would do their best, but what were they supposed to do, drop everything to take care of her? They would, but I didn't want that for them.

Fuck.

I was exhausted, every muscle aching from hours of sitting, my wrists raw from the handcuffs, my mind a tangle of tension and fatigue. Maybe I should just tell them what happened.

I was about to break, and then the officer stood. "We'll give you some more time to think," he snapped, leaving the room with his partner.

That was close.

I shook my head, blinking my eyes several times, because what the fuck was I about to do? They didn't have anything on me. I just needed to keep my damn mouth shut.

The silence pressed in, and my mind drifted between anger and sheer exhaustion. I reviewed film on Sundays with the coaching staff, so all my mistakes were fresh. Even if I got out, that was going to be a fun conversation with Coach about why I'd missed that. And Casey, I had planned to be over there the second I was done, convincing her she was the love of my life. I was going to send her breakfast . . . and flowers. The last thing I needed was to give her space, and now here I was, completely silent for who knew how long.

The door was thrown open, and the cops filed in again, and judging by their faces, the nice-guy routine was done.

How fun.

In my next bout of "quiet time" I couldn't fight it anymore. My eyes drifted shut; my head drooped down onto the cold surface of the table. I let myself slip into sleep, even though I was the opposite of comfortable. My wrists were probably permanently impaired at this point.

I'd just nodded off when the door opened again, the sudden noise jolting me awake. I wearily blinked at the door, feeling like a zombie. But it wasn't the same cops coming back to torture me. Instead, a guy I didn't recognize, with a shock of blond across the front of his dark hair, stood there. He was dressed in a fitted suit, but he looked completely casual, leaning in the doorway as if he owned the place, his expression unreadable.

I blinked, trying to place him. There was something vaguely familiar about his face . . . or maybe it was his eyes. Where had I met him? Before I could ask who he was or why he was here, he took a key out of his pocket and ambled over to me, with a quick click undoing the cuffs around my wrists.

I hissed as the blood rushed back into my hands. Fuck, that did not feel good.

He straightened up, giving me a slow, deliberate look. "The Sphinx sends its congratulations. Sometimes *silence* is trust," he said, his tone low, almost amused.

And then, he turned on his heel, slowly walking out of the room, leaving the door wide open behind him.

THE WRONG QUARTERBACK 183

I sat there, staring after him, my mind reeling. This had been a setup—the cops, the endless questions, the threats. This hadn't been a real interrogation. This had been my second trial.

Fuck.

———————

I had no money, and I had no phone. So it was really fun to step outside the now seemingly empty building and realize I had no idea where I was . . . and that it was night. First chance I got, I was going to go find out what the real police station looked like in town—because this wasn't fucking it.

My stomach twisted as I blinked, trying to get my bearings. I'd lost an entire day—at least. I had no idea where I was, and I was more tired than I could ever remember being.

Which would make this walk fun.

I forced myself to move, barely noticing the trash on the broken sidewalk or the lack of streetlights in this part of town. There were certainly a lot of empty, run-down warehouses. I guess if the third trial was hiding a dead body, I'd have a possible location to dump it.

Fucking hell.

I must have walked a mile before I heard the sound of an engine revving, headlights cutting through the darkness. I squinted, turning my head just as a truck screeched to a halt beside me, the headlights blinding for a split second.

As my eyes adjusted, I recognized the familiar outline of an army-green Jeep Gladiator. I exhaled, relief flooding me as I saw Jace sitting behind the wheel, Matty next to him in the passenger seat.

Jace threw the truck in park so violently, the whole Jeep shook. He jumped out and jogged over, throwing his arms around my shoulder and squeezing.

"Fucking hell. Where the fuck have you been? We thought you died!" he growled, still holding me tight. Matty was out of the Jeep, too, and suddenly I was in some sort of group hug.

"As endearing as this is, can we fucking get back? I haven't slept in—what time is it? What day is it?" I asked.

"It's eleven p.m. on Sunday," Jace said, still not letting me go.

"Crap," I growled, shaking my head. A part of me had been hoping I'd just overestimated the time I'd been gone. I couldn't believe they'd kept me for almost an entire day. "Have you seen Casey? Is she okay? Is she worried?"

184 C.R. JANE

Matty threw up his hands. "We didn't exactly have time to go check on your girlfriend since we've been looking for you all day!"

I stalked over to Jace's truck and jumped in. "Let's go. I need to see her."

Jace and Matty stared at me incredulously.

"I got arrested after the party for our little adventure in the graveyard. They took me to a fake police building and interrogated me for almost twenty-four hours before someone from the Sphinx came in, undid my handcuffs, and told me I'd passed the second test. Can we go now?"

Jace and Matty were still blinking at me. But I didn't have time for that. As crazy as my story was, all I cared about at the moment was making it back to Casey. It had been almost an entire day since I'd last seen her. Completely unacceptable.

"Well, I guess when you put it like that," Jace said slowly, finally walking over and getting into the driver's seat. It took Matty a little longer; his mouth had been so wide with shock, it had taken him a moment to scoop his bottom lip off the ground and get a hold of himself. Neither of them had gotten any Sphinx trials yet, and here I was with two already. Lucky me.

We started driving, each of them peppering me with a million questions that I answered tiredly. They'd covered for me this morning by saying I had a stomach bug—which usually would be code for "hungover" for a college coach. But since I'd never done anything like that before, Coach didn't make a big deal of it. Matty and Jace had then spent the rest of the day trying to find me.

"How *did* you even find me?" I asked, suddenly realizing in my exhaustion how unlikely it was that they'd just happened to be driving in this part of town as I was walking down the sidewalk.

Jace had a very smug look on his face after that question.

"Oh, well, with your friendship bracelet," he said nonchalantly.

Matty made a pained sound in the backseat. "They are *not* friendship bracelets."

Jace smirked. "They're *totally* friendship bracelets."

I glanced at the leather band that I'd forgotten Jace had even given me. We'd gotten them freshman year, and I considered it my lucky charm at this point. I never took it off.

"What does my . . . band have to do with this?"

"It has a tracker in there," he said proudly. "Because best friends stalk each other."

I gaped at him and then looked back at Matty, who just looked resigned at this point.

THE WRONG QUARTERBACK   185

"What do you mean it has a tracker?"

Jace shrugged. "It's not a big deal. It just was annoying freshman year that I never could find you guys when I needed you. So I bought tracking discs for your *friendship bracelets* and gave them to you . . . it's very useful."

There was a lot to unpack with all of that.

"Well, why the fuck didn't you find me sooner?" I griped.

Jace snorted. "When I was eighteen, I was obviously not shelling out for high-tech machinery." He raised an eyebrow at me like I should know that . . . even though the thought that my man-bun best friend had been actively stalking Matty and me for the past three years had never even come up as a possibility in my mind before.

Although now that I was thinking of it . . . Jace had always just popped up. I'd assumed it was some sort of superpower he had that he always was able to find us.

I was going to have to reevaluate my life after this.

"Anyways. It was just telling us your general location, but not the exact building. We've been searching warehouses all evening, trying to figure out if you'd been kidnapped or something." He nodded to himself as we continued to drive. "I'm definitely going to upgrade now."

I didn't have the energy to address that revelation. Matty was also being surprisingly silent about this. But I guess Jace had all day to beat Matty into submission. He was very good at that.

"We'll discuss this tomorrow," I finally said tiredly, and Jace started whistling, like he wasn't worried about that at all.

"I did come up with a really good one today," Jace commented as we turned at a stop sign and I finally began recognizing where we were. "All the driving around frantically because we thought you died was really good for my creativity."

Matty snorted in the back, and I could only imagine the day that he'd had.

"Hit me with it," I told Jace, needing something to distract me from the fact that I had a thrumming need to be with Casey that was only getting worse.

"What does a robot do after a one-night stand?" he asked.

I tried to think of something, but my brain had no interest in performing. "I have literally no idea."

"He nuts and bolts," replied Jace proudly.

I huffed out a laugh. "Good one," I told him, and Jace preened.

Matty clapped me on the shoulder. "Really glad you didn't die, QB."

186 C.R. JANE

I nodded, feeling oddly . . . choked up at the moment.

"Me too."

———————

The dorm was silent. I strode through, barely glancing at the girl at the front desk who gave a half-hearted protest as I passed. No one was going to stop me from seeing my girl.

I took the stairs two at a time, reaching Casey's floor, and her door at the end of the hall. I knocked, not caring about the hour, my pulse steady and determined. A moment later, Nat's sleepy face appeared in the doorway, her eyes barely open as she blinked at me in confusion. She started to say something, but I pushed past her gently, my gaze already fixed on Casey.

She was curled up in bed, hair splayed across the pillow, her brow creased, lips pressed together, like something was haunting her even in sleep.

Without a word, I walked over, pulling off my shirt before I eased myself into the bed. Gently, I slipped my arm around her, brushing a kiss against her hair, breathing her in. "I'm here, baby," I whispered, my voice soft, the words more for myself than for her.

She shifted, her face relaxing, and I held her close, feeling the stress of the day lift. Nat's bed creaked as she climbed back in, but it barely registered. All I could feel was Casey beside me, her breathing slow and steady, and then I closed my eyes, letting sleep finally pull me under.

I was back where I belonged, at last.

CHAPTER 21

CASEY

I woke, and the first thing I felt was warmth—solid, steady, comforting warmth. I blinked, trying to shake off the remnants of sleep, but there he was, a shirtless Parker, tangled up with me in my tiny dorm bed, his arm wrapped around me like he'd been here all night. I took a moment to drink him in, the soft light filtering through the window casting shadows over his face. He looked like an angel right now, a perfect being that had somehow fallen out of heaven and ended up here . . . with me. Parker's face was relaxed and peaceful, like he'd finally found a place he could rest.

I glanced over at Nat's bed and saw she'd already gone, and then my gaze was right back on Parker's beautiful face.

His blue eyes slowly opened, and he looked at me, a sleepy smile tugging at his lips. "Hi," he murmured, his voice low and warm, like a secret meant just for me.

"Hi," I whispered back, a smile breaking free as my heart did its usual flip. I'd thought I'd been dreaming last night when I'd felt his arms around me, but he was here, his gaze soft.

What would it be like to wake up with him like this every morning?

It would probably be impossible to have a bad day.

"I missed you yesterday," he said, his lips curling into a frown, like he really was devastated we hadn't seen each other.

I hated that I actually *had* been upset about it. Since that moment in the library, when he wasn't at practice or other team-related activities—he was with me. We had breakfast and lunch together. He brought me coffee. He walked me to and from class.

188   C.R. JANE

It was ridiculous to think that could be an everyday thing, but my pathetic self had soaked in his presence like a cracked desert getting its first rainfall.

I'd spent the entire day glued to my phone, waiting for him to text.

But he never did.

I looked away, afraid he would see the *pathetic* in my eyes, but he gently tugged my chin back to him. His ocean blue gaze was filled with promises as I stared, and I wanted him to keep each one.

"Did you miss me, too?" he asked, and the desperation in his voice seeped into my veins.

"Yes," I told him, my voice serious. While I'd been waiting for him to text yesterday, my thoughts had been filled with all the ways that I'd fucked up. I'd been doubting him, and he'd been doing things like kissing me on national television. And it wasn't just that. It was the way he knew my favorite drink order, the fact that he'd memorized my schedule, how he held my hand every chance he could . . . and how he made me feel like he was aware of me every second—even when other people were around.

When I'd gone to bed last night, I'd been sure I'd made the biggest mistake of my life. I'd been prepared to find him today, to tell him how I felt, even if he rejected me.

At some point yesterday, I'd realized that Parker wasn't a loss I was willing to take. I at least needed to fight for him.

"I thought—I thought maybe I'd messed everything up," I whispered, my voice embarrassingly emotional.

He pulled me closer, so every inch of me was pressed up against every inch of him. His dick was like a steel bar, digging into my stomach.

"Just ignore it, he can't help himself," he said, his voice still sleepy.

"There you go with calling it 'he' again."

His grin was brilliant, the kind of smile that made you lose your breath, that made you desperate for a camera so you could capture it forever.

"You could never mess us up," Parker said, his thumb stroking my cheek as he held my face. "I wouldn't let you. You could run, and I would run after you; you could hide, and I would find you; you could go to the other side of the fucking planet . . . and I would spend my entire life trying to track you down."

I blinked at him and let out a soft laugh, because of course he wasn't serious. But Parker's expression didn't waver. His eyes were clear and steady, no hint that he was teasing, no smirk or grin tugging at his lips. He was looking at me like he'd never believed in anything like he believed in what he'd just said.

THE WRONG QUARTERBACK   189

He lifted a hand, gently brushing a strand of hair away from my face, his fingers lingering on my skin. His thumb traced a soft line across my cheek.

"Parker . . ." I began, but my voice faltered, because my brain was still fighting against the notion that after breaking up with the boy I'd thought I'd loved for most of my life . . . that I could stumble right into my soulmate.

And not just my soulmate, but someone who shone so brightly that it was hard to see anything else.

Parker watched me calmly, like he could see everything inside my head, and he was giving me the space to figure it all out, for me to understand what he actually felt.

"I—" he began, but I couldn't let him say it. Because once he said it, I would be forced to say it back. And I couldn't say it back yet . . . right?

So I cut off his words with a kiss. A kiss that I poured my soul into. A kiss where I said all the things I was too afraid to say out loud.

And I think he got it.

He didn't try to speak anymore. Instead, he kissed me back . . . desperately, making a low possessive sound as his grip tightened around me.

I couldn't say *I love you* yet . . . but I could give him something else.

"Parker," I whispered in between breathless, urgent kisses. "I want you."

"You have me, baby. I'll give you anything you want," he said roughly, plunging his tongue into my mouth. I sucked on it, just how he liked, and he groaned, his hips thrusting against me.

"No, Parker," I said. "I *want* you." I pulled at my sleep shirt, sliding it up until I could awkwardly pull it off. I hadn't worn a bra to bed, so I was bare-chested against him.

"Look at you. You're fucking perfect, baby. And you're all mine," he purred as his hands slid up my inner thighs, and his thumbs briefly caressed the edge of my underwear. His eyes stayed locked on mine as he slowly tugged my panties off and threw them toward the end of the bed.

Parker suddenly pushed my thighs apart, holding me down as I squirmed under his perusal, his fingers slowly parting my folds as he took his fill and slid down my body.

His tongue delved into me, hungry and messy, every movement raw and consuming. There was nothing shy or restrained in his touch; it was intense, an unrestrained worship. He was tasting, savoring, his lips and tongue exploring with feverish need. His fingers followed, gliding through my slit, parting me, so he could taste everything he wanted.

His mouth closed over my clit, drawing me into a dizzying rush, his tongue dipped deeper, coaxing me open, his thumb circling and pressing just where I needed it. My body tensed, then shattered, every nerve alive as I fell apart around him. He didn't let up, lapping up every tremor, my muscles still fluttering as he lingered, his tongue continuing its gentle rhythm. As the waves eased, he continued, kissing and caressing, every swipe of his tongue sending me into a starry haze.

He stayed down there for what felt like forever, keeping me coming over and over until I was hoarse from screaming from all the pleasure he had given me.

I felt high, like I was floating above the stars. As he crawled up my body, settling close, his eyes heavy-lidded and his lips shiny from *me* . . . I wanted more.

"My turn," I told him, and my voice came out more animalistic than human as he obediently lay back.

His dick was halfway out of his sweatpants, and I was out of my mind as I pushed them all the way off so I could have what I wanted. I knew he was huge from feeling him through his pants before, but actually seeing his dick in all of its glory . . . it was life-changing.

His cock was huge and hard, the head red and swollen and already shiny with his cum.

"Can I taste you?" I murmured, an edge of sanity rushing back to me as I remembered this was all new to me. What if I sucked at it? What if I didn't like it?

I took in the sight of Parker's form lounging like a caged animal waiting to pounce, and I almost laughed. Of course I was going to like it. I was beginning to think this god was made just for me, designed to give me everything I could ever want.

Lucky me.

I leaned over, watching him as I tentatively licked along the mushroomed head. I slid my hands along the slick, solid shaft as I lapped at the bead of moisture that had just appeared.

He moaned, his gaze hot and almost crazed looking, like I was playing with fire and any minute he was not going to be able to control himself.

I wanted that. I wanted that unhinged, all-consuming lust. I wanted everything he was willing to give me.

I squeezed, immediately licking at the moisture that seeped out.

"Please, baby," he breathed. His hands were clutching the sheets, every muscle in his chest and arms tensed and outlined. And it was all because of me.

It was a heady, otherworldly . . . powerful thing to know I was the one who was making this beautiful creature react like this.

THE WRONG QUARTERBACK 191

I slid my lips around the head and took him as deep as I could. I didn't care what girls bragged about; there was not a throat on this planet that could take this cock all the way down. I sucked harder and harder, my hands sliding and gripping and squeezing along his length as I concentrated on the head. I was sure that I was awkward, and there were a million things I could improve on. But what I lacked in experience, I was trying to make up for in desire. I'd never wanted anything the way that I wanted him.

He was moaning, his hands tangling in my hair as he guided me up and down his dick. I loved it. I might not be able to say the words to him, but I could think it . . . I loved his dick.

I loved every other part of him, too.

"Baby," he rasped, sliding out of my mouth and dragging me up his body, his length hard and sticky between us.

"I'm going to come in your sweet cunt this time. Your perfect mouth will have to be later," he growled before pulling me in for a hard, dirty kiss that had me dripping against his thigh. "Are you ready for me, baby? There's no going back, you know that, right? You're already mine, but once I get inside you, it's permanent."

He kissed me one more time before he rolled us over, so he was hovering over me.

"I'm on birth control," I blurted out as he slowly slid his dick through my sopping-wet folds. It was hard to get the words out because it already felt better than anything I'd ever experienced.

There was a strange gleam in his eyes as he took in that news . . . almost like he was disappointed.

"Are you—"

"Am I clean?" he murmured, pressing a bruising kiss against my lips before he pulled back, his forearms on either side of my head, so I was completely covered by him. He was so much bigger than me. I loved this, this feeling like he owned me. It was a strange thought, but I realized . . . I'd never felt so safe.

"As soon as I saw you, I went and got checked. I knew you were it. I knew I'd never have anyone else." My eyes widened at his words, and he smoothed my hair out of my face, kissing me all over like he wanted to make sure he touched every part of me.

"I trust you," I said softly, and he closed his eyes for a second, as if the words had reached some important part inside of him.

He brushed against my skin, stroking my breasts and my stomach. His fingers slid through my slit for a moment before he brought his fingers to my lips, spreading my wetness along my bottom lip and into my mouth so I could taste myself.

"You're so sweet, baby. My sweet, perfect girl," he murmured, his tongue sliding down my neck before he suddenly bit down on my shoulder, admiring the mark for a moment before he licked away the pain.

He reached down between us and guided his dick to my opening, pushing barely inside as he watched with a wild, wide-eyed gaze.

"Baby," he slurred. "You feel so fucking good."

He pushed further in, my legs parting even more, every piece of my body ready for him. I whimpered; what I was feeling was better than anything I'd ever experienced.

This was what it felt like to fly. To burn. To become something more than just yourself.

"You're doing so good, Casey," he said as he brushed a soft kiss against my lips. "So fucking good."

His hand reached between us and circled my clit in a light, rhythmic glide, the sparks of pleasure making it easier to accept him as he pushed inside me, inch by enormous inch.

He thrust deeper, his words a constant stream of praises as tears gathered in my eyes. There was so much pressure. My breath was erratic as I tried to adjust to the fullness, to the feeling that I was being split in half.

"Just a little more, baby. You can take it," he said soothingly, and I whimpered again, because I wasn't sure I could. He was so fucking big.

He laughed, and I realized I must have somehow said that out loud.

"Please, don't stop," I whispered, and he kissed me, thrusting in one final time until he was seated in all the way, filling me so completely I couldn't think. Parker had become a part of me; that's what this felt like.

"Never," he murmured roughly in my ear, and I forced myself to open my eyes so I could look at him. "You were made for me." He licked a falling tear off my cheek. "I've never felt anything so good. So right."

Parker pushed my knees up as he drew back, his glittering eyes glued to where he was stretching me wide.

He slammed forward, sinking deep as my scream filled the room.

"That's so good, baby. Look at you taking all of my big dick. That's so good, my sweet girl."

He thrust in and out, his muscles flexing under my fingers. The room was filled with the sound of us. My cries, his groans, a soundtrack I could listen to for the rest of my life.

"I love you, baby. I love you so much," he suddenly rasped.

I came.

The pleasure was almost painful because it felt so good, like I was being possessed. Like he was ripping open my veins and replacing my blood with something new. Something transcendent. Something that only he could understand.

I'd always wanted a love like he was promising. His words were a gift. A scary, terrifying, overwhelming gift that I wanted to live with for the rest of my life.

Parker's kiss gave me life, his tongue tangling with mine desperately as his hips drove into me, harder and harder until he was moaning against my mouth, and his hot cum was filling me in magical, life-changing bursts.

It was spilling out of me, dripping down my thighs and onto the bed, and I had the insane urge to reach down and shove it back into me because I wanted him inside me . . . forever.

Pushing in deep, he stayed there, relaxing against me with almost the full breadth of his weight so I couldn't move at all. He nuzzled my neck, kissing me lazily. "You're fucking amazing, Casey. I love you so much. This is the best moment of my life." His words wrapped around me as my arms pulled him closer.

I never wanted this moment to end.

―――――――

We fell asleep like that, him still inside me. He rolled us over so I wasn't taking all of his weight, making sure we stayed connected the entire time.

I woke to Parker's hard cock pushing into me again. He was behind me now, his hand massaging my breast, his other hand playing with my clit as he eased in and out.

"I have to go to practice, baby. But I couldn't help it. I needed more," he murmured.

I sighed, sinking into the pleasure, his groan spreading warmth across my skin.

"I love you, Casey," he said, his pace speeding up as his fingers led me into a rolling, delicious orgasm. My hips moved with him, like he'd possessed me or reprogrammed me so that we'd always be perfectly in sync.

"I'm going to have all of you, baby. Every part of you is going to belong to me," he whispered against my skin. And maybe I should have been alarmed at the possessiveness in his voice. At the words he continued to say that told me this love he was claiming . . . it was laced with an obsession as well.

194   C.R. JANE

He groaned, his tongue licking along my shoulder as he filled me once again. Parker shuddered against me, his breath warming my skin as his fingers slid along where we were connected.

"I love you," he whispered again as I fell back into a deep, dreamless sleep where I was safe and loved . . . by him.

Parker

I think if you weren't at least a little nervous before you stepped into your head coach's office . . . you were doing something wrong. Although the fact that I'd just left Casey naked in bed, after the best morning of my life, was definitely helping with those nerves.

He called me in after practice, barely glancing up from his desk as I stepped inside. The door clicked shut behind me, and I got the sense this wasn't going to be a quick pep talk. Coach Everett leaned back in his chair, eyeing me over a stack of playbooks with this strange, hard-to-read expression.

Coach had the build of an ex-lineman who never quite let himself go—broad shoulders, a bit of a gut, but still solid. His face was weathered, with deep-set eyes that held a permanent squint, like he'd spent too many years staring down sunlight and tough decisions. Gray hair peeked out from under his cap, and his jaw was almost always clenched, a rough scowl marking his features, even when he was pleased.

"Davis," he started, his voice gruff. "I need to know if your head's on straight."

I straightened, bracing myself. "Yes, sir. Is there a problem?"

He held my gaze for a beat longer, like he was trying to read my mind, then sighed, rubbing a hand over his jaw. "Look, Parker, you're the most talented quarterback I've had come through here. You could have it all—the records, the scouts drooling over you, number one in the draft. I mean, all of it."

"Thank you, sir," I said, nodding. I'd heard this before, but I could tell there was something else eating at him.

He shifted in his chair, clearing his throat, looking more uncomfortable by the second. "Rumor is," he said, his voice dropping like he didn't want anyone else in the world to overhear, "you're pretty serious about a girl. Real serious."

I couldn't stop the grin from stretching across my face. "Yeah, Coach. As a matter of fact, I am."

His brows shot up, just a little. "Girls can be distracting. You're a junior in college, with your whole life in front of you . . . you've been behaving out of character lately." He hesitated. "Are you sure this girl is a good idea?"

"She's not a distraction," I said as I leaned back in the chair, crossing my arms, feeling that rush of satisfaction hit me just from saying it out loud. "She's my future wife."

Coach blinked, stunned, his mouth opening and then closing like he wasn't sure what to say next. "And, uh, does she know that?"

"Not yet," I replied, smirking. "But she will."

Coach let out a heavy breath, leaning back in his chair, just staring at me, like he was trying to figure out if I was kidding . . . or if I'd lost my mind. "Davis, one wrong move . . . one little slipup, and this could all blow up in your face. You know that, right? You're putting a hell of a lot on the line here."

I nodded, my face dead serious. "I've got it all under control, Coach. Trust me."

He shook his head, but there was a hint of a smile hiding beneath his usual scowl. "Yeah, I'm sure you think you do," he muttered, picking up a pen and tapping it on his desk. "Now get the hell outta my office. I've got work to do."

I pushed up out of the chair, feeling that surge of energy that only Casey could give me, even just talking about her. "Thanks, Coach."

"Yeah, yeah," he grumbled, waving me off. But as I hit the door, I heard him mutter under his breath, "Damn kid sounds like a fucking psychopath."

I grinned, letting the door click shut behind me . . . because maybe I was.

CHAPTER 22

CASEY

There was a knock on my door, and a smile was instantly on my lips thinking it was Parker. I swung it open, expecting his gorgeous grin, but my stomach dropped when I saw Gray standing there instead.

He stared at me with an intensity that made me uncomfortable. It was something that I'd wanted not that long ago, but now it felt all wrong. "Casey," he breathed, a trace of desperation in his voice. "I miss you. And I'm willing to do anything, anything, to get you back."

I bit down on my lip hard, keeping my face neutral, refusing to let him see the ripple of uncertainty stirring in my chest. "Gray, this isn't—"

"Please, Casey." His voice softened, searching. "Remember how it used to be? All those good times we had? You were the one I turned to for everything. And I was that for you too. Don't you remember?"

My pulse quickened, but I pushed the memories back, steeling myself against the way his words tried to dig under my skin.

He took a step forward, his voice barely a murmur. "I can be that person again. The one you needed, the one who's known you since the beginning. I haven't had a drink since that night. I *won't* have a drink. I'm going to do everything to get you back."

"Gray, I need you to leave," I said, my voice coming out firmer than I felt.

But he didn't move, his expression twisting in something that almost looked like pain. "You think Parker is gonna love you like I do?"

The words stung, lacing their way under my skin, but I pushed them down, my hand gripping the edge of the door.

THE WRONG QUARTERBACK   197

I pressed my lips together, fighting the knot tightening in my chest.

He leaned toward me. "He can never love you like me, because he'll never *know* you like me."

I stared at him for a long, tense minute, and then without another word, I closed the door in his face. Leaning back against it, my mind was a mess of memories.

It was hard to say goodbye to memories that had once been held in strict reverence in my mind, the only things that had kept me going in years filled with nothing but pain.

But no matter what Gray wanted, Parker's glow was too strong. Gray wanted to pull me back into the past, but I didn't live there anymore. I'd learned that what I thought were highlights, sparks of brightness that were all because of Gray . . . they were actually nothing but shadows.

Swallowing the tangle of emotions clawing at my chest, I pushed myself off the door. I needed clarity, I needed to feel grounded again. I grabbed my keys, knowing there was only one place to go when my heart felt torn apart like this.

It was time to talk to Ben.

Parker

"You look suspiciously rosy-cheeked," Jace quipped as we walked into the locker room. "I wonder why that is."

I grinned. I wasn't going to deny it. Well, I wasn't going to say I was rosy-cheeked. Because what the hell was that? But I *was* supremely happy, like someone had stuck me with fucking happy juice and this was my new state of being.

"What's the opposite of *dickmatized*?" Matty asked, leaning his arm on Jace's shoulder as they both gave me smug smiles.

"*Pussy-conquered*?" Jace offered, cocking his head as he thought about it.

"Oh, yes. That's a good one," Matty said, giving Jace a fist bump.

"I don't like this," I said, pointing to the two of them. "When you two gang up on me."

"It's because you're a little scary now, QB. You've got that crazy look in your eyes. We've got to shore up our defenses," explained Jace.

"What?"

"Just in case it's catching, he means," said Matty. "We didn't sign up for . . . what was the word again?"

198   C.R. JANE

"*Pussy-conquered.* We didn't sign up for that," supplied Jace helpfully.

I scoffed. "I'm pretty sure that's not a word."

"I'm pretty sure that your picture is the definition of it in the dictionary," said Matty.

I threw my jockstrap at him, and he ducked, laughing when it smacked the wall behind him.

"I'm just saying, Matty. If you let your little stalker get within ten feet of you . . . maybe you will get a little crazy too."

Matty shuddered like that was his worst nightmare. "Take that back right now."

"I don't know, Matthew. She might be just the kind of crazy you need in your life."

Matty snarled, and Jace and I both snickered.

Still laughing, I reached into my bag for my phone, my smile fading when I saw the text from Casey, canceling our dinner plans.

> LOML: I'm not going to make it to dinner. I'm sorry. I'll see you later.

"Uh-oh, he's not rosy cheeked anymore," whispered Jace.

I scoffed at him and grabbed my bag. "I'll see you guys later," I told them, leaving the room to a chorus of "pussy-conquered" chants.

Pulling up my phone, I checked my Find My Friends app and saw that she was in her dorm room—Jace's stalking tips were actually very useful.

So far there had been a different girl manning the desk every time I'd come by—thank fuck—and this one just gaped at me as I walked by. Once I got to Casey's door, I pounded on the wood, tapping my finger against my leg impatiently because I needed to see her.

Five hours was too long. It would probably be too much to ask her to sit in the stands during practice, right?

The door opened, and Casey appeared, her red-rimmed eyes telling me that my baby was having a tough day.

"Tell me what's wrong," I demanded. "Let me fix it."

She wiped at her eyes. "I just went to see Ben, and . . . it's hard. It never seems to get easier." A tear slid down her cheek, and I growled as I pushed my way inside, scooping her into my arms as I walked over to her bed and sat down. I continued to cradle her in my lap as she buried her head in my neck and sobbed.

"I know about grief," I murmured. "The kind that eats you from the inside out. The kind that you don't think you can escape from. When I lost

THE WRONG QUARTERBACK 199

my dad, I used to go sit in his office. I'd sit in the same chair that I'd always used when he was working late into the night and I'd wanted to hang out with him. And I think I was waiting. I think a part of me thought that maybe he'd walk in. And he'd grin when he saw me. And then we'd just talk while he worked, about everything and anything. I kept sitting in that chair for a month until it really hit me . . . he was gone."

She pulled her face from my neck and stared at me somberly. "I'm sorry about your dad, Parker," she said quietly as her gaze searched mine.

"Me too, baby. Me too."

I pressed a kiss to her lips because I couldn't help it, and she kissed me back with a breadth of emotion I hadn't expected.

"Next time you want to go, I'll take you," I murmured against her lips. "I don't want you to go by yourself anymore. I don't want you to be alone."

She looked away, her lower lip trembling. "It's a long drive, and you're so busy. I'd never—"

I gently grabbed her chin and made her look at me. "Don't go alone. I'm never too busy for you. You don't get this yet, but you're my number one priority. There's nothing more important than making you happy. Nothing."

Casey was looking at me like I was crazy, and I got it. She didn't understand yet that I'd looked at her and knew that the most important piece of my soul . . . the one I'd always known was missing—it was in her.

"When you say that, I don't know what to say. When you say that . . . it feels dangerous." She closed her eyes. "My brother was Mama's favorite child . . . and I was okay with that. I really was. Because he was my favorite too. He was popular and handsome; everyone who met him thought he was the best. He *was* the best." She opened her eyes to look at me again, as if it was important to her that I understood what she was saying. "That meant, though, that I wasn't seen very much. I was the afterthought in our family, the afterthought in school, the afterthought in . . . life. And then when Gray did that . . ." She bit down on her lip, trying not to cry anymore. "When he did that, it was just a reminder of who I am. A nobody," she whispered.

I opened my mouth to vehemently reject what she was saying, but she placed a trembling finger to my lips. "So when you, a person who literally outshines everything and everyone, tries to tell me that you see me, or that I'm important . . . or any of the other crazy things that keep coming out of your mouth . . . it's hard for me to believe. The sun was never meant to be with the stars."

I snorted then, and she looked at me, shocked. "The sun *is* a star, baby. Not to cut you off. A bunch of those stars are in fact brighter than the sun . . . they're just farther away. We're both stars, Casey."

200   C.R. JANE

"You kind of are a nerd," she joked. "Are you sure that you actually need tutoring?"

I grinned, because if she only knew.

"Promise me that you'll tell me next time you want to go," I pushed.

She bit down on her lip, and I knew she wasn't going to.

"One day, baby . . ." I whispered.

"What?"

"One day you're going to wake up, and you're going to realize you're safe with me. That out of anyone you've met in your life, anyone you'll *ever* meet in your life, I'm the person you can trust."

"You're doing it again," she murmured.

"Doing what?" I asked with a grin, because I was pretty sure I knew what she was going to say.

"You're talking crazy," she said, hovering by my lips, so I had no choice but to kiss her until she couldn't breathe.

I love you was trying to burst out of my chest, but I held it in.

I'd said it to her when we had sex, but something told me saying it again right then . . . it would probably drive her over the edge.

Soon, I told myself. Soon I'd be able to say it whenever I wanted.

And she would believe me.

The night was still, the parking lot empty and quiet under the glow of the streetlights as I walked up to her car. Her car was what you called . . . a piece of shit. It already sputtered when she started it, and every time she hit a bump, it rattled like it was going to fall apart. It was barely hanging on, which tonight was very helpful. Casey got into this car every time and expected it wouldn't start.

Tomorrow, her expectations would be met.

I popped the hood, glancing around to make sure no one was around to get curious. I'd spent enough hours working in a mechanic's shop back in high school to know my way around an engine, even if my boss had been a dick. Loosening the negative cable on the battery terminal was easy—just a quick twist, and it wobbled enough to disconnect. It would look solid from above, like nothing was off. I grinned, then reached for the ignition fuse and pulled it out for good measure, pocketing it. That'd buy me enough time to make sure she wasn't heading to the cemetery alone again.

THE WRONG QUARTERBACK   201

It wasn't healthy for her to go there alone. She was used to handling everything by herself, but that didn't mean I had to let her take off whenever she felt like burying herself in that place. Not without me there, to ground her, to keep her steady.

As soon as she trusted me, I'd get her a new car. One that didn't look like it was one pothole away from falling apart. My baby deserved better than this shitty safety hazard.

For now, though, I needed her safe, and I wasn't above a little sabotage if that's what it took.

I closed the hood with a firm click, straightening as I looked up at the night sky, a grin spreading over my face.

Casey

I slid into the driver's seat, turning the key, and . . . nothing. The engine didn't even try to turn over. Groaning, I smacked the steering wheel and leaned my forehead against it, trying to think.

I didn't have the money to fix this junker right now, and calling Mama for help wasn't going to get me anywhere—even if she actually answered. I sat there for a moment, tapping my fingers on the wheel, feeling the knot in my stomach tighten.

Finally I got out, accepting that snack shopping was not going to happen. Right as I'd slammed my door shut, I heard the rumble of an engine, and Parker's truck pulled up next to me. He rolled down his window, eyebrow raised, that infuriatingly adorable smirk tugging at his lips.

"What's up, baby?" he called, his voice all teasing, but there was concern in his eyes.

I sighed, leaning back against my car. "It won't start," I groaned.

Parker hopped out of his truck and strode over, glancing under the hood with that casual confidence that always seemed to cling to him. "Let's try a jump," he said, already grabbing the cables from his truck.

I popped the hood, watching him work, his movements smooth and familiar as he connected the cables. He slid into my car, turning the key a few times. But the engine didn't so much as sputter. He turned to me, shrugging, that grin of his back in place. "Well, I gave it my best shot, but looks like your girl here is just not having it."

I sighed, frustration building up. It wasn't the biggest deal not to have a car, but it was definitely going to be annoying asking for rides. Parker nudged me gently with his shoulder. "Hey, don't stress. I'll drive you. Consider me your personal chauffeur."

He flashed me that sexy smile, the one that somehow melted all my worries, every time. The words hovered on my tongue, the words I knew he wanted to hear, but I kissed him instead.

"You're way too sweet, you know that?" I murmured against his lips.

He just shrugged, a mischievous spark lighting up his blue eyes as he opened the truck door for me. "You keep telling me that, baby, and it might go to my head."

I got in, and he drove me to dinner, and I didn't think about my car . . . even once.

CHAPTER 23

PARKER

The phone vibrated in my pocket, its sharp buzz breaking through the quiet peace I was sharing with Casey as we lay in bed. I sat up so abruptly that Casey startled.

My phone buzzed again, and my heart rate spiked.

When I put my phone on Do Not Disturb, there were only three people who could get through, and they all knew not to try unless it was important.

I pulled out my phone, seeing Martha's name flash across the screen. My stomach dropped. Martha only texted when something was wrong, and she didn't call unless something was *really* wrong.

Fuck.

I shot Casey an apologetic look for scaring her and answered. "Hey, Martha, what's going on?"

"Your mother passed out again." Martha's voice was tight, strained. "She still hasn't been eating. I went to give her an IV, and she just passed out before I even got the tube in. I called an ambulance, and she's on her way to Farragut Memorial." She paused, and I heard her take a deep, shuddering breath. "I'm sorry, Parker," she finally said, her voice filled with emotion. "I did everything I could."

I closed my eyes, trying to push down the surge of emotions flooding my insides. The sinking dread, the frustration, the helplessness. This wasn't the first time my mom had landed in the hospital because she refused to eat. But every time it happened, it felt like we were one step closer. Like a countdown to an ending I couldn't stop.

"I know you did," I finally said, keeping my voice steady, even though it felt like the ground was shifting under me. "I'm on my way."

Martha sighed, and I could hear the exhaustion in her voice, the same weariness I carried. "Parker . . . I don't know how much longer she can keep doing this."

I swallowed hard. "Yeah. I know."

When I hung up, I felt Casey's hand on my arm, her fingers soft but firm. "Parker? What happened?"

I buried my face in her hair, my whole body trembling as I soaked in her scent, using it to ground me so I could get through the night ahead.

"My mom passed out, and she's on the way to the hospital," I murmured into her skin, trying to convince myself to let her go.

Casey stiffened, a little gasp caressing the back of my neck. I forced myself to pull away, not sure how to explain the mess of emotions twisting inside me.

For a second I got caught in a memory of Walker and Cole being gone somewhere and me as a little kid trying to get my mom to make me lunch. She'd sat in her chair by the window as if she couldn't hear me, staring out . . . I shook my head, trying to clear my head of the past.

Casey's eyes were filling up with tears, and I immediately pulled her into my arms. "I'm so sorry, Parker," she whispered, pressing a shaky kiss to my cheek. What a fucking sweetheart. "Do you want me to come with you?"

I looked at her, shocked by the offer . . . although I didn't really know why that was. I guess it was because I hadn't even thought about asking, because I'd been dealing with this by myself for so long. I hadn't even asked Jace and Matty to help me.

But suddenly the idea of facing this alone felt un-fucking-bearable. "Yeah, baby. I'd . . . I'd really like that."

She nodded, squeezing my arm. "Then let's go."

We walked to the truck in silence. But the drive wasn't as terrible as it normally was. Casey's presence was an anchor, keeping me from spiraling into the dark thoughts that would normally be consuming me.

As we got closer to the hospital, though, the reality of what would be waiting for me in that hospital room started to hit me hard.

"I should explain," I said after a few minutes, my voice tight. "About my mom."

Casey turned to me, her eyes soft with understanding. "You don't have to if you don't want to."

"No, I do," I said, gripping the steering wheel harder. "You should know what's been going on. Even if I fucking hate talking about it."

THE WRONG QUARTERBACK · 205

I took a deep breath, trying to figure out where to start. "After my dad died . . . everything changed. My mom just . . . it's like she lost the will to live. She barely eats, barely talks. She's been like a ghost of herself for years now."

Casey listened quietly, her eyes soft and understanding.

"That's why I came to the University of Tennessee," I continued, my voice rougher than I intended. "I couldn't leave her. My brothers didn't have control of where they needed to be, and it's also harder for them—they've got too many memories of her from before. But I . . . I thought maybe I could help. She's been fading ever since, though. It's like she's just waiting for the right time to give up completely."

I paused, letting out a shaky breath. "And now . . . now I don't know if it's even better for her to keep living like this. I mean, if she doesn't want to be here anymore . . . should I even try to stop her?"

The silence stretched between us, heavy with the weight of what I'd said. It wasn't something I'd admitted to anyone before.

But it felt freeing to tell her.

I was already gripping Casey's hand when she lifted our intertwined fingers, softly brushing her lips across my knuckles. She didn't say anything right away; she simply held on to me, her thumb gently soothing my skin. And somehow, that was enough. I didn't need her to give me an answer or tell me everything would be okay. I just needed her.

By the time we pulled up to the hospital, my chest felt tight, every breath suddenly strained. Casey stayed close, her hand still in mine as we walked through the automatic doors and into the sterile, cold environment of the hospital. The fluorescent lights buzzed overhead, and the smell of antiseptic hit me like a slap to the face.

I'd been here too many times before.

We checked in at the front desk, and the nurse gave us an update on how my mom was before directing us down the hall to her room. My steps slowed as we got closer, because I didn't want to see her like this. I didn't want *Casey* to meet her like this.

I prided myself on being in control of almost everything in my life.

But I'd never been able to have control over my mom's unwilling-ness . . . to live.

When we reached her room, I hesitated for a moment before pushing open the door. The sight of her lying in that hospital bed, pale and fragile, made my chest tighten. She looked so small, so . . . breakable. Like one wrong move would shatter her completely.

206   C.R. JANE

I let go of Casey's hand and walked over to the side of the bed. My mom was sleeping, her breathing shallow, her skin almost translucent in the harsh hospital light. It was hard to reconcile this woman in front of me with the mom I remembered from before—before everything fell apart.

I stood there for a moment, just looking at her.

"Hey, Mom," I said softly, though I knew she wouldn't respond. "It's me. Parker."

She didn't stir, didn't move. Her chest rose and fell with each slow breath, but it felt like she was already gone, like she'd checked out long before she ever landed in this hospital bed.

I swallowed hard, the lump in my throat making it difficult to speak.

The words that I knew I should say felt like knives in my chest, each one cutting deeper than the last. I needed to say them. I needed to let my mom go, but I didn't know how.

Casey came up next to me and leaned her head against my arm.

"I don't want her to suffer anymore," I whispered, my voice barely audible now. "But I keep thinking that one of these days she'll decide to fight. Hope is a fucking dangerous thing, though."

The silence in the room was deafening, and I could feel the tears burning in my eyes. I hadn't cried in years—hadn't let myself—but now, standing here, I was close.

My phone buzzed, and I pulled it out of my pocket, grateful for something else to do but stare at my mom and will her to wake up.

"Hey," I said to Walker, putting it on speakerphone in the hopes that Mom would hear his voice and come to.

"Sorry, Parker. We had a game tonight. I just saw your text."

I could hear people talking in the background. He must have still been in the locker room.

"Yeah, I figured you would see it when you were finished. Did you win?" I asked. Usually I'd be watching the game or at least tracking the score closely, but obviously I hadn't had a chance tonight.

"Yes, thank fuck. We were down by one, and Linc tied it in the last minute. Then Rookie ended up scoring in the first thirty seconds of overtime. It was a fucking game."

There was a pause.

"How is she?"

I knew my brothers felt guilty that I carried the majority of the load of caring for Mom, but it was more of an unspoken thing between us.

THE WRONG QUARTERBACK   207

"She hasn't woken up. They've got an IV going. They're going to do a feeding tube if she won't eat on her own. But . . . she's at least stable."

I turned back to my mom, hoping—praying—that maybe she had opened her eyes.

But, of course, she hadn't.

"Casey's here with me, though," I said, glancing at Casey who was listening quietly at my side.

"Meeting the parents. It's getting serious," he said, a hint of laughter in his voice. He didn't realize he was on speakerphone, obviously. Casey was suddenly trying to pretend she couldn't hear anything.

"Very," I told him, watching as she started blushing furiously.

There was a surprised pause.

"Well, then, I can't wait to meet her," he said quietly. "Let's make that soon."

I said goodbye to him and promised to update him about Mom.

And then we were back to sitting in silence.

We stayed there for hours, the room quiet except for the sound of her breathing and the faint beeping of the machines that monitored her vitals.

"Tell me something about Ben," I murmured, my eyes locked on my mom's face.

Her hand squeezed mine for a second. "He considered himself my protector. Every morning, before Daddy would go to work, he'd kneel down and look Ben right in the eye. 'Now you're the man of the house while I'm gone, Ben. You need to take care of our ladies,' he'd say. Ben would puff himself up and nod, and for the rest of the day, until Daddy got back, he'd try to take care of us." Her hand trembled in mine, and I rubbed her knuckles with my thumb. "One day, Daddy didn't come back, he got crushed on a construction site. But Ben never forgot what he'd told him. He was always our protector."

"I love you, Casey," I murmured, not expecting anything back.

But to my surprise, she took a deep breath and said, "I love you, too."

My breath hitched, and my chest got tight, like maybe I was having some kind of heart attack brought on by getting something I'd been wanting more than anything else. When I looked at her, her face was tense . . . scared, like she couldn't believe she'd said the words either.

I'd have to make sure I never gave her a reason to regret that.

"Thank you," I answered, feeling like I'd been given a gift. I pulled her into my lap. My emotions were raw, exposed in a way I hadn't let them be

208   C.R. JANE

in a long time. But I felt lighter, like maybe, just maybe, I could carry this sorrow a little longer. Because I wasn't alone anymore.

A soft knock broke through my thoughts, and when I looked over Casey's shoulder, Martha stood in the doorway, her frame backlit by the morning light spilling into the hall. She held a steaming cup of coffee in her hand, her expression calm but warm. Martha was in her fifties, with silver strands woven through her dark hair, which she always wore in a neat braid down her back. Her face was lined and kind, and her gentle eyes seemed to see everything without judgment.

She walked over, taking a sip of the coffee. "You should get back to school, Parker," she said gently, a reassuring smile on her lips. "I've got this. She's in good hands."

I nodded, feeling relieved that she was here. There was no way I could miss another practice today. "Thank you, Martha," I said, the words thick with gratitude. She patted my shoulder softly.

I leaned over and gave my mom's cheek a kiss. "Bye, Mom," I whispered, and then I led Casey out of the room, not sure what kind of goodbye I'd just said to her.

"Thank you for coming with me," I said quietly, turning to Casey.

She gave me a small smile, her eyes soft. "Always," she answered, repeating my word back to me.

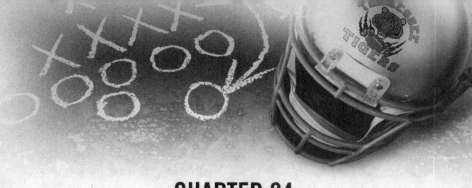

CHAPTER 24

PARKER

We'd gotten our asses kicked in practice, and I was looking forward to food and a fuck . . . not necessarily in that order, as I rounded the hallway that led to Casey's room, stopping dead in my tracks when I saw him—Gray, standing in front of Casey's door.

My jaw clenched, and I stepped back, slipping into the shadow of the hallway so I could watch. He looked desperate, his posture tense as he ran his hands through his hair frantically and stared at the door.

"Casey, open up," he yelled, banging on the wood so hard that all the doors in the hallway rattled.

I didn't like that. I didn't like that at all.

I wanted to kill him.

The door opened a crack, and Nat stuck her head out, her eyes narrowing the second she saw him. "Get lost, you fucking asshole," she snapped, her voice sharp and dismissive.

I grinned at that, happy my lady had such a good friend. I hadn't been too sure of her when I'd met her—if she was being nice to Casey to get in with the football team or something. But so far, there hadn't been any red flags. Which was good. I had enough red flags to go around.

Andrews didn't back down. "I need to talk to her," he insisted, his voice low and pleading. "Just for a minute."

"Fuck you," she hissed, slamming the door in his face without another word.

You go, girl.

His shoulders sagged, but he didn't move. He stood there for a moment longer, staring at the wood as if he could *will* the door to open. Finally, he turned and started to walk back down the hall, toward me, frustration and agony all over his face.

I understood what he was feeling. I would do anything to get Casey back if I lost her—I was doing all sorts of things right now to *keep* her.

But my understanding didn't mean that I was going to allow it.

I waited around the corner, listening to his steps approach as he neared the end of the hall. As soon as he turned, I grabbed his shoulder and slammed him against the wall, feeling the solid impact, the satisfaction of his body colliding with the concrete.

Gray's eyes widened as he looked at me; shock . . . and a hint of fear flashed across his face. I kept my hand firmly on his chest, pressing him into the wall, leaning in until there was barely an inch of space between us. I knew Gray had played basketball in high school, and he still worked out now, but he was no match for a football player in his prime.

And he knew it.

"What do you think you're doing here, Andrews?"

"Trying to talk to my girlfriend," he hissed.

I knocked his head against the wall for good measure, because obviously he had some kind of screw loose. Apparently breaking his nose wasn't enough, so I guess things would have to escalate.

"Listen to me, Andrews," I said, my voice low, cold . . . and deadly serious. "I don't want to see you near her again. You're done. She doesn't need you. She doesn't want you."

Gray's face twisted, and he sneered at me. "She just needs to be reminded of what we had. Once she remembers, it won't matter that you're the star quarterback, Davis. Casey will want to come back to me."

I grinned. "You should know this now, before you get yourself in any more trouble. It will really help you out." I leaned in closer. "I win," I said mockingly.

His face paled, but he wasn't done. "I know you did something that night. I don't know how, but I know it was *you*."

I adopted my best mocking, Bambi eyes. "I have no idea what you're talking about," I answered innocently. "I don't see how I could make you 'cheat' on the most perfect girl who exists in the world. That was all you, Andrews."

"I didn't cheat on her!" he yelled. "It doesn't count if I was pissed out of my mind and I had no idea what I was doing!"

"See, that's the difference between you and me. I love her so much that my dick wouldn't even work on other girls."

THE WRONG QUARTERBACK   211

He scoffed. "It was a kiss. Nothing but a kiss."

I flashed my teeth at him. "It was a betrayal and my way in. You're just going to have to accept that."

He opened his mouth to say something else idiotic, and my hand creeped to his neck . . . squeezing and cutting off whatever bullshit was about to come out of his mouth. His eyes widened. "Casey belongs to me now. You so much as look at her again, and we're going to have a problem. You don't get to haunt her. Not anymore."

I released his neck, and he coughed. "Casey know you're a fucking psychopath?" he growled, and I laughed as I stepped back as he tried to regain his balance, his face red with barely contained rage.

Without another word, he turned and walked away, his steps echoing down the hall. I watched him leave, anger still simmering in my veins.

I finally straightened my shirt and walked down to Casey's door, knocking on it lightly.

Nat opened the door just a crack, relief flooding her features as she opened the door wider and let me in. I immediately went to Casey, pulling her in for a deep kiss because I'd missed her so fucking much. It should be illegal for her to ever be away from me.

When I pulled away, I tried to keep my expression neutral. "Was that Gray I just saw outside?" I asked, keeping my voice easy.

Casey hesitated, her gaze flickering away. But before she could answer me, Nat jumped in, her tone annoyed. "The asshole just won't leave her alone."

I kept my mouth from twisting into a scowl, forcing myself to nod and act like it wasn't anything to me. "Let me know if he tries to talk to you again," I said, locking my eyes on Casey's.

She nodded, her voice soft. "I will."

Relieved she hadn't tried to argue with me, I pulled her back into my chest, lowering my voice so only she could hear me. "Let's go to my place," I murmured, letting the words linger as my lips brushed against her skin. "I'm feeling . . . hungry."

Her eyes lit up, and without another word, I slid my hand into hers and led her toward the door.

And as we walked out of the dorm all I could think was . . . it was time for her to move in.

I handed Casey the card, watching the flicker of hesitation in her eyes. She always acted so shy when I tried to buy her anything. She hadn't realized yet

212   C.R. JANE

that I would buy her literally anything she wanted. Since the moment I met her, everything I had done was to set us up for the future and make it so I could. "I've got a late practice tonight. Grab some dinner on me," I told her.

Casey shook her head. "Parker, you don't need to—"

Before she could finish, Nat snatched the card right out of my hand with a wide grin. "Don't mind if we do. Your man just got a deal with Nike, he can definitely afford to treat us to a nice dinner, Case." She flashed the card at Casey like a victory. "We're going to get steak, by the way," she said, tossing me a mischievous grin.

I smirked, raising an eyebrow as I looked at Casey. "You better."

Nat made a swooning sound while I kissed Casey, and then I left their dorm room, heading to practice, which was in fact scheduled to be an hour shorter than usual.

When I got out, night had fallen, and when I checked my app, I saw that Casey was headed to the restaurant, a fancy steak house on the outside of town.

Perfect.

"I need you to distract someone for me," I told Jace as we changed and headed out of the locker room.

He squinted at me. "Why does that sound so . . . foreboding? But yes, I'm in."

"Why aren't you asking me to help?" said Matty, sounding annoyed.

"Because he needs someone with a big dick, *Matthew*," said Jace, sounding completely serious. "Mine is obviously the better choice."

Matty blinked at him. "It's A HALF INCH."

I snorted. "You have tutoring tonight . . . and morals. I'm trying to be nice. Give you a break for once. Wouldn't want you to be haunted or anything."

Matty wrinkled his nose . . . and shivered as he no doubt thought about our little night in the cemetery. "I can be *nefarious* . . . but I do have tutoring." He side-eyed me. "Real tutoring, might I add."

"See, right there, that was judgy. You need to work on that, Matty, if you're going to be in the Pussy Posse," said Jace, acting like he was giving him really important advice as he slapped him on the back.

Matty flipped him off. "I'm vetoing that one."

"Me too," I agreed, glancing at my app again. They were almost at the restaurant. "But we can discuss that later. We don't have a lot of time."

"Let me know if I need to bail you both out of jail." Matty sighed as we parted ways.

THE WRONG QUARTERBACK 213

I grinned at him. "We'd only need that if I get caught, and that's *obviously* not going to happen."

Matty was shaking his head as Jace and I got into the truck, a small smirk on his lips.

"That guy totally likes nefarious things. He's just lying to himself."

"I agree," I told him, before launching into an explanation of my plans for the evening.

Jace was gaping at me as I finished.

"Let me clarify this real quick. You're going to get your girlfriend kicked out of her dorm by having me distract the front desk so no one sees you breaking in. Then you're going to light a fire so that the sprinklers go off and ruin the room. And *then* you're going to use a fire escape ladder that you bought online to scale down the building so that no one sees you leaving. Did I get that all right?"

"Well, it's not breaking in anymore since I have a key," I corrected him as I pulled into a parking lot a few buildings down from Casey's dorm.

"THAT YOU STOLE AND COPIED."

I winked at him. "I don't see the problem in that sentence."

Jace sighed, blinking his eyes a few times. "Alright, so we're doing this. I didn't have it written on my calendar to add breaking and entering and *fire* to my dossier today, but I can pivot."

I snorted as I got out of the truck and grabbed my bag out of the back. "It's just a little *fire* if that makes you feel better."

"Hey, I didn't say *fire* like it was a bad thing," Jace said as we started walking toward the dorm.

"Except you just said it the same way again."

"Yeah, but I didn't say it like it was a bad thing, so it doesn't matter if I add a little emphasis to it, don't you agree?"

"Sure," I murmured as we reached the edge of the building.

I jumped up and knocked the fixed security camera up so that it wasn't aimed at the door anymore. No one actually manned those things—the college was too cheap—but I didn't want us to be on the camera footage just in case.

"Okay, just go in, do your little charming thing and get her *out* of the building somehow so that I can sneak in."

"Yeah, I've got all that, except I'm going to need you to rephrase that. It's not a *little* charming thing. It's a *big* charming thing," he argued.

"Alright, yes, that. It's a big . . . charming thing."

"That's what she said," he quipped as he began to creep toward the door like we were in some spy movie.

214   C.R. JANE

"What are you doing? That's the opposite of the charming thing."

"Oh, right. Just thought that creeping was part of our villain era."

"We're not villains," I hissed after him as he began walking normally again and had made it to the entrance. "We just don't let things interfere with true love."

"Riiiiiight," Jace said, sounding very sarcastic. "That's all we're doing."

I peeked through one of the windows as Jace leaned over the counter, working his magic as he flirted hard with the girl at the front desk. *He was definitely going to get an orgasm out of this.*

I wasn't going to owe him shit.

Two minutes later, she was somehow following him out of the building. Where he was taking her . . . I had no idea. But at least she wasn't manning the front desk anymore.

Perfect.

Walking inside, I jogged up the stairs, somehow not seeing anyone. Using my key, I let myself in and snapped a quick photo of the room . . . since this was where Casey had given me her virginity . . . and this was the last time I'd be in here.

I moved a few things so they wouldn't get completely ruined, like the photo of her and her brother, and then I reached into my bag and pulled out the rain poncho I'd brought with me, shaking it out before sliding it on and zipping it up to my chin. The plastic crinkled softly as I pulled out the pack of cigarettes. With a quick flick of the lighter, I sparked all of them at once, the orange glow intensifying as they caught, releasing thin streams of smoke almost instantly.

Holding the lit cigarettes under the sprinkler, I watched as the tendrils of smoke curled upward, swirling toward the ceiling like a ghostly signal. The scent thickened in the air, mingling with the faint traces of Casey's perfume that still lingered in the room. I waited, the seconds stretching until finally—*click*—the sprinkler system activated with a sudden jolt. Cold, chemical-laced water sprayed down in thick streams, coating everything in its path.

The fire alarm began blaring out in the hall. *Shit.* I needed to be quick.

Water hit the bed in heavy splatters, seeping into her comforter, her pillows, her neatly stacked textbooks on the nightstand. Her posters curled as the mist reached them, edges darkening, the ink running as they began to peel. The photos Nat had taped up on the wall buckled and blurred, the memories fading under the onslaught. Every trace of her was slowly wiped away.

THE WRONG QUARTERBACK   215

Satisfied, I tossed the smoldering cigarettes onto the floor, watching them sizzle against the wet carpet, then turned to the window. I unlocked it and pushed it up, cool air rushing in. Pulling the fire ladder from my bag, I hooked it onto the windowsill and climbed out, closing the window as much as I could behind me.

Once I reached the ground, I pulled the ladder down and unzipped the poncho, tugging it off in one swift motion, before stuffing both into my bag. With one last glance up at her window, now clouded with condensation from the inside, I jogged into the woods behind the dorm, disappearing into the shadows before anyone could notice.

It wasn't long before my phone buzzed, and Casey's name lit up the screen. I answered on the first ring, keeping my voice calm and steady.

"Parker . . ." Her voice was thick, choked with panic. "Our room—it's completely ruined. Everything's soaked, and campus security found cigarettes. They think we did it. They're saying . . . we're getting kicked out of the dorms."

I could hear the tears, the shock and frustration clinging to every word she spoke. I tried not to smile. Not because I was happy she was upset, of course, but because the plan had come together *perfectly*.

"Stay where you are, baby," I murmured, letting a note of concern lace through my voice. "I'll be right there."

Ten minutes later, I found her waiting outside the dorm, eyes red-rimmed, hugging herself tightly as if she could hold herself together. Nat was next to her, pacing and muttering under her breath, looking as furious as Casey was distraught. As soon as Casey spotted me, she broke from Nat and walked straight into my arms.

"They really think it was us," she said, burying her face into my chest, her words muffled against my shirt. "They won't even listen."

I ran my hand up and down her back, feeling her steady, little by little, against me. "It's going to be alright," I told her softly. "We'll get it figured out."

Nat folded her arms, shaking her head as she glanced between us. "I tried to show them the fucking receipt from dinner, and they weren't interested," she fumed. "I can't believe this is happening."

A moment later, Nat's phone buzzed, and she glanced down at the message, her eyes widening. "Oh, thank God. It's from my friend Mia—she has a spot off campus. She said I can crash with her until things get figured out."

She looked back up at us, her gaze worried. "But what are you going to do, Case?"

I could feel Casey tense against me, and I looked down at her, brushing a strand of hair from her face. "She's going to stay with me," I said easily, slipping my arm around Casey's shoulders.

Casey looked up, her brows knitting together, uncertain. "Parker, I don't know . . . I don't want to just show up and crash your place."

I laughed softly, shaking my head. "Baby, it's not 'crashing' if I want you there." I leaned down, my gaze locking onto hers. "I'd feel a whole lot better knowing you're somewhere safe. Besides—" I let a smirk tug at my lips. "I wanted you to move in with me the moment I saw you."

Nat gave me a knowing look, like she could see right through me, but she still decided to help me out. "It's true, Casey. You'd be way more comfortable at his place than trying to find a place off campus with a stranger. I don't even know if we could find a place right now. And what if they're snack stealers?"

Casey huffed at what must be an inside joke for the two of them, and I was absurdly jealous.

I wanted to be in on all of her inside jokes.

I also needed to buy Nat more steaks because her little spiel had helped.

Casey bit her lip, glancing between us, still hesitant. "But—I mean—are you ready for that? To live with me? It hasn't been that long . . ."

"Ready?" I repeated, feigning offense with a playful smirk. "Trust me, I'm not going to be complaining." I tilted my head, lowering my voice so only she could hear. "It will just give me a chance to convince you that you should stay . . . forever."

She glanced at me and mouthed "crazy," but I could see I was wearing her down.

"Just say yes, baby. There are a lot of things you should say no to in life, but *this* is not one of them." I reached down and grabbed her hand, bringing it to my lips for a kiss—because for some reason she melted every time I did that. "Look, stay for a night or two. See how it feels. And if you're not comfortable, we'll find another place. But right now, I just want you to give it a chance."

Casey looked at Nat, who gave an encouraging nod, and finally, she let out a sigh. "Alright . . . just for a few days. Until I can figure something else out."

A small victory. I wrapped my arm around her, pulling her close. "Perfect," I murmured.

THE WRONG QUARTERBACK **217**

My phone buzzed at that moment, and I pulled it out, smirking when I saw the text from Jace.

> **Jace: We are definitely in our villain era, QB.**

Maybe we were.

CHAPTER 25

CASEY

I was boarding the airplane with Nat, getting ready to fly to Parker's away game in Alabama. It had only been a day since the dorm incident, and I'd somehow found myself living with him. But we'd only spent one blissful night together before he'd had to fly out with the team.

Nat pushed me to the window seat and sat in the aisle. "I'm under strict orders that men are not to associate with you," she said, her eyes watchful, like a guy was going to jump out at any moment in first class and try to get me.

"No one's going to try to 'associate' with me," I said exasperatedly. "I've literally been a nerd who plays piano her entire life. There's been no *associating*."

Nat giggled like I'd just said the most hilarious thing she'd ever heard. Then she took my hand and leaned close, staring into my eyes like she was trying to hypnotize me. "Someday, you're going to wake up and take your power. You're going to see what everyone else sees. Why Gray wanders around campus all day like he's in a daze because he lost you. Why a literal walking god thinks you're the best thing he's ever seen . . . and he's not wrong. Why I decided that you're my bestest friend . . ." She grinned. "And let's be real, I have extremely good taste, so that should be the biggest factor in this equation."

I laughed and then gave her a quick hug . . . because how could I not?

Nat continued to do her weird watching thing until everyone had boarded. Then she laid her head back against her seat.

"Phew, being a bodyguard is exhausting. Thank fuck your hot boyfriend shelled out for first class, Case. I need to rest."

THE WRONG QUARTERBACK 219

I snorted and read the text he'd just sent me.

> Parker: I miss you. And he definitely misses you. Hurry to me quick.

I typed out a quick response, hurrying because I was a rule follower, and they'd already asked us to put our phones in airplane mode.

> Me: Tell him I miss him too.

"Who's *him*?" Nat asked, reading my text over my shoulder. She paused for a moment. "Oh, that's a dick joke, isn't it?"

I winked at her, trying to be cool while I blushed. "Maybe," I finally said.

"I need to get dicked," she humphed as I put my phone away. "I'm going through a dry spell."

"Didn't you hook up with that hot lacrosse player two nights ago?"

She pressed her palm against my mouth. "Don't call another guy hot. Parker will somehow hear you. And I like that guy. I don't want him to disappear."

I rolled my eyes.

"Parker's not going to make anyone disappear."

Nat smirked. "You think that. But it's always the hot ones who are crazy."

I laughed, because that was probably true.

Nothing seemed too crazy about Parker yet, though, besides the fact that he was crazy *perfect*.

He'd been so sweet about my dorm, helping me unpack what I'd been able to salvage—in his room and then going out to buy ice cream to celebrate the fact that I was there with him.

"Ugh, you guys are too fucking cute," Nat growled, but there was a twinkle in her eye that said she didn't mind.

"*He's* too fucking cute," I murmured, sitting back with a sigh.

And I couldn't wait to see him again.

The concrete floor of the stands was shaking, the kind that rattled your bones as you stood there. Every seat was packed, a sea of orange and crimson. I clutched the edge of my seat, my fingers tight around the armrest, barely breathing as I watched Parker line up again. Alabama had sacked him twice already, each hit harder than the last. I could still feel the thud of my heart in my throat from the last time he went down . . . and took forever to get up. Somehow he'd kept pushing, though, dragging the team down the field inch by inch until they were close enough for the kicker to line it up.

"He'd better not fucking miss this." Nat's voice cut through the noise beside me. She was on the edge of her seat too, biting her lip, her leg bouncing like she was trying to shake the nerves off.

I swallowed, eyes glued to the field.

The kicker jogged out, positioning himself as he readied for the kick. Alabama fans were going insane, the sound of the crowd becoming earsplitting. I hoped Parker liked hearing aids in his women, because I might be needing them after this season.

Nat and I were nothing but a massive inhale of anticipation as we watched, waiting. The snap was perfect. The holder set the ball down in one smooth motion, and the kicker's foot connected with a sharp, clean thud. And the ball soared. My breath locked up, frozen as I tracked its arc. The ball sliced through the air, barely clearing the line of defenders reaching up to block it, and I held on to that breath, waiting, hoping as it flew . . .

Right through the uprights.

The Tennessee fans exploded, and Nat screamed right in my ear, throwing her arms around me. I gave up on trying to save my hearing and joined in, shouting as loud as I could, both of us gripping each other in a wild, jumping hug.

I searched the huddle of celebrating players for Parker. Even from here I could see his gorgeous smile as he slapped the kicker on the back.

"You know what I don't understand," Nat mused suddenly. I raised an eyebrow at her, keeping half my attention on Parker . . . because how could I not.

"Why does the kicker wear a pad and helmet in the first place?"

"Huh?"

"I mean all he does is kick a ball. It's literally a penalty for the other team to touch him."

"Well—" I began, but she was making some good points.

"He should just wear some kind of beautiful costume or something that shows the team's personality. Don't you think?" she asked.

I thought about what she'd said . . . and then burst into laughter at the thought of the Tennessee kicker wearing some kind of ice dancer costume in the middle of the field.

THE WRONG QUARTERBACK   221

We were all on our feet, screaming at the top of our lungs as the clock ticked down. This was it. We either scored here, or we lost. I leaned forward, my heart pounding as I watched Parker on the field, intense and focused. Besides the grass stains on his jersey, you'd never be able to tell how rough the game had been. Parker glanced at Jace and barked something.

The ball snapped, and Parker dropped back, scanning the field. Alabama's defense surged forward, their blitz closing in. Parker sidestepped one linebacker, narrowly avoiding another sack, and kept his eyes downfield.

Just as the pocket started to collapse, Jace broke free from his defender. With a quick flick of his wrist, Parker launched the ball in Jace's direction, low and fast, cutting through the air straight into Jace's hands.

Jace caught it effortlessly, barely slowing down before he took off down the field. My heart was in my throat, watching as he dodged one last tackle and crossed into the end zone.

Touchdown.

Tigers win!

I watched as he danced around, soaking in the cheers, a smug look on his face. Then, instead of celebrating with the rest of the team, Jace turned . . . and headed straight for me.

Or at least it seemed like he was heading my way. I glanced to the left and right of me, but since we were surrounded by Alabama fans, there weren't a lot of options for Jace to be going.

Jace jogged over, holding the ball out like he was about to crown me queen of the game, a ridiculous, sexy grin on his face. "This one's for you, sweetheart," he said, his voice low and teasing, full of laughter.

I blinked at him, not sure what to do. I hesitantly reached out to grab the ball, right as the stadium's roar grew even louder. I glanced beyond Jace only to see Parker appear out of nowhere, barreling into him and tackling him to the ground.

Right there. In front of the entire stadium. And I was pretty sure everywhere ESPN was being aired.

There was a beat of silence, everyone watching as Parker pinned Jace to the turf.

And then the crowd went nuts.

Was this some kind of stunt? It seemed against how Parker usually behaved in these games, but since I hadn't exactly been a Tennessee fan before this season—I could be watching a time-honored Tennessee tradition—but I wasn't confident in that guess.

Jace was laughing like a maniac, barely fighting Parker off.

222   C.R. JANE

Parker pushed him back down on the turf and then jumped up, pulling his own jersey over his head and striding over to me.

"Put this on," he growled, in a feral, crazy-sounding voice as he jumped up and stood on the railing in front of me.

I was already wearing a jersey with his name on it, but I let him slide his game jersey over my head. He gripped my chin and kissed me. Hard. His tongue sliding into my mouth, claiming me.

"Mine," he rasped when he pulled away, staring into my eyes like I needed to get the message.

I nodded, completely in shock as he gave me one more kiss and jumped down, ignoring Jace who was still laughing hysterically nearby.

I lost him in the crowd of players and coaches and media staff.

"Holy fuck," Nat said, gripping my arm. "Please tell me his dick is just as good as the rest of him. And please tell me he's just as growly as that in bed."

I blinked a few times, still staring after where Parker had disappeared in the sea of people.

"It's all just as good," I murmured, heat flashing through my insides.

"I'm so fucking happy for you," Nat responded, beginning to dance around.

A smile slid across my lips.

I was happy for me, too.

Parker

My teammates kept shooting me glances, like I'd lost my mind.

But I didn't care.

Was it great that I'd tackled my best friend on national television? No, no it was not.

Did my brain shut off when I saw him flirting with her and giving her the game ball?

Yes, yes it did.

All of that was for a future me to deal with, though, because there was only one thing driving me right then.

Need.

I needed her.

I needed to feel her perfect cunt choking my cock.

I needed to slide my dick down her throat and hear her gagging.

I needed to mark her all over with my cum, spread it all over her skin so there was no doubt.

THE WRONG QUARTERBACK   **223**

She was mine.

I grabbed one of the assistant trainers.

"See that girl over there?" I asked, pointing to where Casey was talking to Nat . . . looking like the fucking hottest thing I'd ever seen in my game jersey.

"Yeah," he said, sounding a little scared of me.

"I need you to grab her and bring her to where we watched film right before the game, the small room near the locker room."

He blinked at me. "Ummm, you want me to bring her there?"

"Yes," I said, trying to keep the annoyance out of my voice. I didn't want to scare him any more than I already had.

"Okay, yeah, sure, Parker, I'll get her."

I resisted the urge to tell him not to touch her, hoping that was a no-brainer. The reasonable part of my brain had shut off, and all that was left was the animalistic instinct to fuck and mark what was mine.

"Hey, QB, you alright?" Matty asked, sounding amused. "I thought you were going to kill Jace . . . what's our game plan on how to explain your bout of temporary insanity today?"

"That's just our new way of celebrating," I said, beginning to jog toward the tunnel.

"Where are you going?" he called out behind me. "You're supposed to be interviewing with *SportsCenter*!"

"Fill in for me, will ya, bud?" I answered over my shoulder.

I didn't stop running until I reached the door where I'd asked the assistant to take her. I didn't have much time. Any minute now, one of the coaches would be coming to rip me a new one. I had to fuck her first.

I threw open the door, and she jumped, laughing as she put a hand to her chest. "You scared me—" She giggled, her words cut off as I captured her mouth, gripping her chin as my tongue slid between her lips. The sexy little moans she was making were going to undo me.

She was fucking perfect.

"Sorry, baby," I murmured against her lips. "I need you. Now."

"What? Here?" She gasped.

I couldn't get any more words out. I had to taste her. I had to coat my face with her scent. I needed to drown in her pussy.

Dropping to my knees, I tugged her shoes and socks off, yanking at her leggings and thong after that. She fell forward, her hands bracing on my shoulders as she helped me remove her clothes.

"Spread your legs," I said roughly.

224 C.R. JANE

Casey leaned back against the wall, spreading her legs wider.

I dove in, breathing in her sweet scent. I licked her folds, pulling her leg over my shoulder so I could get deeper into her cunt. My tongue pushed into her, fucking in and out. I licked down, and she stiffened as I rimmed her asshole.

"I can't wait to get inside there," I growled, my voice muffled as I bit down on her inner thigh, marking her like I wanted.

She yelped, and I grinned, probably looking like a madman as I licked at the bite marks before returning to her sweet pussy. Sucking hard on her clit, I pushed two fingers inside, rubbing against her G-spot as I forced her into an orgasm.

"Paaarker," she cried, and I lapped up the drops of her sweetness sliding down her thigh.

Hopefully that was enough to get her ready, because I couldn't wait any longer to get inside her.

I stood up, catching her before she fell, my hands sliding under the jerseys she was wearing, pushing beneath her bra so I could squeeze her breasts.

"You look so hot like this, baby, wearing my jersey, your pussy wet and naked just for me."

I released her breasts and pressed her against the wall, lifting her legs up. "Wrap them around me," I ordered, my voice almost unrecognizable; it was so rough.

Using one arm to hold her up, I fumbled with my pants. "Fuck," I growled as I finally undid them, and my cock sprung free, the head already dripping with my cum.

I quickly lined it up with her slit and lunged forward, groaning.

I was lost after that, thrusting in and out of her, driven by nothing but how good it felt to sink inside her cunt.

"That's it. Choke my dick, my dirty girl. Take my big cock."

I rutted into her mindlessly, telling her everything I wanted to do to her body.

Her whimpers coated my skin, and I slammed my lips against hers, wanting to capture those whimpers inside me.

I forced my hand between us, rubbing on her clit while I praised her for being my good, perfect girl.

"Come for me," I begged, feeling myself getting close.

Her lips parted from mine with a gasp, her pussy clenching around me, her legs shaking as she came.

"Yes, yes, yes," she panted.

THE WRONG QUARTERBACK 225

I pulled out as I came, spraying her pussy and legs with my cum. My cock jerked again and again, until she was coated with me.

I was heaving as I feverishly rubbed the cum into her skin, making sure I was all over her.

"Don't you dare wash any of this off," I rasped against her lips. Her hands were gripping my pads, her body trembling against mine as her breath left her throat in sexy little gasps.

A sharp banging on the door had us both jumping.

"Coach is coming," Jace called through the door, his voice filled with the same laughter he'd had on the field.

I forced my still-hard dick back into my pants and quickly began helping her to pull her leggings back up. The sight of my cum spread all over her skin just made me want to fuck her all over again. Her pussy was red and swollen, though, and between my bite marks and the redness from my stubble . . . my baby needed a break.

"Are you okay?" I finally got out after I'd helped her put on her shoes.

"Yes," she said after a moment. "That was—"

"Perfect?" I asked hopefully, knowing that I'd lost my mind and worked her harder than I ever would have intended.

She pushed some of her hair back, moving off the wall and swaying a little bit, and I winced, expecting the worst.

"Definitely perfect," she finally said as her hands slid to my chest. I'd never seen her more beautiful. Her hair was a mess, her lips were swollen. And now I could picture my cum coating her thighs.

Fucking beautiful.

"But you should probably go right now before you get in any more trouble," she said.

"I love you." I breathed, kissing her a few more times because I couldn't help it.

"I love you, too," she replied, and after telling her how to get back to Nat, I reluctantly left the room, wishing I could bring her with me.

Jace was leaning against the wall outside the door. "Are you feeling better about being *pussy-conquered*?" he asked with a grin. "Less likely to punch me in the face?"

I huffed at him and shook my head, grinning as we walked to the locker room, where I was no doubt about to be reamed by the coaching staff.

"Definitely *pussy-conquered*," I finally responded. "And definitely better."

He opened the door, but I grabbed his jersey, stopping him from going in.

226   C.R. JANE

Jace stared at me uneasily. "Don't ever touch her again," I said, threatening my best friend for the first time ever.

Jace's eyes widened, and he nodded. "Noted, QB. It won't happen again. I like my nuts where they are."

I released him and clapped him on the back. "Glad we have that understanding."

My smile was wide as we walked into the locker room.

Out of all the games I'd ever played, this was my favorite one.

CHAPTER 26

CASEY

I felt the coolness of the arena air hit my face as Parker led me inside, his hand firm around mine. The low hum of the crowd around us, the squeak of skates on ice, and the sharp clink of sticks against the glass made the nerves in my stomach tighten.

I kept my eyes on the ground as we walked down the steps to our seats, trying to ignore the fluttering in my chest. Meeting Walker—Parker's brother—felt like a big deal. I wasn't sure what Walker was going to think of me, but the pressure was enough to make my palms sweat.

"He's going to love you," Parker murmured in my ear, because he seemed to always be able to read my mind. "But obviously not as much as me," he amended, like he was suddenly worried about that.

I laughed softly, and he winked at me, and my stomach did literal flips. I wasn't sure that I could ever get used to the sight of him. It felt like I had woken up in the best dream ever every time I looked at him—one that couldn't possibly be real.

We settled into our seats right in the front row, and I took it all in, shivering as I adjusted to the chill and the distant scent of popcorn and stale beer. The ice stretched out in front of us, a perfect white expanse with the blue and red lines slashed across it. Players in blue and white jerseys skated back and forth, passing pucks, some stopping to tap their sticks against the boards, sending shivers up the glass. They moved fast, like they were floating on some invisible current, each movement sharp, powerful, like the ice itself was their stage.

I caught sight of one guy, balancing on his skates while doing a full stretch, his legs spread wide, rocking his hips as he leaned forward. The

228   C.R. JANE

stretch was . . . well, it looked very . . . sexual. I bit my lip, trying not to laugh. Parker glanced out to where I was looking.

"Fuck," he growled, quickly placing a hand over my eyes. "Maybe bringing you down here was a bad idea."

"I mean it's honestly good that you don't include that in your warm-ups. I'd have to fend off even more women," I joked.

He smacked a kiss on my lips. "Other women don't exist anymore."

I rolled my eyes, but inside I was giddy.

Because I was becoming more and more sure every day . . . that he actually meant it.

There was a knock on the glass, and we glanced over to see a guy in full goalie gear, grinning from ear to ear beneath his helmet.

Fuck. This was Walker.

Parker grinned as he stood up. "What's up, Parkie-Poo," Walker said through the glass as he took off his helmet. My eyes widened.

The Davis family was blessed.

I had to look away for a second because the combined effect of the two of them was too much for me.

There should be a worldwide revolt, where all the men on Earth send in complaints to whatever gods had created them . . . because they'd definitely gotten cheated.

Walker had messy brown hair and intense blue eyes that were just a shade darker than Parker's. I understood now where his *Disney* nickname had come from. He looked just like a Disney prince.

His beauty was intimidating because it also meant that Parker was going to get even better looking . . . which I hadn't thought was possible.

"Are you going to introduce me?" Walker asked, winking at me.

"Hey, no winking," Parker snapped, covering my eyes again. I sighed as I pushed his hand away and saw that Walker's lips were curled up in amusement.

"Olivia loves when I wink," Walker commented.

"Does Lincoln?" Parker smirked. Walker sighed and rolled his eyes.

Another player skated up, stopping suddenly and spraying ice all over Walker.

"Whoops," the new guy said, grinning as he nodded at Parker. "What's up, Little Davis?" He was also freaking gorgeous, with black hair and glimmering, mischievous green eyes.

"Living the dream, Lancaster," Parker replied, obviously at ease with this guy too.

THE WRONG QUARTERBACK   229

My eyes widened when I realized this was Ari, one of Walker's best friends. Parker had told me all about Walker's buddies and how they were in something called "the Circle of Trust."

I'd asked him what that was, and he said nobody knew. I guess I was never going to find out, because I wasn't sure I could form normal words around these guys.

"Is Disney over here simping again?" Ari asked with a sigh. "Because he's been insufferable. Ever since Golden God over there scored his last goal."

"My brother is always simping after Linc," Parker said. "I'm surprised Olivia isn't jealous."

Walker rolled his eyes at Ari's comment, and it looked so similar to how I'd seen Parker react to Jace that I couldn't help but laugh.

"Sorry, I have taste," Walker drawled, glancing at me again. "Don't believe anything they say about me. It's all lies."

A third player arrived then, and it was definitely obvious not only who it was, but why Walker was his simp.

Lincoln Daniels *was* a Golden God, and possibly the only man who could rival Parker in good looks.

Parker's hand went in front of my eyes again.

"Just in case," he whispered.

The buzzer sounded before I could say anything else.

The game was insane. It was a different kind of rush from Parker's football games—the tension building with every second, every shot on goal, every collision that sent players flying into the boards. There was also the fact that they hit each other. Two legit fistfights broke out in the first period alone. That almost never happened in other sports.

The crowd was relentless, too—chants, clapping, the whole arena practically buzzing as the clock wound down. The game was tied until the last few minutes, but then the Knights surged, each play faster, more aggressive, until, with just seconds left, a defenseman, Camden James, ended up scoring—a position that Parker explained didn't score that often.

The final buzzer sounded, and the place exploded. Walker's teammates piled onto Camden, a mess of sticks, pads, and shouting.

"What did you think?" Parker asked as we made our way down the tunnel where we would meet up with Walker and his wife for a bit before we began our three-hour drive back to campus.

"It was amazing," I told him, and he frowned.

"But not as good as one of my football games, right?" he asked, a hint of a frantic whine in his voice.

I grinned. "Not even close," I told him, even though it was a little bit of a lie. Hockey was pretty awesome.

Once by the locker room, Parker introduced me to Walker's wife Olivia, and I almost fainted when I realized that she was the super famous *pop star* Olivia who I'd been listening to for years. The one that had been placed in a conservatorship and whose songs made me cry.

It was all I could do to try and play it cool and not scream. By the amused glances Parker was giving me, I was not doing a good job of it.

Once Walker came out, we went up to a quieter lounge in the arena, and the four of us hung out for a bit, laughing and trading stories. Olivia filled me in on all the team gossip, and Walker made sure to tease Parker constantly, clearly enjoying my reactions every time he let some embarrassing detail slip.

The moments flew by, and I almost forgot that I hadn't known the two of them for my entire life.

All too soon, Walker and Olivia had to leave. Olivia gave me a huge hug. "I'm so happy he found his person," she murmured, winking at me after she'd let me go.

Her words made my heart ache in a weird, unexpected way, and as they left, I had a pang of sadness. I'd only just met them, but somehow it felt like saying goodbye to family.

"Told you they would love you," Parker murmured as he wrapped me in a hug before we walked out of the arena to the truck.

"I—I loved them too," I murmured, and his answering grin was almost heart-stopping.

As we drove home, all I kept thinking was how perfectly our pieces seemed to fit and that maybe . . . soulmates really were real.

CHAPTER 27

PARKER

The second I walked into Professor Hendrick's history class, I could feel the chill in the air—and it wasn't just from the air conditioning. She barely looked at me as I took my seat, but the rigid set of her shoulders and the way her eyes flicked coldly in my direction said enough. Something was off. I didn't have time to dwell on it before she launched into her lecture.

"Ms. Larsen, what's the significance of the Battle of Actium?" Her voice cut through the classroom, icy like a winter's wind.

Casey's head snapped up, eyes wide. She stumbled over a couple of words, clearly blindsided; the professor never did her lectures like that.

"Uh... the... Octavian—um... defeated Mark Antony?"

Professor Hendrick arched a brow. "Barely a complete answer," she said, voice dripping with disdain. "Try reading the assigned materials next time, Ms. Larsen."

I clenched my fists under the desk, trying to keep my cool. I didn't like anyone talking to Casey like that. Hendrick moved on, but her gaze kept drifting back to Casey, tossing her another question every few minutes. Each time, Casey looked more flustered, her face reddening.

"Mr. Davis," Hendrick finally said, her voice dripping with authority as she looked straight at me. "Do you plan on staring daggers at me the entire class, or do you have something to contribute?"

I leaned back, giving her a calm smile. "Just interested in the lecture, Professor. You're... keeping it lively today."

There were a few snickers in the class, and her eyes narrowed, but she didn't respond. Instead, she threw another question at Casey, who barely

232   C.R. JANE

managed an answer before the professor dismissed her with a wave of her hand, as if she were bored.

When class finally ended, Hendrick's voice rang out over the noise of shuffling papers and closing laptops. "Mr. Davis. A word."

Casey shot me a worried look as she packed up, but I gave her a nod. "I'll be fine," I murmured. She hesitated but walked out, leaving me alone with Hendrick in the now-empty classroom.

"Take a seat," she said, her tone still frigid. I dropped into the nearest chair, watching her fold her arms, her stare as hard as granite.

"Is there a problem, Professor?" I asked, keeping my tone polite.

She tapped her fingers against her arm, each one landing like a metronome, and then she went right in for the kill. "Rumor has it you're seeing Ms. Larsen. I think we've had enough conversations about why that's a bad idea . . . have we not?"

I raised an eyebrow. "Rumor has it? Didn't know you kept up with campus gossip, Professor," I responded lightly.

"Careful, Mr. Davis," she snapped, her voice dropping to a steely whisper. "I'm not here to banter with you. I'm here to warn you."

"Warn me?" I asked, leaning back, crossing my arms. "About what, exactly?"

She sighed, leaning closer, her gaze piercing. "You think you're untouchable right now. But you're sorely mistaken. You think fraternizing with a freshman isn't going to come back to bite you?"

I fought the urge to roll my eyes.

Her lips pressed together in a tight line. "You're a talented quarterback, Mr. Davis. You have a bright future. But if you keep this up, your record will be tainted."

I shrugged, trying not to let her see just how little her words fazed me. "I think there are always ways around rules, Professor. Don't you think?"

I was glad there weren't any knives in the room because she kind of looked like she wanted to kill me after that statement.

Since I had no intention of being discreet about how I felt about Casey, I'd been preparing for this conversation, asking around if anyone had any dirt on Professor Hendrick for me to work with. But so far, I hadn't found anything.

"I guess if it comes down to it, I can just resign as your TA," I told her. "But I'm still trying to figure out why this is such a big deal. It's not like I'm a teacher screwing a student . . ."

THE WRONG QUARTERBACK 233

"Resigning isn't going to stop me from informing the admin that you broke the rules. I have enough power at this school to *touch* even you, Mr. Quarterback."

Jace would have had a joke for what she'd just said, but right now I was really annoyed. Between what Coach had said in that meeting the other week . . . and now this, I wasn't excited about all of these people trying to interfere with my relationship.

"I've seen far too many girls ruined by boys like you, Mr. Davis," she sneered. "Boys who think that they are above the rules. Who think that the world and everything in it is their plaything. I promised myself long ago that I wasn't going to facilitate it."

She clasped her hands together. "This is your final warning, Mr. Davis. I expect you to arrive at our next class with a changed attitude . . . and a changed relationship status."

This was bullshit.

I didn't say another word to her, knowing anything I said right then would make it worse.

Casey was in her next class, so I went home, kicking off my shoes and throwing myself onto my couch. I rubbed a hand over my face, trying to think. Hendrick had made it clear she was coming for me. She wasn't the type to bluff, either. She'd had a TA two years ago who she'd gotten kicked out of school. Obviously he hadn't been Tennessee's star quarterback, but it told me she wasn't playing around. If she went to Admin, it would be a headache no matter what. And if she tried to reach out to the scouts . . .

I wasted the next hour trying to figure out what to do . . . when I noticed it: an envelope lying neatly on the coffee table.

It was black, heavy paper with the Sphinx symbol pressed in red ink on the front. Right below, in red, sharp letters, it read, *Courtesy of the Sphinx*. My pulse jumped.

I needed to invest in better security for the house.

I tore open the envelope and slid out a stack of glossy photos. As soon as I flipped to the first one, I froze, then broke into a grin. Hendrick. Younger, but unmistakably her, with that no-nonsense haircut. And she wasn't just posing for some faculty photo, either.

No, she was wrapped up with another professor, locked in a kiss that was way more than friendly. Her hands were tangled in his shirt, his hand gripping her waist. I flicked through the rest, and each photo got worse—more intense, more incriminating.

234   C.R. JANE

Because the other professor in that photo . . . was very married.

I grinned. I'd been wondering when the Sphinx would show it was worth anything besides annoying me. I guess they'd decided to give me a little taste of what they could do, of the power they held. I would think about the fact that they'd known I needed this information in the first place at a later date.

Chuckling, I let the pictures fall loosely in my hands. Hendrick was done.

———————

I walked into Professor Hendrick's office, feeling really good about life. She looked up as I entered, her gaze sharp, a trace of smugness in her eyes.

"Here to beg, Mr. Davis?" she asked, her voice dripping with condescension.

"No," I responded, my voice low, steady. "I'm here to hear *you* beg."

I tossed the photos onto her desk, letting them spread out for full effect.

Her face blanched, the color draining as her eyes darted over the photos, widening with each one. She looked horrified, her voice catching as she whispered, "Where did you get these?"

I leaned forward, making sure she could see the smirk on my face.

"The Sphinx sends its regards."

I didn't think it was possible, but she got even paler, suddenly swaying in place like she was going to pass out.

"I expect my recommendation letter by Friday. No excuses, no delays," I said mockingly, repeating what she told her classes all the time.

She stared at me, eyes wide, like I was a monster she'd never seen coming.

Turning on my heel, I headed out, whistling as I walked down the hall.

CHAPTER 28

PARKER

"What does the horny toad say?" Jace asked as we walked down the sidewalk in front of our houses.

I grinned tiredly, wishing I was already in my bed. We had Georgia coming up next game, and I was pretty sure that Coach was trying to kill us with how hard he'd been working us in practice. We couldn't play if we were dead, but he didn't seem to care about that.

"What?" I responded, pushing back some wet hair that had fallen in my face.

"Rub it," he answered, his eyebrows going up and down, clearly so proud of himself.

Matty and I both snorted, and Jace smirked proudly.

"I think you're getting better," I told him as we got to my house.

"I resent that, QB. I've always been good. I think Casey's just actually given you a sense of humor."

I scoffed and waved at them as they continued to their place next door. Casey was at a Dean's Dinner for freshman students, and then she was going over to Nat's new place to have cake for Nat's birthday. Somehow I was going to have to survive the next four or five hours without her.

Unlocking the front door, I dropped my bag inside and groaned as I stretched my arms over my head. *Fuck.* Seriously, I wasn't sure if I was going to be able to throw any passes tomorrow. Walking into the kitchen, I opened the refrigerator door to grab a bottle of water . . . when something shiny on the counter caught my attention.

A dark glass bottle sat on the countertop, labeled only with two words: *Drink Me*, like I'd stepped into a demented version of *Alice in Wonderland*.

236   C.R. JANE

Right next to it was an envelope stamped with the unmistakable symbol of the Sphinx.

Motherfucker.

My stomach tightened. The gift they'd left after their last breaking and entering ended up being a good thing, but something told me this letter wasn't going to be my favorite.

There was also the matter that my fucking cameras hadn't gone off when someone had broken into the house, *yet again*. I was going to have to upgrade. Heads needed to roll at the security company I'd hired. Obviously their system didn't work.

I sighed and then decided to get it over with, grabbing the envelope and tearing it open, my eyes scanning the letter inside.

This is a test of trust. The Sphinx is a brotherhood beyond any other. To be a brotherhood, there must be trust. To proceed, drink the contents of the bottle. Do not question. Do not share this information. This is a solitary task. Once you've done it, wait.

That was it. No explanation, no hint of what the drink actually was or what it might do to me. Nothing. Just a command to drink it and wait.

These fuckers were really stepping up their game. I don't know what I'd expected when they'd pulled that bag off my head and told me I was going to be tested . . . but what I'd experienced so far had been way beyond anything I'd thought of then. I think I would rather dig up another body than do this.

I read through the note again. I'd heard a rumor that a woman had been allowed in their Darkwood College chapter, so they might want to update their whole *brotherhood* lingo. I also didn't trust any of them worth a shit . . . but if I wanted in with these people, I was going to have to drink this.

Grabbing the bottle, I walked to our bedroom, the sheets still messed up from where I'd fucked Casey before practice. I closed my eyes for a moment, breathing her in. I loved that she was everywhere now. That every part of our house smelled like her. I hadn't known what this place had been missing, but now I realized it's what every place would have been missing my entire life.

Her.

I took my phone out, propping it in the corner of the room and setting it to record . . . just in case. Whatever happened, I wanted some kind of record.

With the camera rolling, I picked up the bottle, twisting the cap open. The liquid inside was clear, odorless. I had no idea what it was. Could be water. Or poison. Or anything in between.

What the fuck was I doing?

THE WRONG QUARTERBACK   237

I moved to my bed, sitting down, bottle in hand. Every part of me was screaming in protest that this was a bad idea. But I'd come this far. At this point it felt like some kind of challenge, like the Sphinx against me. The competitor in me couldn't let them win.

I just hoped that it didn't cost me that much to cross the finish line.

I tipped the bottle back, wincing as I swallowed the liquid. The taste was sharp, a slight burn that didn't give me any hints as to what it was.

I waited. And waited. And nothing happened.

Okay, maybe that's where the trust part came in. I drank it. And I was done.

That was easy. I breathed out a big sigh of relief and stood up—my head swam, the room spinning around me. My knees buckled, and I hit the bed hard, my vision going black in an instant.

I blinked up at the ceiling, feeling like I'd been out for days, my head disoriented and heavy. My brain struggled to piece together where I was . . . why my mouth was so dry . . . and why my limbs felt like dead weight. Had I fallen asleep after practice?

The faint creak of the front door snapped me out of my haze. "Parker?" Casey's voice called, sweet and perfect. It cut through the fog in my brain. I cursed under my breath, reaching around, searching for my phone—I'd told her I'd pick her up. I must've passed out way longer than I thought.

Before I could sit up, she appeared in the doorway, one eyebrow raised in amusement. "Hey, sleepyhead," she teased, leaning against the frame. "Are you okay?"

I managed a rough smile, fighting the pounding in my skull. "Yeah, just . . . long practice. I must've dozed off."

As I pulled myself up, a sharp sting shot across my chest. I winced, lifting my shirt out of reflex, and froze. There was a white bandage taped across my chest.

"What is that?" Casey asked as she stepped closer, her eyes widening. "You didn't tell me you were getting a new tattoo."

"That's because I didn't," I muttered, peeling back the bandage. Beneath it, the unmistakable symbol of the Sphinx was inked deep into my skin, black and intricate, right over my heart. The whole night hit me then, memories crashing against my brain: the bottle, the letter, the way I'd blacked out.

I bolted out of bed, ignoring the ache in my chest, and went straight for my phone, still recording in the corner. Fast-forwarding through the footage,

I watched myself slump over on the bed, completely out cold. And then, a minute later, the door to the bedroom cracked open, and two guys in the same masks as what the members had been wearing the night I'd been kidnapped from my room slipped inside, one of them carrying a tattoo kit.

Casey gasped beside me, watching as one masked guy started setting up, his gloved hands precise and clinical, while the other one scanned the room, idly snooping around. At one point his masked face appeared in front of the camera, and he grinned before continuing his perusal.

The guy with the needle leaned over me, adjusting the angle like he'd done this a thousand times before. He started working on my chest while I lay there like a slab of stone, oblivious. The needle bit into my skin, and I watched, sickened, as he carefully inked the Sphinx symbol, marking me as theirs.

The video played on until, finally, the tattoo was done. The guy in the mask pressed the bandage over it, gathered up his supplies, and gave a nod to the other, and within seconds, they were gone. All that was left on the screen was me, unconscious and oblivious, a new mark branded into my skin.

Casey's hand came to her mouth, her eyes darting from the screen to my chest. "Parker . . . what the hell was that?"

I ran a hand over the fresh ink, my chest tightening. "That, baby, was my final trial for the Sphinx."

CHAPTER 29

CASEY

"That's so fucking good," Parker growled as I lapped at the pre-cum beading at his head. I felt his breath on my core, and a second later he was dragging his tongue along my slit.

I whimpered and sucked harder, trying to get more of his length in my mouth, and he moaned.

No one had ever told me that giving head could make you feel powerful, but the way Parker reacted every time my tongue even got near his dick made me feel that way.

"That's it. Suck my cock, baby," he groaned as he pushed his tongue inside me, and his fingers worked my clit.

I never thought I could do this, grind my core on someone's face while I licked and sucked their dick . . . but I was having no problem with it now.

We couldn't get enough of each other. Morning, noon, and night . . . even between classes. If we had a spare second, he was inside me.

His tongue slipped up to my ass, and he licked around the sensitive ring before the tip of his finger began stretching the muscle.

I lowered my head, trying different angles until I could work him further down my throat, all while trying not to die of pleasure as his finger pushed deeper into my ass.

I gagged around his tip, and he chuckled against my slit.

"Love the sound of you choking on my cock," he breathed as he pushed his finger all the way in, stimulating nerve endings I hadn't known I had.

I cried out, freezing in place as he began thrusting his finger in and out.

"Keep going, baby," he ordered roughly.

240 C.R. JANE

I whimpered but obediently sucked as hard as I could, somehow sliding more of him down my throat.

"That's it. You're such a good girl," he praised. "I want to fuck your throat. Will you do that for me, sweetheart?"

"Yes." I gasped, but just as he thrust forward into my mouth, I came, sparks of light exploding behind my closed eyes as my muscles convulsed with waves of pleasure. I moaned around his dick, my hips fucking against his tongue as he continued to work me.

"Fuck. That was hot," he murmured roughly . . . as he somehow worked another finger in my ass.

"I can't," I cried, my words lost as his dick surged past my lips, and he began to thrust against my face.

His free hand tangled in my hair, holding me in place as he fucked my mouth.

"Take my cock. Take it. Fuck. Yes, relax. Just a little more. There, that's it."

Another inch slipped down my throat. "Yes, yes. You're my perfect, sweet girl. I'm coming . . . fuck."

A few hard thrusts later, and his hot cum was shooting down my throat. My hands gripped his ass as I swallowed as much as I could, ribbons of it dripping down my chin.

And somehow his fingers and tongue continued to work me, never letting up until I was gasping through another orgasm while still trying to drink down his cum.

Parker slowly drew back, sliding his cock out of my mouth and moving so that we were face-to-face.

"Fuck, that was hot," he said, giving me a huge, sexy grin. He pressed a scorching kiss on my lips, and it was erotic thinking of him tasting himself in my mouth while I tasted myself in his.

"I love you, baby," he murmured, pressing his forehead against mine. My breath was still rough, and I was already tired from my two orgasms.

"Mmmh," I breathed as his tongue once again dipped into my mouth.

I fell asleep listening to him tell me how much he loved me, a *very* satisfied girl.

"Casey!" Gray's voice echoed down the hallway as I walked to my next class, a little too loud, and definitely a little too close. My pulse kicked up, and I sped up, keeping my eyes fixed straight ahead. I didn't need this right now. The last thing I wanted was a conversation with him.

THE WRONG QUARTERBACK   241

It was like he had some sixth sense about finding me alone, as if he knew exactly when I wasn't surrounded by people or tucked away somewhere safe from his reach. Even in a place as big as this campus, he always managed to track me down. I kept moving, hoping that if I walked fast enough, maybe he'd get the hint.

"Casey!" he called again, his tone turning sharper, like he was determined. I clenched my jaw and kept my pace, refusing to look back.

"It's about Parker." His voice was low but intense, and serious enough that I slowed down at that. I would just hear him out and then hopefully he would leave me alone . . . for at least a while.

Gray quickly closed the distance, stopping next to me—way too close. I took a step back, wondering how someone who'd once felt like home now felt like a stranger.

He let out a frustrated sigh as he eyed the space I'd just created between us.

"That girl from that night . . . the one I kissed . . . I talked to her."

I closed my eyes, waiting for the pain to slice through me, like it usually did. But all I felt was betrayal. "Okay, thanks for telling me that," I told him sarcastically.

"Listen," he growled, and my eyes widened. "She told me that she'd been sent over to me by Parker."

I blinked at that, but still, I knew that Parker had been after me, even then. Even if he'd sent her over . . . "It's not like he forced you to kiss her," I said, finishing what I'd been thinking out loud.

"That's the thing, Case, I've gone over that night a million times in my head. I know I was fucking up, but I never would have cheated on you. I never would have! If you really thought about it, too, away from that prick, you would agree with me." His voice was pleading as he hurried on. "One of my frat brothers remembered that Parker handed me a drink that night. I think . . . I think he drugged me."

The words hung in the air—completely absurd. I let out a laugh, shaking my head. "You think Parker drugged you? That sounds insane." I moved to push past him. "This is ridiculous. I'm not listening to this anymore."

He grabbed my arm. "Look at this," he demanded, pulling something from his pocket and unfolding it before holding it out. It was a piece of paper, slightly crumpled, but I could make out the medical logo at the top. "It's a drug test," he said, his voice steady. "I had it done after I started putting the pieces together, and I got the results a few days ago. They found something in my system, something *I* didn't put there."

242   C.R. JANE

I yanked my arm from his grasp, refusing to reach for the paper, to even look too closely. "That doesn't prove anything," I whispered, feeling a hollow ache settle in my stomach. "It doesn't mean Parker—"

"But it's not the only thing he's lied about, Casey." Gray's eyes bore into mine, unwavering. "You've been tutoring him, right?"

I swallowed, not liking where this was going. "Yeah . . . ?"

He took a deep breath, almost as if he didn't want to say what came next. "Case, you're tutoring him in a class he took two years ago. A class where he got straight A's."

The world tilted slightly, and I fought to keep my voice steady. "No. That's—why would he do that?"

"Think about it," he said, his voice softer now. "Think about everything. The way he always knows where you are, the way he got you to move in with him in a matter of days. He's manipulating you, Casey. This guy is not who you think he is."

A wave of doubt crept in, scratching at the corners of my mind, but I shoved it down. I didn't want to believe any of it.

"Gray . . ." I trailed off, unsure of what to say, the words caught in my throat.

He stepped closer. "You know there's something off about all of this. If you really let yourself think about it . . . you know."

"I've got to go," I told him, beginning to back away.

"Casey!" he said, reaching for me. But I turned and sprinted, to where I wasn't sure, but trying to outrun the questions . . . and doubts now running through my head.

My fingers pressed down on the keys, each note echoing in the quiet room, but today, even the familiar rhythm didn't help. Gray's words kept looping through my mind, unsettling and sharp, filling the spaces between each chord. The harder I tried to lose myself in the music, the heavier everything felt.

Parker had surprised me with this piano. I'd walked through the door, and he'd been standing right by it. He'd even wrapped it with a huge bow— orange, he'd said, for the Tigers. He'd sat right by me every day since then, helping me steady my hand when it started to shake.

He'd done that and a million other sweet, perfect things that had made me feel seen—made me feel loved. There was no way that kind of man could do what Gray was claiming . . . right?

THE WRONG QUARTERBACK 243

I moved to play the next part of the piece, pushing down on the keys harder than necessary, letting out some of the tension. But my hand froze, an uncomfortable twist shooting through my fingers and up my wrist. I grimaced, flexing my fingers, but they wouldn't relax. The pressure kept building, and I could feel a tremor starting.

Tears pricked my eyes, blurring the keys in front of me.

I heard the door open, and my head whipped up. Parker stepped in, his face lighting up as he caught sight of me, but I couldn't return the look. I could barely breathe as I stood up to face him.

I took a deep breath, my heart hammering. "Did you lie about needing help with math?" I began, starting with the lightest accusation—something that could even be considered romantic—if what else Gray had said wasn't true.

Parker's expression went blank, his usual ease slipping away. For a long second, he just stared at me, unreadable. Then his face settled into something smooth, too smooth, as he reached back and locked the door with a quiet, deliberate click. "Why are you asking me that?" His voice was low, almost calm, but it only made me more uneasy.

"Gray told me," I said, feeling my pulse quicken, hands tightening into fists by my sides. "He said that you took that class years ago, that you got straight A's . . . is that true?" I laughed. "It's not, right? I mean—"

"It's correct. I took that two years ago. Straight A's on every test," Parker said calmly.

I blinked at him. "Oh . . ."

He shrugged, crossing his arms in front of him. "I needed a way to spend time with you. That's what I came up with." Parker grinned. "You can't say it didn't work." He licked his bottom lip, like he was tasting me on his lips right then.

I blushed and then swallowed. I didn't need him distracting me. If that was true, though . . . that didn't necessarily make anything else true. Or at least that's what I was telling myself as I prepared to ask him. He was probably going to be upset that I'd even believe that. I was already feeling bad that I had to ask.

But I had to.

"What else did he say?" Parker asked calmly, his eyes glimmering with something I couldn't read. There was a different energy surrounding him, like a giant coiled cat before it pounced.

"Gray thinks that you drugged him," I whispered, my eyes wide as he took a slow step toward me.

244 C.R. JANE

"He had a drug test that showed . . . something was in his system. He said you sent that girl to him. That you organized it all."

A flicker of something I couldn't read flashed across his face, but he stayed perfectly still, his eyes never leaving mine. "Gray thinks a lot of things," he said quietly, taking a step closer. The way he looked at me, like he was trying to gauge my reaction, only twisted the knot in my stomach tighter.

"It sounds almost like Andrews thinks I'm some kind of mastermind," he mused lightly, taking another step.

I swallowed, feeling trapped between wanting to pull back and needing to know the truth. "I need you to tell me, Parker," I said, my voice barely a whisper, each word feeling like it might shatter the ground beneath us.

"And what would you say if I did, Casey? What would you say if I got the drugs from Jace's brother, and I tossed it into a drink and gave it to Gray? What would you say if I watched him drink it with a smile on my face before I sent a girl after him. What would you say if I told you I've planned everything to make sure you were mine." He grinned. "Hypothetically, of course—"

I stood frozen, his words sinking in like stones, each one heavier than the last. My mind screamed to move, to put distance between us, but I couldn't force myself to turn away.

Finally, I found my voice. "I'd say . . . I'd say you might be a monster."

I turned, my legs barely carrying me as I stumbled toward the hallway, each step echoing in the silence. The walls seemed to close in, and I felt his gaze follow me, piercing and unyielding.

"Where are you going, Casey?" His tone was almost gentle, but I knew better. I didn't answer, just kept moving, my mind racing with the next steps—steps I didn't want to take.

"I'm going to pack," I managed to say, my voice trembling.

A pause, then his footsteps, close and fast. "I don't think so."

Before I could react, his hands were on me, strong and unyielding as he lifted me off my feet and slung me over his shoulder.

"Let me go," I screeched, struggling to get away from him—but his grip was ironclad. He opened a door and carried me down a set of stairs, each step echoing ominously as we descended. The basement air was cool, the walls dark and unfamiliar, and when he finally set me down, I staggered back, taking in my surroundings.

The basement was . . . finished, like a small apartment. A bed was pushed up against the far wall, a TV mounted nearby, and I could see the edge of a bathroom door. It was clean, orderly, and set up with unsettling precision.

THE WRONG QUARTERBACK 245

"Why am I down here?" My voice wavered as I tried to make sense of it.

He didn't hesitate. "Because I told you, Casey—you're my endgame. If it takes you a little while to realize that, that's fine. But you're not running away from me."

I blinked at him. "So—so what, you're just going to leave me down here?" I said with a laugh . . . waiting for him to laugh too.

But he didn't.

"Yes. Until I'm sure you're not going to run," he said calmly, turning to go up the stairs. "I'm going to go make dinner," he called over his shoulder. "Your favorite—chicken Parmesan."

He closed the door, and I heard the sound of a lock clicking into place. A few seconds later, I heard the door closing at the top of the stairs.

I still tried the knob, though, pounding on the door after I realized it was locked, screaming for him to let me go. Even then it took me at least an hour to realize this was really happening.

Parker Davis had just locked me in his basement.

CHAPTER 30

PARKER

I cracked some eggs into a bowl and then added some salt and pepper, setting it aside to dip the chicken in as soon as I pounded it down. I paused for a second, listening to hear if Casey had stopped screaming and banging on the basement door yet.

Bang. Bang. Bang.

Nope. Not yet.

Would it make the situation any better if I told her that the basement setup was pre-existing? The house was meant to be rented out to four students, with three bedrooms on the main floor and another apartment in the . . . basement.

Had it come in handy when she tried to leave me? Yes.

But I hadn't prepared it for her, like a serial killer. That should mean something, right?

I had no idea when I'd joked with my brothers about having someone in my basement a few months ago that I'd find myself here.

Sounded a little like fate if you asked me.

I heard the unmistakable sound of a key turning in the front lock. Before I could even register the thought of visitors, the door swung open, and Jace strolled in like he owned the place, holding a gallon jug of milk in one hand and a corn dog in the other.

"'Sup, QB," he said around a mouthful, nodding as he gave the milk jug a casual shake, as if that justified his sudden entrance. He took another bite of the corn dog, completely unfazed by my silence.

THE WRONG QUARTERBACK 247

I raised an eyebrow, resisting the urge to look at the door that led down to the basement. "A corn dog and milk? Really, Jace?"

"Protein and calcium, my man," he said, holding up the corn dog like it was some sort of winning lottery ticket. He plopped himself down in a chair, and took a swig straight from the milk jug without missing a beat.

"It's actually not a good time," I began.

"Ooh, are you making chicken Parmesan?" he said, excitedly hopping right back out of the chair.

"Get out," I huffed, pounding on the chicken so I could get it the right thickness. When I'd found out that Olive Garden chicken Parmesan was Casey's favorite, I'd looked up every copycat recipe I could until I'd perfected it. All the flavor and none of the bad chemicals.

Hopefully it would soften her up.

"You have to give me some of that. Otherwise, I'm going to eat this corn dog over the sink like a fucking rat," Jace begged.

Casey chose that moment to scream. I froze, the meat mallet clenched in my hand.

I really hoped that I wasn't about to have to use this on my best friend.

Jace was frozen as well, the corn dog halfway to his mouth.

Casey banged on the door . . . and then screamed again for good measure.

It was a testament to her lung capacity that she could keep going like that. Probably one of the factors in why she was incredible at giving head.

"So . . . QB. You and your lady playing hide-and-go-seek, and Casey just forgot the rules?" Jace asked.

I thought for a moment. "Yes, that's definitely it."

Jace tapped on the counter and took a long, exaggerated gulp of his milk.

"Is there a reason you have your girlfriend locked in the basement?" he finally asked after he'd set down the milk. "Or have you officially lost it, and a meat suit *really* is next."

I snorted. Jace was perhaps the only person who could make me even think about laughing at the moment. "Her ex decided to give her information about some . . . of my more questionable activities, and she's a little bit upset. So I'm giving her some time to get used to that."

Jace scoffed, taking another huge bite of his corn dog before he responded, his mouth still full. "She tried to leave you."

I set the mallet down since it seemed like he wasn't going to run and go try and free her, and nodded. "She tried to leave me," I confirmed.

Jace nodded, like he was thinking harder than he ever had in his life.

248   C.R. JANE

"So, uh, how long are you going to keep her down there, exactly? And what's your plan to make her . . . not want to run away?"

I dropped the chicken into the egg mixture and made sure it was coated before moving it to the seasoned breadcrumbs.

"For however long it takes. And I'm still thinking," I murmured as I lowered the chicken into the oil-filled pan.

And she screamed again.

"Alright, well, I'm going to go check my stocks."

I eyed him. Jace barely passed most of his classes, but for some reason he was *literally* a genius at stocks. He managed both Matty's and my portfolios from the endorsement deals we got, and he'd tripled what we had.

But not what I'd expected him to say.

"What? That's your response to me telling you I'm keeping my soulmate in my basement?"

He blinked at me like I was stupid.

"As a fellow No Drama Llama member, I need to be prepared in the inevitable event that I have to bail you out. Which means my stocks need to be better."

He walked out of the room, taking his milk and corn dog with him.

"I didn't vote for that name," I called after him, a smirk on my face as I flipped the chicken.

"I'm going to call some lawyers too . . . just in case. Can't let my fellow Pussy Posse member down," he added as he opened the door.

"I'm not going to need one," I yelled to him, but he'd already left.

I sighed as Casey banged on the door again, and I plated the chicken, arranging her favorite Caesar salad on the plate. Usually she would be in the kitchen with me, and I missed her. I needed to figure out a way to fix this soon.

I brought our plates down the stairs, and she didn't soften at all, refusing to eat even a single bite.

As I walked back up the stairs, I was thinking I was going to have to work really hard to make sure Jace didn't need to get that lawyer.

Losing Casey's heart wasn't an option.

————

"What are you doing?" she growled at me later when I came down for bed.

"Going to bed," I replied calmly.

"You've got to be shitting me. You are *not* sleeping with me," she snapped. Her eyes were red, and her hair was a mess. And as usual, she was the most beautiful fucking girl I'd ever seen.

THE WRONG QUARTERBACK   249

"Can you honestly say you're going to sleep well without me?" I asked, sliding into the bed. She tried to get out, and I grabbed her around the waist and pulled her against me.

She only kicked me twice before she gave up and lay there quietly.

That was a good sign, right?

Except a few seconds later she started crying. I pulled her into my chest and stroked her hair.

"I can't believe you did this," she whispered. I squeezed her closer.

"I can't believe you didn't know I would."

She sniffled again.

"I told you that we're endgame, Casey. I'm going to help you remember that."

"You can't keep me down here forever," she answered.

And I didn't say anything after that . . . because I was pretty sure she wouldn't like my answer.

I held her close to me all night.

"Tell me a story about Ben," I murmured as I held her in bed the next night. I was hoping that this question would lower her defenses a little. This was something we'd done the past weeks, tell stories about the two people we'd lost.

She was still mad at me, but at least she'd eaten tonight.

So that was progress, right?

I'd made sure to get all of her schoolwork by telling her professors that she was sick, so she'd be able to keep up on her assignments while we were in this . . . stage.

She'd tried to hit me with one of her textbooks when I'd given it to her, but it was so cute that I'd laughed.

Which had then made her refuse to talk to me.

"Well, he definitely wouldn't have approved of this," she snarled, sounding more like a cuddly kitten than the terrifying monster I was pretty sure she was going for.

"Noted. Now tell me another story," I said, softly stroking her hair.

She huffed, but her body relaxed against mine. "He was a star, like you," she said softly. "He was offered a spot on Tennessee's basketball team, and he was so ready to shine. Ben was the first person in our small town to get an athletic scholarship like that, and everyone was so proud."

"They weren't proud of you with your piano skills?" I asked.

250   C.R. JANE

She hesitated. "Not like they were with Ben," she finally said. "That's why I came to Tennessee, though. He didn't get to come here, and once I knew my dreams of playing at Juilliard weren't going to happen, then at least I could live a little part of his dream."

"You know I would do anything to help with your dreams. Your brother would want you to shine. I don't know him, but I know that much," I told her, my mind racing as usual with ways that I could help her make her dreams come true.

Casey turned in my arms. Her eyes were less red-rimmed and more . . . resigned. I wasn't sure I liked that either.

"When are you going to let me out?" she asked softly.

"When you promise not to run, and I believe you."

"And what if I did run?"

I laughed softly. "Then I would spend the rest of my life chasing after you. As you know, though, I'm pretty dedicated when I want something. I don't think you'd be able to run far."

She rolled her eyes, the ghost of a smile on her pretty lips.

Don't think about her lips, I told myself, shifting my dick away from her since it was starting to harden from just that.

"You know, I kept telling myself you were too good to be true. And I guess I was right," she whispered as her smile faded.

I brushed a kiss across her lips before she could jerk away.

"Everything I've done is for you," I said. "I love you more than life itself. There's your truth."

She sighed, but her forehead was scrunched, like she was thinking hard.

I was wearing her down.

———

I woke up from a really great dream, to something even better . . . Casey naked on top of me, sliding onto my dick.

"Don't talk," she whispered when she saw I was awake. "This doesn't mean I don't hate you."

"Of course not," I answered, even though that's exactly what it meant. I grasped her hips and helped her work me all the way inside her.

I couldn't help but groan when she sank all the way down, taking every inch of me like the good girl she was.

Her hips tilted, and she rocked up and down. I pulled her forward, changing the angle to the one I knew she liked best that also rubbed her clit.

THE WRONG QUARTERBACK 251

"I love you," I murmured, nuzzling into her hair. She stiffened for a second but ignored me, her pace increasing as I grasped her hips and fucked into her.

It had been forty-eight hours since I'd been inside her. Absolutely unacceptable.

I was addicted to her, and even a few hours felt like eternity. I was glad that my efforts to train her body to feel the same way had evidently worked.

"We're never going to talk about this. I should be biting your dick . . . not riding it," she murmured unsteadily as she pushed her hips all the way back and then slammed forward.

"Mmmh," I answered, pressing down on her lower back so her clit rubbed against me harder.

She was close. Her breath was coming out in gasps, and her cunt was tightening around my dick.

"Yes, yes, yes," she breathed as she rode out her orgasm. Her head thrown back, her chest flushed, her nipples beaded into hard, rosy points. It was the most erotic sight I'd ever seen.

And then she flipped off of me.

"What?"

"This is a reminder that I'm mad at you," she said, her gaze trained on my cock as I started feverishly stroking myself.

"That's fair," I grunted, even though I wasn't happy about it. I came, cum splattering all over my stomach, my moan echoing around the room.

Her eyes were dilated as she continued to watch me.

"Want a taste, baby?" I said, sliding my finger through the mess and bringing it up to her lips.

She bit my fucking finger, hard, before her tongue lapped up my cum.

"You love me too much to stay mad at me forever," I told her after I'd cleaned off my stomach and came back to bed.

"We'll see about that," she responded, but I didn't worry about that.

Her body was already back on my side, and with a little more work . . . her heart would be too.

CHAPTER 31

CASEY

I woke up furious with myself.

Furious that I'd been so weak and that I'd been the one to instigate last night's sex session—no matter how hot it had been.

It's just he'd been having some kind of sex dream, moaning my name as he rubbed his hard, perfect length against my ass.

A girl was only so strong.

I told myself I was just using his body to get off. But that had been a huge lie.

He was too tangled up in my heart for sex to ever not be *more*.

And I hated that.

The fact that I was so conflicted over what was happening could only be because of my upbringing. Parker had been the first person to ever make me feel seen. Like I was more than a shadow, more than a nerd, more than . . .

Ben's sister.

I really was fucked up.

There was a part of me that craved Parker's attention . . . that needed it. After a life of not being seen, I didn't know if I could go back to that.

Parker had made me addicted to him, and he wasn't giving me a chance to get him out of my system.

I also didn't know if I could, even if he gave me that chance.

"You're going to have to let me text Nat. She's going to get worried," I told him as I watched him pull his shirt down over abs that were so perfect they almost looked fake. He'd brought a bunch of his stuff down here, so he was with me constantly when he wasn't in class or practice.

THE WRONG QUARTERBACK **253**

"I've been texting her from your phone," he said calmly, as if that wasn't a big deal at all.

My eyes widened, but I couldn't honestly say I was surprised. Every time my defenses started to go down . . . I would be reminded again . . . my boyfriend's a psycho.

And yes, I would examine later why I was still calling him *my boyfriend* in my head.

"If I promise not to run away, can we end this hostage situation?" I sighed, still not believing that I was saying that.

He snorted. "I prefer the term 'basement time-out.' And yes, I know you won't run. But I'm still not letting you leave the house until after my game tomorrow."

"How do you know I won't run?" I asked, offended that he'd think I'd be won over so easily.

Parker stared at me for a moment, a piece of his dark hair falling into his face. I still didn't understand how he could have put me down here. How he could have done that to Gray. Everything else about him was so perfect, so . . . beautiful.

It was that unsettling beauty, though, that left me feeling the most confused, because I couldn't reconcile it with everything he'd done. A villain shouldn't be allowed to have a pretty face.

"Because you love me too much," he finally murmured, his tone perfectly confident.

And I couldn't argue with that.

Parker's face softened. "Do you need anything while I'm gone, baby?" His voice held that low, easy tone, the one that usually made me melt.

"For you to let me go," I immediately said, more to myself than to him. He flashed a quick grin, that irresistible, boyish charm trying to batter at my heart.

"Impossible." He moved closer, his fingers lightly grazing my cheek as he brushed a stray hair from my face. The gentle warmth in his touch sent a pang of doubt spiraling through me, tugging me in two different directions.

I didn't know how he could be both the protector and the affectionate lover while also being the man who could trap me in a world of his own making. It was like there were two people beneath his skin, and I wasn't sure which one would come to the surface next.

I wanted to ask him, to see if he could explain the pieces that didn't fit. But as his hand lingered, and he leaned down, pressing a soft kiss to my forehead, my questions tangled up in my throat.

254 C.R. JANE

"I don't know how I'll ever forgive you for this," I whispered, a tear sliding down my face. "I thought you were my hero and now . . ."

"There are villains and there are heroes, and then there are men who are in between," he said idly, softly stroking my cheek as he stared at me like I was his whole world.

"And which one are you?" I whispered.

"Depends on what your answer is, Casey," he mused. "Because there's no world where you're not mine. Whether you give me you . . . or I have to take you, it doesn't change the outcome."

"Which is?" I asked, even though I was quite sure I knew the answer.

"That you're going to be mine until the day we die and for all our lifetimes after that. There's no me without you."

"That's crazy," I told him in a hitched voice, a swarm of mixed emotions in my chest because I was pretty sure I should be running.

He smiled, and the swarm of mixed emotions took on a glittery haze, something that always happened when he looked at me like that.

"No, baby," he finally murmured. "That's called true love."

And I wasn't sure I could argue with that.

"Don't leave the house," Parker cautioned me that night when he'd let me out of the basement, and he was about to leave for the hotel that the team spent the night in before home games to make sure no one got in trouble.

"I have cameras at every entrance . . . and watching the windows on the side. I *will* leave my hotel to come find you."

I scoffed. "And what if I tell someone before you do."

He grinned, and he didn't have to speak the words out loud for me to understand him.

Who would believe you . . .

What did it say about me that a little thrill went through me at his confidence . . . that he had everything planned out . . . a way to handle every circumstance.

I was becoming more and more convinced that leaving him was not really a possibility.

I was also becoming more and more convinced that . . . I liked this. I actually liked this twisted game of control. To see the depths he'd go to keep me.

For my entire life, I'd wanted someone to see me. I hadn't expected it to come in this form, though.

But maybe broken things *needed* extraordinary measures to fix them.

Maybe Parker Davis was exactly what my broken soul needed, because he'd hold me tight enough that all my broken pieces would come together again.

"Make sure you watch the game tomorrow," he ordered, dragging me out of my thoughts before he pulled me in for a breath-stealing kiss.

"I'm not going to," I called after him as he strode to the door. He threw me a dazzling smile over his shoulder.

"Beautiful little liar," he said.

And then he was gone.

I didn't leave. Instead, I tossed and turned all night, the empty space next to me feeling like too much without him.

It got so bad that I even picked up when he called after his team meetings.

"Hi," he murmured, his voice warm and sleepy and delicious. "I miss you."

"I—I miss you, too," I said after a moment, his absence clearly affecting me.

"You look beautiful right now."

I blinked, and it took me a moment to understand what that implied.

"Parker Fucking Davis, are you watching me on camera right now?" I screeched, jumping out of bed and frantically searching around the room for a device.

"It's like FaceTime." He laughed. "What's the big deal?"

I opened my mouth to argue, until I realized I had that confusing, warm feeling inside me again. The idea that he was so obsessed with me that he wanted to watch me when he was out of the house was . . . hot.

Psycho, but hot.

Fuck. I needed a therapist.

I gave up on finding where he'd hidden the camera and crawled back into bed.

"That's my girl," he murmured, and I tried to snarl at him.

Which only made him laugh at me more.

"Tell me that you love me," he finally said.

And my reply was instant. "I love you. I love you, even though . . . I shouldn't," I admitted.

"There's no *shouldn't* involved. No one gets to say how the greatest love stories are told. We can make our own rules."

I didn't have anything to say to that . . . because I was beginning to think he was right.

"Put the phone down next to you, but keep the line connected," he ordered.

"Why?" I asked.

"Because I want us connected all night. Just keep the line open, even while you're sleeping. That way, if you need anything . . . I'm here."

Ugh. Why did he have to be like that, already anticipating that I wouldn't sleep well without him? Why did he have to make me feel like I was the center of his world?

"Okay," I whispered, tucking my phone next to me on the bed, a warmth settling over me. I put the phone on speaker so I could hear him.

Because if he was going to be my stalker . . . I wanted to be his stalker, too.

"Good girl." His voice softened, filling the empty space between us. "Sweet dreams, baby. I love you."

I fell asleep listening to the sound of his breaths.

Watching him on the screen the next day, my chest felt tight, like I could barely breathe. Tennessee had won, and then Parker stood there with the announcer, sweaty and triumphant. His eyes were still blazing with that fierce focus that seemed to power him through everything.

When he leaned into the mic, his gaze was steady, his voice firm. "This win . . ." He paused, almost like he was gathering the right words. "It's for someone special. My soulmate's brother, Ben Larsen. A man I never got to meet, but wish I had. I respect him immensely, and I know he's watching out for her and us, wherever he is."

Hearing those words hit like a punch, softening me in a way I hadn't expected. Ben. He'd just said Ben's name on national television, dedicating his win to him. The respect in Parker's voice was real, solid, and the whole world was watching him honor my brother in a way that made my heart twist and ache. No one else had ever done that, no one else had ever thought of Ben like this—not even Gray.

Beneath the warmth swelling in my chest, there was a crack, something uncertain and heavy.

I closed my eyes for a second, feeling a confusing mixture of emotions—pain, warmth, anger, and a strange sort of gratitude. I wanted to hate him, wanted to believe he was as twisted as Gray insisted he was. But he did things that no one else had ever done for me. He fought for me. Protected me. Every move he made seemed to be about giving me the best, even if his methods were sometimes . . . unhinged.

I realized right then, I loved him. He was willing to be unhinged for me, to do whatever it took to have me.

I opened my eyes again, the screen still frozen on his face, his expression soft and serious. It was like he was looking right at me, saying things that I was finally hearing.

The lengths he'd gone to weren't conventional. They weren't even *right*, but maybe it didn't matter what the world would think. Because with that dedication, he'd just proven he knew exactly how to honor my heart.

And that's when I knew . . . I'd stay.

I was waiting for him at the door when he got home. He dropped his bags and held out his arms . . . and I ran to him.

"Finally," he murmured as he squeezed me against him, letting out a breath like he'd been holding it this entire time.

I lifted my head off his shoulder and held his face in both my hands.

"I think you're crazy," I told him as I stared into his blue eyes.

He grinned.

"Yes. Crazy for you."

"And you are absolutely *never* allowed to put me in a basement again— or anywhere else—without my permission," I continued.

His smile widened. "I'll consider it."

"But I love you," I told him, my voice breaking. "I love you more than anything. You own my . . . soul."

I watched as a tear slid down his cheek, the happiness radiating off him making me light-headed, like we now existed in our own little world.

"You've owned my soul since the moment I saw you, baby," he finally whispered in a choked voice. "I've just been waiting for you to realize it."

His lips brushed against mine once, twice, before settling against me. Our tongues slowly tangled together, our clothes coming off as he walked me further into the house.

"Casey," he breathed as he *finally* pushed into me.

His touch was reverent, savoring, like he was memorizing every pass against my skin.

I cried as our hips moved together.

Parker completely enveloped me, so there was no space for any doubts or anything else to slip in. There was only him.

"I love you," he moaned, his cock stretching me over and over as we moved in a slow, exquisite rhythm.

"It feels like too much." I gasped against his lips, the tears streaming down my face as he pushed deeper. I didn't know how to handle this feeling inside me. It was too encompassing.

I didn't know how to exist in this new world where my soulmate was a living, breathing person that I couldn't exist without.

I understood now how his mother could have faded away after she lost his dad.

If she'd had something anywhere close to this, how could she exist when it was gone?

I wasn't sure that I could.

It was terrifying . . . exhilarating.

It was *everything*.

"I've got you, baby," he murmured, licking my tears away, soft slides of his tongue that eased some of the ache. "Just feel me. I'm right here."

His teeth bit down gently into my shoulder, and the slight pain centered me enough for my body to pull me into a deep climax.

"I love you," I cried as my core squeezed him tighter.

"Keep saying it," he said roughly, his hips jerking in a staccato motion before he pushed deep and held himself there, his cock jerking inside me as he filled me with his cum.

I wrapped my legs around him, trying to get as close to him as I possibly could.

"Mine," he murmured as he rolled us over so I was cradled against his chest.

"Yours," I agreed, letting myself drift off with him still inside me.

CHAPTER 32

CASEY

Parker and I were walking down the street a few days later when we turned a corner . . . and there he was.

Gray.

He stopped in his tracks, his face turning pale as his incredulous gaze darted from the way Parker's arm was wrapped around my waist . . . to my face.

"Casey?" he asked.

Parker's fingers pressed into my side for a second, like he was tempted to grab me and carry me away . . . but then they softened.

"I'm going to talk to him for a second," I whispered to him, staring up into Parker's torn face.

There was a tic in his cheek as he closed his eyes and took a deep breath before opening them. "I'll be over there, baby. But if he touches you . . ."

I smiled reassuringly. "It will be fine."

"Just remember that I'm never letting you go," he said, his lips claiming mine as his hand slid down to grab my ass, and he pulled me against his hard body, his dick stiffening between us.

I got lost like I always did. The world around us disappeared, and this moment became my only point of focus.

A throat cleared, and my eyes flew open as I broke away from Parker's lips with a gasp.

Whoops.

I sheepishly glanced at Gray, a wave of shame rolling across my skin because he looked like I'd just stabbed him in the heart.

260   C.R. JANE

Parker reluctantly released me, a small smirk on his lips telling me *he* hadn't forgotten Gray was there during that kiss. "I'll be right over there," he murmured before he slowly walked over to a bench and sat down, somehow making the park bench look like a throne as he lounged back like an insolent king.

"So you're with him, even after everything I told you," Gray spat, his fists clenched at his sides. "After everything we've—"

I held up my hand. "I'm not letting you use Ben against me anymore," I whispered.

Gray staggered back like I'd shot him.

"I—"

"That's what you've been doing. You took me for granted, and every time you saw me slipping away, you used Ben to reel me back in." My lip quivered as I stared at the boy I'd once thought that I'd loved.

And maybe I *had* loved him.

Maybe it was just hard to think of it as love because this thing between Parker and me was so overwhelming, so all-encompassing—it drowned everything else out in the world.

Maybe that had been love, and what Parker and I had was a soul-shaking obsession.

But whatever it had been with Gray . . . I didn't feel it anymore. Parker's light shone too bright. It had burned everything else away.

"Gray," I whispered, his name catching in my throat, like it hurt to say. Maybe it did. It felt like a goodbye already, a word weighed down by a thousand memories that wrapped around my heart and squeezed tight. I swallowed hard, tasting the salt of unshed tears.

"Don't say it," he said stubbornly.

"I'm letting you go," I whispered.

I stared at him, the boy who'd been my constant, my refuge, my home for so long.

But he'd also deserted me when I'd needed him the most.

And then he'd treated me like I was an afterthought instead of the love of his life.

The streetlight cast a soft glow over us, its flickering creating shadows that danced across his face, catching the deep furrow of his brow, the pain that swam in those familiar eyes.

"We're not kids anymore," I said, the words a knife between us. "And whatever we once had—it's not enough now. I thought it was everything then, but . . . it turns out I didn't know what *everything* actually was." My

THE WRONG QUARTERBACK 261

chest ached, the pain raw, like I was being hollowed out from the inside. The streetlight flickered again, casting us in and out of shadow, like the universe couldn't decide if we should be seen or forgotten.

He took a step closer, and I held up my hand to stop him.

Gray's eyes glistened, unshed tears making them shine. "I can be better," he said, voice cracking, raw and desperate. "Case, please—"

I pressed my lips together, the tears finally breaking free and slicing hot, silent paths down my cheeks. "I love him. I love him so much that I can't imagine breathing without him. I love him so much that it feels like he's carved into my soul."

He dropped his gaze, the fight leaving him, and it was like watching a light go out. The silence stretched between us, a chasm that neither of us could cross.

"Goodbye, Gray," I whispered, the words breaking me apart even as I said them. He didn't move, didn't try to stop me as I turned back toward Parker. I left the boy and walked to the man who made up my whole future.

And with each step I left a trail of my memories with Gray behind me.

Parker had stood up from the bench, and he was waiting for me with outstretched arms. I fell into his embrace and let him lead me away with a soft kiss to my hair as we walked.

I didn't look back until we were far away.

The night had swallowed Gray, and with it, the last pieces of who we'd been.

CHAPTER 33

PARKER

My brother was a fucking rock god.

We were backstage, watching him perform. He'd been touring with the Sound of Us for the past year, and he'd finally made it to Tennessee for a concert.

My chest was tight with pride as he sang to the packed crowd that filled the whole fucking stadium.

Even if he was wearing feathers in his cowboy hat again.

I glanced at Casey as the music blasted through the speakers. She looked mesmerized, her eyes wide, her body frozen in place, like she couldn't quite believe where she was. I knew she was nervous; she had been the whole car ride here, but now? Now it was like she was in a trance.

I covered her eyes.

"Hey," she cried, pushing my hands off.

"Cole snores terribly loud, and his farts literally clear rooms," I told her.

She blinked at me, the same look she always had when I said something fairly crazy.

"Why are you telling me this?" she asked slowly.

"Just making sure . . ."

She grinned at me knowingly.

Cole was deep into his song, leaning into each note, when suddenly, a high-pitched wave of screaming broke through the music. He barely had time to register the sound before a group of girls burst through the security barriers in front of the stage. They somehow bypassed the security guards and ran across the stage floor with determined looks and hands already reaching out for him.

THE WRONG QUARTERBACK 263

He froze mid-strum, eyes widening as he took in the scene. The first girl was just a few feet away when Cole's survival instincts finally kicked in.

"Oh, hell no," he muttered, and bolted around the mic stand as more girls pulled themselves up onto the stage, their arms outstretched like they were zombie extras in an episode of *Walking Dead*.

His guitarist started playing a fast-paced riff, adding an absurd soundtrack to the chaos. Cole dashed behind the drum kit, ducking as one girl lunged at him. He laughed nervously, sprinting to the far side of the stage as security rushed in, grabbing fans left and right.

"I'd rather not!" he shouted over his shoulder, just as another fan managed to get up close. He hopped backward, narrowly avoiding her grip. Cole half ran, half laughed his way across the stage, dodging the crowd like it was a bizarre game of tag.

Finally, security managed to get a handle on the situation, ushering the determined fans back down. Cole caught his breath, hands on his knees, shaking his head as he looked out at the crowd.

"That's going on YouTube, isn't it?" He laughed into the mic, brushing off his shirt and adjusting his hat with a dramatic flourish. He'd lost a feather while he'd been running, so it looked slightly less ridiculous. "Love the enthusiasm, Nashville, but let's leave the tackle moves to the Tennessee Tigers when they kick Florida's ass this weekend, okay?"

The audience roared, and Cole grinned at me before he held up his guitar triumphantly and launched right back into the song.

"Walker is going to hate that he missed that," I muttered to myself, thinking that a video wasn't going to do it justice.

"That's the kind of reaction I want when I walk in a room," said Jace as Matty gaped at him. "Don't look at me like that, Matthew, you have a stalker. That's an affront to nature, especially because of the size of my—"

"Don't talk about dicks," I growled, covering Casey's ears this time.

The three of them laughed at me like I'd done something funny.

The final chord struck, the crowd exploded in cheers, and I grabbed her hand.

"I've got a good one for your brother this time," Jace said. "Want to hear it?"

"Don't say yes. This one is not good," groaned Matty.

"Well, now I have to hear it," I said.

Jace rubbed his hands together, obviously really excited about this one. "Okay, prepare yourself."

"I'm prepared. Hit me with it."

"What kind of bees produce milk?"

"I literally have no idea."

Jace grinned. "Boo-bees."

Casey giggled, and I glanced down at her, only smiling because of her laugh. And not because it was funny.

"See what I mean?" said Matty.

"Cole's going to love it. He appreciates me for my comedic humor," Jace retorted, scowling at the two of us like we'd deeply betrayed him.

"Cole also wears birds on his head, so I'm not sure you can trust him," I mused as the man in question waved to the crowd and strode toward us off the stage.

I got ready to hug my brother in all his sweaty glory, but to my horror, he had something else in mind.

Before I could blink, he swept Casey up into a huge hug that made her squeak in surprise. "Hello, future sis-in-law," he crowed as he spun her around.

"Put her DOWN," I growled, seeing red as I forced myself not to tackle my oldest brother.

Cole's smirk stretched across his whole face as he set her down and watched as I immediately pulled her against my body. "So touchy about touching," he said, taking off his hat and pulling back his dark blue bandana so he could use it to wipe his sweat-slicked face.

I took in what he was wearing while he was distracted, because one of Walker's and my favorite things to do was to make fun of his . . . colorful style.

I would call this one his hobo cowboy look.

His shirt, some kind of loose linen deal, was unbuttoned halfway down his chest, revealing a glint of silver from a chain with a small emerald stone at the end, swinging slightly as he shifted. His leather pants were so tight that I wasn't sure how he'd actually gotten them on in the first place.

I snapped a picture and sent it to Walker. His response was instantaneous.

> Walker: Burn it.

I snorted, and Cole lifted an eyebrow at me. "You're laughing at me, aren't you?"

"Only a little."

Jace started his joke, and I turned my attention to Casey, who had gotten extremely quiet.

THE WRONG QUARTERBACK 265

"What's up, baby?" I asked.

She glanced up at me, and I realized she was blushing. Now I really wanted to know what was going on in that gorgeous head of hers.

"He called me his 'future sis-in-law,'" she whispered shyly, and I brushed a kiss against her lips.

"'My future wife' is better, but if the other one gets you going, I'll take it as long as it gets me to the same place."

"The same place?"

"At the altar, with you in a white dress, telling me you're going to belong to me forever and ever."

"I like the sound of that place," she said, her blush deepening. I kissed her again.

"That place is going to happen. Soon."

CHAPTER 34

PARKER

I moved down the winding paths of the cemetery, my hands shoved deep in my pockets, every step feeling heavier than the last. The place was quiet, like the silence here was something alive, pressing down over the rows of headstones around me. No sounds, no distractions—just a hushed kind of stillness that made me feel like I was walking into something sacred.

I'd been here once before with Casey, but this was my first time alone. I still found Ben's grave easily, though, the location embedded in my mind.

When I reached his grave, I paused, looking down at the headstone. Simple, barely more than his name and the dates. It looked plain, not nearly enough to capture who he was to Casey. I crouched down, brushing a bit of dirt from the edge, running my fingers over the rough stone. "Hey, Ben," I started, my voice rough, feeling a strange mix of nerves settle over me. I hadn't talked when I was here with Casey, I'd just been there as emotional support.

It felt strange now talking to someone I'd never met, but I kept going. "I don't know if you can hear me, but . . . I guess I just wanted to introduce myself. I'm Parker."

I rubbed a hand over the back of my neck, feeling the importance that this moment carried. "Look, I know you probably would've had a lot to say about me being with her," I admitted, managing a small, wry smile. "And I don't blame you. But I love her, man. More than I can even wrap my head around. She's . . . everything."

I let out a shaky breath, my gaze dropping to the name etched in stone. It hit me then—everything he'd missed, everything he'd left behind. "I'm

THE WRONG QUARTERBACK **267**

sorry we never met. I wish we had." I paused, letting the silence settle before going on. "But I want you to know . . . you can trust me with her heart. With her life. She's safe with me."

The words hung thick in the air, like a physical representation of everything I'd been carrying. I stared at the headstone as if expecting an answer. "I'm going to take care of her. I promise. You don't have to worry—your sister's going to be okay."

I shifted, digging my hands into my pockets, the words feeling heavy on my tongue. "Ben . . . I know what it's like to miss someone after they're gone," I said, my voice barely a whisper. "Hell, I know what it's like to miss someone even when they're still walking the Earth. To carry around that ache, day in and day out. It never really leaves you."

I swallowed, letting that truth sink in, feeling the raw edge of it in my chest. "But I'm going to be there for her. I'll help her keep you with her, always. She's never going to have to carry that alone." My voice cracked, but I forced myself to keep going, to make the promise as real as I could. "I'll make sure she remembers every story, every memory, every bit of you. I'll keep your memory alive with her."

I took a shaky breath, the truth in those words grounding me, a vow that felt more real than anything I'd said in a long time.

A gust of wind suddenly blew across my skin.

And somehow, standing there, I felt that Ben understood.

The drive to my mom's house felt as heavy as what I'd just left in the cemetery. Every mile stretching with the enormity of what I was going there to say. And when I walked in, it was obvious that nothing had improved since her stint in the hospital.

I made my way to her room, finding her curled up in bed, covers pulled to her chin, her face pale against the pillow. She was still eating nothing, and now she didn't even have the energy to get out of bed.

She barely stirred when I came in, and a burst of anger flooded through me. Taking a deep breath, I tried to remind myself that I didn't know what it was like, to lose my soulmate.

I tried to remind myself that I'd probably be worse than my mom. I'd probably be trying to follow Casey as soon as I could.

I tried to remind myself of all that as I sat on the edge of the bed. The springs creaked beneath me, and I reached for her hand, covering it with mine. Her skin was cool, fragile, like she was slipping away even as I held on.

268 C.R. JANE

I knew what I needed to do.

"Mom," I started, my voice low as I tried to steady myself. "I know you're tired. And as much as we want you to fight . . . we can't do that for you anymore. Not if you don't want to."

She didn't move, but her fingers twitched just slightly, like she could hear me.

"I brought Casey to meet you at the hospital," I continued, my voice softening. "This girl, Mom, she's everything. And I'm gonna marry her. Soon. We're going to have kids, the whole thing. I'd love for you to be there for that. I'd love for you to see me play in the NFL, to watch me build a family, to be a part of it." I stopped, feeling the words catch in my throat, the honesty feeling like heartbreak.

"But I get it, if you're done. If it's too much. You've been gone for so long, and I don't know how to reach you anymore. If you really don't want to be here . . . if you're ready to go . . . I just . . . I just need you to know I'm letting go if that's what you want."

I waited, searching her face for any sign that she was still there, that the mom I used to know was somewhere under the surface. But she stayed silent, unmoving, and that heavy ache in my chest grew. I squeezed her hand gently, trying to make my peace with it, and stood up.

"Take care, Mom. I love you," I whispered, patting her hand one last time before I turned and walked out, leaving the house that had long ago stopped feeling like home behind me.

On the drive back to school, my mind was a mess of memories and hope tangled up with grief. And then my phone chimed, breaking through my thoughts. I glanced at the screen, and the words hit me like a punch:

Mom: I'm ready to get help.

I pulled over to the side of the road, the message blurring as the tears came, hot and unrelenting. The burden I'd been carrying for so long finally cracked open, and for the first time in years, I truly let myself cry.

CHAPTER 35

PARKER

Months Later . . .

"I'm going to be sick," Griffin muttered, hunching over the bench with a green tint to his face.

"Come on, Griffy. Get your shit together. This is what we live for," said Jace, spreading eye black under his eyes, even though it was dark outside. He claimed that it helped with the glare of the lights.

Whatever worked.

The NCAA championship. This is why I played. This is why I dripped sweat and blood all over the field all season long.

For games like this.

I was never going to admit it . . . but I also felt a little sick.

My phone buzzed on the bench next to me, and I grabbed it, hoping for a distraction.

> Walker: Good luck out there, little brother.

I frowned.

This was bad luck. I couldn't go out there with them sending me a . . . nice text.

> Me: Absolutely not. Take that back!

> Walker: What?

270   C.R. JANE

> Me: You can't go the whole season spouting non-sense and then decide to play it safe for the last game.

Jace fell onto the seat next to me and peered at my phone. "Are my brothers from another mother wishing me good luck?" he asked, his foot tapping up and down furiously.

I was glad to see that he was nervous, too.

> Cole: Sorry, just making sure I heard that right, Parkie. You're saying you want us to insult you? And that's good luck . . .

> Walker: Well, you actually should be making sure you "read" that right. Unless you have your assistant reading your texts out loud again because you like the sound of her voice.

That definitely called for a . . . So I typed one out.

> Walker: Good one.

> Me: Stop being nice.

> Cole: I'm flipping you both off right now. Does that help?

> Walker: Still have a thing against emojis?

> Cole: They're unnatural.

> Walker: . . .

> Cole: I'm going to report you to the Circle of Trust for continual misuse of . . .

> Walker: Well, at least you got the name right this time.

THE WRONG QUARTERBACK 271

"I should have trademarked that name while I had the chance," Jace mused—still reading my texts. "Remind me tomorrow, after we win, to apply for *Pussy Posse* before that gets snatched up too."

I side-eyed him. "I most certainly will not."

"Literally any other name would be better than that," said Matty, coming to sit next to me. He had a rubber band stretched between two fingers, and he was plucking at it, over and over again.

Another nervous teammate for the win.

"Oh really, Matthew. *Any name*? Are you sure about that?" Jace asked sarcastically.

I glanced over at Matty. "Seriously, *are* you sure about that? Why would you want to give him that type of power?"

Matty snarled at us. "Why do we have to have a name at all?"

"Because all the great ones do, Matty-kins. All the great ones do," Jace said, suddenly very serious.

Matty and I blinked at him, but then my phone buzzed again.

> Walker: Alright, how about this . . . Parker, you fucking suck. Try not to mess it up too bad and embarrass us. Was that good enough?

Jace and Matty both snickered next to me because obviously they were the worst, and both had decided to read my text messages now.

> Cole: He's pouting. I can sense it. Parkie-Poo the pouter.

"Oh, that's a good one," said Jace. "I'm going to use that from now on."

"He *will* kill you," said Matty, and I high-fived him, because he was right.

"Noted," answered Jace with a grin.

> Me: That was perfect. Thank you for your donation. Now enjoy watching me kick ass.

Fuck. They were going to be at the game. With Casey. I quickly typed out another text.

272   C.R. JANE

> Me: Please make sure that Olivia and Casey's friend are in between you and Casey at all times.

Matty snorted, and I shot him a look.

> Me: Actually, take out the please. DO NOT SIT NEXT TO MY GIRL.

"So shouty," Jace mused, and I held myself back from elbowing him because I was a team player like that.

My phone buzzed again, and I glanced down, expecting it to be something else from my brothers.

But it wasn't.

It was from my mom.

> Mom: Good luck tonight, Parker. I'll be watching it on TV with some of the nurses.

Another text followed as if that one text wasn't enough.

> Mom: I'm so proud of you.

Football players weren't supposed to cry before the championship game. But it was all I could do to hold myself back.

Matty clapped me on the back and stood up, so his body was blocking me from most of the players in the locker room. They didn't need to see their quarterback freaking the fuck out before the game.

I took a few deep breaths and finally typed back.

> Me: Thanks, Mom.

After she'd sent me that text that day, she had accepted help. We'd agreed that she needed more than Martha could give her, and a week later we got her into an in-person care center that specialized in therapy and rehabilitation for those suffering from severe depression. She'd been in there for a few months now, and she acted and looked like a completely different person. There was always the chance that she'd relapse, but I was grateful I'd gotten this time with her. And that Casey could see her like this.

THE WRONG QUARTERBACK 273

I took a few deep breaths, trying to center myself, before I tossed my phone into my locker. Done with distractions and filled with gratefulness that I had the support I did around me.

Matty and Jace both gave me head nods as we grabbed our helmets and got ready to go.

Coach Everett came in then to give us his usual motivational speech, and I stood up from my seat.

LFG.

I'd never heard the stadium this loud. It was hard to think with my ears threatening to burst.

But this was it.

We had four minutes left, we were down by four . . . and it was fourth down.

I was either going to fucking love the number four after this game . . . or I was going to hate it until the end of time.

My teammates huddled around me, their faces tight with tension, eyes locked on me, waiting for the call. I could feel everything in their stares, their trust and their desperation. We needed a touchdown to win. A field goal wasn't enough.

But right now we needed a fucking first down.

I leaned in, keeping my voice calm, steady. "Alright, boys, this is what we play for. We know Oregon's bringing heat on the blitz, so I need the line to hold strong. We're gonna wear them down." The guys nodded, a few grunted, the nerves fading as we found our focus.

"We can fucking do this," I told them, locking eyes with them all so they could see that I wasn't just saying it—I believed it.

We broke the huddle and lined up, the clock ticking down. I barked out the cadence, and the ball snapped into my hands. Dropping back, scanning the field, my eyes darting left, then right. I saw Matty slipping through a gap down the middle. I fired the ball, a quick, sharp pass, and he hauled it in, charging forward as he was swarmed by defenders. We picked up twelve yards and moved the chains.

"Atta fucking boy, Matty," I yelled, and he nodded, his eyes sharp and determined. The clock was still running, and I motioned for everyone to get back in formation.

Three minutes left. The line held firm, and I dropped back, scanning for an opening. I saw Jace sprinting down the sideline, hands up, ready.

274   C.R. JANE

I launched the ball, a perfect spiral arcing through the air, and he leapt up, snagging it midair and coming down just inside the line. Another first down.

Oregon's defense was fucking relentless, though. They were crowding the line, trying to stop every play before it started, pushing back hard, daring us to run. I called a quick play-action pass to keep them on their toes. We snapped the ball, and I faked the handoff before darting to the right, slipping out of the pocket as the pressure built around me. Jace was open in the flat, but a defender was barreling toward him. I had to move fast.

Two minutes on the clock. I glanced over at the sidelines to catch a glimpse of Casey. She was in the front row, wearing my jersey, gripping onto the railing in front of her with a terrified look on her beautiful face.

I blew her a kiss and then called an audible, adjusting to Oregon's coverage, and took the snap. The pocket collapsed, and I dodged left, then right, my eyes scanning the field. Finally, I saw my slot receiver, Jordan, cutting across. I lobbed the ball over the defender's head, and he snagged it, dragging two Oregon defenders for a few extra yards. But he couldn't make it out of bounds to stop the clock.

Less than a minute. Coach had to call our last time-out. The team huddled around me, breathless, faces slick with sweat. "This is it," I said, locking eyes with each one of them. "We've got this. Focus. Protect the line, keep it tight, and we're bringing this home."

We lined up again, every muscle in my body tense, every instinct tuned to the game, the stakes, the clock ticking down. I took the snap and saw a gap open up. No time to think—I darted through it, barreling forward as the defenders closed in. They hit me hard, but I held on to the ball, my eyes fixed on the far side of the red zone, just a few yards away now.

Thirty seconds. We lined up one last time, and I felt the weight of everything in that single moment. The snap came, and I took a quick drop back, searching for an opening. *Nothing.* The pressure was coming fast, collapsing the pocket around me. *Fuck.* I tucked the ball and ran, pushing through the line, every step taking me closer to the end zone.

Five yards. Three. A defender dove at my legs, but I hurdled over him, stretching out as I crossed the goal line. *Touchdown.*

We'd fucking won!

Jace reached me first, knocking his helmet against mine hard as he tackled me to the ground. "Fucking hell, QB. You beautiful, beautiful man. You fucking did it!" he crowed. Matty jumped on me next, and my eyes widened—because I might be about to die when more of the team came.

THE WRONG QUARTERBACK 275

The rest of my teammates did pile on me after that, laughing, cheering, and, in Chappie's case—crying when he joined the throng of our teammates.

When my oxygen was about gone, they started getting off me. It was complete chaos in the stadium; the fans had started pouring out of the stands.

The energy was infectious, and the crowd was pushing us toward the middle of the field, but I needed to get to the sideline.

I needed to see *her*.

Pulling off my helmet, I pushed through the swarm of people—my teammates, coaches, and the fans trying to touch me, dodging reporters and cameras as they tried to get interviews. Someone slapped a championship hat on my head as I moved through the crowd.

"Parker, how does it feel to have just won the championship?" one reporter asked, shoving a microphone into my face as I tried to pass by.

"Awesome," I yelled, before I ducked under her hand and kept moving.

Finally, I spotted her still in the stands, flanked by Olivia and Nat, and guarded by Walker, Cole, and Olivia's bodyguards, who were staring daggers at anyone who dared to get too close.

Her starlight eyes were locked on me. I could see the relief, the pride, and something else—something that made my heart race even faster than it had on the field.

I dodged bodies left and right until I finally reached the stands. Without a word, I reached up, grabbed her hand, and pulled her down onto the field.

"Baby," I murmured, and she jumped into my arms and wrapped her legs around my waist.

I kissed her, hard and fast. I'd been waiting all night for this moment. She melted into me, her arms wrapping around my neck as she kissed me back, the world around us fading into nothing.

The noise of the crowd, the chaos of the celebration—it all disappeared. All that mattered was her.

When we finally pulled apart, she was breathless, her eyes shining with emotion. "You did it," she whispered, her voice full of awe.

I smiled, brushing a strand of hair away from her face. "It was all for you."

Casey snorted and scrunched her nose at me. "Corny as usual."

I laughed and leaned in, pressing my forehead to hers. "It's the truth."

The moment stretched between us, perfect in every way. But eventually, the world came crashing back, the sound of the crowd and the celebration pulling us back to reality.

276 C.R. JANE

I turned, spotting Walker, Olivia, and Cole crawling over the barriers, all of them grinning wide. I raised a hand in acknowledgment, and they all cheered, pumping their fists in the air.

The reporters eventually caught up to me, shoving microphones in my face, asking a million questions at once. I didn't want to answer them; I didn't want to be anywhere except with Casey, but I knew I had to say something.

I glanced down at her, squeezing her hand before turning to the cameras. "We worked hard for this," I said, my voice loud and clear. "We never gave up. This team, this university, we've been through it all, and we came out on top. I couldn't be prouder of my guys."

The reporters shouted more questions, but I held up my hand.

"Sorry, y'all, I have one thing that I need to do before I do any more interviews."

They watched, shocked, as I fell to one knee and looked up at the love of my life as I took her hand. I'd wanted to do this since almost the moment I'd seen her in class that day. I had just been waiting for her to be ready too.

Casey's eyes filled with tears as she covered her mouth with one hand in shock.

"Baby," I began, my voice catching. "I knew, from the second I laid eyes on you, that you were the one. That you were the other half of my soul, that I'd known you in every lifetime before this. That you'd always been mine."

I pressed a kiss to her hand and took a deep breath.

"There's not a single thing in this world that I want more than to spend my life with you, to build something amazing, something that's just ours." I could feel my chest tightening, my heart racing, but I pushed through. "Casey . . . marry me. Be my forever, my home, the person I get to wake up to every day for the rest of my life."

Jace popped up in my peripheral and tossed me the box he'd been in charge of retrieving. "Get it, QB," he called.

I caught it and opened it, smiling at Casey's gasp.

It was a really big ring.

I tugged her closer and motioned for her to lean over. "You don't really have a choice," I whispered to her, and she scoffed . . . because she knew I wasn't joking.

I released her with a big grin. "Baby, will you marry me?" I asked loudly—for propriety's sake.

She sank down onto the ground in front of me and grabbed my face, kissing me hard before she leaned back, sobbing.

"Yes," she cried.

THE WRONG QUARTERBACK   277

I grabbed her hand and slid the ring onto her finger, my hands steady but my heart feeling like it was about to skip out of my chest. And when she kissed me again, tears streaming down her face, it felt like everything— every plan, every dream, every bit of who I was—had finally fallen into place.

Casey

"That's it, baby," Parker growled as he drove into me.

I'd asked him how he wanted to celebrate winning the national championship.

His answer . . .

Fucking me on the fifty-yard line at the Tennessee stadium when we got home.

And that's how I'd found myself on my hands and knees, being railed into oblivion.

"Say it," he ordered, his fingers digging into my hips as he thrust his dick in and out.

"I love you," I murmured.

"Again. Keep saying it," he growled.

And so, I said it over and over again. Parker pushed me further into the ground so that my breasts, covered with nothing but his thin jersey, dragged along the turf, stimulating every nerve ending in my body.

"Parker," I moaned as he pounded into me.

His hand slapped my ass. "Say it."

"I love you. I love you. I love you," I chanted.

"That's my good girl," he murmured, leaning over me and biting down softly on the sensitive part of my neck.

"You're going to come for me, aren't you, baby? You're going to choke my big dick."

"I love you," I cried, the combination of his dirty words and his cock hitting the perfect spot inside me sending me into a pleasure freefall. I writhed against him, my arms giving out.

He caught me just in time and pulled me up so that we were sitting up and facing Tennessee's end zone.

"One more time, pretty girl," he murmured, his finger circling my clit as he continued to push deep inside.

It didn't take long until my body was on fire again, my whimpers filling the air around us as I squeezed his cock.

278   C.R. JANE

I felt his dick jerk inside me, and then he was coming, long streams of his hot seed filling me up until it was running down my legs.

"I love you," he said, his chest heaving. "I can't get enough. I want to live inside you."

My answering giggle morphed into a groan as he slowly pulled out.

"Let's get your leggings back on, baby. He's going to come back any minute now."

He being the grounds manager who had given Parker a key in the first place.

We got our clothes back on, and Parker kissed my ring, like he was reminding himself it was there.

"I love you," he whispered as we made our way out of the stadium.

A sense of warmth settled deep inside me, a feeling that went beyond love or belonging. It was the quiet peace of no longer feeling alone in the world. Of walking side by side with the person who'd been meant for you.

For the longest time, I thought loneliness was just . . . inevitable. A constant I would carry in my heart wherever I went.

After losing Ben, and then Gray, with my family splintered in ways I couldn't fix, I didn't think I'd ever find that feeling again.

A feeling of completeness, like I'd found my home.

Parker didn't just see the broken, empty parts of me—he stepped into them, filled them with something I hadn't realized I needed. He made me feel like my heart could beat steady again, like I could let go of the past and let something new, something real, take root. Parker had become everything I'd thought I'd lost.

He pulled me closer, his heartbeat steady against my cheek. I didn't have to say a word, didn't have to explain the way he made all the broken pieces of me feel like they belonged. He already knew. Somehow, he'd known all along.

And maybe that's what love really was—not just filling a void, but building something beautiful out of the empty places. He'd become my world, my everything, the person who made me feel safe in a way I never thought I'd feel again.

In his arms, I knew I wasn't alone anymore. And I was ready, achingly ready, to start my happily ever after . . . with him.

EPILOGUE

CASEY

One Year Later . . .

The announcer's voice echoed through the stadium, loud and clear, and then . . .

"With the first pick of this year's NFL draft, the Dallas Renegades select . . ." He paused as we all held our breath. "Parker Davis."

The world seemed to freeze, then burst into a thousand colors. I squeezed Parker's hand so hard it probably hurt, but he didn't flinch. He turned to me, his eyes bright with excitement and disbelief. The smile that spread across his face was everything—years of dreams, sweat, and sacrifice shining in that one moment.

I couldn't stop the tears as I whispered, "You did it."

Without another word, he pulled me in and kissed me, not seeming to care that there were a million cameras pointed at us. When he pulled back, he was still holding on to my hand, his thumb brushing over my knuckles like he needed the steadying just as much as I did.

Parker glanced over at his mom, who was standing beside us, misty-eyed, proud . . . and the healthiest I'd seen her. She'd made it her goal to be here for this, working hard every day so she could leave her treatment center and be here for Parker.

He kept hold of my hand as he leaned over to hug her. "I'm so proud of you, son," she said, her face beaming. "Your dad—he would have been so proud, too." She was crying then, but unlike in the past . . . they were happy tears. Which was a huge step up from how it had been since I met her.

280   C.R. JANE

Walker and Cole came over, each of them giving him a hug . . . while Parker still held on to my hand.

"Parkie-Poo, showing us up," Cole said with a grin, like he hadn't just won a Grammy two weeks earlier.

"Someone had to make this family legitimate." Parker smirked.

Walker rolled his eyes. "So cocky already. You're going to be insufferable, I can tell."

Parker winked at me. "Looks like Dallas just got an upgrade in the Davis brother department. Hope it's ready."

Walker scoffed. "Tell me that when you've won a Lombardi Trophy, like I've won a Stanley Cup."

Parker's smile widened. "Fair."

He turned back to me. "Shit. This is happening," he said, sounding nervous as they stepped away.

"I think they're waiting for you," I whispered, wide-eyed because everyone was staring at us. Parker may have been used to that—but I still wasn't.

He kissed my hand. "I love you," he murmured, before he finally let go and walked toward the stage. I watched him go, feeling like my heart was going to burst because I loved him so fucking much.

Parker stepped up, took the hat from the commissioner, and looked out over the crowd, grinning at Matty and Jace across the room before his eyes found me again. He winked.

He was going to give me a heart attack one of these days.

But what a way to go.

———————

"You are so sexy," he rasped, pulling at his tie as he backed me into our living room.

"Mmmh, right back at you," I breathed, stumbling on air . . . because I was very drunk. Parker caught me right before I fell, and I giggled.

"My hero," I crooned, and he grinned.

"Sometimes."

"Feel free to be as bad as you want tonight," I purred, and his eyes widened.

"It sounds almost like you're offering me a present, baby." He grabbed me around the waist and hauled me to his chest.

"Yep. Whatever you want." I smacked a kiss on his lips, tangling my fingers in his hair because I couldn't help myself. "I need you," I whispered.

Parker glanced around wildly, his gaze finally setting on something behind me.

THE WRONG QUARTERBACK 281

I glanced back and saw he was staring at the Steinway in the corner. In celebration of my surgery with the country's foremost hand surgeon—that he had found and paid for as a surprise—he'd replaced the one he'd already bought me with my dream piano.

The surgery had been a success. I still had tremors occasionally, and I wasn't going to be playing professionally like I'd once dreamed, but I was able to play whole songs now. Which had greatly improved my mental state.

It was another thing he'd given me that I'd thought I'd lost.

"I want to eat you out on that piano," he murmured, walking me backward.

"I'm pretty sure there's a movie with that kind of scene." I laughed, the sound coming out as more of a moan, because I was already wet thinking about his tongue and all it could do.

"There is. And I've been thinking of reenacting *that scene* since the moment I found out you could play."

Parker lifted me effortlessly, guiding me back until I felt the cool, hard edge of the piano keys underneath me, a cascade of rich, resonant notes echoing through the room. I braced myself, hands gripping his shoulders as he moved between my knees, his eyes locked on mine with that fierce, unwavering intensity that made everything else fall away. The low notes hummed quietly beneath me, each movement a gentle chord.

"Well, this is a good start," I said breathlessly.

He laughed, the wicked sound sliding over my skin.

His hands slid from my waist, up between my breasts, and then he firmly pushed me back until I was sprawled across the piano top.

I watched as he sank onto the piano bench, his gaze glittering in the faint light of the room.

"Spread your legs," he murmured, and I obediently hooked my legs on his shoulders, more dissonant chords filling the room as I moved.

"And I think these need to go." I had been wearing a dress, and so he had easy access to slip his finger under my thong line . . . and pull.

I moaned as the cool air of the room hit my core . . . and then I was really moaning as his hot, wet tongue slid through my folds, spreading me open.

"Yes," I whimpered.

As his tongue slid into me, a gentle pressure, the piano keys responded with a soft, accidental melody, each note blending into the next in quiet, haunting echoes that would stay in my mind as the sexiest soundtrack to our love I could ever imagine. The sound filled the room, rising and falling as his body pressed against the keys.

282 C.R. JANE

And when I came, the music seemed to crescendo, the final note lingering, hanging in the air as exquisite pleasure soared through me.

"You're mine," he murmured as he stood up and undid his suit pants.

And as he slid into me, I could feel his claim. I could feel how much I really was his. But the most amazing thing was . . . he was mine too.

SECOND EPILOGUE

PARKER

Two Months Before the National Championship Junior Year . . .

I kept my eye on Casey, who was swaying dangerously while holding up Nat as they tried to spell *H-O-T-T-O-G-O* while incredibly drunk. Matty and I were laughing as we watched. Her girls' night was in full, wild swing, and I had designated myself as my girlfriend's personal watchdog, making sure nothing happened to her in the process.

"Where's Jace when I need to make a bet?" Matty grumbled, looking around the room for the man in question.

"Why can't you make a bet with me?" I asked, offended.

Matty smirked. "Because the bet is *on* you. I'm just wondering how long you're going to be able to hold yourself back from punching that guy who's staring at Casey's ass."

I quickly studied everyone who was around Casey, but didn't see who he was talking about.

"Where?" I growled, pushing off the bar I'd been leaning against.

Matty started laughing hysterically. "This is too fun."

I huffed and rolled my eyes. They liked to give me a hard time about how obsessed I was with Casey, but I liked to think that someday they would understand the irrational feelings I experienced on a daily basis.

I sat back down, content that Casey was safe . . . for now, when Jace finally reappeared. He was looking . . . well, wrecked, staggering like he'd just stumbled off a roller coaster. His shirt was half-untucked, collar askew. His hair was a total mess, sticking out at wild angles. His face was flushed, and there were faint red lipstick smudges along his neck, standing out against his skin. He plopped down heavily on the barstool, his face a mix of shock and something close to awe.

"What's wrong with you?" I asked, raising an eyebrow. Matty and I exchanged a glance, the beginnings of a smirk already forming on Matty's lips.

"And what, or rather *who*, did you just do?" Matty added.

Jace looked at us, his expression so serious it was almost comical. "You're never going to believe this."

"You got funny since you went to the bathroom? Yeah, I'm probably not going to believe that," Matty muttered, leaning in with an exaggerated sigh.

Jace didn't even blink. His eyes were still wide . . . kind of crazy-looking, actually. "I just . . . I just found the love of my life."

Matty and I stared at him, both of us trying—and failing—not to burst out laughing.

"Where?" Matty asked, biting back a grin. "In the bathroom?"

"No, man. She was out there." He gestured wildly toward the dance floor. "We were dancing, and then . . . well, you know."

I choked on my drink, laughing. "Wait, you did that just now—"

"Yep. Right out back. Best fifteen minutes of my life—and don't give me a hard time about fifteen minutes. I had to work my ass off to even last *that* long." He sighed, staring down at the bar like he was lost in a daydream. "She was perfect."

"Okay . . . so where is she? What's her name?" Matty asked, glancing around the room like he thought he could pick her out of the crowd.

Jace's face started to turn red, and he looked genuinely distressed. "She left. And . . . I don't know her name. She wouldn't give it to me." He leaned back in his chair, rubbing at his chest like he was having a heart attack. "Fuck. I don't know her name. What the fuck am I going to do?"

Matty was practically doubled over at this point. "Let me get this straight. You think you met the 'love of your life' and she wouldn't give you her name?"

Just then, the bartender appeared in front of us. "Hey, man, that blonde you came up to the bar with—was that your girlfriend?" he asked Jace.

Jace sat up in his seat. "Yeah. Why?" he said casually as he lied through his teeth.

"She left her credit card behind. Figured you might want it back."

"Thanks," Jace responded, his voice coming out two octaves higher than usual. He cleared his throat as he took the card with shaking hands, glancing down at the name on it. He looked up, his face breaking into a slow, ridiculous grin.

"Gentlemen," he announced, holding the card up like he'd just been handed the Holy Grail. "Do you know what this is?"

"What?" Matty and I asked, almost in unison. We were hanging on Jace's every word at this point . . . because we'd never seen him like this.

"This—this is a sign."

Matty rolled his eyes, clapping him on the shoulder. "Or it's just her credit card, man. Either way, let's get you another drink before you have another revelation about your future wife."

Jace ignored him, clutching the card like it was his ticket to paradise. His face curled up in a smug, confident grin as he tucked the card into his pocket. "Nope. I'm telling you. Mark my words. I'm gonna find her."

BONUS SCENE

Want more Parker and Casey? Come hang out in my Fated Realm for an exclusive BONUS scene! Get it https://www.facebook.com/groups/C.R.FatedRealm

PARKER'S CHICKEN PARMESAN

SERVINGS: 4

INGREDIENTS

2 CUPS TOMATO-GARLIC SAUCE OR MARINARA
2 BONELESS SKINLESS CHICKEN BREASTS
½ CUP ALL-PURPOSE FLOUR
2 EXTRA-LARGE EGGS
1¼ CUPS PANKO BREADCRUMBS
1 CUP FRESHLY GRATED PARMESAN CHEESE
1 TABLESPOON ITALIAN SEASONING
1 TEASPOON GARLIC POWDER
1 TABLESPOON TABLE SALT
½ TEASPOON FRESHLY GROUND BLACK PEPPER
2-4 TABLESPOONS OLIVE OIL
1 CUP FRESHLY GRATED MOZZARELLA CHEESE
2 TABLESPOONS CHOPPED FRESH PARSLEY
PARSLEY SPRIGS FOR GARNISH

INSTRUCTIONS

ADD THE TOMATO-GARLIC SAUCE TO A SAUCEPAN SET OVER MEDIUM HEAT. WHEN IT IS HOT, REDUCE THE HEAT TO LOW, AND ADD THE CHICKEN BREASTS. COVER AND SIMMER WHILE COOKING THE CHICKEN TO A MINIMUM INTERNAL TEMPERATURE OF 165 DEGREES FAHRENHEIT.

USING A SHARP, THIN KNIFE, SLICE EACH CHICKEN BREAST IN HALF HORIZONTALLY TO MAKE TWO CUTLETS. IF NECESSARY, FLATTEN TO AN EQUAL THICKNESS. BLOT EACH BREAST WITH PAPER TOWELS TO REMOVE THE MOISTURE.

SET UP A BREADING STATION WITH THREE SHALLOW DISHES. PLACE THE FLOUR IN THE FIRST DISH. WHISK TOGETHER THE EGGS IN THE SECOND DISH. COMBINE THE PANKO BREADCRUMBS, PARMESAN CHEESE, ITALIAN SEASONING, GARLIC POWDER, AND SALT AND PEPPER IN THE THIRD DISH.

WORKING WITH ONE CHICKEN CUTLET AT A TIME, ADD IT TO THE FLOUR MIXTURE, COATING IT ON BOTH SIDES, THEN DIP IT INTO THE EGG, THEN INTO THE BREADCRUMB-PARMESAN MIXTURE, PRESSING DOWN LIGHTLY SO THE BREADCRUMBS STICK.

PLACE THE COATED CHICKEN CUTLET ON A PLATE AND PROCEED WITH THE REMAINING CUTLETS.

IN A LARGE SKILLET SET OVER MEDIUM-HIGH HEAT, HEAT 2 TABLESPOONS OF THE OIL UNTIL IT BEGINS TO SHIMMER. PLACE TWO OF THE PREPARED CUTLETS IN THE SKILLET AND COOK FOR 3 MINUTES. DO NOT MOVE THE CHICKEN!

AFTER 3 MINUTES, GENTLY NUDGE THE CHICKEN WITH A SPATULA. IF IT DOES NOT LOOSEN, CONTINUE TO COOK FOR ANOTHER 30 SECONDS. IF THE CUTLET IS CRISP ON THE BOTTOM IT WILL MOVE EASILY.

FLIP IT OVER AND COOK THE OTHER SIDE FOR 3 MORE MINUTES. TRANSFER THE CHICKEN CUTLETS TO A PARCHMENT-LINED BAKING SHEET AND PROCEED WITH THE REMAINING 2 UNCOOKED CUTLETS.

WHEN ALL THE CUTLETS ARE COOKED AND ON THE PARCHMENT PAPER, ADD 2-3 TABLESPOONS TOMATO SAUCE ON EACH CUTLET, THEN ADD 2-3 TABLESPOONS MOZZARELLA CHEESE, COVERING MOST OF THE SAUCE.

TURN THE OVEN TO BROIL AND RAISE THE RACK TO ITS HIGHEST LEVEL.

TRANSFER THE BAKING SHEET TO THE OVEN AND BROIL UNTIL THE CHEESE MELTS, 1-2 MINUTES. IT IS OKAY IF IT BEGINS TO GET TOASTY. USE A MEAT THERMOMETER TO CHECK FOR DONENESS OF 165°F.

GARNISH WITH THE FRESH PARSLEY AND SERVE WITH SPAGHETTI OR YOUR DESIRED SIDE.

ACKNOWLEDGMENTS

I've always said that my favorite things come from my darkest times. I wrote this in the midst of a failed IVF cycle. If it weren't enough to have a million hormones running through me, the process itself was excruciatingly emotional. And so disappointing. It's a trial that I wish no one has to go through, and I honestly wasn't sure if I'd be able to write. The second I started typing, though, it was like I was transported somewhere else, somewhere away from the emotional pain I was feeling. Parker, Casey, and their friends were just what I needed to help pull myself into a more positive mindset. I laughed and I cried and I swooned while writing this book. And I hope you do too.

Ben's death and Casey's grief were symbolic to me. Grief comes in many forms, and is different for each of us, and it's a lifelong lesson learning how to navigate and overcome it . . . or to just live with it.

Thanks for letting me live in their world and sometimes escape from mine.

XOXO,

C.R.

A few thank yous . . .

To Sky: You make this life possible. You're the best decision I ever made. I love you forever.

To Raven aka My Moon aka Bird aka My Best Friend: At this point, I can't remember what life was like without you. You're remarkable and a blessing that I never expected. I don't think I know how to write anymore

292   ACKNOWLEDGMENTS

without your support. You're brilliant and talented and the very, very best. ILY.

To Alexis: My tier 1 friend. Your support means everything to me. You're the voice I hear when I write these characters and I love your kind heart.

To my beta readers, Crystal, Blair, and Lisa: You three have become some of my dearest friends. I'm so grateful for your support and your love and your enthusiasm. I'm so lucky to have you in my life.

To Stephanie, my editor: You are such a gift. Your passion for your job and your attention to detail is so appreciated. I love working with you and I'm so grateful for the time, love, and passion you put into my books.

To my PAs and BFFs, Caitlin and Sarah: You know I love you. Always have. Always will. Words aren't enough.

And to you, the readers who allow me to live my dream. I love you and I'm grateful for you every day.

Thank you.

ABOUT THE AUTHOR

C. R. Jane is a *USA Today*–bestselling author of romance, fantasy, and whatever else she feels like writing. Her stories are designed to make readers cry, scream, and eventually . . . swoon. Welcome to her world, where heartbreak and happy endings rule.

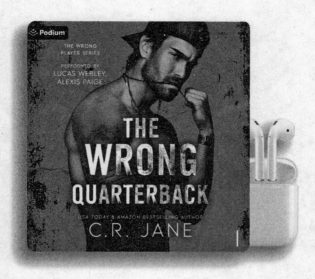

TOUCHDOWN!

Obsessed with Parker and Casey?

Get lost in the tension, temptation, and twists all over again in the audiobook. Their story comes to life in duet narration performed by Lucas Webley and Alexis Paige.

Listen now!